THE GLORY BOYS

Also by Gerald Seymour:

HARRY'S GAME

THE GLORY BOYS

A Novel by

GERALD SEYMOUR

Random House
New York

Copyright © 1976 by Gerald Seymour. All rights reserved under International and Pan-American Copyright Conventions. Published in the United States by Random House, Inc., New York. Originally published in Great Britain by Collins Publishers, London.

Library of Congress Cataloging in Publication Data
Seymour, Gerald.
    The glory boys.
    I. Title.
PZ4.S5192Gl3   [PR6069.E734]   823'.9'14   76–10807
ISBN 0–394–40773–3

Manufactured in the United States of America
9 8 7 6 5 4 3 2
First American Edition

To Rosalind Wade

THE GLORY BOYS

One

There was quiet in the car now, all attention riveted on the twin headlights far behind in the darkness. The man in the back seat had swiveled around and wiped the condensation from the back window, and was now peering hard out into the void of the retreating road. The passenger in the front was also twisted in an attempt to follow the passage of lights, while the driver kept scanning the tilted mirror above him. The road was not straight, and on the sharp curves where the high hedges came close to the tarmac, they would lose the lights, and then find them again as the course of their route leveled out.

For the three men the tension had begun some fifteen kilometers back.

The driver had been the first to speak, but that was long after his companions had noted his continual and hurried glances up at the polished mirror.

He'd spoken in the slow, high-pitched dialect of the pure Palestinian Arab. "It's been with us a long time now, the car behind. I've surged three times, pushed the speed up seven or eight k's an hour. It doesn't affect him, he's just maintaining the same distance. By the big farm, near the wood, you remember, I slowed then. Right down, cut back by about twenty. He didn't close up."

That was when they'd all started to take notice. Picked up the two powerful beams away in the distance, begun to sweat a little, allowed the nervous silence to take over.

The front passenger pulled the glove compartment open and rummaged with his hands for the plastic envelope containing the maps that had been supplied with the car. He felt in his pocket for the cigarette lighter he carried, and then, with the maps and the small flame, he bent himself double, the papers down on the floor and the light shielded by his body. He ran quickly through the pages that showed in detailed and intricate pattern the road system of Northern France. He hesitated on one, his finger tracing a line with difficulty in the flickering, shaking light.

"We're just past Béthune, that was the last town. Another two or three kilometers, there's a turnoff to the left. Runs through some villages. Auchy . . . Estrée. It's difficult to see like this. It looks as though the road winds round the villages, a by-pass. It's a broken line on the map, not for lorries. We can get through that way, and still be in good time for the boat. We have the time?"

"There's time enough," the man in the back said, his words carrying away from the other two as he continued to search the road behind. "He's still there. I'd lost him a moment, but he's there again."

The road was straight now. Clear and fast, high trees on either side, their headlights swung past the tall trunks and melted away into the night across the fields. An occasional lighted cottage or farmhouse, but no other sign of the living. Three in the morning, with the soulless cold of the early hours settled deep on the countryside. The men in the car shivered, the small fear they felt accentuating the chill. From the back came a request for the heater to go on, declined by the driver.

"We've just cleared the mist on the windows. I don't want it again. I want to be able to see from all the windows. I want to be able to see all the way round."

As if to emphasize the point, he wound down the window on his door, letting the bitter night air flood into the car. There was a howled protest as the wind and draft cut in from the space above the glass.

"Don't worry," shouted the driver, lifting his voice above the noise. "The turnoff is very soon now. He'll be gone then. Look for the signs and remember the names of those villages." Optimism, the way they all wanted it.

The man beside him said, "Auchy and Estrée, those are the two we want."

They came too fast to the junction, and the driver had to brake hard to avoid overshooting the narrow road that curved away to the right. The car protested fiercely as it was swung around, tires indenting the gravel chips. He changed down through his gearbox.

The watcher in the back was flung across the wide seat. To steady himself he clung to the heavy grip bag that shared the seat with him. When he looked again, the twin lights had disappeared.

It was a winding, delaying road now. An uneven surface, pocked by the use of tractors and heavy farm machinery. Hay from the fields showed up high in the overhanging trees, where it had been whisked from the carts by the branches. The speed came down.

The driver still returned to his mirror, but there was only the message of darkness to confuse him.

"We'll not know for a bit yet. The curves are too quick . . . he'd have to be right up our bottoms for us to know he was there. Right up."

He laughed, and the others joined him. Too loud to maintain the pretense that they were still calm, the apprehension came through with the successive giggles. It had been a long drive, three days of it already gone, across hundreds of kilometers of Italian and French roads. So little distance left. Less than two hours to the ferry port, far less. And now the first crisis, the initial moment of the unexpected.

The minutes went by as the driver carefully threaded his way along the center of the road. The man in the back allowed his eyes to wander, the compulsion of his vigil at the rear window waning.

"Can we have the window closed now? I'm frozen. All right for you bastards, but here I'll die of cold."

"Just a while longer, just a few more minutes. Till we are sure we will keep the air coming in and the windows clear. You should not feel it that hard. You said you spent your winters in the Jordan mountains, you will have known the cold then, the snow on the hills—" The driver was interrupted.

"Not the Jordan mountains, the mountains of Palestine."

The laughter spread through the car. The driver turned to look behind him, his face huge with the smile. "Accepted. There was no snow, no mountains for it to fall upon in Haifa. Palestine Haifa. No cold there."

"What can you know of Haifa? Too long ago when you left for you to have memories there."

The driver said, "No, I have a slight memory of it. I was four years when we left. There is memory, though it is faint. One does not know how much is memory and how much is the image of what one has been told in the camps of the former life."

"I have been to Haifa," the front passenger interrupted. "I went by lorry to work there on a site, a building project. They took us daily from Jenin. It must have been beautiful once. They were spreading concrete over the earth when we came. It was just stopgap work before I went to Beirut to study, just to fill in the time while I waited."

They drove down a gentle incline into a small, tight-knit, snug village. Big church, civic building, market across to the right, and a ribbon of houses. Few lights. A grey, hostile, closed hedgehog community, battened down for the night to repel strangers, no movement except for the long-legged dog that scurried from their path. They laughed again as they saw the animal take refuge in the shadows. This was a private place, offering no refuge to visitors. Road running straight through, without hesitation. No reason to stop, nor even to slow. There was a bridge, and then they were past the village and climbing again.

The driver was still smiling as he looked again in the mirror. Two bright circles of light, perfectly and symmetrically framed in the chrome fitting. He stared hard, watching their progress down the same hill they had traveled over on their way into the village. He said nothing, but flicked his head between the view in front and the one in the mirror. The man in the back saw his movements and swung heavily around on his seat.

"It's still there," he said. "The bastard is still with us. Coming into the village now, perhaps three, four hundred meters behind us. Go faster. While he's dawdling through the village, get some distance between us."

The car surged forward, the power of its engine pulling it over the road surface. There was no consideration now for the ruts and holes. The chassis jolted and bounced as the wheels undulated on the uneven road, lurching where the deeper pits had been half filled with stones. The face of the driver was total concentration, his hands far up on the wheel, feet alternating between brake and accelerator, body deep into the well of the seat. The new-found speed communicated his anxiety to his passengers.

"Get me a route mapped out," he snapped, talking coldly between barely moving lips, eyes not diverted from the front. "We don't want to find ourselves boxed in some miserable farmyard. I want all the options, and good notice before the turnings."

The front passenger had the maps on the floor again, and was struggling with the lighter. "I can't do it, not with the wind, and not with the banging. I can't see a thing, the scale is too small."

"You can have the window up, but I can't slow it, not now. What's at the back?" The driver yelled the last question over his shoulder.

"He's there still. The lights were gone for a moment just as he was coming out of the village, but they're back again. You can see them yourself, now we're on the ridge and in the open. Staying with us. As we've speeded, so have they. Who do you think they could be? What bastards are they?"

Questioning, lack of decision. Anxiety welling up, about to flood out.

That angered the driver. "Don't waste yourself worrying about that sort of nonsense. Makes no difference who the bastards are. What matters now is that we know what road we are on and where it goes to. Shut up about everything else."

Tortuously the man with the maps traced out a path. He'd folded the sheets so that only that part of the region they traversed was visible. It made a small square. His nose and eyes were very close, but it was some time before the flame of the lighter, stronger now that the window had been wound up, permitted him to find the route they were taking. Every movement of the car jolted his finger from the lines that he was tracing out for them. He was aware of the frustration building inside the car as his colleagues waited for his information. It was a network of country lanes and minor roads that they were asking him to ferret through. He took his time. Perhaps no opportunity to rectify a mistake; one alone would be disastrous. Let them wait till he was ready, and certain and definite. When at last he was satisfied, he drew an envelope from an inner pocket of his anorak and began to write. He had trouble with the spelling of the villages, the printing was so miniature, and several times was obliged to look again and work slowly through the longer words.

He flicked the lighter closed. "It will be the last time we can manage it for such a long time. The flame has little more power. We are well I think. We are on the road to Fauquembergues. First we must pass through Estrée, but it looks to be the same road. At Fauquembergues there are three roads, which divide just beyond, just past, the village. We take the most northerly, the one to the right. After that, on to Liane and so to Samer. Boulogne must be signed there."

"How far to Estrée?" said the driver.

"Two, three kilometers, perhaps. We go straight through. Then Fauquem . . ." His voice tailed away as once again he sought to read his scribblings in the half-light of the dashboard illumination.

"You're sure, now. No doubts about the route?"

"None at all," the passenger snapped back.

Irritation forcing forward. He thought: We hardly know each other, have been together for days now, but have no personal contact. Had never met before the planning of the mission. Had only talked in the most general and superficial way; that was as it was intended. Each one of them dependent on the other, needing to trust totally in the skill and resolution of his colleagues, but without the deep-rooted certainty that comes from long-standing knowledge and companionship.

The driver swerved on a bend, nearly taking them off the paved surface and onto the raised and heavily grassed verge. Preoccupation, anxiety bending him away from his principal role, driving the car. Friction would follow, fanned by the man who sat beside the driver—the driver quiet and resentful at the lack of implicit faith shown in him. In the back the third man gazed out through his window at the lights, held as if by elastic at the same unincreasing and undiminishing distance. It was standard in these operations, they knew, that the attack team would come together only at the final stage, that they would have been drawn from different camps, different backgrounds. They were briefed to keep clear of questioning their comrades on personal histories. From involvement, follows breakdown and collapse under interrogation. Know the code name only. What more do you need to know? they had said. But without an understanding of each other, the strains in adversity were so much greater, fueling the apprehension inside the car.

The driver stamped his foot on the brake. On the speedometer dial the needle sagged back from beyond a hundred kilometers an hour to below forty. Both his passengers hung on to their seats.

Straddled across the road was the solid, unyielding mass of a Friesian herd. Perhaps on the way to milking, perhaps being transferred from one field to another further away, perhaps being collected for market, perhaps . . .

"Murdering hell, what in the whore's mother's name do we do with this?"

"Blast the horn. Get the old fool in the front to shift them."

"The car behind, it's closing quickly."

"Use the grass at the side of the road."

"The bloody peasant with them, at the front . . ."

"Get on the grass, that's the only way round."

"The car behind us, it's less than one hundred and fifty meters. It's slowing but still closing on us."

Inside the near-stationary car there was a babble of shouting. In front the herd seemed unmoved. Sad and heavy eyes looked at the car, more concerned, though, with the black and white dog that snapped and yelped at their hoofs.

"Shut up. Shut up. Stop goddamn well talking," yelled the driver.

He wrenched the car across onto the grass. Momentarily the wheels began to spin, before they bit into the soft ground.

"Take it easily, slowly, or we'll be stuck."

More instructions for the driver. But he alone was remaining frozen cool, ignoring, closing his mind to the shouting.

The car moved on, bumping over the loose earth that had

been excavated from the ditch that ran beyond the grass and short of the field's hedge. The bumper nudged aside a cow, sending it butting its way into the safety of its fellow creatures. Huge, dark figures, snorting and scraping their bodies against the paint work of the vehicle. Their smell crept into the sealed car, drawing twisted grimaces from the men inside.

"He's right on us. Not sixty meters away—" The shout from the back was cut off as the glare of the pursuing headlights illuminated the interior of the car. The passengers ducked down, only the driver remaining still upright.

"All right. All right. We're nearly out now. He has to come through this crowd too." Before he was clear of the herd he was changing up, running through the gears, accelerating his speed, weaving to avoid the leading animals before bursting back onto the open road. He caught only the briefest sight of the farmer, walking proud and straight at the head of his livelihood.

The car rushed forward. Ahead, the road was clear, stretching into the emptiness beyond the reach of their lights.

The three men heard the first blast on the siren as the vehicle behind them attempted to untangle itself from the obstacle, the shuffling barricade. The piercing, singsong wail of the amplified call drove through the windows and doors and roof of the car, filling it with noise. Flashing amongst the confusion of the cows' backs and heads was the blue rotating police lamp.

The man in the back pulled the bag toward him, slid back the zipper and plunged his hand in among the shirts and socks and underpants and books, before he fastened on the hardness of the Luger pistol. Some of the contents spilled out onto the leather seat, snagging on the raised foresight of the gun as he pulled it from the case. The magazine was in position.

"There's your answer," he said quietly. "Now we know who we have running with us."

There was no reply from the front. He cocked the gun.

From his office at police headquarters in St. Omer, twenty-five kilometers to the north, the man who had been issuing orders for the last hour could plot with exactitude the position of the fleeing car. His size, not grotesque but huge, belied his efficiency at his work. The big wall map where an aide continually moved color-headed pins demonstrated this. The position of the car, kept up to date by the constant radio calls from the pursuing police vehicle, was shown by a yellow marker; his own men, barely separated, by red. Stretched out ahead of the path of the three Arabs was a near-continuous line of blue pins, straddling the minor and principal roads that led to the coast and the port of Boulogne.

He had not expected the turnoff from the main coast road across which his major force was concentrated, but as a precaution, had placed single police cars, each manned by two officers, on all parallel-running B routes. It had been his intention that the car which held his interest would be unaware that it was under surveillance before it was stopped by any one of the sixteen blocks now in place. The use of the pursuit car's siren and lamp had changed that.

It had been a brutal day's work since the teletype message bearing the instructions from Paris had forewarned him of the need to set a major operation in readiness. By late afternoon, at a time when he would normally have been thinking of home and his supper, the fleet of black Citroëns had started to arrive in the discreet yard at the back of his headquarters. He had shaken several hands. Men from the Ministry, from the security services. There had been one who wore no tie, who was dressed in creased jacket and slacks, and to whom everything was relayed. That one had spoken his French adequately, but was not fluent, had a Central European accent and dangled a silver six-pointed Star of David around his neck. He was treated with something close to deference.

The local man had been told little, informed of only a part of the background of the event, but had established, and forcibly, that if a car was negotiating his personal territory, then it was preferable to have his own men on its tail.

"These lanes will swallow you up," he'd said with the certainty of intimate knowledge. "If you have no local experience, you will lose them, easy as a flea in a rug."

The point had been taken and accepted. One of the canniest of his drivers had taken over from the security services' surveillance that had shadowed the car across two-thirds of French territory. It had been going well, earning congratulations from the big men of the Paris counterespionage division, until the angry and staccato bursts over the radio had warned of the intervention of the cows. But little, he had reflected, was lost. The men he hunted were still being shepherded into the fine mesh net that he had laid for them.

"When will they reach the blocking point, on their present route?" He spoke to his aide.

"Four to five minutes, sir. Not longer. Just the far side of Fauquembergues, at the crossroads. Where the petrol station and the café are."

"Two men?"

"Two, sir. Roben and Miniux. We're in touch with them. They are alerted and have been told they have only to hold the fedayeen a few minutes. The larger force is already heading toward the point."

"Tell them to go carefully," and as an aside, because he too was now consumed with concern, "it was not intended only two should make the interception."

It was the driver who spotted the red light in the center of the road.

It was being waved slowly up and down, the international sign to halt. As he closed the distance the gendarme's fluorescent arm band gleamed back at him above the brightness of the torch, and he shouted to the others, "There in the front, a police check, they're waving us down."

It was the moment for one of the three to take control. The man in the back reacted to the situation first, perhaps because it was he who clasped the only firearm in the car. Someone had to lead now. There had been too much indecision in the previous few minutes, too many voices raised, his own amongst them. He leaned forward, head and shoulders pressing over the top of the front seat. His voice was shrill, but clear and commanding. "Burst right past him. Don't hesitate, don't slow at all. Go to his left and speed faster as we go by. He'll be armed, so keep your bodies low as you can . . . right down. Don't hesitate . . . And when you get very close, put down the front lights . . . then on again."

The car hurtled toward the lone policeman, bearing down on him at some twenty-seven meters a second. The driver could see the whiteness of his face above the darkness of the uniform and rain cape, could see the shape of the torch, beam now agitated, and the movement of the illuminated arm wrestling with the webbing strap across the right shoulder. The driver could see the fear fill his face, the eyes grow large. His feet rooted to the ground rabbitlike, the policeman stood transfixed.

"Kill the lights."

The command was barked from the back of the car, and the driver instinctively carried out the instruction. Easier for him now, too much initiative heaped on his shoulders before, now just able to obey, to react. Fifty meters in front, the policeman disappeared in the blackness. Almost immediately came the next order.

"On again, the lights."

The driver shrieked with horror. Ten paces beyond the front of the car was the policeman, directly in their path, his submachine gun close to his right hip, pointed directly at the windshield. He never fired.

The radiator of the car smashed into his upper thighs. His body jackknifed into the air. The car recoiled from the impact, then shuddered again as the policeman clipped the roof before arcing over the top of the car. The driver swerved across to the right, late and with effort, to avoid the blue-painted patrol car, parked at an angle and filling half the road. The man beside him felt the nausea rising deep in his intestines and into the constricted pipe of his throat. The third man had closed his eyes just before the fragile toylike figure was brushed aside, trying to shut out the vision of the gaping, incredulous mouth.

As Roben hit the road surface, shattering his vertebrae and destroying what faint source of life was left in him, Miniux opened fire.

From the car they never saw the policeman who crouched back from the road and close to the ditch. At his shoulder was the steel-framed butt of the squat MAT-49. There were thirty-two nine-millimeter rounds in the magazine, and he fired them all at the car, moving his finger from the trigger only when the hammering kick of the weapon subsided. The listed maximum effective range in the manuals Miniux had read was more than ten times the distance between himself and the stricken vehicle.

The bullets plowed their way first into the engine of the car, then worked their pattern back toward the interior. The first to die was the front passenger, four shells hitting him in the upper chest. He went wordlessly. The driver too was struck, feeling the pain spreading endlessly from his left arm and then into the torn wounds in his side. But the man behind, protected by the bodywork and the seats of the car, survived the low-velocity spray.

The car veered first to the left, and then wove a way down the center of the road as the driver fought with his weakening strength to maintain a direction against the contradictions of the damaged steering system. His head went down once, but he jerked it upward, taking in again the contours of road, hedges and fields. A few more meters, perhaps, but not a journey. He was incapable of that, he knew it. Only strong enough to get clear of the awfulness of the noise of the bullets, and the smell that they brought, and the terror that followed the caving in of the windshield and the side windows.

He managed another three hundred meters down the road, then with great effort dragged his foot across to the brake. It took so much force to bring the car to a stop. Vermilion blood, his own blood, billowed and spilled across his knees and ran to a pool on the rubber mat under his feet. That was death, he could recognize that. There was no way to staunch that life flow. Too much going too fast. He looked at it, abstract, and the desire to rest and end it all was supreme. The rear door opened and he saw the face at his window and then his own door was gaping. He felt himself sliding out, the rough earth coming to meet him, and a hand arrested his fall and held him upright.

The voice, familiar but couldn't put a name to it, was close to his ear. "Dani, Dani, can you hear me, we have to run from here. Bouchi is dead, he has to be. So still. The siren is closing. But I can help you . . ."

The driver shook his head, very slowly, very deliberately. "You go alone. There is nothing further for me. Over. Gone." Little more than a whisper, near-deluged by the frantic approach of the following police car. "I don't even know your name, only a code. You don't know anything of me, nor any of us about Bouchi. Idiotic." He paused, seemed to suck in air, which his carved lungs could not accept. "For Palestine, for a free Palestine. You'll remember that when you meet with him. Remember Palestine, and remember me, when you meet with the Mushroom Man."

His eyes blinked, not enough strength to laugh any more, just to move the delicate soft-brown eyelids, and he died.

The sirens came no closer. Stopped at the block, the survivor thought, as he reached inside the back of the car and pulled the bag clear. The Luger was now in his pocket. He ran to the back of the car and unscrewed the petrol-tank guard, and thrust his hand into his trousers for a packet of cigarettes. The fist crumpled the carton, enough for it to fit comfortably into the petrol aperture. With his matches he lit the thickened paper, dropped it into the hole, and sprinted for the comfort of the darkness.

He heard the explosion behind, but didn't turn.

An official black car brought the Israeli secret service officer to the crossroads. Roben still lay in the road, a policeman's coat draped over his face, and the car skirted him at crawling pace. Further up was the parked patrol car with a knot of uniformed men around it. They were feeding Miniux with brandy from a flask, and a long way beyond that, difficult to discern, was the smoking skeleton of the burned-out vehicle.

"How many have we found here . . . of them?" The Israeli pointed down the road.

"We found the two men. They are still inside, unrecognizable of course. There will be problems of identification. The car reached that far; the policeman who fired on it says after it stopped, it caught fire. That could be expected, it took many bullets."

The Israeli looked back at the detective who had spoken, then stared out into the short horizon that would soon be broken in the first pencil line of dawn. He said, "It's very strange. Just two of them. The information that we gave in Paris was that there were three who were traveling. Perhaps we have lost one. Mislaid him somewhere on the way."

Two

The young Arab's sole preoccupation now was to put distance between himself and his pursuers. He'd sprinted the first few hundred meters, till the sodden fields and the churned mud of the farm animals had taken their toll as his feet sank into the softened ground, causing him to heave and pull to withdraw them each time he struggled to renew his stride. Soon he had switched to a more gentle jog trot. Not to safeguard his strength, but simply because he was not capable of faster movement. He punched his way through thick hedges, tore his coat on a strand of wire, fell once when trying to keep up his momentum and clear a dried-out ditch. But all the time he kept on his way.

He reasoned that if he were fortunate, the gendarmes would be satisfied with the debris of the car. They would poke about amongst the charred bodies, find little justification for launching a manhunt for him. But that was if he was lucky. If they were coming after him now, it meant that the following car had spotted the three of them when the lights swept the inside, where they had sat the second before they ducked down to avoid the brightness and the recognition.

Or the one who had fired from the side of the road, the one they had never seen—what if he had seen them in silhouette as they sped past him? If he had counted three, then they would now be massing with their dogs and their cordons and their large-scale maps. But the bag, which dragged him down with its weight, would be his salvation. Here was the vital change of clothes, the travel documents, the mold back into society when he arrived at the ferry port.

There was barking once when he slipped past a darkened farmhouse, old, rectangular and alien. There would be no help for him in this wet and clammy countryside. He must keep going, however much the pain in his stomach, caused by violent exertion and no food, slowed him down. It would be difficult to move once the sun rose away behind him, where the car was, where Bouchi and Dani lay, but till then he must continue to run, whatever the agony.

This was what the training had all been for. This was why they had urged and pummeled the recruits up the soft shale hills of Fatahland, why they had screamed and kicked them to the point beyond exhaustion, toed them into activity when they collapsed, and then when they could move no more, left them to find their own slow path back to the tented camps. And the next morning it had been the same, and the next . . . and the next . . . They had gone on driving the young men till their stomach sinews had hardened, their lungs were cavernous, and their thigh muscles rippled and rolled in use. After all that, and only then, they taught them the weapons drills, the craft of being in open country. Then had come the sophistications of disguise and concealment.

When he had first arrived at his camp, he had been a raw, attractive and intelligent young man, but they had spotted the bitterness, and turned his hatred of Israel into overwhelming obsession. It had not taken them long. Seven weeks of the intensive course had been enough. The product was ready for use then. The determination sharpened, the viciousness honed, the mark of the killer, that was the role they had fashioned for Abdel-El-Famy. They were pleased with what they saw, and confident of success when they gave him his orders.

The man who now struggled and heaved his way over the fields of Northern France, hugging the hedgerows for protection from the eyes of the country people who would soon be rising from their beds, peering through their curtains, opening their doors, was a very small pawn in the complex power game of the Middle East. Individually he was insignificant, unexceptional, unremarkable. Under his given name he featured in none of the tens of thousands of personal files maintained by the Israeli and Western European intelligence services.

Back in Nablus, the sprawling valley town on the Israeli-occupied West Bank of the Jordan River, he had flung stones at the Israeli soldiers who massed close to the school gates every afternoon a little before one o'clock. There was nothing particular about that. All the high school children did it; all of them were at some stage caught in the pincer nets of sprinting Jewish soldiers, thwacked on the head and shoulders by the billy sticks, and taken off in lorries to the barbed-wire compound and left to cool their heels for a few hours. He'd been through the process, known that when the officer and the political advisor came to interview them, the time for insolence was not ripe. He'd bided his silence then, and been sent home, with an army boot in the seat of his jeans to help him on his way. Nobody filled in papers about boys like that; it would have tied up the bureaucracy for a lifetime.

But the regular afternoon rock-throwing, and the race back to the safety of the labyrinth of alleys and deep shops in the Casbah, affected young people in different ways. Some grew beyond it, learned to control their dislike of the occupying force, and as age and responsibilities increased, were able to co-exist with the new order. A few, a very few, were left scarred by the experience. Abdel-El-Famy was one of those. At eighteen he left Nablus, took the bus that wound into the Jordan Valley, and crawled for fourteen hours across the Jordanian and Syrian plains before dropping down through the winding Lebanese hills to Beirut. There were always places in the Palestinian-oriented universities for those from the Occupied West Bank. Those who had lived under Israeli rule, and rejected it, were traditionally lionized. He enrolled for a course in English studies, was a good student, but throughout, was brushing against a quite new science, one that the military governor had effectively stamped out in Nablus. That was the science of revolutionary politics.

Through the long dryly hot afternoons after classes, the students sat at the café on the Corniche, disputing the road to the recovery of Palestine. Choking them were the exhausts from the huge Fords and Cadillacs which paraded the tourists and visitors through the city. A few hundred yards down the road was the looming bulk of the United States of America's embassy complex, complete with heavily armed personnel carriers manned by Lebanese troops. The open jeeps of the Squad 16 militia, with their angled crimson berets and toylike Armalite rifles, would cruise past the young people, watching them, eying them, letting them have no doubt that they were in a foreign country, without rights, without privileges. They were strangers, tolerated, not welcomed. They could only afford the thin upright bottles of Pepsi-Cola, and had to drink them with patience and restraint to make them last.

And while they sat and watched the affluence and arrogance of another country, they argued and bickered over the way to regain their own state. In the old days it had been clear, abundantly clear, that the answer lay in violence, and they had clubbed together their piasters to buy papers, Arabic, French and English, which carried the long and detailed reports of the activities of Black September and the Popular Front for the Liberation of Palestine. Two bottles had lasted all day in the roadside café where they had settled with their papers and a transistor radio to hear the news of the assault on the Olympic Village in Germany. September 5, 1972—it had been a long-drawn and heroic day. They had worshipped the fedayeen who died on the airport apron at Fürstenfeldbruck, reviled what they called the treachery of the German police in ambushing them, rejoiced at the death of eleven Israeli sportsmen.

But out of the violence of Munich was spawned a degree of respectability for the Palestinian cause; and the leaders, so the young people in the cafés said, were beginning to get wind of the leathered seats around the conference tables, the scent of the huge black official cars that would carry them there, wanting to finger the gold-cased pens that signed and initialed treaties. The arguments in the bright heat, with the sea shimmering to the front, became more heated, more divided. There were some who said any Palestinian state was better than nothing, however small, however much an exercise in diplomatic geometry, wherever the lines were drawn. There were others who saw only the complete return of their former lands as being sufficient, the argument of no compromise. This was the view of Abdel-El-Famy. He understood that the table-based arguments, which he was becoming more and more frequently sucked into, would only sap his resolve and desire for revenge. His presence at the cafés became less and less frequent as he sought out the men untainted by weakness who were prepared to fight on regardless of any moves by the leadership of the Palestinian refugee community toward a half-peace.

He joined the Popular Front for the Liberation of Palestine General Command, a small but deadly organ in the so-called "Rejection Front." He became one of fifty-five young men, aged between seventeen and twenty-five, who had taken a solemn initiation oath, who knew they would be sent on missions with little prospect of return or survival. It was as he had wanted it.

Just eight days ago he had been called forward from morning parade and instructed to present himself at the tent of the General Command's leader. There were three others inside when he opened the flap door, their faces all in shadow from the diffused light that passed through the grey-canvas roofing. Apart from the man who directed the General Command's operations were the figures he knew only as Bouchi and Dani. New arrivals, placed with different training sections, and therefore virtual strangers. They were all told they would be traveling to London, that their mission was regarded as of the utmost importance to the whole Arab movement. With a code name, and an operational plan to work to, and a target to seek out, Abdel-El-Famy was no longer a penniless nothingness from a bare bungalow in the hill above the marketplace of Nablus. Like a stoat hungry for rabbit's blood, he would not be easily deflected. His threat to the uneasy peace of the Middle East was enormous, and if he succeeded, the earthquake-scale reverberations of his action would be felt by millions throughout the Western world.

Famy lay high up amongst the bales in the roof of the barn. It was past eight and he had been resting there for more than twenty minutes, but the breath still came hard for him and the sweat rolled in great rivers from the shiny dank hair down across his face and onto his shoulders. He had stripped off his clothes, except his yellow underpants, and was prone on the hard, irritating surface of the packed straw. He estimated he'd come twenty-five kilometers. Four hours' traveling. One more such effort and he would be in Boulogne and ready for the ferry. He'd thought about it, and decided better to arrive a day late in England by traveling rough across country to the ferry port, than to risk all in the hope of finding a bus or a lift on the roads in the immediate aftermath of the interception. He would stay in the barn all day, emerging only as the darkness fell again over the fields.

He heard children playing far away, high-pitched voices carrying to him, and when he moved to peer through a hole in the wooden planking, he saw them, bright in their school clothes and with their filled satchels on their backs, skipping and playing as they went away from him up the road. They offered no threat to him, harmless and unseeing. And he began to rest, body splayed out on the bales. Once he was aroused from his sleep by a dog's sharp bark, and from the same vantage point he watched the progress of a farmer across his land, with the animal far in front trailing a scent. Otherwise there was nothing to disturb the tranquillity he so desperately needed. In his sleep he was far away: in the hills above the town where he had been born, playing on the slopes and rolling stones down at the imperturbable goats, playing at football in the dusty schoolyard, working beside his father on Saturdays in their ramshackle garage.

Perhaps it was the evening coming on, as the sun dipped and the warmth fled from the aging timbers of his refuge, but his dream switched abruptly in mood from the happiness of his childhood to the day just after his fourteenth birthday when the big tanks had rumbled their way into the square at Nablus. Echoing machine-gun and rifle fire, the wail of the Red Crescent ambulances, and the fear on the faces that huddled in steel-shuttered doorways. It was the first time in his life he had seen terror on grown men's faces. He would not forget it. He was not asleep much longer, waking quickly, but then finding himself confused and needing a minute to work out his situation, where he was, and why.

It was dark in the barn when he set off again. It was difficult to walk at first, as the stiffness and damp of the previous night seemed to have locked the suppleness of his knees. It would be another hard trek, but by dawn, if he pushed himself once more, he should be near to the boat, ready to dispose of the muddied, drenched clothes and substitute the clean garments he preciously carried in his grip bag. With laundered clothes he could assume his final identity, and take on the name of Saleh Mohammed, Algerian passport Number 478625, born August 22, 1953, at Oran.

There is a restaurant, specializing in fish delicacies, that over-looks the sea at Sidon. It's roughly halfway between Beirut and the nest of tents far to the south where the General Command maintained its headquarters. Before the Palestinians took their war into Israel, and before the retaliatory air strikes and com-mando raids that inevitably followed, this was a place that tou-rists delighted in. But the package-holiday makers, or so the tour operators discovered, are not seeking any great excitement when they pay out their dollars and francs and marks. They are prepared to give the possible excitement of the war zone a very wide miss. Flights of Israeli Phantoms this far north are rare, but the sightseers have needed more convincing.

So the restaurant is almost deserted, and the square-built Crusader castle that stands just to the front of the white table-cloths no longer groans under the armies of stiletto heels and sandals. Out on the terrace is as comfortable and as discreet a place to discuss matters greatly confidential as any in the town.

The leader of the General Command seldom came to Beirut. His independent stand had won him many enemies inside the overall Palestinian movement, and his presence in the Leba-nese capital would make him vulnerable to the attentions of the Israeli agents who at a few hours' notice could call in their country's assassination squads from the sea. He was high on their death list, perhaps even ranked number three after George Habbash and Abou Iyyad. He had received a phone call on a secret unlisted number in the little village close to his tent camp in midmorning, urging him to make the rendezvous. The message was from a journalist who sympathized with the poli-tics of the General Command and who was on the staff of one of Beirut's biggest dailies, which had its offices and printing works on the chic, well-heeled Rue Hamra in the heart of the most fashionable part of the Lebanese capital.

As the dark intense-eyed man picked the flesh from a small bone-packed mullet, the journalist passed to him a piece of news agency copy ripped from the teleprinter in his office that carried the reports of the Agence France Presse exclusively. He was aware of basic details in the organization's operations and had realized the significance of the eight-line story. It was the first news that the General Command had had of the progress of their unit since the three men had flown from Beirut to Athens, with an air and road journey mapped out for them via Naples, Rome, the Italian-French border, Paris, Boulogne, and across the water to London.

"They are reliable, this agency?" asked the General Command leader through his mouthful of fish.

"One has to believe them. They are taking just the main points from all French sources, but most of this story is taken direct from the Sûreté statement. There would be little room for error. But the other agencies, Associated Press and UPI, are carrying much the same. In less detail it was carried on the Overseas Service of the BBC as well. The facts are not in dispute."

"It speaks of roadblocks. Roadblocks stopping them. Of the car being machine-gunned. Now, at that time in the morning why are there roadblocks, why have countryside police been issued with weapons of the size of submachine guns? There is only one interpretation, I think you will agree with me. There is only one explanation for such precautions to be taken in circumstances such as this."

The journalist nodded, and sipped at the water in the narrow-stemmed glass in front of him. He said quietly, "It has to be the Israeli service; our people have been compromised. The French would do nothing on their own. If our people were going right through France, they would be allowed to do so. The Israelis have prodded the French, poked them into action. Did they have arms?" It was a bold question for him to ask; normally he would not be privy to such minute mission details.

The leader smiled. "Not much, perhaps a pistol, not more than one. No grenades, no explosives, no rifles. They are further on down the road. To be collected. But that is not for your paper. Perhaps you could let it be known from a high source in the men's movement that they were not armed. But not identify the group. Yes?"

"There is no difficulty in that. Two unarmed Palestinians gunned down by the French police, that will make good reading, perhaps the Paris office of our paper can work up the involvement of the Israeli secret service. The two can be married together." On his pocket-sized pad, the journalist began to make quick notes of the form of words he would use.

The two men now attacked their meal, pulling with their fingers at the larger bones, spitting out the smaller ones, and dousing their hands in the bowls provided. When they had finished, the commando leaned forward. Except for the diners at this one table, the terrace was quite empty, there was no one within yards who could have overheard what he said, but old habits die hard.

"The reports speak of two men being found in the car. There could be no doubt of that one fact?"

"No doubt at all. That is common to all the stories."

"And if they had captured a prisoner, a third man, would they have released that information?"

"Most likely," the journalist replied. "It is not the sort of thing they would be likely to hold secret. There is no reason for them to."

Again the smile played around the mouth of the General Command's leader, dallied there a little, was mirthless, and then faded. He was not one given to conventional humor. One would not expect that from the man who was responsible for a morning's carnage at the bright, modern Fiumicino airport of Rome that left thirty-one dead, nor from the man who ordered his subordinates into the northern Israeli settlement of Kiryat Shmona, an operation that filled seventeen coffins. But irony amused him. And it would be ironical if the death of that one's colleagues were in fact to enhance the safety of the man who lived. It was no part of the journalist's role in the movement that he should be aware of such interests.

The leader said, "I would be interested to hear if there are any further arrests, or sightings, or . . ." He let it tail away. He had said enough.

The journalist waved his arm at a distant figure who hovered at the entrance to the kitchens, gestured a writing motion with his hands to signify the meal was over and he wished to accept the bill.

"Before you leave, there is a message I want you to deliver. It is sensitive. I want it handed only to the man whose name I shall give you. He is in Beirut, and it must reach him this afternoon." The leader drew a sheaf of papers from inside his khaki combat jacket, revealing for a moment the polished light-brown shoulder holster he wore through all his waking hours, and with a ball-point pen, began to write. Had he looked, the waiter who brought the reckoning for the meal could not have seen what was being written, as the leader protected the message with his hands as he bent low over the table. The pen moved hurriedly and with bold strokes across the paper, the Arabic symbols firm and decisive.

While the banknotes were away being sorted out at the cash till, he said, "It must go straightaway to the commercial secretary of the embassy that I have written on the folded paper. I'll tell you what it says, I know you pressmen, you'll want to open it if I don't tell you, and I would rather not have it delivered as if it's been halfway through the souk in Baghdad . . ." He laughed, and the journalist shuffled in embarrassment and muttered his protestations. "No, I know you, you are all the same. It merely says that we go on as before, but at reduced strength. There, that tells you all or nothing. For you, my good friend, I think it tells you nothing. Nothing. And you should be happy that way."

And he was gone, striding between the tables inside the restaurant toward the car park where his Fiat waited. Once he raised his right arm above his shoulder, a final farewell to his luncheon informant. One of his bodyguards had stayed at the front door of the building, and he now fell in behind; two more were sitting in the car. As the leader settled into his seat the driver engaged the gears, and they moved off.

"We have to be patient awhile," he said. "Two of the men on the European operation have been intercepted. They are dead. There is no word of the third, nor of whether the French even know of his existence. If there were to be one who has survived, and could go on with the task, which one would we select?" He was speaking to the man who sat beside him, an older man whose judgment he trusted implicitly, whose loyalty was unquestioned, and who cradled a Kalashnikov automatic rifle across his lap.

"Of those three?" The other paused for a moment's reflection. "It would be the one we code-named Saleh. Saleh Mohammed. The one that calls himself Famy."

"That is good judgment. Pray to God it is that one who lives. They were all fine boys, but he was the best of them. The youngest, but still superior. It is a great problem that he faces, the one who has lived, if that is indeed the case."

His companion stroked the sleek steel darkness of the rifle barrel, his eyes playing on the cars that flashed by them, watchful, alert. The leader was talking softly, half to himself, and there were no interruptions.

"Much will depend on the people he meets there. These Irishmen, they represent an unknown factor, and one man on his own must be more dependent on them than we had planned. More is required now than a simple availability of weapons, explosives, transport and a safe house. The foreigners must provide a different dimension. They must become involved."

He was silent. The other man said, "Will they provide that?"

"It is imponderable," said the leader. "Probably, but I cannot say with certainty. In Tripoli they were friendly enough. They wanted to cooperate then, were anxious to buy weapons. They were making a gesture toward us then. That was the conception of the plan. They have killed many times in their own struggle, but always have been fearful of the scale of mission that we are prepared to stage. Perhaps their cause is only worth fighting for, not worth dying for. There were promises in Tripoli, endless promises. As I have said, we shall have to be patient."

Again the smile. No warmth. The smile of the killer whose senses tell him death is meandering close at hand.

After their swim the young man and the girl had taken their towels, draped them on the grass away from the pool and close to the high wooden fence that shut it off from the road and the car park, and sprawled themselves down. It was hot that evening in London's southwest suburbs, and facilities were overstretched. But few wanted to be in the shade and far from the water, and so the couple found the privacy they searched for.

Five and a quarter miles down the road were the main run-ways of Heathrow Airport, and every 105 seconds their voices would fade out, losing the competition against the Rolls-Royce and Pratt and Whitney engines that surged overhead gulping down aviation fuel as they powered the huge passenger airliners toward the ground. But in between the cacophony there was time for them to talk, not of anything special, nothing heady, just the things that young people want to talk about, endlessly repeated by other couples who shared the grass with them but were out of earshot.

She was seventeen and a half, called Norah, and punched a cash register in a supermarket from eight-thirty in the morning till five-fifteen in the afternoon, lived at home, and thought the boy she had met beside the pool the previous evening quite the most interesting she had encountered in her limited experience. She wore last year's bikini, which had been right for Benidorm and the ten days of concentrated Spanish Mediterranean heat but now seemed tight and restricting, as if unable to cope with the developments of the previous twelve months. He seemed to like it, though; his eyes were seldom off it. Most of the time they lay on their backs, stretched out and relaxed, fingers touching, his short-cut nails searching out the lines of her wrist, the crannies between her fingers, the soft sensitive places on the underside of her knuckles. He'd kissed her last night, after the cinema and the ditching of her friend, quietly and gently in the lane behind her house. He'd held her rather loosely, with none of the frantic endeavor she was used to submitting to from the series of boyfriends who took her for a coffee and a dance or a film and then believed in their right to maul and explore her afterward as due return for a pound's expenditure.

This one was different. No thigh pressed hard between her legs, no fumbling under her blouse, no hand trying to get inside her jeans. The boy had kissed her, long and easily, seemed to think that was what they both wanted, was right, told her he'd see her tomorrow, same place. She'd come to the pool, and he'd been there, where he'd said he'd be, looked happy enough to see her again.

She had done most of the talking, last night and again this afternoon. He seemed to want that, didn't interrupt, looked interested. He said very little himself as she chattered about her holidays, her friends, her mother and father, her work, the prices in the shops, the television programs she saw when she was at home, the films she went to on her nights out. He didn't reciprocate. Last night, when she was in her bed at the front of the semidetached house a mile and a half away, she'd blamed herself for that. " 'Course he didn't say anything, didn't give him much of a chance to get a word in," she'd said to herself.

Soon the dew would be forming on the grass, and the coolness of the middle evening was beginning to embrace her bared shoulders. She shivered a little and reached out for the jersey she had brought in her bag. She'd come equipped this time to be out late in the open air, uncertain what the next few hours would bring, but excited and expectant.

"I'll catch my death, dressed with nothing, like this." She giggled and turned toward the boy, anticipating he would be smiling back at her, laughing with her.

But he was sitting up now, his head arched back, neck taut, long fair hair pressed against the shoulder blades, eyes staring and intent at the huge obliterating frame of the Boeing 747 three thousand feet above them.

"You're late, big bird," he said soundlessly against the roar of the aircraft. "Don't be late next week, not for the plucking of the Mushroom Man."

"What did you say?" she shouted, wriggling closer to him to hear his reply.

"Nothing, nothing. Just that they're flying late tonight." Her ear was close to his mouth, and he spoke softly, his delicate Irish brogue flavoring the words.

"What plane is that?" she said to him, watching over his shoulder the vast airborne mass, almost beautiful with its white fuselage and the deep sky-blue livery line running its length, tail erect and crowned with the simple star on the pure background.

"That, my little girl, is a Boeing 747, manufactured at Seattle, in the State of Washington, U.S.A. It's valued at a little more than fifteen million pounds, and that one is flying in Israel's color. El Al, and late again."

He got up from the grass and began to pull on his trousers over the dried-out swimsuit. Before he draped his shirt over his shoulders she saw again the reddened disfigurement of the healed puncture wound, diameter little more than a pencil width, low on the left side of his chest. She'd asked about it the day before, been told of a stumble while carrying a pitchfork, on the farm and many years back.

"Are we doing anything tonight?" She mentioned it hesitantly, though she'd already told her mother she'd be out late —at her friend's home.

"I'm sorry," he said, seeing her face fall open with the disappointment. "I'm sorry, I really am, but I can't tonight. I have to meet a man . . ."

"About a dog," she said.

"No, it's real. I have to meet a man tonight. It's been planned a long time, and he's coming over from abroad to see me. Really. There's some business I have to do, take a few days. I'll see you then, again. Definitely. Definitely. Come on, I'll walk you down to the bus stop."

She was near to tears when he left her waiting for a red double-decker to take her back to an early night at home.

For two hours Ciaran McCoy stayed beside the train departure board at Waterloo Station, waiting for the man he was to meet to come forward and introduce himself. He had fulfilled all his instructions. Red tie, light raincoat over his right arm, Avis Rent-A-Car sign displayed in his hand. It was futile and frustrating—endless faces scurrying past him, running to catch their trains, running to leave them, all anxious about being left in the belly of the great terminus a minute longer than was necessary. He'd been buffeted, pushed and shoved by those who saw him as an obstruction in their path, but never noticed, not acknowledged. Close to midnight he walked across the now near-empty concourse to the battery of telephone booths and dialed the seven-figure number he had been given.

His call was answered by a switchboard deep behind the Edwardian façade that housed a North African embassy in a smart SW7 address overlooking the favored Rotten Row and the spaces of Hyde Park. McCoy asked for an extension, was surprised when the operator did not say that there would be no one there at this hour, and was further surprised when the phone was again answered. Couldn't remember the word he was supposed to give. Been waiting too long, too wrought up to remember it. Bloody foreign word, and he didn't know what it meant.

"It's McCoy here. Ciaran McCoy. I was told to call this number. Our friend hasn't shown."

The voice at the other end was calm, reassuring, perfect English. Unconcerned at the lack of the code word. There had been a delay. The situation was uncertain. The project might be called off, might not. Developments were awaited. He should telephone again tomorrow evening, but not so late. The voice wished him goodnight, and the call was terminated.

Five seconds after McCoy put the receiver back into its rest, the tape recorder stopped rolling. It was standard procedure that all calls to that number were automatically monitored, and had been so ever since the extension number was obtained from a second officer of that embassy in exchange for Foreign Office silence about his drinking habits. The diplomat had done well from the bargain, the conservative Moslem government that he represented in London would have looked badly upon his behavior.

The tape would be one of scores of conversations recorded that night which would be replayed by shorthand typists working from the basement of a substantial building in Curzon Street, Mayfair, a bare mile from the embassy.

Three

David Sokarev always carried the Mauser pistol in the glove compartment of his car. It rested there on top of the maps and the packet of boiled sweets that his wife had bought him as an aid to ending his smoking habit. On top of the gun and hiding it was the rag that he used to clean the overnight moisture from his windshield. The pistol was loaded, but with the safety catch in force, and was fired only twice a year, when he went on the shooting range to the east of Beersheba. Left to himself he would have placed it in a drawer and forgotten about it. But he had been ordered to possess a gun, and therefore it was easier simply to leave it in the car. If the occasion had arisen when he was obliged to fire in anger, he would probably have missed. His chunky iron-rimmed spectacles were a witness to his poor eyesight. The pistol was never disturbed, rejected like the boiled sweets, but like them, of insufficient importance to make an issue out of.

There had been a suggestion that his work made him too sensitive a man to be driving himself to work, and there had been talk that he should have a driver pick him up from his home, take him to the laboratory, and then, late in the day, bring him back to Beersheba. He had railed at that as being preposterous, asked them whether there were so many able-bodied men without proper jobs to do that they could spare one for such sterile activity. He had won his case, and drove himself.

He was a careful and methodical man, and unlike so many of his fellow countrymen, drove slowly and with circumspection. It took him between forty-seven and fifty minutes between the time he left the flat up on the third floor of the block, till he presented himself with his identity card at the gate at Dimona. Colleagues using the same route would flash past him, hoot their horns and wave cheerfully at the old "Tortoise," as they had nicknamed him. It was a boring ride to have made most days a week and most weeks a year for the last sixteen years, but his mind was seldom concerned with the other traffic. The problems of plutonium, subcritical masses, fission, isotope separation, neutrons—they were what enveloped him as the little car trudged its way back and forth the twenty-four miles across the Negev desert. He would read, too, as he drove, the book propped against the steering wheel, apparently able to take in the printed word while successfully avoiding the fast-moving hazards which shared his road; few of his colleagues lightly accepted the offer of a lift.

When he had started to work at Dimona, the project had been at the apex of Israel's secret list. He had not been able to tell any of the family friends where he went each day, nor what his work consisted of. The buildings, tucked away amongst the sandhills and well back from the road, were described to the outside world as housing a textile factory, and no one who knew him could comprehend a link between David Sokarev and man-made fibers.

But the Bedouin who used to pass, listlessly urging their camels between the dunes, had taken the news of the cranes and bulldozers and cement-making apparatus across the border to the military governor of Egyptian El Arish. The message had gone to Cairo of huge construction works deep in the Negev, of wire fences that were sprouting, of armed troops patrolling. The concern in Cairo was passed to the American State Department in Washington. There, too, anxiety was expressed and the foolproof method of international espionage set in motion.

From a U. S. Air Force base in northern Iran a U-2 spy plane had taken off with orders to overfly Dimona and photograph the new complex. The pilot had violated Israeli air space at an altitude of fractionally more than fifteen miles. At the IAF field which had specific responsibility for Dimona they could only watch the radar blip of the American reconnaissance aircraft and contain their frustration that it was beyond their own operational ceiling. It had been a brilliantly hot October day, back in 1960, when the photographs were taken. Sokarev had been working in his temporary prefabricated wooden offices, awaiting the fulfillment of the director's promise that he was high on the list for more suitable and permanent premises. He, like everyone else who pored and bent over charts and diagrams and formulas, was unaware of the pictures being recorded in the upper stratosphere.

When the U-2 landed in Turkey, the rolls of film were rushed under conditions of great secrecy direct from the cameras in the plane's nose to another aircraft standing ready and fueled to fly to Washington. They showed the little wooden hut where Sokarev worked, or, rather, its roof, but there was small interest in that; what concerned the viewers was the bulky shape discernible a hundred yards away across the sand and surrounded by the lorries that were needed to bring up the materials. The men expert in interpreting altitude photography identified a medium-sized nuclear reactor, the integral plant necessary in the manufacture of the plutonium that is at the heart of an atomic explosion.

When Dimona was washed out into the open, the news made slight adjustments in Sokarev's life. The degree of security that had been wrapped around the very existence of the project was relaxed. The Israeli government issued statements about the requirement for nuclear energy for peaceful uses ranging from electricity power to the extended life of vegetables on shop counters.

Sokarev was pleased. Fewer of his friends regarded him with curiosity. Life became more normal.

In the halcyon days after the June victory of 1967—when the nation's defenses seemed secure and the Arabs had taken a bloodied, broken nose, been pushed far back from the Israeli settlements, across the deep buffer zones of Sinai, the Jordan Valley and the Golan Heights—there was little to concern Sokarev about the pace of his work. At forty-one he was a man young for his job, on the way up, regarded by his colleagues as brilliant, and directing his energies toward what his project director blithely called "the agro-nuclear complexes": the reclaiming of desert land through the use of thousands of millions of gallons of sea water distilled through nuclear power. The project did not last.

The war of attrition across the Suez waterway exacted a toll both in life and in terms of the fragile Israeli economy. New tensions rose along the Egyptian and Syrian borders. And on the day in October 1973, when Sokarev and his family were at prayer, Yom Kippur, the Arab armies breached the great defensive lines that lay along the Canal and bestrode the Golan. The peace was hard-won this time; none of the trumpeting of 1967 followed the cease-fire. Reports filtered through the foreign press of new, far-reaching Soviet rockets, sited on the plains behind Damascus and protected by nests of antiaircraft missiles, rockets that could reach any Israeli town, either with a conventional high-explosive warhead or armed with a localized nuclear device.

To Sokarev, and to many of his team, it was clear the time had come, perhaps belatedly, to consider hard what was called—in the common rooms around the world where men specialized in physics—the "nuclear option."

The days at Dimona started earlier, ended later. Sokarev and the team that was built around him wrestled with the problems of abbreviations in time and expenditure for the fashioning of the bomb. Extraction of uranium from the phosphate ores of the Negev was increased as the plant gulped up more than twenty-five tons a year. Some of the ablest men in the department were sent to the United States to work in laboratories, and to West Germany to study at the European nuclear center. The costly Jericho missile system was developed, with a range of more than three hundred miles, the country's own and independent delivery weapon.

The politicians began to talk. "The possibility of nuclear weapons moving into the Middle East theater should not be eliminated," said Moshe Dayan. Israel's president proudly announced that his country had assembled the knowledge and equipment to construct the bomb.

And from the reactor in the desert came the tiny quantities

of plutonium 239, at little more than eight kilograms a year, in bulk the size of a fruit from the Beersheba orangeries and with the capability to create a twenty-kiloton explosion. The bombs, equivalent in destructive capacity to those dropped more than thirty years earlier on Hiroshima and Nagasaki, could not be tested, but at least the stockpile was starting.

It had been a brutal twenty months for Sokarev, months of fierce hours, interminable arguments over money, government money, that never extended to the budgetary minimum he maintained his department must have if research were to continue. He took his papers home at night, but increasingly they were covered with the columns of figures that represented the finances of the program and were expressed in the currency of the inflated Israeli lira. He longed for the days gone by when his working brain had been overwhelmed only by the horizontal characters of the equations he sought to set up and then disprove, and if he could not find the flaw, then to rejoice in the knowledge of perfection.

That he was tired showed on him. His face was greyer, and overcast with the pallid shadow of yellowness that comes from perpetual artificial illumination, denial of sunlight, the harassment of worry. His trousers were poorly fitting and stretched, and his shirt bulged over his lower abdomen; the tennis that he had played twice a week, and which had been his principal form of enjoyment, was now denied him.

But the guard who stopped him that Thursday morning at the first of the security perimeter gates, and who knew the personnel that came and went at the plant, noted that the normally worn face of David Sokarev was a little brighter, a little livelier. As he looked into the car window, waiting for the Polaroid identity card to be produced, he saw almost a spark of recognition in the other man's eyes. Generally there was no acknowledgment, just the handing over of the document and its acceptance back. Today there was the inclination of the head, near to a greeting.

"You're looking well today, Professor," the guard said as he handed the plastic-coated card back to the waiting hand.

"So I should be. Off out of here for a few days. My last day, and then away for a bit."

"Holidays?" the guard asked before moving back to swing up

the red-and-white-painted Stop barrier that blocked advance. "Of a fashion. A few days in London, then on to New York, and perhaps San Francisco after that. The last isn't finalized. A few lectures, to meet old friends. Something of a holiday, yes."

Twice more the car was stopped by grey-brown-uniformed guards. Each time they swung their Uzi submachine guns across their backs and walked forward to check the card. All three men who spoke to the professor as he arrived that morning were to notice the fractional bounce that had lifted him.

"I'm late in," he said to his secretary in the outer office. "Was held up talking to the man on the gate." She said nothing. It was one minute past eight o'clock.

"What have we today?"

"Mostly meetings. The director wants to see you also, preferably in the afternoon. Two subcommittees in the morning, so that will fit well. And there was a call a few minutes ago from the Foreign Ministry. They want to drive down from Jerusalem to see you, but they'd like us to fix a time for the afternoon, and call them back. I would suggest about four, after you've seen the director." She was a pretty girl, tall, straight-backed, and wore an eye-riveting miniskirt high up on her sun-browned thighs. Efficient as well, and the office was chaos every time she left for military service.

"What do they want in Jerusalem?" He was behind the desk now, scooping at the papers from his tray and scattering them over the wooden surface.

"It was the security division from the Foreign Ministry. Protection branch. They said they wanted to talk about your trip."

It was closer to six in the evening, and many of the Dimona workers were already on their way home, before David Sokarev's desk was clear enough for him to feel able to abandon it for the three weeks of his visit to Europe and North America. There were no more letters to sign, charts to check, scribblings to be made in the margin of reports. No more excuses to prevent his seeing the two men who waited in his outer office.

When they came through the door, he saw they were both young. Fit and good-looking. They shook his hand. He did not apologize for keeping them so long, and they did not seem to expect it. Joseph Mackowicz had come to talk, Gad Elkin to listen.

Mackowicz said, "I am glad you could see us, Professor. We are both to be traveling with you throughout your journey. We will be very close to you at all times. It is best on these visits that we get to meet the people we accompany before we leave, rather than just seeing each other at the airport a few minutes before departure. I think you have little experience of being escorted on a visit abroad?"

"I have not been away for some years. It is a long time ago, and then I traveled only with my secretary." He saw Elkin smile. "Not the one I have now, I can assure you. A rather more formidable lady. But when I intended to take Anna to handle my correspondence, type my speeches, things like that, it was refused. Not enough for her to go, I was told. I did not anticipate that if they could not scrape together the lira for Anna, that they would be able to send two gentlemen such as yourselves. I had resigned myself to traveling on my own."

"Your typing will be taken care of, the embassies will find a girl for that." Mackowicz did not react, was not one to rise to even the most gentle humor. "We have the places that you will be visiting, and we will supervise your program. What we want for the moment is a guarantee that you will afford us your cooperation and take most seriously our advice."

The professor looked hard at the young man, adjusted his glasses back to the bridge of his nose. "I would never knowingly not cooperate."

"That, Professor, is excellent news. Not everybody in a position similar to yours is happy to have us in immediate proximity. Some talk of embarrassment for their foreign colleagues. I can assure you, if there is embarrassment, it is a necessary cross to bear."

"I had not given myself such importance," said the professor slowly, the tinge of sadness there, "nor had I realized that I might be at risk. It is not the sort of situation that one considers."

Mackowicz said, "We had not considered our athletes at Munich to be either politically important or at risk. We knew an Arab attack, from the Black September faction, would come at about that time somewhere in Europe. No one put the sum together, and no guard was given to our people. They died defenseless, and it will not happen again. A single tennis player, or swimmer or runner, if they represent Israel, then they are protected. It was all laid down in the reorganization that followed Munich. Inevitably. So, too, for a politician, a diplomat or a scientist of your status."

Anna carried in a tray with coffee. No milk, too expensive, sugar coarse and with the granules overlarge. They stopped talking while she was in the room and handing out the mugs. The professor thanked her, said he would send a post card, see her on his return. She should go home, he told her. He could lock up. She waved, a small, feminine gesture, at the door, closed it behind her.

"Gentlemen," said Sokarev, "I am only a scientist, perhaps only a technician. Not versed in the ways outside Dimona. I read the paper, not often, but I read it, and I hear the wireless in the evening. Though I had not imagined it before, I can accept the possibility of a threat. But I would not take it as a great one, a small risk only. So I ask myself these questions. Firstly, why did you come here tonight, a long journey—and we have discussed nothing of importance so far? Secondly, I ask why two men are needed to look after me. Why cannot this be done by our own people from the embassies when I get off the plane, or by the police forces of the countries that I visit?"

There was silence in the room. Sokarev held his gaze at Mackowicz, waiting for the answer. Watched him light his cigarette, unhurried, patient with the ignorance. In the distance there was the noise of a car starting up. The scientists would be gone soon, and the cleaners would be on their rounds. Permeating the room was the semi-audible moan of a faraway electric generator. A fly played around the professor's nose, till he swatted it away.

It was Elkin who spoke. "It had been intended there would be just one of us. The situation changed, and we have to change with it. You are regarded by government as high-risk category. You have much specialized knowledge from your work here. You head an important team. All those things make you an important target, but then, all those things we knew weeks ago when your itinerary was filed. Since that time there have been movements; we have had information that suggested to us that your protection should be increased. Our work, in a way, can be considered perhaps as sensitive as yours. You would not wish me to say more."

"You have said nothing," retorted Sokarev.

"We have listening posts," Mackowicz cut in. "We have people who listen for us, and we have people who interpret what they hear. It's a difficult, long-drawn-out process, and many times we are wrong. Often there are several factors in the air at the same time; rarely do they come to land together. But from what we learn, we try to form a shape, anticipate actions. This is what we are doing at the moment. The pattern is not yet whole in this instance, but it has a form, an outline."

"Specifically, there is a threat to me?" There was puzzlement from Sokarev, confidence about to drain.

"We cannot take it that far yet," said Elkin. "We know a squad from one of the Palestinian terror groups has been moving north across Europe. They were intercepted, on our advice, by the French authorities. At least two of them died. We believed from our informants that there were three. If so, one is not accounted for. They were on the road to Boulogne when they were blocked. It is reasonable to assume from that route that their destination was a cross-channel ferry and Britain. We have no political leaders, no military men in Britain in the next month. Only yourself, Professor."

Sokarev was quiet. Subdued. Unhappy in the presence of these chilling young men, growing resentful of the message they brought.

The silence, long and perceptible—to the point of shuffled feet—was broken by Mackowicz. "You will not have read about this, nor will you need to repeat it. Six nights ago the same group that has held our interest in Europe mounted a raid from their advance base in Lebanon across the fence toward Ramat Naftali, south of Kiryat Shmona. They were ambushed by an army patrol. There were five in all, and we captured one. The rest we killed in the action. The IDF statement that evening announced that one of the terrorists had escaped, though he was in fact in our hands. He talked to us. Under interrogation. They often do, you know. We gave him his life by barter. He would survive, but he would take back with him a radio transmitter. He could give us further information about operations.

That was the agreement we made with him. There were no messages, and he is dead. We have many eyes and ears in Fatahland, and yesterday we were told. He died not nicely, but in pain, and choking because his testicles were blocking his windpipe. Not the pleasant way to go, Professor. But from what I say, you will see that information is not easy to come by, and when we do have access, then we listen to what we are told."

Sokarev wanted to vomit. He rose up unsteadily from his chair and moved across the room. He felt more than his age, and a great weariness. By the door he switched on the light, banishing the spreading shadows, flooding the office with the fluorescent ceiling-hung bar. Apart from the chart that showed him which members of his team had booked their annual leave or were on extended sick leave, and a single photograph, the walls were bare. Uncomplicated, as he wanted his office. The photograph showed his three children: two girls in army slacks and regulation V-necked navy-blue sweaters; between them his son, a head taller, in light summer khaki with his pilot's wings on his chest. He'd taken the picture when he had them together for a Shabbat leave, and they'd be together again, same opportunity, tomorrow. They expected to fight, understood the new conflict, could comprehend the modern war fought crawling at belly-level beyond the frontiers of their country. But to Sokarev the dark and sinister images that the two security men had introduced to his office were hostile and alien.

"You are presumably going to tell me what this terrorist said under questioning?" He had stayed by the door.

Mackowicz and Elkin stood up. Mackowicz said, "He told us they had been planning an attack in Europe. He did not know the location, he did not know the target. He'd known only the code word for the operation. Under extreme interrogation he gave it to us. The PFLP General Command is the terrorist grouping, and they have given to this operation the word *kima*. It is an Arabic word, of the Palestinian dialect. Translated, it is 'mushroom.' Not the small button-shaped one of the restaurant kitchen, but the larger, free-growing plant that magnifies and flourishes. That is why we consider a man from Dimona to be at risk. That is why there will be two of us at your side when you travel."

*   *   *

After they had gone, David Sokarev sat a long time in the room.

Then he collected together the papers he would require for his journey, packed them into the old frayed leather briefcase, and locked the door behind him. There were few lights left on in the office blocks and laboratories as he walked to his car, but all around were the brilliantly lit wire fences. The watchtowers were manned after darkness and he could see the men high up on the stilted platforms, and below them the dog handlers with the proven attack Alsatians. This was the oasis that he knew, safe, rewarding, isolated. Severed from the two men powering their way back to Jerusalem.

When he reached for his keys he found that his hands were trembling, that he had difficulty selecting the correct one to open the door. He rested in the seat for a few moments, to calm himself, mollify the breathiness that affected him, then drove off for the gates, and the road, and home. At the three check-points the guards called out a greeting, but won no response.

He drove home faster than usual, arriving at the flat a full eight minutes earlier than his established habit would have permitted. His wife noticed the drawn look that spilled out from the side of his mouth, and the tension about his eyes. For the first time in his adult life he was experiencing fear. It was a fear of the unknown. Of a strange city of millions of people, but where one man . . . or two . . . or three . . . or four had a solitary and inflexible purpose: the destruction of David Soka-rev, of himself. He'd seen the photographs of these men in the *Jerusalem Post* and the afternoon paper, *Yediot Aarenot;* they were on their backs, broken and spent, cut down by gunfire, surrounded by the circle of elated soldiers. They always died, always seemed to end their missions dragged by the ankles to an army jeep, flung onto a bloody stretcher with the reverence of a turnip sack. Refuse. Garbage. But there was no reason that Sokarev could see to believe their commitment would be any the less in a foreign capital.

She brought him his meal. Some liver, the monies for it dug deep from the housekeeping purse. She watched the way he toyed with the meat, eating to please her. He told her nothing of Mackowicz and Elkin, and what they had said inside his office.

Four

A city is a vulnerable, flaccid target for an act of terrorism. Huge and preoccupied and indifferent. The ideal hunting ground, and never more so than if the stalkers are a small, motivated group of men whose numbers can be counted on the fingers of one hand. In time of war the city can be mobilized, organized and put into uniform, with specific tasks to perform. But when peace reigns it absorbs the danger, turns the other cheek, has too much to concern itself with to be agitated by the puny cancer flowing at will in its body. Breeding and dying, buying and selling, hurrying and resting, all these consume its restless energy.

The Provisional IRA proved conclusively how defenseless a great international capital is—148 bombs in twenty-two months and the mighty carcass barely knew it was under attack. Cars packed with gelignite disintegrating amongst shopping crowds, duffel bags exploding on busy railway platforms, mutilated bodies ferried away in fleets of ambulances. But the next time the sirens screamed, the crowds still gathered to watch, amused sometimes, always interested, never involved.

Where eight million people are gathered together over an area of some four hundred square miles, everyone is a stranger, no one belongs. No man has the right to be suspicious, aroused by his neighbor's behavior. For the terrorist, there is anonymity here, the opportunity to blend into whatever background he so chooses. If he has funds he can take a smart flat—Mayfair or Belgravia, where a porter will salute him as he goes out, but will ask no questions, expect no answers. Without money he can turn to the myriad of small hotels behind the big railway termini of North London, pay his pound notes when he registers, and abandon himself to total privacy. In the big city the man who is careful and patient and skilled in the art of guerrilla warfare should survive. He can blame only himself if he fails.

The forces ranged against him are meager. The principal and most obvious bastion that he must avoid is the headquarters of the civilian police force, at Scotland Yard and close to Victoria Station. Confronted with the increasing problems of conventional crime, whether serious or minor, of public apathy and lack of manpower, the Metropolitan police have been forced into a crash course in combatting international violence. They started without experience, and it has been a hard road over which to make up ground, with no luxury of time permitted. The whole concept was far from officials' minds when they moved the offices and files and laboratories into a towering glass-faced structure so vulnerable to car-bomb attack that policemen now have to patrol the pavements outside to prevent any vehicle from parking unattended within fifty feet of its walls. But of the hundreds of detectives who scurry in and out of the main swinging doors, flashing their warrant cards at the bemedaled commissionaires, relatively few are engaged in antiterrorist operations. Those who are belong to Special Branch, the wing formed close to a hundred years ago to counter the Irish Fenian threat.

The Irish problem still dominates their work, tying men down on the long-drawn-out surveillance of buildings, meetings, pubs, airports and homes, along with the constant search for reliable informers.

The Branch men also have to concern themselves with the potential of subversion, and keep their paper work up to date on the fringe anarchist groups, the most militant of the trades union officials, the activities of the Iron Curtain bloc diplomats. They have the responsibility of personal protection for important Britons, from the Prime Minister down, and also for foreign persons of rank arriving in the country.

They are not generously endowed with funds, nor with manpower. Less than five hundred men, and the country to cover. They had been informed of the planned visit of David Sokarev to Britain, but with only four days to go until his arrival at Heathrow Airport, were unaware of two crucial factors: Sokarev's importance to Israel and the extent of the threat against him. At a later stage there would be a discussion over the telephone between the Middle East desk and the security attaché at the Israel embassy, probably the night before the professor flew in. In the normal way of things, the decision on the need for protection would be taken then, with consideration given to the availability of officers and more pressing priorities.

But, for the survival of David Sokarev on his journey through London, there was another group of men far more important than the officers of Special Branch. They worked from little-known premises in one of the most fashionable districts of the capital. Close to the Playboy Club, the London Hilton and the Londonderry Hotel is a gaunt five-story building. It is in need of painting and pointing and general repair. Its windows in the uniform metal-rimmed rows so beloved by between-the-wars architects are shielded by lace curtains to prevent outsiders from seeing the personnel who work inside; those on the lower floors are protected by half-inch-thick concertina steel meshes. Side entrances to the block have been bricked up, as have the upper windows at the corners of the building, which still show the defensive rifle-aiming slits hurriedly fitted in 1940. Visitors are discouraged by the lack of any plaque on the walls beside the main doorway that would give a clue to the occupation of those who work behind the closed windows. The parking meters set into the pavements outside the front entrance are masked by red plastic hoods to prevent the casual motorist from legitimately leaving his car there. Above the doorway, and needing the attention of the cleaners if passers-by were to be able to read them easily, are the words *Leconfield House*. The building carries no other visual identification.

It is the nerve center of the country's most secretive organization, the one responsible for the deeply undercover counterespionage and counterterrorist operations; the British Security Service works from here.

                    *   *   *

Eleven hours after the tape recording of Ciaran McCoy's conversation with the Arab diplomat had been completed, the spools were on the desk of a man who used a small office on the second floor of Leconfield House. A transcript had been made by the duty clerks who had first listened to the playback, and that, too, lay on the high-polished oakwood surface. The room occupied by Philip Whilloughby-Jones was bare to the point of starkness. A regulation square of carpet, determined by his civil service grade, covered the center floor space and was surrounded by aging, though systematically polished, linoleum. Set in one wall was the doorway, opposite the only window; on the third wall was a calendar sent out by a firm that specialized in the postal sales of garden bulbs; against the fourth was a grey-painted steel filing cabinet. Grouped in a semicircle in front of the desk were four chairs, framed in metal tubing, seats covered with yellow plastic, not designed for comfort but for working men who would leave them when their business was completed. The chair in which Jones sat offered only slightly more concessions in that it boasted two vaguely cushioned armrests.

Jones—he detested the hyphenated name his father had taken to using after his admittance to the Masonic order of a small East Midlands industrial town—was short and sparely built, not admitting to superfluous flesh. He had a sharp gull nose which jutted out above the brush mustache that was a legacy of his Royal Air Force service before he had joined Security. His thin cheeks, concavely merging into the shape of his bone structure, lacked the color and verve of a man who can regularly spend time out of doors. His hair, which he tended hurriedly and carelessly each morning, was wispy and greying, in shape only for the time that the water he had used on his comb maintained order. The brightness lay in his eyes; narrow, deep-set, but alert and alive. It was his lower jaw that separated him from other men, the way the skin, lacking in wrinkles and hair, had been transplanted from his right buttock to cover the incinerated layers that he had lost so many years before. The replacement had no gloss, no animation, and at the point where the new had been grafted to the old, it irritated and annoyed. Jones was responsible for the general surveillance of the activities of Middle East embassies located in London.

Duggan, of Irish Affairs, would be down in fifteen minutes to talk with him, and Fairclough, Arab Affairs (Palestinian). Before they came, there was time to look again at the file on the embassy in Princes Gate. So much of it was done with the files; the most thorough and successful course of action invariably followed the writing down of minutiae—that was the Director General's belief, and the way he expected his subordinates to operate. Jones shifted his chair back and stood up, feeling for his keys as he did so. He unlocked the center of the three drawers of the cabinet, and rolled it out. Hundreds of typed reports confronted him. Observations, assessments, personal biographies, recorded telephone transcripts. At the particular embassy, several telephone lines were listened to, each extension warranting a separate brown folder. He flicked through them till he came to the one he wanted and lifted it out. Few sheets there. The number was only recently known, and it had been noted that little traffic came through it. Back at his desk he began to read, quickly and expertly, occasionally writing a few words in a neat, trained hand on the memory pad. There was time for a pipe before the others came, and he lit up, sucking far down into the charred bowl of the wood.

Wait till there's a big party, then move, they'd told him. Abdel-El-Famy had delayed going through the French Customs and Immigration, waiting till the student group swamped the blue-uniformed officials. He had merged with them, one moment on their fringe, the next right amongst them. But the checks at Boulogne were casual, guided only by the report from St. Omer that they should be vigilant for a man mud-spattered and probably unshaven. The precautions the battery-shaved Famy took were unnecessary as he stood in his laundered jeans. The orange shirt that had been neatly ironed and which had not suffered from its time in the grip bag, the hip-length navy corduroy jacket—they were his protection. He fitted no description that had been issued to the harbor police. The pistol and the soiled clothes were successfully buried beneath the previous autumn's windfall of leaves in a wood to the east of the town. They would be found eventually, but long after he had completed the task that had been set for him.

On the crossing, short and calm, as the Sea Link ferry

plowed its way across the narrow corridor of water, Famy deliberately made acquaintance with a section of the party. His knowledge of French was variable, but sufficient to allow him to strike up conversation. Spirits were high, as they always are at the start of a holiday, and there was no shortage of young people to laugh and joke with. The lecturer into whose care the students had been entrusted for their eight days in London was vaguely aware that the tall, swarthy man, a little older than the others, had not been at the station in Paris. It puzzled him, but he knew only a few of the group, had had little time on the Paris-to-Boulogne leg of the journey to get close to them, so he shrugged it off. Perhaps a friend from home, or from school, or from . . .

Famy saw the white ribbon of cliff as the boat swung to port and began its run to the long jetty. Not as clear white as he had thought, nor as formidable a barrier as the one he had read of back in the University of Beirut. Rather shallow, and with the fields coming further down toward the sea than he had expected. The castle caught his eye, powerful in its toad squatness, but old-fashioned, antiquated. He smiled to himself, savoring it; that was his enemy, tired now, outdated. Unable to compete in the new and modern world that he sought for, unable to comprehend the hitting power of the Palestinian movement, unable to defend itself against the new philosophy of revolution and attack.

The two girls from Orléans and the boy from St. Etienne were a long time getting their baggage together after the complicated process of docking and tying up. Famy was patient; the rest of the group less so. There were cries for the three to hurry themselves, from the lecturer and other students. It suited Famy well. Out of the delay would come anxiety about the train connections for London, and that would mean a concentrated, excited rush at the Customs and Immigration barriers.

And that was how it was. As Customs quizzed the first four of the party the lecturer began to shout and wave the folder with the rail tickets. Other students joined in, all hugely enjoying the performance. The officials were good-humored enough, didn't get bloody-minded, and the party went through. Famy handed over his filled-in white immigration card at the desk, and was deep in talk with the two girls as they swept past the duty Port Watch Special Branch men. He didn't rate a glance from them. His passport was still close in his inner pocket, unrequired, unexamined.

For Famy there was now a moment of indecision. His orders, the orders for the three of them when they left Beirut, had been specific about the next stage of the journey. The instruction was that under no circumstances were they to travel via the direct Dover-to-London rail connection. If for any reason you are suspected, they had said, the authorities have two and a half hours' grace to make up their minds and intercept at the terminal at Victoria. His people had been adamant about this, and thorough enough to provide the bus timetable that would enable the squad to move down the coast and then link up with a train not connected with the cross-channel services. Famy reasoned that although he was traveling a full day behind the schedules that had been prepared for him, the timetables would remain constant.

He had felt safe with the group and was reluctant to leave them, but his orders made no allowance for personal initiative at this stage. When the girls looked again for him, he had disappeared.

There were endless waits at bus stops, interspersing the tedious stages of the journey. Dover to Folkestone, seven miles. Folkestone to Ashford, seventeen miles. Ashford to Maidstone, eighteen miles. And in all that time, sitting cramped in the leg-restricting seats, nobody, with the exception of the ticket man, spoke a word to him. Not a greeting, not a smile, not a syllable of conversation.

In Maidstone, a dull little town it looked to him as he walked with his bag through the streets busy with late Friday afternoon shoppers, he reverted to the railway system, and a slow-stopping train to London.

As he climbed into the carriage he could reflect with satisfaction that he was within an hour of his destination, and the streets on which it had been determined that David Sokarev would die.

It was a difficult meeting in Leconfield House. Three men close around the desk, close to their copies of the recorded transcript, attempting to read more into the badly typed words than they could find. There were many silences, and a brief adjournment had been forced on them by the necessity for Duggan and Fairclough to return to their offices and search among their own paper work for anything that might throw light on the single brief conversation they had begun with. After an hour of sparring around the problem, Jones had felt it was time for some sort of summary and analysis.

"Let's just stop a minute," he said, wearying of the general, wanting to be back with the specifics. "Let's establish what we have from our own material before we start going elsewhere and picking other people's stuff. First, the number our friend McCoy telephoned is rarely used, but was considered of some importance or that little sod wouldn't have given it to us and looked as though he thought he was doing us the favor. When we spoke to him last he seemed to think we were getting the bargain out of it. So, it's sensitive. That's born out by our second point of reference, the call itself. It's different from other calls on the line, on the number. They've been in some code, but we haven't enough on that yet, and it's not broken."

He reached into one of his files, taking out four foolscap sheets, each with only three lines printed on it. "Stuff like this. Doesn't make much sense, but this is what we have. 'Accommodation 173.65.312.' That was put over three days ago, bit of preamble, not much. English accent, probably disguised. Next night something similar, same sort of style. 'Rendezvous as arranged 77.1.6.' Both incoming calls being given the information. On to the message last night. To my mind it represents a failure of rendezvous. Clear to the deaf that, nothing remarkable in that piece of deduction. But where the pattern breaks down is that though the voice is the same as the first two calls, this time he uses a name. Introduces himself. Doesn't use a code word, busts straight in."

Fairclough spoke. "Try the simplest way through. McCoy, the name we have and which is perhaps genuine, he's hanging about last night. Cools his heels waiting for someone. Gets fed up. Wants to know what's happening and calls the number, the contact number he's been given. Uses the call box. But he's got to be angry—hopping, bloody mad. Too angry to remember the drill he's been given. What's the code word used in the first two calls?" It annoyed Fairclough that he couldn't remember it; a concise, organized man, he liked to have things at his fingertips. "Just one word, it seems," said Jones. "Just the word 'Mushroom,' then straight into the message, and whatever that means. No delay, very professional. No possibility of a trace on a call of the length they've been using."

"Bloody impossible," interjected Duggan. Didn't like the way it was shaping, the pattern that was building. Too ominous, too much that smacked of planning—and who plans, and takes this trouble over the casual, the unimportant?

"Back to the scene, back to the facts." Jones knew the way a meeting could disintegrate into sidetracking, theory, and end up with a morning gone, and nothing for the paper, for the file. "We establish that for last night's call there is no use of the code. We also establish that our little diplomat feels it's worth sitting in his miserable hutch half the evening waiting for the incomings, long after the crowd he works for are off swigging sherbet and tomato juice on the merry-go-round. When we look at him, what we have on him, there's damn all. New here, within the last few jobs, ostensibly small job, visas and passports. Oilmen and a few businessmen, not that many, but he has a phone line of his own and extension not listed in their directory. Takes calls at any time, either arranged or he sleeps in there."

He paused, talking too much, doing the bloody schoolmaster bit again. Shouldn't be like that with his colleagues, but he'd caught the Duggan chill, didn't want it to spread. Even among friends, doubt and apprehension are corrosive. Bloody daft, though, wasn't it. Three grown men playing schoolboy riddles, working on a brain tease. Fun this one, because they've torn up the answers, won't tell you whether you're right or not. Can change the questions halfway through, can't they, just when you're warming. Their initiative, always the same, always the bastards have the initiative. And the three of them were there, pushing the hot air up, seeking another justification for another lost weekend. Ought to have the head examined, working himself into a lather, eighty-hour week, another fraught telephone call home. Bloody stupid. Plow on, Jonesey, they're all waiting. "So we come finally to the complication. Mysterious Irish voice, the magic accent that gives us all wet dreams at night."

Duggan looked pained. Fairclough smiled.

Jones went on, "What is McCoy doing—waiting for his mate, and when the blind date doesn't show, phoning a confidential embassy number? Thoughts, gentlemen."

He'd finished. Let the others pick the bloody bones out of that lot. Nasty old smell it left, not too tangible yet, but enough of a stench to alert him.

Duggan's turn. He'd contributed little so far. The area he covered in his work was very different from that of the other two men. They were long-range, working on hypotheses, dealing with the possible but the unlikely. His concern was the probable, an exact and known threat that went under the initials of PIRA—Provisional Irish Republican Army. When he had slipped back to his office earlier he had checked against his own list of suspects, and the cross references, looking for any mentions, any traces of Ciaran McCoy. None existed. He had telephoned the headquarters of Military Intelligence at Lisburn, County Down, in Northern Ireland. They would begin their searches, feed his request into the computer. Negative or positive would be on the Telex by lunchtime at the earliest, midafternoon by the latest.

"If the boy's PIRA, it's difficult to explain. They've had contacts with this government. Bought arms there. The Claudia and the Kalashnikovs that we intercepted, they were from this source. They've had meetings there, discussions, but their politics are the width of the Sahara apart. If there is a liaison, then it would be of direct necessity. It's to do one thing, then forget it. They couldn't hold together for anything sustained. But we have to know about this boy, we have to localize him."

"It's the place we have to start," Fairclough chipped in. "Only bloody place we can begin. It's from McCoy we start pulling the pieces together. But if they're talking about linking up, then we're not far off the spectacular. After rendezvous they don't hang about knitting, they move onto target. That's the Arab way, what we have to be thinking about if we believe the liaison exists. They come in late and they hit and they shift. Munich's the best example. The crowd that went into the Olympic village arrived two and three days before the attack. But they'll have done the planning, and with thoroughness. Go back to Munich again—they were setting that up seven months earlier."

"Don't know why we bloody bother," said Duggan, determined to depress.

"Perhaps they're not available to come at all," Jones mur-

mured. The smile playing around his lips, contorted somewhat on the graft line, accentuated the divisions in the age of the skin. "You saw the morning papers. Shoot-out near Boulogne. Two men believed Arabs cut up at a roadblock. But nothing from the 'Firm' yet."

"Nice thought," agreed Fairclough.

There was a gentle knock on the door. The girl who came in was tall, a little plump, fair hair back over her shoulders, her skirt an inch too long, her sweater an inch too tight. Too many bulges. She was Helen Anderson and had been personal secretary to Jones for the last eight years.

"Sorry to interrupt, sir," she said quietly.

No, you bloody aren't, thought Duggan. You run this bloody office, come and go when you please. Sorry, my arse.

She repeated, "Sorry, sir, I didn't put it through, but there's been a message for Mr. Fairclough from Foreign Office. The Israelis have made a contact with our people in Cyprus. The report will be coming over the wire later on. When they've put it through the mincer, found the right code book, it'll be sent over. They said it was important, that you should wait on for it." She nodded her head, accepted that the message was understood, and was gone.

"That's the bloody evening gone, for the lot of us," said Fairclough. "You'll be waiting all ears and pencils for the phone chat-up, Duggan for trace, me flogging through this lot."

They all laughed at that. They bitched and moaned every Friday night when work saturated their desks, and always stayed.

Only a very few of the businessmen who dropped in for a quick one with their wives or secretaries or mistresses at the White Elephant or the Curzon House Club on the other side of the street would have any inkling of the work of the men whose lights burned late into the night in the gaunt building opposite.

The Israeli who had flown to the Akrotiri Royal Air Force base in southwest Cyprus was traveling under the direct instructions of the director of Military Intelligence in Tel Aviv. He came anonymously, the only passenger in an aging nine-seater Aero Commander. Much of the exchange of information between the various wings of Israel's security services and the

British Secret Intelligence Service—SIS, or the "Firm," as the trade called it—was conducted in the immense, sprawling RAF camp. Sent to meet him was one of the resident British team, who had driven the seventy-five miles from Nicosia in response to a telephone message from the Israeli embassy there to the British High Commission. The British took note of the warnings that were flashed to London from the island; on at least half of the occasions that troops had been drafted into Heathrow Airport, it followed close on information received via the harsh sun-reflecting tarmac at Akrotiri.

That evening the two men wasted little time, and the Israeli was in the air again less than twenty-five minutes after their conversation had begun. It was sufficient for him to make five points. First, that a Palestinian assassination squad had been intercepted on its passage through Northern France. Second, the Israeli security representative in Paris was both unhappy with the French authorities' follow-up of the incident and uncertain that all the members of the gang were accounted for. Third, the Israelis had gained the knowledge that the operation was code-named "Mushroom." Fourth, that his country's premier but largely unknown nuclear scientist would be leaving Tel Aviv for Britain on the following Monday to fulfill a long-standing speaking engagement. And fifth, his government would react extremely unfavorably if any incident should mar the visit. Understatement was the man's style, but he repeated the last three times.

"He is important to us. Very important in certain fields that we consider vital to our national defense. You understand what I have said?"

The Englishman looked across at the ground crew, standing beside the plane out of earshot but curious about the two men. He said, "If he's so important and the threat exists, why not call the visit off, forget about it?"

"If we did that every time there was a threat, we would become immured, be sterilized. We do not bend the knee to these bastards, and we expect the support of your agencies in the United Kingdom."

"Anything else that could help us?" said the Englishman. He thought: The little sod, he's enjoying it. Always do when they can wrap someone else up in their interminable problems.

"Nothing more. Just keep it tight round him, our professor. As you would say, tight as a guinea pig's arse."

Always the bloody same, thought the Englishman. They revel in it, rest of the world jumping to their bloody orders, little sod. He, too, would have a destroyed evening, writing and then encoding his report, but unlike the men in London, he would be scratching out of a cocktail party. The big girl from Chancery would have . . . Made you bloody sick.

The information that Duggan had requested was brought from the basement bank of teletype machines at four o'clock. He read the paper with care, the frown deepening on his forehead, the anxiety growing as he waded his way through the lines of blue-punched capitals.

Timing: 15.52 hours. Friday 28/6.
Subject: McCoy, Ciaran Patrick Aloysius.
Address: Ballynafeigh fm, nr Crossmaglen, SArmagh, NI
Age/DOB: 22 years, 14.3.54.
Security File: For last three years McCoy has been member Crossmaglen Bn PIRA. After one year was reported I/C Active Service Unit operating Cullyhanna area. Believed expert rifle shot comma natural leader. Arrested Sec Forces 8/12/74. ICO and detention order. Held HM Prison Maze where became PIRA cage commandant. Freed on Sec of State's instruction 3/7/75. Since then active in political work and would return again to violence if situation further deteriorates. Last is Mil Intelligence and SB assessment. Believed to be responsible for various shootings incidents in S Armagh area, specifically RUC patrol car 17/8/74 and sniping of paratroop killed 10/10/74. Pix and Prints following.
Background: Undermentioned is person to person confidential from Mil Intelligence HQ 13BDE Lurgan, NI and not for release outside your department. "We are astonished at release of McCoy and protests were via Commander Land Forces appropriate political offices. Reply was that as McCoy only detainee from that area and response to local PIRA required in existing cease-fire situation he was being freed. Exclaimer. Regarded as of high calibre and exception to colleagues in that has good educational standards with full secondary education from Armagy City. Deceptive in manner, could pass well in all company.

Re your specific requests:

1. Last seen in area approx 10/12 days ago.
2. No known visits to London, but sister once worked St Mary's Hosp, Paddington London NW
3. Would have considerable disguise capabilities witness long period before pick up.
4. Last interrogated by Maj Ian Stewart, Int Corps, Rtd, address obtainable Ministry of Defense (Personnel).

Upsummer: Hard boy. Bestest luck.

Duggan photocopied the paper three times. One for Jones, one for Fairclough, one for his departmental head. The original he put into the new folder, marked with McCoy's name on the outside, which up till then had contained only the transcripts of the phone calls to the embassy.

He reread the information, interpreting the officialese of the message. The implications to his trained mind were fearsome. A top man, in a top-grade Provisional setup, leader of an active service unit, arrested, served with an interim custody order, then a detention order, and then released by some bloody politician in order to keep a cease-fire going when everyone knew the bastards were on their knees and suing for peace. Responsible for at least two deaths. Poor devils, gunned down, and not even the satisfaction of having their man spend the rest of his natural behind bars. Not even the General able to get the decision reversed. Made you want to heave, have a cry, pack it in.

So what was little McCoy, the little bugger, doing running around London, calling up embassies, missing his links? Duggan hurried to the lift and the floor below where Jones had his office.

Five

His wife had noted the preoccupation that gripped David Sokarev. The listlessness, the unwillingness to contribute anything in conversation, the desire just to slump in his deep chair, the books at his desk left unopened. There were often times when his work had seemed to force him down, literally bowing his shoulders with the pressures of the speed and finesse and intricacy required for the study of nuclear action.

But on previous occasions the signs of extreme exhaustion and depression had been well telegraphed, and they had been able to discuss them, thereby lessening the load. But not this time. She found little response to her gentle feelers for information about what was weighing on him, was just shrugged off, and left with a feeling of frustration and inadequacy. She hoped that the arrival of the children, as she still called them, would be enough to rouse him when they came later in the day.

Sokarev himself thought continuously of what the security men had told him, wondered why they had found it necessary to take him into their confidence, regretted that they had. He was not a man used to fear and could not remember a similar sensation of such intensity. Like an infant afraid of being left alone in an unfamiliar darkened room, he had come in the last capsulated twenty-four hours to dread the visit to the strange city.

When his wife had suggested just before nightfall succeeded dusk that they take a walk together, he had shaken his head, heavy with the negative. He heard her sigh her disappointment as she fidgeted with a duster behind his chair.

"We've time," she'd said, "before the children come. We could go down to the new swimming pool, just a few hundred meters, a few minutes. We'll be back well before them."

He'd shaken his head again, and she'd dropped it.

He sat for a few more minutes, then got up abruptly. "I'd like a walk," he said quietly. "I'd like to go on my own. I won't be long." Her face clouded, he watched the pain he had inflicted. Her jaw seemed to tighten, her eyes to close a little. "There is a problem. I have to think about it. It has no place for you. Not long-term. Resolved very soon. I'm sorry."

There was a warm, dry heat out on the street. The children were on the pavement playing with footballs, and they made way for the professor. Spiced kitchen smells came to him as he walked past the blocks, and mingled with the scents from the flowering trees that had been planted when the flats were built. There was a noise. An argument high above him. A couple shouting abuse at each other, fiercely combative.

It was difficult for him to concentrate on the question that dominated his thinking; too many extraneous sights and senses forced their way over him. He walked little more than half a mile, then turned and came slowly back. When he had reached the entrance on the ground floor that led to his apartment, he saw parked outside the Mini his son drove, and he went on around to the back of the building where the garages were. He unlocked the door of his own garage, and then the door of the car on the passenger side, and slid into the seat.

His hand wavered a moment before he opened the glove compartment. Underneath the duster, where it always was, rested the Mauser pistol. Sokarev took it in his hand, weighed it, felt the black hard shape of the butt pressing down onto his palm. The magazine was fastened into position. Live bullets, the power to kill, or to protect, was there, uncomfortable, in his hand. They're dragging you down, old man, he said to himself, pulling you into their own pit, where crude, insensitive violence settles all. What learning, what thought, what intellectual capacity is demanded to ease the stiff and metallic lever of the safety catch that transforms this from a useless piece of engineering into a killing instrument? So vulgar, so alien. To the men who would accompany him to London, the gun would be as familiar as their shoelaces, their toothpaste, the belts that held their trousers on their hips.

He would take it with him. Whether they liked it or not, those two young men would have to accept it. A part of his destiny he would keep in his own hands. Retain a say in his own survival chances. He put the pistol back and covered it again with the duster.

As he paused at the door of his flat, searching in his pocket for the key, he could hear his wife talking, her voice anxious, excited, and the quieter tones of his son. But he felt calmer now, more steadied. When he walked inside, there was the smile of greeting on his face.

At Victoria Station the Arab pushed his way past the crowds of surging homeward commuters toward the telephone kiosks. He waited his turn till the box in front of him was vacant, nodded his gratitude to the man who held the door open for him, and went inside. It smelled in the dank cubicle. Perhaps a man had vomited there. The cleaning had been inadequate. He read the instructions, found a twopence coin and dialed the number he had memorized. When the call was answered, and there was the vibrant noise of the beeps instructing him to feed his money into the appropriate slot, he panicked for a moment. The coin slid through the mechanism, emerging in a small tray below. He fumbled for it, and pushed it again into the machine. A pause, then the answering voice. He spoke the number of the extension they had given him. Through the earpiece pressed close to his head he heard the click that denoted the reconnection. Another voice announced the number he had just asked for, confirming it for him.

Famy said, "Mushroom, one has arrived."

From the other end, curt and hurried, "Same rendezvous, as if you had been here last night. You know it?"

Famy said, "Yes, I have it memorized, I . . ."

The line was dead, the voice replaced by the purring constant sameness of the dialing tone.

Three hours to kill. Time to be lost, evaporated. Famy walked
out into the late evening sunshine and onto the London pavements. In front of him was a tourists' stall. Union Jacks, dolls in
guardsmen's uniforms, post cards of Buckingham Palace, cardboard replicas of "Gentlemen's Lavatory" and "Piccadilly."

His voice seemed diffident as he asked the elderly man sitting
on a stool beside his counter, "Excuse me, excuse me. I wonder,
do you have the *AZ Book of London?* A map called the AZ."

The man looked at him, boring into his face, no reason, just
a mannerism. He handed the blue, white and red paperback
book to Famy.

"A *to* Z," he said patronizingly, repeating it. Look of contempt on his face. "Thirty pence it'll cost you."

Famy moved away with the book. Across the fast-flowing
road he could see a sign. *Sandwiches and Snacks* it proclaimed.
He felt hungry, tired. He waited till a group of pedestrians had
gathered by the traffic lights, and joined them as they scurried
across the wide space. Safety in numbers. He looked at the huge
white-fronted porticoed houses of Lower Belgrave Street. It
was what he might have imagined of London: grand, majestic,
privileged. In the café an Italian brought a coffee to his small,
constricted table, and he ordered some bread and salad. He
flicked at the book, taking in the labyrinthine network of lines
and words that made up the Greater London area. When his
food came, he reached inside his coat for the slim diary he
carried, and amongst a jumble of figures in the section for accounts at the end of it, selected the top line. It read "77.1.6."
He shouldn't have written those numbers in his diary. The
order had been to memorize them. Dani and Bouchi, they
wouldn't have written them on paper. But Famy had been
nervous of forgetfulness. He was aware that for the first time he
had broken an instruction of the mission.

The sensation of guilt, though faint, caught him as he started
to work the code system he had been given. He noted the
numbers, printed heavily in black at the top extremes of each
page, and went carefully through the book till he came to page
77. There was a 1 printed smaller below it, marking a series of
squares. He counted through his alphabet, learned years ago at
school, searching for the letter that corresponded to the number 6. On his fingers he came to the letter F. He peered closely
at page 77, directing his sight at the square marked laterally by

the figure 1 and vertically by the letter F. In the square there was a shaded-in area, a quarter of an inch across, marked "Waterloo." They had said the rendezvous would be at a station, but that there were several, and he would be told which one only when he had arrived. If for any reason, his briefing had gone on, it is not suitable for a rendezvous to take place, you should go straight to the accommodation, but that would not be desirable. He checked with the figures for the accommodation code. "173.65.312." This time he turned to the back index of the map, sought out page 173, and began to work his way down the extreme left-hand column of street names. The sixty-fifth in the descending order read "Englefield Road, N.1. 4C 46." The accommodation address was 312 Englefield Road, on the fringes of Islington and Dalson in North London.

A transcript of Famy's call to the embassy was hurried up to Jones's office.

"There's no chance of a trace," said the man who brought it. "Lasted about fourteen seconds, the whole thing, and that includes fumbling with the money and getting transferred. There's a fair bit of background where the call originated, probably a public place, but that's where most of the phone boxes are. It's not inside a building, anyway."

"We definitely can't pick up a call like that?" Jones queried.

"Not a cat in hell. No way at all. Need an awful lot more than that."

"And the voice," persisted Jones.

"Need more time with that. Foreign, and we can go a bit further than that. Not U.S.A., not North European, not African, not Asian. I'd put in a bid for Mediterranean, not Latin but East."

"Thank you," said Jones, and the man made his way out of the office.

There were men in the department trained to work on phonetics and speech. Experts who would be able to pinpoint the origin of the caller, or at least the region in which he had spent time long enough for it to affect the vowel and consonant construction of the syllables. It would take them no great time, but Jones was certain that whatever they came up with would merely be the professional confirmation of what in his own mind he already knew.

So he had arrived, their little friend. Missed his first appointment, but was now in and ready to make up the lost time for the rendezvous. Right code word, right part of the bloody world, and ready to meet up with this sodding little Provo.

Jones reached across for his white telephone, the one which carried the Department's main number and an extension. The one beside it was red, carried a separate number, and was left clear for incoming calls. He dialed 9 for an outside line, and then his home number.

"I'll be late, dear. No, it's just come up. Usual old story, isn't it? I say I'll be late, but it's conceivable I won't be back at all tonight. Boys all right? Good. I'm sorry . . . I always say that. Mean it, though. Love you. 'Bye, darling."

There were two files now. One for the embassy calls, one for McCoy. He took them both with him as he went down to the basement. In cubicles sat the men who listened to the calls that the Director General had authorized as suitable for monitoring. He pulled up a chair beside the man who listened to the number he was concerned with. The man greeted him silently, plugged in a separate pair of earphones and passed them to him. He offered Jones a cigarette, which was declined. And then they waited. Concentration building up, the metal of the earpieces digging into Jones's flesh, anticipating the next call.

He reflected that there was no complacency amongst his small team. They were too old for that, too well versed. All appreciated that they were starting late, having to catch up in a few hours on the homework it had taken the enemy weeks, perhaps months, to prepare. There was never enough time in this business for indulgence. Always running from behind, handicapped, racing against the passing of the calendar.

The major from Intelligence Corps was able to tell Duggan little of McCoy that was not already apparent. The major enjoyed his retirement and the gratuity the army had given him. And now he devoted his attention, once directed toward interrogation, wholly to his rose garden. He had been there in semi-darkness when Duggan had called the cottage in Wiltshire, and the former officer's mind was more fully attuned to the problems of green and black aphis fly and its risk to his blooms than to the young Irishmen he had met so many months earlier.

"He was a hard little bugger," he remembered. "Very cool,

difficult to shake. Cut above the usual cement-between-the-ears boyos. We had more than one session, didn't budge him at all. Things had got pretty easy for them by then. Clamps were well down on what we could do with the bastards by the stage we got our hands on him. He didn't tell us anything."

Duggan read him over the first section of the report from Northern Ireland intelligence.

"I didn't see any great political leanings. So few of them have," said the major. "He reacts to orders, like most of them. But he's tougher, harder. Has a lot of hate. Patient. One of those that would lie up on the hedgerows for days at a time, ready to set off a bomb under an armored truck. Plans well. We know that from some of his operations. They're a hard breed down there in South Armagh, harder than anywhere else in the bloody place." He paused, seeking for anything else that could be of use to the man in London, then went on, "One thing. If you're looking for him in London. He had a sister, a bit older, perhaps a couple of years. Worked in a hospital somewhere in London . . ."

Duggan prompted him.

". . . Well, the girl went a bit haywire. McCoy thought she'd been in the wrong just by coming over. We were told that from other sources. He didn't think she should be working across in the mainland. Seemed quite normal girl, apparently, then got mixed up with a load of hippies. Packed her nursing in and went to live with them. He didn't approve of that. They're a very puritan crowd, the hard-core Provos. I tried to talk about it to him, tried to shake him up a bit, get him angry. Didn't work. Not at all. Water off a duck's back."

"That could be very helpful," said Duggan.

A courier came by car with the report, decoded, from the meeting at RAF Akrotiri. Fairclough had to come down to the lobby of the building to sign personally for the plain buff envelope that carried only his name on the outside. He slit open the envelope when he was back in his office, and read the typed sheets with attention for detail. It was very thorough, word for word, but then, SIS in Nicosia was well known for its exactness.

He buzzed through to Jones's extension, received no answer, and tried the outer office. Helen had not gone home.

"He's down below. Eavesdropping. Said he won't be up for some time. He asked me to stay behind. Said there might be some typing to do, some reports to make up."

Annoyance surged through him. His own girl had disappeared hours ago. Jones's girl was always there, never went home, watching them the whole time when they worked late, amusing herself at their expense.

"Get a message to him," Fairclough said. "As soon as he's taken the business down below, we need to see him. Mr. Duggan and myself. Say whatever time he's through, we'll be waiting."

When he'd rung off, he, too, phoned his home to warn of a late departure from the office. Duggan had already done the same.

"Here it goes, sir," said the man hunched intently in the cubicle, stretching his bulk closer over the machinery. Jones could hear the sounds of the amplified beeps searing through his earphones. He winced at the noise.

The man reacted to it without turning around. "Have to have 'em up full blast. They can whisper, and you've lost the lot while you're fiddling the volume." He had switched on the tape recorder, the two wheels revolving steadily and without the impatience the listeners were caught up by. A third man was behind them, holding to his mouth the receiver of an open telephone to the GPO exchange nearest the embassy.

"It's McCoy," muttered Jones as the Irish voice came through. The man behind was speaking into the phone, urgently. Jones heard the switch made to the extension inside the embassy, heard the code word given, and the single sentence in reply before the connection was broken. It had been shorter than the earlier call, by two to three seconds.

"Not a bloody hope," said the man who was standing at the back. "It gives them next to nothing to work on."

"Didn't say much anyway." Jones spat the words out. "Two hours' bloody waiting for that. Used the code word, though—that's all."

His note pad carried a few hastily scrawled words: "Mushroom—same as yesterday, but confirmed."

Helen was standing by the outer door of the basement when he emerged. She said, "Mr. Duggan and Mr. Fairclough want

to see you. They said they'd wait till you were through with
whatever . . ."

"Get them to my office, and quick." And he was past her,
hurrying along the corridor, not waiting for the lift, and then
attacking the broad central staircase, three steps at a time.

From amongst the crowd by the mobile tea trolley, Famy
watched McCoy as the Irishman stood in front of the high
wooden board that gave out the destinations and the times of
the trains from Waterloo Station. Wearing the right clothes.
Shirt correct, draped coat correct, sign correct. Nervous, that
was as it should be. Not furtive, but just anxious, that was to be
expected. Passengers swayed around the tall, fair head of the
Irishman as his eyes swept the concourse, searching for recognition and the contact. While he waited, Famy could reflect that
this was a completely new departure for him, beyond the range
of his experience. He had had no contact with foreign groups
in the camp. Older, more senior, more influential men in the
movement had, but not Famy. If it had happened as planned,
Bouchi would have been the one to go forward. Associated from
the early planning stages, he was the one that should have made
the approach. But Bouchi was in a morgue, cold on a slab in
Northern France, a darkened, shapeless obscenity.

Famy drank his tea, his hands scalded as the heat pressured
its way through the fragile sides of the plastic cup. His eyes were
never far from the Irishman, but intermittently they strayed to
take in the rest of the concourse, watching for any other man
who lingered overlong. He took many minutes to be satisfied,
then began to thread his way forward.

He moved deftly, picking his way through the running beings, circumnavigating the problems, avoiding confrontation.
McCoy saw him some fifteen feet away, and stiffened. He felt
the rigidness settle through his limbs, his breathing come a little
faster. Contact just a few seconds away. He was slightly built,
this man who approached: dark-chocolate skin, short well-
groomed hair, brightly dressed. A stranger, something separate.
McCoy watched him roll his hips and sway past the mass, saw
the head turn once for reassurance and look behind, and then
he was close, and pausing, hesitating, and then speaking.

"The mushrooms are—" Famy broke off. Waited a moment.

"I think you are here to meet me." There was a questioning in his voice. The word they had told him to say—how stupid and idiotic it sounded, spoken by a grown man to a fellow human in the chaos of a railway station.

McCoy just said, "Come on. No need to hang about. Let's move." As an afterthought, "You speak English, understand English?"

Famy nodded. Like all these British, never believing anyone knows anything but themselves. McCoy was on the move, the Arab half a step behind him. McCoy pushed a path for himself toward the steps that led down to the bus station in the street below. Almost out into the open again, he shortened his stride and said over his shoulder, "Where are the others?"

"It is just me," said Famy.

There was a tint of suspicion in the way McCoy tilted his head, swerving his eyeballs to focus on the other man. "That's not what they told me"—he rapped it out staccato—"they said there'd be three of you. They told me I'd meet three men."

"It is just me," repeated Famy.

"What's happened to change it?" McCoy hissed the question, hurrying again now, confused.

"Read your papers of today. Read of the events in Northern France. When you have done that, it is simple."

McCoy shook his head, his lack of comprehension overwhelming. They were standing at the bus stop, the street ill-lit from the high lights.

Famy went on, "There was a shooting, at a roadblock. Yesterday in the early hours. My friends did not survive, only myself."

McCoy turned around fast, his body close to Famy. Shorter than the Arab, he looked up into his face. "Dead?" The one word, very quietly.

"They did not survive," said Famy.

"Is it called off, is it over? Finished, the plan?" McCoy was speaking fast, but trying to keep his voice suppressed.

"It is not over. There is no possibility of our abandoning the plan. We have been launched. It is not infrequent there should be setbacks. But it is not a thing to talk of here. Later we can talk."

McCoy shrugged. Wanted to say more. But it was difficult against the unfamiliar logic spelled out in the curiously pitched voice of the other man. He noticed he ran the words together; strange, really, seemed to join them together, but very precise, very clear. Like a sort of textbook, he spoke, reckoned McCoy, not natural. Nothing more was said as they watched for the approach of the brightness of the big double-decker bus. What sort of bastard game is this? thought the Irishman. The bloody team shot to pieces, and this little bugger carrying on as if sod all had happened. Daft, bloody mad. He saw the face of the other man, masked, unemotional, staring down the road. Out of their bloody minds, this bugger and the ones who set it all up. What can one man, what can two, achieve compared with four? Four was the minimum number, all agreed and locked up, that had been. Should have been more, but for the problems of shifting a bigger group. And now it's halved, and this eejit says it goes on. God Almighty, put some sense into these thick buggers' heads. He mouthed the oaths, silently rolling his tongue around them, savoring and enjoying the words that somehow slashed at the anger he felt. When the bus came, he motioned with his head and went up the stairs to the top deck. A couple sat halfway, and the two men took the front seats, Famy pushing his grip underneath his knees.

"We can talk up here," said McCoy.

"There is no problem, my friend," said Famy, his voice gentle and lilting as he pronounced the words. There was no rush as he spoke, only a calmness and a certainty. "We two are sufficient. There is a plan? I was told there was a plan that could be executed. That is correct?"

McCoy nodded his head, numbness setting in along with the knowledge that he was no longer in control, that the tall stranger had taken command.

"If there is a plan, we can execute it," said Famy. He broke off as the ticket collector arrived at their seats. McCoy paid, and pocketed the thin white paper strips he received in return. Famy went on, "He is only one man, the one we seek. He will be guarded, but not thoroughly. If we are determined, there is no difficulty that can arise."

There was no more conversation as the bus jolted its way from stop to stop, leaving the heart of London far behind and climbing the hill beyond King's Cross to Islington's Angel. The upper deck filled, taking on the teenagers disgorged from the cinemas. McCoy looked sideways occasionally at the Arab, and realized that the man who sat beside him showed no interest in the journey, that his eyes never shifted from their relaxed, unseeing gaze to the front. The bright fronts of restaurants, advertisement hoardings, pin-table arcades, cinema hallways— all passed him by. A group of drunk, noisy West Indians, loud and aggressive in their shouting, roused no reaction. He's like a bloody train, thought McCoy, on course, all signals green, and couldn't give a damn about anything else. He tried to put himself into the same situation. New city, contact man he's never met before, close to target, half the back-up dead behind him, and the bugger doesn't even turn his head. Not a drop of sweat on his head, no perspiration around his balls making his trousers stretch too tight so that he has to wriggle for comfort. Just bloody relaxed, like he's on a bus outing.

The time he had shot the paratrooper was very clear to McCoy. He could recall the clammy nausea in his throat as the gangling soldier in his smock and his red beret had come into sight. He'd waited so long for him, but when the soldier came he'd hardly been able to focus his eyesight down the smooth, crisp barrel of the Armalite. Cold sweat running in rivulets under his shirt, fashioning freezing paths of movement across his skin. The unreal distraction as the man in khaki had called to the sergeant patrolling in front of him, a remark that McCoy had tried to overhear, and in the effort, recognized his concentration eroding away. He'd fired then, watched the soldier heave and clutch at himself, seen the disbelief that comes before the pain and before death. He'd sprinted then, fast, with the adrenalin pumping through his veins, and for hours afterwards, even in the womblike safety of the barn where he lay up after missions before returning to the farm, he had panted with the excitement, close to exhilaration, of the moment when he had fired. A near-orgasmic movement of release as the butt of the rifle thudded into his shoulder, his finger coiled on the trigger—he could relive it hour after hour.

But this bugger sitting next to him . . . something different. It's animal when you don't care, thought McCoy, unnatural when you don't feel the tension. Subhuman. The Irishman had read of these people when they went into Israel. Suicide squads, kamikaze, there to kill and be killed. Take the greatest possible

number with you. Seen the pictures on the television of them
training with the explosive packs strapped around their waists.
Madness or motivation? McCoy didn't know which it was. And
the man beside him, with the vacant, contented eyes, would he
be one of them? Had to be, didn't he? Could be certain of that.
One of the hard, mean bastards.

"We get off here, next stop," said McCoy.

The two men gripped the backs of the seats as they made
their way down the center of the moving bus to the staircase.
They waited by the top step till the bus had come to a halt.
Down on the pavement they began to walk, Famy fractionally
behind McCoy. After a hundred yards McCoy turned left, then
realized the Arab was not beside him. He turned and saw him
pressed against the well of the pub on the corner. Bloody play-
acting, said McCoy to himself, and walked on. He'd gone another fifty yards before the running feet caught him up. The
explanation was not slow in coming.

"Makes certain we're not being followed. To wait a moment
at a corner when one goes on. The tail will hear the feet, and
have to keep going. That way you spot him. Nobody is following," said Famy.

The street was made up of four-story Victorian terraced
houses. Up to fifty years ago these were the homes of the middle
classes, complete with maid and cook to work in the basement
kitchens and sleep in the attic bedrooms; expensive and sought
after. But those families had long since abandoned the houses
as ghostly, costly white elephants and fled to the cheaper, more
territorially secure suburbs. The houses had disintegrated into
flatlets owned by landlords who lived far from the premises.
McCoy stopped outside a house at the far end of the street.

"Just a word of explanation," he said. "We thought about this
a fair bit where we were to hole up. We've tried to find quite
a new territory this time. None of the haunts our people use, the
regular dormitories. It's what we call a commune here. Young
people who just couldn't give a fuck for it all and drop out,
absolve themselves of the rat race, they say. This place is up for
sale, one property owner selling to another, and it's sitting
empty. The kids have moved in, taken over, till there's an
eviction order, till they get chucked out. But it's safe, safe for
us. People come and go at all hours of the day and night. No-

body asks questions. Just don't get involved with them, don't ask questions, don't give answers. Just keep to yourself, and no one will bother you. I've got them to clear a room for us, when I thought there were four. Just don't let them bother you, and remember, nobody gives a damn who you are here."

They walked up the paving steps to the front door. McCoy pushed the handle and the door swung open. They were met with a flood of hard rock—shrieking pain-bearing music.

Inside the diplomatic bag being sent out of the embassy that night was a cryptic note, in code and in a high-security sealed envelope. It would be flown the next morning to a North African capital. Upon receipt, the envelope would be transferred again inside the web of diplomatic immunity to Beirut. A telephone call would then be made to the newspaper offices of *Al Nahar.* The call would be person-to-person from the commercial secretary of the embassy in the Lebanese capital to a particular writer. The message that the man code-named Saleh Mohammed was now in London would then be just a hard drive away from the camouflaged tent of the leader of the PFLP—General Command. By Sunday evening he would be aware that his plan was still in motion.

Under the harsh fluorescent light, the files in front of the three men who sat around the desk had begun to thicken. Every half-hour or so Helen would bring in the mugs of coffee on which the department seemed to exist. The men's jackets were off, ties loosened at the collars, hair disheveled by constant fingers pushed through in search of inspiration. Twice the secretary had been called in to type out assessments handed her without word by Jones. They were all tired now, weary from the strain that had begun more than twelve hours earlier, but aware that no sleep could be taken until the next day's plan was prepared. Jones knew the danger of exhaustion, had seen it sap men, make them vulnerable. That's how it had been in the war, the last half-dozen raids before the end of a tour, but he'd been little more than a boy then. More than thirty years later, and close to the decreed age of retirement, a similar work load was still expected of him. But no way around it. No point in mobilizing the forces at their disposal—police, detectives, army—not until there was a plan, something for the masses to do. And that was the problem which he knew confronted him: to find the shape of the threat. Then, and only then, could the big battalions be drawn in. He'd begun to wonder more frequently what retirement would be like, how he'd feel the day after they'd given him the silver pen, or the cut-glass decanter set, or the shining gardening kit; no train to get on in the morning, no conferences to prepare for, no problems . . . didn't know whether he would welcome it or not. But irrelevant that night.

Past midnight Jones dialed the home number of the Director General. It was rare for him to be called at home, let alone at that hour. To the head of the department, one of the triumvirate who sat on the Joint Intelligence Committee, Jones spoke with deference. He sketched through the outline of the papers that confronted them. The taped conversations, the identification and background of McCoy, the arrival and rendezvous with the unknown man, the Israeli warning. The DG liked his briefs kept short, and listened without interruption as he sat pajama-clad on the side of his bed, his wife of thirty-one years asleep beside him.

"Suggestions?" the DG said at the other end of the line.

"Perhaps you could come in tomorrow morning, sir," Jones replied. "Have a conference with us. Then I think we should meet Special Branch with a view to hunting out the Irishman. The Israeli security attaché will have to be brought in, get the lines buzzing a bit on the newcomer. We'll have to do a card check on airports and ferries, though that will probably narrow down simply to the channel ports. This Israeli professor comes on Monday, in the afternoon. There's not a lot of time."

"Right. Thank you, Jones." The winds on the Sussex Downs wrapped around his house; the central heating was long off, cut on the arrival of spring. The DG shivered. "I'll be in a bit after eight. Give me a few minutes, then the three of you come in at eight-thirty. Get some sleep in the meantime." He rang off.

Jones repeated the instructions. Duggan and Fairclough shuffled their papers together.

"Not worth making much of a move at this time of night," said Duggan. "I'll doss down in the office." Fairclough agreed. As they were leaving, Helen came in, alerted by the scraping of the chairs on the lino fringe of the carpet.

"What time in the morning?" She said it casually, matter-of-fact.

"Eight-thirty, my love. We're seeing DG then. You might as well make it same time. Far to go tonight? Or Jimmy's, is it? He the lucky man?"

No trace of a blush, just a light laugh. "Jimmy said he'd sit up, make me some cocoa."

Lucky bugger, thought Jones. "Tell lover boy not to burn the candle too hard. Might be needing him before too long. All fit and fighting fresh. Tell Jimmy that."

And she was gone, leaving him with the task of setting up the canvas-and-metal bed that fitted so snugly when collapsed into the bottom drawer of his filing cabinet, and which took such an age to make sleepworthy.

Six

The music went on through the night, deafening, raucous. It blasted its way through the walls, the floorboards, under the door, coalescing in the room, the deep rhythm concentrating around Famy. He tossed and rolled in his sleeping bag, heaving it about on the narrow blue canvas cot. They were high in the building, up many stairs, with the walls angled by the roof, but still the noise sought him out, wresting him from the sleep he craved for. A few feet away McCoy lay still, his breathing regular and heavy, impervious to the cacophony. For the first hour the Arab had sought refuge, burying his head under the cushion that McCoy had handed him before they had undressed down to their underpants and crawled into the envelopelike bags. But his stank. There was the cruel stale smell of perspiration about the faded material. His nostrils had turned and coiled and he had hurled the cushion far across the darkened room, then tried again to find comfort by drawing himself down into the bag so that his ears were covered. The bag at least was clean. New, with the price tag. No one had slept in it before.

There were no curtains at the window and the moon of the clear night threw sufficient light into the room for him to make out its bareness. Rough, uncovered boards indented with nails, peeling floral wallpaper. A length of wire hanging twisted from the low ceiling; bulb but no shade. In a corner, a plastic bag, bulging, and around it a scattering of orange peel, newspapers and the cigarette butts that had spilled out. Apart from the cots, and their clothes and their bags, nothing else. His shoulders felt the cold that could permeate the great unheated house.

They'd offered him food when he'd arrived. Talked of beans and stewed meat and bread. He'd declined, and watched the Irishman help himself from a scarce-washed plate. It had revolted him. Later he'd relented sufficiently to take a cup of milk poured from a half-empty bottle. That was all he had allowed himself.

He had waited out in the hall when they had first come to the house, while McCoy had entered a downstairs room and over the music made himself heard. Famy had not been able to distinguish the words. A group, a foraging party, had come to look at him, to survey the visitor. Without meaning he had smiled at them as they stood by the door. They did not come closer, just watched and evaluated. Long dank hair, straight to the shoulders, boys distinguished from girls by beards and mustaches, but in the mutual uniform of tightened jeans and sweat shirts and jerseys. Some had worn sandals; others were barefoot. There were beads and badges embroidered on the clothes. Further into the room, and over their shoulders, he could make out in the candlelight others who were sitting or draped on chairs, all intent on him. McCoy had not led him in, but up the stairs to the room.

There was no life like this in Nablus. Some might live unwashed, and in clothes that were little more than rags, but not from choice. No one sought such degradation, he thought, made it a purposeful way of life. In the camp away up the hill on the Jerusalem Road, where existence was married to the open drains, where a roof was corrugated iron, where walls were fashioned from wooden or cardboard packing cases, there was no satisfaction in the awfulness—there was no option. Those who lived there in the camps had come in 1948, bred their children there, built their shanties, and when the Israeli advance had rushed further forward nineteen years later, the movement had been too fast for them to walk on again and seek a new refuge in new filth on the far side of the dividing Jordan River. The tanks had outstripped them.

But the Irishman had said it was safe to stay here. That was sufficient . . . while the operation went ahead. It was justification.

There was movement below the floor. Doors opened and closed, shouts on the landings. And the undulating and controlled heaving of a bed, starting softly, carefully, rising minutes later to a frenzy. He had listened then, almost ashamed, his mind conjuring the faces and the forms of the olive-skinned girls he had known in Beirut, whose arms he had touched, gentle skin sensitive to his fingers. He strained to listen, drawn awake by the steady, driving persistence of the sound. The half-sleep left him. Imagination delving into fantasy; coiled bodies, searching and passion and closeness, enacted in a near room. It was almost nauseating for him to imagine anything so precious, in that stench, in that dirt. In the camp there had been girls, not many, but they had slept in their own tents; they joined in the laughter and the gaity, shared the training sessions, but at night they were gone, leaving the men to sleep alone on their close-packed trestle beds. In his student days there had been girls too, beautiful, supreme, but with mothers awaiting them as the city darkened. He had never slept with a girl, never known the reality of his imagination, and now, close to him, two of these creatures, with their smears and the hair, coupled. And then the sound died, and the house was at rest.

It was near to dawn, when the thin grey light had begun to penetrate the room, that he was alerted by the turning of the door handle. If he had been able to drift back to sleep, he would not have noticed the action, as it was done quietly and with care.

He lay very still, tensed, eyes slitlike, watching the entrance to the room. He saw his coat and trousers, suspended from a metal hanger, move toward him as the door opened. The movement of the hinges was heavy, and made the sparse scraping sound that whoever was on the other side of the door strove to eliminate. Famy controlled his breathing, taking it to the pitch of McCoy's, and watched the darkened shape glide, without sound, into the room and across the boards. For a moment there was a silhouette against the window, and he could make out long hair and the shape of a coat thrown shawllike over shoulders, then it had merged again into the blackness of the far side of the room and gone beyond his power of vision. He was fearful of moving his head, vulnerable on his back, unable to assert his strength. A small shaft of light, hand torch, edge of his sight field, and the hands pulling and probing in his grip bag. Then doused, and the sound of the feet on the floorboards became indecisive, as if uncertain where next they should travel. Meandering across the room, back toward the door and hesitating there, at his clothes, those that were not beside him. The chink as his belt clasp was shifted, and the smooth rifling of a hand inside his trousers. And then the shape, inanimate and shadowy, was gone, and there was the sound of the catch being fastened again, the door closed. No movement of footsteps away from the door immediately, and he stayed motionless in his sleeping bag. Waiting to see if I'm aroused, he told himself. Like a rat that comes for the cheese and lingers by its hole to see if the dogs are out and have the scent. Fifteen seconds, perhaps more, then the noise on the landing, the shuffling of bare feet, and then lost, emptied into the hugeness of the house.

Famy found that he was sweating, cold moisture on the folds of his stomach, dampness in the hair at the back of his neck. Anything, anything he would have given for the company of Dani and Bouchi, for the presence of his friends from the camp, someone to confide in, someone other than the stranger who slept and ground his teeth in the other sleeping bag across the boards.

The fool had said it was a safe place they were taking him to, a place where he could relax, where there would be no requirement to remain vigilant twenty-four hours of the day. Half a night, and his possessions and clothes precisely and systematically searched. Should he have intervened? Thrust himself at the intruder? But how, how would he have done it? The bag was like a strait jacket, so how to create the element of surprise? It could not have been accomplished, he told himself. He lay on his bag, waiting for McCoy to awaken and the morning to come.

It was past seven on his watch when the Irishman began to struggle and fight his way out of sleep. Famy leaned over to him and shook his shoulder, firmly, communicating his impatience. McCoy awake, eyes focused instantly, the man who sleeps constantly on his guard, traversing the room, seeking explanation and justification for the interruption.

"What is it? What's the bloody matter?" he said.

"There has been someone in here. Someone has been in the room." Famy said it with urgency, seeking to impress with his information.

"So what. People come and go in these places. Looking for a place to doss down, sleep for a bit?"

"Not like that. Someone has been to search . . . the bags and clothes. To examine."

McCoy stared hard across at him. "Been in here, giving us a look-over?"

"I was awake," said Famy. "Couldn't sleep. And someone came in, went through the pockets. I didn't move, pretended sleep. Nothing was found. It was about two hours ago, just before the light began to come."

McCoy forced his lids further open, bruising them with the motion of his arm, and sat up. Famy thought his white skin curiously weak and without sinew, till the body swiveled and he saw the reddened, angry puckered mess of a bullet-entry wound, left side below the rib cage.

"Probably just some bugger on the scrounge looking for a few pence . . ."

Famy cut across him, excited, talking fast. "Nothing was taken. I couldn't see all that was searched, but no sound of money being taken. My trouser pockets they were looked at; the money remains. It's the wrong place for us here, not the place I was expecting, not familiar."

"Well, it's here you're bloody well staying." McCoy was close to shouting. "You'll stay where I bloody well say so, and that's here. It's out of the way, quiet, a no-questions place. If some eejit sod comes wandering about in the middle of the night, frightening you, I can't help it. Shouldn't believe in bloody fairies."

"And if you're wrong?" Famy said.

"If I'm wrong? What the hell does that mean? What I say is we're better off here than with the usual crowd, the ones who might want to know about us, our bloody lot." He quieted suddenly, recognized the anxiety as genuine, was anxious to allay and calm. "I'll ask around downstairs, put a bit of heat on, but gently. There's all sorts of buggers just drifting round these places, looking for a bed, looking for something to pinch. Nothing extraordinary about the night. Remember, it's London you're at now, and it's Saturday, and the man you want is here on Monday, whatever it is you call him . . ."

"Al Kima."

"Whatever that means."

"It is the man who grows mushrooms. The Mushroom Man. My friends would like to see me meet him. They would believe that I would avenge them."

Crisis over, calmed the little bugger down, chance of more sleep. He turned away from Famy to face the wall. "There's nothing much to do today, lie up. Tomorrow we start working. For now, it's sleep we want; there's nothing today but a walk round the university. Tomorrow it gets interesting."

The Irishman could not see the gleam in the other's eyes, the brightness that comes from erotic and compulsive anticipation: the dream of the shudder of gunfire, blood smears on the concrete, the international headlines, the adulation in the tents far away in Fatahland.

When Famy looked again across the floor of the room, he saw McCoy was asleep with his left arm high around his head to shut out the light; the bullet wound below was exposed. The thought of it bruised the Arab. He who had come so far, and who now assumed leadership, was virgin and had never known the reality of conflict. He could not know how it would affect him, the moment, when it came. Famy lay on his back, stared at the ceiling, while deep in the sleeping bag his legs trembled.

Jones was padding down a ground-floor corridor at the back of Leconfield House on his way to the canteen kitchens, which would be empty but where he could heat a kettle, make himself a cup of tea with the tea bags he kept in his desk drawer, top right. He was without shoes and socks—washed the socks last thing before getting into his bed and they were still damp and he would leave putting them on till the last minute, before the walk up the stairs to the early-morning meeting. After the tea he would shave, make himself presentable, the way it was supposed to be in the department.

As he stood facing the window, running the water from the taps into the opened top of the kettle, he saw the Director General's Humber car turn into the narrow entry to the underground car park, wire portcullis raised as the vehicle was expertly maneuvered by the young man in the front. In the back nothing much to see, an opened newspaper masking the figure well down in his seat.

The alarm bell, furious, demanding attention, woke Helen.

She reached forward, pressing herself up with one hand, the other straining across Jimmy toward the bedside table and the offending clock, till she found the button and the silence. He hadn't moved all night, the bastard. Still on his back, with his eyes tight and hermetically sealed, mouth open, pajamas top-buttoned protectively to his neck, sprawled in the middle of the bed. Bloody good weekend entertainment you make, Jimmy boy. Bloody great porpoise up a beach and no prospect of another high tide. She made one more concentrated effort to work some life and awareness into the marooned carcass next to her, slipped her hands down underneath the material and worked with her nails at his chest, slowly and with consideration sketching out small patterns of the skin. Jimmy slept on.

"You're bloody hopeless," she told him, mouth close to his ear. "Understand, bloody hopeless, a great dump of garbage. Come on, wake up, stir yourself."

No response. She moved her hands lower, indenting the line where the beginnings of his paunch slunk down to his hips. Then there was movement. Convulsive, total, as his arms came up and around her, gripping the shoulder blades, pulling her down onto him. Eyes opened for a brief flicker, closed again, and his arms went slack.

"Better, Jimmy, fractionally better. One out of ten for trying, zero for everything else."

He hadn't seen a razor the day before, nor the one before that, and his chin was close-set with a tight brush of hair. It bit into her skin, penalty of the fakir, a myriad of needles.

"Not so fast, lover boy, or we'll have the bloody department wanting a blow-by-blow account if I turn up with half my face scraped off by your beard."

He spoke for the first time, but as if the effort were all but beyond him, the ultimate struggle. "It's bloody Saturday, you're not going in today, and what bloody time did you get here last night. I'm sitting here half the bloody evening waiting for you."

"I'm going in today, and I'm going in now. Jones's special request. There's a big flap, big panic, all hands to action stations." She slid out of his grasp, swung her legs over the bedside. She wore no clothes. Wishful thinking, you silly bitch, she told herself. Leave him past midnight and you're always the loser. Jimmy had begun to take an interest. Not in me, she thought, wave him the boobs and the backside. But it'll take second place to the Department. He was half up, almost sitting, pained at the awareness that another day had risen for him to go and do battle with.

"What's going on, what's the flap?"

"Don't worry, lover boy, you're included in the cast. Some hit-and-runners reached inside base with a nice plum Yiddisher target all to themselves, and second, third and fourth floor running round like it's declaration-of-war day. Big enough for the DG to be arriving before breakfast, then a full-scale bit of summitry at 0830 hours on the precise stroke."

He was still trying to focus on her, rounded, pink, but not clear lines yet. Striving for concentration. "What way is it for me?"

Helen moved off the bed toward the chair draped with her clothes. Began to pull them on. "Don't know yet. Jones mentioned you just as I was pulling out in the wee small hours. Said he might be needing you. All fit and fighting fresh. Be bloody lucky, won't he? That was all he said, and I was just on my way. Wasn't social chat, I was on my way then."

"He didn't say anything else?"

"Nothing at all."

"Bloody fine message for crack of dawn Saturday. What am I supposed to do? Sit here all through the weekend, hanging on the edge of the phone, waiting for him to ring?"

"That's what you do every weekend. God, these bloody tights smell. Not as though anyone will notice. They all slept in there. Jones, dreary old Duggan, Fairclough, all doing the boy scouts' bit, all kipping on the premises. They'll all be high, smelling to the ceiling. I'll be in good company." She eased her skirt into position and grimaced as she looked at herself in the mirror. "Look like a bloody wreck," she said.

Jimmy called across from the bed, "But he said nothing more?"

"Patience, lover boy, patience. They'll be in touch. It's just that one hell of a panic started up yesterday. Huddles, chats, meetings, files for me to type, dispatch riders bombing over from the FO . . . God I'm late. Never get a taxi at this bloody time, and I said I'd be in. Have to take the bloody car. Now be a good lad, and go quietly back to sleep and shed some of that load, so you sound all sweet and sober when the gaffer comes on for you."

"One more time," he said. "Give us a kiss and tell me again what it's all about. Come on." He said it quietly, the thickness of his voice evaporating.

She leaned over. Let him kiss her on the throat. He was considerate enough not to spoil her make-up. "I don't know much. Really. But there's an Israeli coming over to stay here, comes sometime next weekend, and they've hooked onto a couple of boys. One's IRA, the other they're not sure of, but Phonetics say probably Middle East. The code word they're using is something involving 'mushroom,' and the man they're having the flap about is a nuclear scientist. Seems a nice easy equation. Quite a pretty little code name, better than all those Greek goddesses we're forever calling our fiascos after. But don't tell Jones what I told you. Let it come to virgin, suitably surprised ears. I'll see you tonight, I'll try not to be late again, and we'll cook something."

Helen stepped up quickly, gave the prone figure on the bed a wave and was on her way out of the flat. Early enough not to meet the neighbors on the stairs; stupid bloody looks they gave her. Two years she'd been coming now. First time after a Department party, and Jimmy too drunk to notice she'd driven him home, and waking in the morning and taking his time to remember who she was. And then a sort of habit had set in, and she'd come more often, and taken to cleaning up and washing his smalls and cooking his meals. The Department governed both their lives; the restrictions about social contact with people who did not share an existence governed by the Official Secrets Act ensured a curtailed horizon of friends. They began to accept each other, enough to make love in a perfunctory and clumsy style that satisfied the immediate needs of both of them. There was no talk of marriage.

The curtains were still drawn, and Jimmy switched off the bedside light, darkening the room, resisting the sunlight trying to infiltrate the cotton curtains. Be a bugger of a day, he thought, waiting for the telephone to ring the summons. Be by it all day in case Jones called, just as the girl had said he would, just as he always did when there was something rumbling at the Department. Wouldn't go out, not even to stock the larder, not even to get liquor. Whiskey was thin, drained after last night. He could see the bottle over on the table, by the divan in the living part of the room. Barely an inch left, and it had been two-thirds full at the time she should have come back last night. Not much else on the table, just the ashtray, big cut-glass effort, and piled high with butt ends, stubbed and strangled to extinction, and the water jug. He could remember that he'd started by mixing it with water, but the last two inches they'd been neat. Constant refills, the way it generally worked out when he sat up on his own. Need another bottle if any possibility of another late night. But couldn't leave the phone, not if Jones was going to call. There was a nerve-breaking ache in his head now, split from side to side, and a deep throbbing somewhere far inside and behind his temples. Always the bloody same, Jimmy boy, self-inflicted wound.

Jimmy lay back, trying to shut out the pain, wallow in the situation. This was the way it worked out. Big scene down at the Department, high-level stuff top men nattering to each other, twisting their knickers, and at the end of the day finding a place for Jimmy somewhere in the setup. Hadn't been anything for four months, not since the MP, bloody little grovel merchant. Represented sixty thousand miners and their families and cohorts up in the West Riding. Smug little sod, with too much to say till they worked out the links—the Hungarians, how he afforded the London flat, the rendezvous points, what he had to offer from the Select Committee on Defence Expenditure. Found it only after Jimmy had slipped the kitchen window while the man was in the House, picked the lock of the drawer in his working table, pocketed the overfilled, concisely documented diary. Must have missed it, the little bugger, but never reported it. Just looked crestfallen, as if he might weep when they read the charge out. Asked for his solicitor, lot of bloody good it would do him.

But life had been hard since then. The Department's retainers don't go that far.

*   *   *

For Jimmy the existence on the fringe of the Department had
started a long time ago.

Recruitment was haphazard, following few fixed patterns,
depending mainly on personal recommendation.

Jimmy owed his connections with the Security Service to his
actions on a glorious moonlit night on August 24, 1944. He was
aged nineteen, with the exalted wartime rank of flight sergeant
(rear gunner) in a Lancaster bomber squadron. He flew in
"Charley Apple" off one of those eternal concrete runways
littering the flat, uninteresting Lincolnshire countryside. The
whole eight-man crew, officer included, had bitched about
flying that night.

"Should have their bloody heads examined, those desk bastards," the pilot had said.

"Sitting bloody duck for whatever they send up" had been
the contribution of the navigator.

Jimmy had been neither old nor experienced enough to add
to the condemnation publicly, but he'd recognized that the
cursing was counterfeit for fear. They were more than a hundred and fifty miles short of the target when the nightfighter
was guided onto them. Jimmy had a fleeting glimpse of it before
the firing started, enough time to shout a warning and bring his
own machine guns to bear. Then the cannon began to rake the
airframe of the Lancaster. Fire quick to follow, and the order
to abandon the aircraft. It took Jimmy what seemed endless,
stretching minutes to realize that the heavy canopy through
which he should have made his individual escape would not
move. One other way out, and he crawled more than sixty feet
down the length of the belly of the plane to where the roaring
wind drove an entry through the opened forward escape hatch.
Six men had already jumped into the night that stretched more
than three miles beneath. As Jimmy had been about to lever
himself into the hole, commit himself to the slipstream, he saw
the movement beyond the flapping door of the cockpit. Then
the pilot, edging toward him. There was a look of surprise on
the officer's face, and he'd shouted something like "I thought
they'd all gone," and his attention was turned from the effort
of movement and the pain from the fire that had caught at the
upper fabric of his flying tunic. But Jimmy had not heard him,
the words lost in the noise of the wind and the tearing metal as

the superstructure of the aircraft struggled to hold together in the face of its unnatural and contorted descent.

They had jumped virtually together. Jimmy first, then the officer. First time for the rear gunner, only the tower and the simulator before. He had felt the moment of stark panic before he had pulled the metal hoop fastened to the harness across his chest, and then had followed the decisive and successive sensations of the jolt of the parachute opening, the surge upward as it billowed out, the silent descent, and then the terror as the earth catapulted up to meet him before impact. The officer had landed less than a hundred yards away, the fire on his body extinguished by the air rush of his speed of fall.

They had barely disentangled themselves from the cords and webbing of the parachutes when the German soldier had reached them, shouting instructions and calling to his colleagues further away across the fields. Not a front-line man, middle-aged, reservist, for use behind the shock waves of contact. Jimmy had gestured into the middle distance behind the soldier, and as the man had turned in his inexperience, the heavy flying boot had thrashed into his crotch. As he jackknifed, the hard outside edge of the right hand chopped down on the neck in the bare and exposed inch between the helmet and the thickened collar of the great coat. The German had died there, instantly and without whimper, giving Jimmy and the officer time to fade into the sanctuary and shadow of the trees. The next morning when light came, Jimmy had seen the pilot's face, seen the mashed raw damage, legacy of the clinging cockpit oil. The sight had not unduly upset him. He had been sympathetic, interested, nothing more.

The pilot's name was Philip Whilloughby-Jones. He was two years older than the rear gunner. He would never forget the speed and ruthlessness involved in the death of the German. He would never put out of his mind the fresh pleasure that played in Jimmy's eyes, reflected by the moonlight, before they reached the trees, the delight in success that showed on his young downy mouth. Via the French resistance they had been smuggled to the Spanish border, and after their return home, had lost touch. There'd been different postings, different stations. Following the war, when he became a full-time deskman with the Department, Jones had let it be known that there existed a man who could kill without scruple.

His assessment of Jimmy had not been disproved.

The nearest police station to Englefield Road is some six streets away and to the north, beyond Dalston Junction and close to the Balls Pond Road. It's a forbidding grey-brick building dingy from lack of paint and the general state of misrepair. Inside, attempts had been made to brighten the cavernous passages and interview rooms with quantities of paint; they had been largely unsuccessful.

Police Constable Henry Davies, Alsatian dog handler, nine years in the force, was going off duty. That in itself didn't entail much work, just signing the time sheet, confirming that his overnight reports were completed and ready for the day duty inspector. It had been a quiet night, no pub fights at the start, no premises broken into at the end. Time for him now to go to his ground-floor flat to sleep through the daylight hours, with Zero out in the kennel beside the coalbox. It would be a dull and boring weekend, his principal source of company denied him.

As he passed the main desk at the end of the front hall, the dog on its lead and head pressed close to his left knee, the sergeant, old and cheerful in spite of the surroundings, spoke to him. "Off home, then, Henry? Not been much for you tonight."

"Not a damn thing, Sarge."

"Seeing Doris this weekend?" He'd need that for his dossier, knew every damn thing about everyone, the old boy.

Davies paused near the door. "No way, she's staying in through today and tomorrow. Won't be coming out till Monday."

"Need a bloody good bath and all, then," said the sergeant. "I don't know how she does it. Nice clean girl, living with all that muck."

The constable smiled. "She doesn't seem to mind. Gets a bit deep about it all, says it's what police work is all about. Laughs at me for lugging this piece of dog flesh about."

"Well, I couldn't do it. Might manage if it was nine to five, Monday to Friday. But not living in amongst them, twenty-four hours, weekends and all."

The sarcasm was gentle and kindly meant. "No one's going

to ask you to blend into the hippie scene, now are they? Not your style, Sarge. But seriously, she says all the coming and going is during the weekend. When she was at the place behind the Angel, they got the pusher during the weekend. You have to be there the whole time, part of the furniture."

An old lady moved across the hall and to the desk, diverting the sergeant's attention. Lost her bloody cat, most likely, thought Davies. He gave the lead a very slight pull, and the Alsatian was off its haunches where it had been sitting while they talked, and they went together to his van.

He'd told Doris, but only half-heartedly, that he wasn't that keen on her living in the communes, and she'd dismissed it. Told him it was a damned sight more interesting than driving around with a dog for company. But he'd see her on Monday, when she came out of the half-world that she'd infiltrated to file her twice-weekly report.

Seven

It was Lord Denning who wrote in his report in the wake of the Profumo scandal: "The Security Service in this country is not established by Statute, nor is it recognised by Common Law. Even the Official Secrets Acts do not acknowledge its existence." Since its conception way back in the late sixteenth century, the Department has insisted that its moves and practices are cloaked in total secrecy. For years it was successful, and the Security Service remained shrouded in mystery, with its operators able to congratulate themselves that they had found a near-divine formula for the working of the Department. But all good things come to an end, and that very secrecy, once so jealously protected, had now brought the Security Service into hard times. Politicians, looking for economic savings in the 1960s and early 1970s, found a familiar back to carry the burden of financial cutbacks; few of them understood what went on in Leconfield House, and those who wanted to discover the strange activities of the personnel there were actively dissuaded from pursuing their inquiries.

The number of men employed in the Department shriveled as fewer and fewer funds were channeled toward them. Worse followed when their political masters decided that the autonomy of the Service should be curtailed, and appointed a conventional career civil servant to take charge. Only recently, after a series of well and publicly castigated mishaps, had the Prime Minister reverted to tradition and put a senior man from the Service itself into the Director General's office. His name was unknown to the mass of the population, and was covered by a "D" Notice, requesting that the media keep it confidential.

The present DG spent much of his working day wrestling with the budget the Security Service was allowed by Parliament, striving to keep his force efficient while at the same time remaining in the black as far as the accounts were concerned. It was a soul-destroying job, and one which he detested; and he was paid little for his pains, slightly less than the Fleet Street average for a middle-ranking columnist. But inside the Department, the new man had revitalized morale and effectiveness, simply because his subordinates knew that the man who controlled them comprehended the work, was sympathetic to their problems, and was always available. The Irish problem had also played its part in lifting the tempo in Curzon Street. Instead of dealing almost to the exclusion of everything else with the activities of the Iron Curtain embassies and the huge Soviet trade mission on Highgate Hill, a new dimension had been brought into the work, and on top of that came the more recent wave of Arab terrorism throughout Europe. The DG could note with satisfaction that the building no longer operated on a five-day week, and that many of the key section heads would be at their desks through the weekend, even in high summer.

He was a short, heavily built man. Spread across his desk, eyes only a few inches from the paper, occasionally breaking off to pencil a few words on a pad, he sought the relevant facts from the files that had been left for him to digest. There was monumental concentration, head quite still, eating into the typescript, seeking for flaws in the arguments, high spots in the information. He believed totally in paper work, required it to be short and explicit, but demanded that all relevant facts be set out in the files. He had hooked his coat over the end of the chair he sat at; his tweed tie hung down, loosened at the neck along with the top button of his shirt. He smoked incessantly, non-filtered and one of the strong brand, drawing deeply on the stubs till there was hardly enough of the rolled paper left for him to hold without burning his fingers.

Promptly at eight-thirty came the knock at his door, and Jones, followed by Fairclough and Duggan, came into the bright first-floor office. The DG looked up from the desk top, gestured to them to pull up chairs, and continued reading the last pages of the file on Ciaran McCoy. The section heads made a half-moon as they sat down at the far side of the desk and waited for him to finish. The office was bare, but not to the point of being Spartan: picture of the Queen; water color of a bowl of fruit; a table littered with yesterday's newspapers; wall-to-wall carpets as his position decreed; heavy plain curtains drawn back to let in the sunlight. Not much for them to gaze at, but all felt the aftereffects of weariness from the long night just past, none were in the mood for daydreaming and staring at irrelevancies, had they existed in the room.

When he had finished, the DG closed the McCoy file and neatly piled it with the others, threw an eye quickly over the notes he had made, and looked up at the three men facing him. He could see their tiredness, read it in their hastily shaven faces. A short meeting was required, nothing rambling that would escape the main issue.

"There's not much time, gentlemen," he started. Voice calm, easy, fluent from his Welsh background, the traces of which had not deserted him. "Our guest here on Monday night, his public appearance on Tuesday, and the flight out undecided between Wednesday and Thursday. We can probably ensure that he goes on Wednesday. The threat seems to me to be real enough on what we have at our disposal. There is one factor that we should consider before recommendations are made to the Home Office. If this was simply an IRA affair, I would say that saturation protection would probably see us through—they tend to like to make it home all in one piece at the end of the day . . . if they see the odds placed heavily against them, I think they like to try again when conditions are more auspicious. But there's the added factor of the Middle East involvement. Different people, different philosophy, more prepared to go with the target. If the other half of the team is Arab, Palestinian, then we must accept that he is prepared to die along with our scientist friend. It makes the entire operation of protection infinitely more complicated. The suicide killer always has things stacked in his favor. It means for us that we have to widen the number of people involved, and mount a much wider screen than I would otherwise advocate. That means police, uniformed and CID. Thoughts, gentlemen?"

Duggan spoke. "This McCoy is a hard operator. He's given them a long chase across the water, but he's on strange ground here. It's reasonable to suggest he'll need a safe house, somewhere he can hole up with the other man. He has two alternatives. He can go in with the usual crowd, Provo supporters, that lot. On the other hand, he can go elsewhere, somewhere right outside the norm. The only line we have on that could be some connection with his sister. She's no longer in London, back in the Republic, but she went through a spell in a commune, one of those in North London, but drifting. McCoy was reported as disapproving, but it could have given him the contact."

"Half the raids the Special Branch mount are aimed at communes," said the DG. "It's a good suggestion, but it'll take time to check out, and that's one for the police."

"Presuming that the Palestinian has joined up with McCoy, and we have to believe that from the rendezvous call," said Fairclough "then we can just about guarantee that he's dependent on McCoy for his accommodation, and probably for the guns too. We've had the French report in overnight and no firearms were found in the car, the one that was shot up and burned out. If the third lad made it away from the car, there's little chance he could have carried the necessary firearms, explosives, whatever, for three men. And it makes sense that the Arabs would provide the attack team; the Provisionals, what local knowledge they needed."

"It's strange they should have chosen McCoy, then. No history in London. But ready access to firearms—he'd have no problem finding them." The DG was thinking aloud, picking his words carefully and slowly. "The firearms would be McCoy's part. But what we have to consider is this. If the original team is decimated, and the one man wants to go on with it, how far does McCoy involve himself?"

"He's a killer," said Duggan. Decisive, without hesitation or doubt. "It's clear from the file. He'll think about it, he'll try and make sure he walks out of it, but he's a killer. He won't step back, not unless the odds are tight against him."

"And our unknown friend will need him?"

"He's essential. The Arab, whoever he is, needs him, and badly. But the two make a formidable threat. Make quite a handful."

"To become more general"—with a slight wave of his hand the DG terminated the tack of the conversation—"to delve into the theory of the attack, what brings these two together? No common ideology . . ."

"Necessity only," said Duggan. As the protégé of the head of the Security Service, and one whose career was well mapped and his future charted, he had the confidence to speak his mind. "The Palestinians must have the accommodation and transport; if it's provided locally, then the trails can be that much better covered. It's infinitely more satisfactory from their point of view, particularly if they can also travel clean of firearms. Same for the Provisionals. They'll have become involved because of the advantages that will come to them. They've tried hard enough to get their hands on Iron Curtain weapon systems . . . Europe's difficult as a supply source, nothing coming direct, they don't want to know over there. American market is not adequate and difficult on resupply. But the Middle East offers them a major opportunity. If they pull this one in successful harmony, then it'll be a guarantee that Kalashnikovs, rocket launcher RPG-7s, perhaps even a SAM-7 missile, will be turning up on the border for the boys in South Armagh and Tyrone. I'd put it down as a straight swap—immediate help by the Provos, and they get top-grade hardware in the close future. And talk to any army men, not HQ but the guys in the field, and ask them how they'd feel about having that sort of gear on tap for the opposition."

"And the man Sokarev . . ."

"Important to the Palestinians; big coup if they drop him. Irrelevant to the Irish. If we lose him, heaven forbid, the chances are the Provos wouldn't even claim him, nor their part in it."

"And this bomb that the Israelis keep so much under the table, and that our Mr. Sokarev is credited with, what state is that in?"

"The Americans call it 'screwdriver' state. That's a good description. Probably not assembled, but way off the design bench. Just needs putting together."

There had been enough talking, the DG decided. He straightened up in his chair. "I think we'd better get the following done this morning. Details on McCoy to all police stations in London, particular reference to communes. Run a check on all immigration forms coming in via ferries from Boulogne yesterday— that's for Ports Unit of Special Branch. Liaise with the Israelis, the security attaché. Not here, though. Fix a meeting with him at Home Office, and don't let him think that he's running the show. Jones, I'd like you to coordinate. Final point. I'd like a man on the ground beside this professor night and day, not just Special Branch, they can look after themselves, but one of our own. So we know what's going on."

Jones spoke for the first time, mock-hesitant, a smile on his face. "There's Jimmy."

"Is he on the bottle or off at the moment?"

"About halfway. He'll fit the job."

"There are plenty of others," said the DG.

"He's the best of them." It was Jones's opinion. None of the other men in the room were prepared to make an issue of it.

For differing reasons, both Fairclough and Duggan were disapproving of the choice, but neither spoke. Jones's loyalty to the men who worked for him was familiar to his colleagues. It was recognized that there was a personal bond between the section head and Jimmy; the details of it had never been explained to them. But to criticize the judgment that Jones had made of his man would be futile, and both stayed silent.

The DG nodded. He knew Jimmy, had known him for a long time, liked his results, stayed ignorant of his methods. He said, "I'm going to see the Minister this morning, I'll be back at lunchtime. If you want me, try about a quarter to one. That's it, gentlemen. Remember, there's very little time."

From the outer office Helen called the home number of the Commander in charge of Special Branch, and connected him through to Jones. Copies of McCoy's file, and the fingerprint and photograph folder that had now arrived from Northern Ireland, were sent by motorcycle to Scotland Yard. The conversation also served to activate the search of the immigration

forms, thirty-nine thousand of them, representing the number
of persons who had crossed to Britain on ferries from Boulogne
the previous day.

She called the Israeli embassy, introduced herself as Home
Office, left a number, the direct one to Jones's desk, and asked
that the security attaché should call back as soon as he had been
located, with a view to an urgent meeting in midafternoon.

Next she traced the Assistant Commissioner (Crime) to a golf
club in North Hertfordshire. He arranged to see Jones in his
office at Scotland Yard straight after lunch. That would set in
motion the sifting of scores of reports and observations made by
undercover drug-squad detectives who worked in the communes. The conversation with Jones was impressive enough for
him to scratch from the four-ball game he had arranged, make
his apologies to his partners, and drive home for a morning's
work on the telephone before going into London.

And lastly she raised Jimmy, still waiting beside the receiver
but dressed now. Pretty shabby. Trousers creased at the back
of the knees, jacket with great lines carved across the flap at the
back, shirt not quite clean. But dressed. Would he come in at
four-thirty? 'Course he bloody well would. And after that? She
didn't know. Going at it like a lot of maniacs, she'd said, and
rang off.

The Cabinet Minister who rejoiced in the title of Secretary of
State for Home Affairs liked to keep in touch with his constituents. On Saturday mornings he set aside time when the electors
who had returned him to Westminster for the past eighteen
years could meet him with their problems, and talk to him. His
local political opponents claimed it was simply window dressing, and that as he allowed each of his visitors a bare four
minutes of his time, there was little that could effectively be
talked about in that time. Clogged-up drains and the lateness
of school buses were about all that could be managed. Anything
as detailed as council-house rents or the lay-offs and redundan-
cies at the local car-body factory never made it off the ground.
He had dealt with fifteen constituents in the straight hour

that he set himself, and was preparing for the drive across country to the hall where he would eat a sandwich lunch with the faithful and make a short speech, when the Director General of the Security Service was put through on the telephone in his agent's office on the first floor of the constituency headquarters. On matters of state security, the Director General had direct access to the Prime Minister, but there were occasions when that was not suitable. Going too high up the ladder too fast, and then leaving no one senior to fall back on if the initial contacts with government went sour. The DG liked to leave his options a little open. But it was rare for him to seek an interview with his Minister outside normal working routine. Rare enough for the Minister to be puzzled, and left confused after he had arranged that they should meet at the hall and talk while the tea and food were being consumed.

When the Director General arrived in midmorning, he was shown into a room behind the stage of the hall, and he waited there amongst the piled chairs and old scenery props for the Minister to come in.

"I'm sorry to trouble you," he began.

"I'm sure you wouldn't have done so if you hadn't thought it important." The Minister was wary of the other man.

Security was fraught with whirlpools in the political ocean; when everything was going well you never heard from them, they only surfaced when the gales were blowing.

"I think we're running into some bother, something you ought to hear about."

The Minister aquiesced. The Director General could see he was nervous, uncertain of what was to follow, fearful of its implications.

"Briefly, it's this." He paused, long enough to take in the babble of chatter outside in the hall and be certain there were no footsteps at the door. His voice was subdued when he went on.

The Minister felt trapped, caged in. "What do you want me to do?" he asked.

"It's not so much a case of doing anything, sir. It's a question of your knowing what's going on, what the situation is."

"How important is this Israeli?" The question was barked, staccato.

"One of their backroom men, not a well-known personality. Named David Sokarev. They regard him as critical to their nuclear program. He doesn't work on the power-station side, not on the civilian programs; he's with the other crowd, the one they don't talk about. Sensitive men, sensitive work."

"Is it an important meeting?"

"Not that we know of. We haven't seen a guest list yet; this has been developing only since yesterday evening, we'll have that sort of thing by tonight. But there's nothing to suggest it's world-shattering . . ."

"Which it would be if these bastards get to him." He lingered, concentrating his mind on the problem. Always Security providing the problems, never any good news, always anguish and heart-searching. And now, with not a civil servant of his staff within fifty miles, with the Prime Minister touring Lanarkshire, some sort of a snap decision to be made. I know what this blighter wants, he thought, can read him a mile off. Wants me to tell him he's doing a grand job, let him run off and take charge on his own, and when the fiasco comes, when the scandal breaks, then he can tell the committee sitting under the learned judge in camera, that the Minister was aware of the situation right from the start. No way you get me that easily.

"The Prime Minister should be told of this. He takes a great interest in Israeli affairs. He'd want to know. I'll do that. My first reaction is that the Israelis should call off the visit. If it's not an important meeting, not an important personality, then what's the point in risking him?"

"You won't find that so easy, sir," said the DG. "Foreign Office have tried that one, down the rather more torturous channels than the ambassadorial ones. Got a straight shutout on the suggestion. But I agree it would be the easiest solution to our problem. I'd be grateful if someone could let me know how the suggestion is taken."

The Minister shook the other man's hand, then walked back into the hall. The plates were empty by this stage and the tea was getting cold. His words were awaited. He prided himself on talking off the cuff without a note, but by now his mind was clouded by the conversation that had just terminated. It would be a bad speech, and he knew it.

*   *   *

As the sun rose high that Saturday morning, it moved beyond the compass of the attic window to the room that housed Famy and McCoy. While its brightness and warmth streamed through the glass the Arab dressed, pulling on his clothes secretively and with a shyness that came from never before having been separated from his people. As he dragged his trousers on he turned his back on the Irishman, who still lay in his sleeping bag, picking at the dirt that had accumulated beneath his fingernails. McCoy called across to him. Not to worry about shaving. Don't want to look too pretty in here. The voice had said, "Doesn't fit with the rest of the surroundings," and then a quiet laugh. When he had dressed, Famy paced about the room, taking in its length in a few strides, going constantly to the window, peering down onto the street below, then walking again. He waited for some movement from the other man, and was loath to go beyond the door on his own. The street fascinated him, indistinct voices reaching up the height of the brickwork as he strained to hear what was being said. The dogs that ran free, cocking their legs at the lampposts, the black men and women and children that he had not seen before, the house along to the right where the old façade had been painted a bright scarlet, with the wooden window fittings and the door in vivid yellow —all were strange and beyond his experience.

Beneath him there were more sounds, and the music had started up again. Not so vibrant as when they had arrived— being saved for nighttime, he told himself.

Never far from his mind was the image of the darkened, cloaked figure he had seen moving dreamlike in the room. He felt a sense of frustration that the Irishman had not taken it more seriously, was affronted at the casualness with which his revelation had been greeted. And when the sun was gone, and still McCoy showed no sign of moving, Famy had just squatted down on the sleeping bag and waited for him to get up.

"You can go downstairs if you want to" McCoy said.

Famy shook his head, irritable at his own reluctance.

"They won't eat you, you know. They're just ordinary kids."

"I'll wait."

"Please yourself," McCoy said. He lit a cigarette, smoked it with consideration while Famy silently watched, flicked the ash successively onto the floor, and then when it was spent, ground the tip out on the boards. Then he climbed out of the bag.

Standing in his underpants and shirt, he stared directly at Famy. "Have you done this sort of thing before?" he said. Not much more than a whisper, but demanding an answer. Famy wavered, avoiding the other man with his eyes, reluctant, hurt.

"No. No, I have not before. It was planned that I should have moved into Israel, that I should fight there, a mission over the fence into the North. Then they had the information about Sokarev and his visit, and all was changed for me. I was taken from the original plan."

"Have you been in action before? I mean, have you fired a gun—in anger?"

"Only in training. I have never fought." Famy struggled to control what he thought were the inadequacies of his answers.

"It'll be difficult to get near the bastard, you know that?"

"With preparation, there is alway a way."

"You don't mount a thing like this on wishful fucking thinking." McCoy showed his impatience. "You have to know what you're about. You can't just breeze in—"

"It is unnecessary to talk to me as a child." Famy cut McCoy in midsentence. His speech was very clear, soft, almost singsong.

The Irishman retreated. "Don't get me wrong. I wasn't suggesting . . ."

"Well, don't speak to me as if I were a fool. If you want no part in the rest, say so now. We can separate. Your role forgotten."

"There is no question of that." McCoy stopped. The voices and music carried up to them. Neither spoke for four, five, six seconds. Then McCoy said, "I say there's no question of that. I'm under orders. From the Army Council. They've made a decision, and they'll stick to it. They won't renege on it, won't go back on it. Our chief of staff has given his word." He smiled, weak at the side of his mouth, feeling the cold on his skin, waiting for the response.

The relief flooded through Famy. He reached out and patted McCoy's shoulder, girllike, but a gesture meant as affection and gratitude. "What do we do today?" There was excitement in his voice.

"I thought this afternoon we'd take a look at the university. Can't do that on a Sunday, all the students are back in their bloody digs, in their lodging houses. There won't be many of them about, but a few. Would have been better yesterday, if you showed up on time. Don't worry, I'm not blaming you. You were a bloody genius to make it here at all. I've got a car, and tomorrow we go down into the country. Where the guns are. I've got some grenades. We don't use those much, but I was told to bring them."

"We know about them," said Famy.

"We'll try and hit at the meeting. It's a public place. Should offer the best hope."

"In Lebanon they thought there might be two opportunities. The meeting and at the airport, not as he is coming in, but when he leaves."

McCoy said, "The airport will be sealed, it's difficult there. The best chance has to be at the meeting. How close do you need to get to him?"

"As near as is necessary."

"There has to be a way out."

"We have not come here to escape. We have come to kill Sokarev."

McCoy fumbled with his socks, turning them inside out, trying to decide which one belonged to which foot. He felt the chill of the moment. Could see again the pictures. Those arching bodies spilling from the windows of the flats at Beit Shean, crumpling on the paving below and welcomed there with knives and axes and tins of petrol, and then the smoke and the flames; the sacklike shape pulled from the wreckage of Tel Aviv's Savoy Hotel. Palestinians who had gone as near as was necessary.

"There has to be a way that leaves us a chance of escape," said McCoy.

"Perhaps," said Famy, and the Irishman left it there. He was a bloody madman, this Arab, suicide merchant. Well, good bloody luck to him. But what to do about it? Couldn't back out, couldn't fade away from it. Orders too implicit. Just . . . at the time, he'd hold him back. Make his presence felt then, and when the shooting came, do it with a bit of skill with an aimed shot, not close in and blasting over open sights.

But they were not a team, and both men longed for the companionship of their own.

McCoy led the way downstairs. They saw no one till they

came to the big front hallway and McCoy opened the door into the main room that faced out on the street. The conversation in the room, carried on in a series of separate huddles, was uninterrupted by their entry, but eyes, and heads and bodies, swung to look at them. The talking went on, but attention was diverted toward them. Like the bloody zoo, thought McCoy. He stood in front of the open door, staring back, waiting for someone to speak. They had little resolution against his gaze, and one by one the sitting, standing, crouching youths and girls returned to their own groups. All except one girl. Famy noticed her before McCoy did, then the Irishman saw her. Not pretty, rather plain, he thought. A long loose black dress and heavy wool button-up jersey pulled over her shoulders, shapeless and performing a function of warmth but nothing else. Ugly witch clothes, accentuating the dullness of her skin, which was devoid of cosmetics, empty of anything feminine.

Doris Lang had noticed that the two new arrivals were out of place from the moment they had come through the door of the house the previous night. She was trained to observe and make deductions from what she saw. These two did not fit the pattern that governed the other young people who lived in the commune. She had seen the Irishman's complexion, too bright, too countrified, too healthy for life amongst the dropouts, had noticed that his stature and bearing were divorced from those of the hand-to-mouth hippies. There was too much command in his face for him to belong to those who could not cope with the pressures of the life outside. This one she had decided was strictly a transit traveler, on his way through and using the commune for a particular purpose.

She could sense now the nervousness and lack of ease in the movements of the tall, willowy dark-skinned man who stood a pace behind the Irishman. He, too, did not belong there. His hands must have been sweating, because twice he rubbed them against his trouser leg. He had cold, cruel, purposeful eyes that roamed, without settling, across the room, always coming back to her. It surprised her that she had found nothing in their possessions last night to give her any indication of their business in the house.

She felt the two men stripping her, boring into her with their eyes, and turned away, unwilling to appear too curious. There was marijuana smoke drifting, cool and gentle, heady in its texture, from the far side of the room. Smoking had started early.

Eight

The car of the Israeli ambassador came to the back door of the Foreign Office.

It was a Mercedes, low on its wheels because of the armor plating that was standard for the senior members of that country's diplomatic corps. Unlike the principal transport of other embassies, it carried no suggestion on the number plate as to the identity of the passenger. There was a large radio aerial attached to the rear of the bodywork at the side of the trunk, which maintained communications with the fortified embassy building set back from the private Kensington Palace Road. Most ambassadors accredited to the Court of St. James's traveled with just a chauffeur for company, but in this car there were two other young men, both of whom had been issued licenses from the Home Office to carry Uzi submachine guns. The guns lay on the floor now, one in the front beside the driver, one in the back beside the ambassador, and both covered from careless gaze by coats. As it had made its way through the London traffic, the Mercedes was shadowed by a powerful three and a half liter Rover, painted anonymous blue, unmarked, and in which sat two men from the Protection Division of Special Branch.

When the car pulled up, one of the bodyguards stayed in his

seat; that was the man in front, his hand a few inches from the hidden Uzi. The other, who had ridden with the ambassador in the back, unlocked the door, climbed out, scanned the pavement where it ran down from Birdcage Walk toward the Horseguards Parade, and nodded. The ambassador was out fast, and was shepherded through the narrow door in a matter of seconds. Both he and his bodyguard ignored the Special Branch man who had also stepped onto the pavement. The London detective assigned to the Israeli embassy was used to that, familiar with being treated as an unnecessary bystander, there to make up the numbers but not to be consulted.

Through the working part of the week a liveried official would have been there to escort the ambassador to the second-floor office where the Under Secretary who specialized in Middle East affairs now waited. But on the weekend there was simply a man in a dark suit. The wide passages were darkened, electricity switched off as part of the recent Civil Service economics, leaving the portraits of the great British Foreign Secretaries mysterious and shadowy.

"Thank you for coming, your Excellency," said the Under Secretary as the door closed behind the ambassador. The Israeli said nothing. "The Minister would like to have been able to see you personally. It is regrettable that he is in the country, unable to return to London in the time we felt was available." Liar, thought the ambassador. More likely, half up his thighs in a trout stream somewhere in his beloved Yorkshire. "On the basis of the information that your own security service was able to provide us with, and because of additional information that our own departments have obtained, the Minister has asked me to request of your Excellency that further thought and consideration should be given to the visit to Britain of Professor Sokarev."

The ambassador said, "You say 'further thought and consideration.' To what end?"

Spell it out in words of one syllable, thought the Under Secretary. God protect us, they're a gauche crowd. "With a view, Excellency, to deciding whether or not the visit should continue as planned, in the face of what your service and ours regard as a serious threat."

"You are asking me to recommend to Jerusalem that the visit be canceled?"

"I am asking you nothing. I am merely suggesting, on the

direction of my Minister, that you might wish to reconsider the value of the visit."

"There is only one set of circumstances which would lead me to tell my government that in my personal opinion Professor Sokarev should cancel his lecture on Tuesday night and by-pass Britain."

The Under Secretary inclined his head, and the ambassador went on, "If I were to believe that the police forces and other agencies of Britain were incapable of providing the necessary protection for Professor Sokarev, then I would suggest to my Foreign Ministry that the visit should be canceled."

Cunning fox, the Under Secretary said to himself. "There is no question of that. We will provide protection . . ."

"Then there is nothing further to discuss." The ambassador's voice was cold. "When you report back to the Minister on this conversation, I would be grateful if you could relay a sentiment of my government. We are not prepared to be taken simply as a nuisance child, a bothersome problem that will go away if the door is barred to it. Professor Sokarev has been offered the hospitality of a learned and illustrious body in your capital. We intend to make sure that he honors the engagement. The rest, my dear fellow, is in your hands."

The Under Secretary bridled. "You must understand that I was passing on a request from my Minister."

The ambassador smiled without friendship, puckered his eyes fractionally, and said, "And I will pass on to my Minister that the British government will be providing—what was the word you used?—yes, adequate protection. Perhaps you should know, since it seems you have not been informed, that while we have been discussing the suitability of the visit, the security attaché at my embassy has been talking with the relevant people at your side on the very question of Professor Sokarev's safety. At times like this, Under Secretary, it is liaison that is needed."

He turned on his heel and made his own way out of the room.

In the early afternoon McCoy took Famy from the house and to the car parked fifty yards up the road on the far side.

"I didn't bring it down to the station last night," he said. "It's nicked, stolen, and that's too public a place to leave it lying around. It's all right in a street like this, half the bloody cars here have been stolen."

It was a two-door Ford Escort, painted green and un-scratched, "M" registration. "I got it over in Wembley, that's on the far side of London, out in the suburbs, night before last. Goes okay, though it's a bit small."

Famy looked at the car, disinterested, and waited for the passenger door to be opened for him as McCoy wriggled his way behind the driving wheel. They headed past the Angel Green and stopped at the lights, indicator clicking, ready to turn right down the Pentonville Road and the run in to the main university complex. McCoy could now realize the extent to which he was involved. It had begun simply, and without complications: providing backup, assistance. The shooting in France had changed that, and ensured that if he carried on with the enterprise, it would be as an equal partner.

There's no bloody help from this bastard, he thought to himself. Talks in spasms, then goes silent, saying nothing, just gazes into bloody eternity, like no one else exists. Doesn't give a damn whether we come out of it or not. A different war from the hedgerow actions that he had perfected amongst the fields of South Armagh. Political assassination . . . something that his Active Service Unit had never contemplated. A soldier or a policeman, or a Proddy politician, that was different. That was attrition.

This was a totally new concept to him: a killing on such a grand scale that the shock waves would fill world headlines for a week. One thing to drop a Para, one thing to blow a Wool-worth's, one thing to take out a policeman, but this . . . And he was being drawn into it, he recognized that, and thought even now that the point of retreat was already lost, that the moment of no return had already passed. He was experienced, had known the tension of guerrilla combat in the hills around Cross-maglen, had fired the cumbersome RPG-7 rocket launcher at the tin-fenced, screened and barricaded police station on the edge of his town, had given orders, had men follow him. And yet, this other man who had known none of this was directing him, controlling him, had taken charge, outstretched him in commitment.

Perhaps it was the hate. He'd heard it, read it, the simple hatred the Palestinian hard men felt for the Israelis, and he knew he couldn't match it. Even in the cage at Long Kesh, when he had paced beside the interior perimeter wire and

watched the camouflaged uniformed soldiers in their watchtowers, arcing their machine guns and jeering down at the men
below, even then he could not hate to the exclusion of all else.
When these people blasted their hostages, threw their grenades
without hesitation, without remorse, into cinemas, they put
themselves beyond the reach of McCoy's understanding. His
men could never do that. There had to be a purpose to killing;
every victim ought to know why he would die at McCoy's hand.
But just for the sake of it, just for the gesture . . . that was not
enough.

At the bottom of the Euston Road, in the last lap to the
university, he asked the question. "Why this man? Why Sokarev?"

There was no urgency in the reply. Famy said, "Three times
the Arabs fought the Israelis and were shamed. At their Yom
Kippur we fought them again and surprised them with our
technique and with our bravery, but we did not win. The next
time we fight we will do better, and the time after that we will
have greater success. One time in the future we will take them
close to defeat. Then they will have no option, then they will
threaten their ultimate weapon. They will tell the world of their
bomb, they will tell the world they will use it to survive. Sokarev
is an architect of that bomb. To us he represents a symbol of
what would be their last throw in desperation. We feel if we kill
Sokarev, we have demonstrated that we fear nothing from
them. If we can eliminate a man so much at the center of their
whole basis of national survival, then we have achieved a great
victory."

"There'll be others, others who know as much as this one
man," said McCoy.

"That is unimportant. It is not Sokarev's knowledge that we
will deny them. It is the symbol that we attack. It meant nothing
in manpower for Israel to lose her athletes at Munich, nothing
to lose their attaché in Washington, the man here in London we
took with the letter bomb. It is the symbol that matters. That
we can prove to them that we are at war, that we can strike
where, when we please."

McCoy was still silently repeating to himself "Bloody maniacs" when he drove past the Students Union building and
pulled up outside the massive mausoleum structure that

marked the administrative and academic center of London University.

"Just relax. Take it easy. If anyone asks, you've left some notes behind, coming back to get them. But don't look furtive, look as though you belong," McCoy said as they walked up the great cement steps and into the building.

Famy said quietly, "Do we know which entrance he will use?"

"No, there are a stack of them. This is the main one, the natural one, but there are alternatives."

There was almost a tranquillity about the Arab's voice, that of someone who has had a great rest and awakened refreshed. His breathing was relaxed, unhurried, as he peered around him in the great echoing, high-roofed hallway. "But the room, we know which room he will use?"

"It's marked on the invitation." McCoy pulled his wallet from an inner pocket. From an inside flap he took an embossed white square of card. He smiled as he showed it to Famy. "It's the real thing," he said.

The Arab recognized the name of David Sokarev in ornate copperplate writing in the center of the card, followed by a string of academic initials. He saw also the words: Lecture Room D, ground floor, fourth entrance to the right after entering the main hallway. "Where did you get it?" he asked.

"Acquired it. Long story. I'll tell you sometime."

"What time does he arrive? And when does he speak?"

"He'll come about fifteen minutes before the speech. There's a reception, sherry and sandwiches; he'll probably take in the end of that. He's due to talk at eight."

But Famy was not listening, just taking in the pillars, the various shadowy entrances that led off the hallway to offices and other lecture rooms. Assessing cover, the room he would need, the speed at which a small man could travel across the floor space, the angle required to see him if he were to be surrounded by guards and the welcoming committee. Without seeing the room, he already decided there would be no possibility of gaining direct admission to the lecture, particularly with the bulky firearms that would be needed for the killing. "It has to be from outside," he said, vaguely and to himself.

Famy turned and walked back down the hallway and out into the light; he went left across the car park to the edge of the building, then moved down its side, his attention locked on the windows just above the level of his head. High above him the building towered, with rows of windows set in geometric patterns. Massive, functional and intimidating in its grey strength. It rose in a narrowing column to a topmost point from where half of London could be viewed. The fortress to which Sokarev would be brought. But since time started, there had been a way —had there not?—into every citadel. Brick and stone and cement in themselves do not provide protection, Famy thought; there will be a gap in the defenses, caused by the error of man.

The construction of the lower floors was in the form of a giant and flattened cross, the main doors at the north end, the lecture room off to the west extremity of a protruding arm. Famy hurried across from the front toward the wall where the lecture room would have its windows, and in his step there was a lightness and excitement. They had taught him the art of what they called "using dead ground," moving in terrain which was denied to the vision of the enemy. Those who stood at the main door would have no sight of the windows he wanted; the butting corner would deny them. And where would they assemble the security men that would come with Sokarev? They would be with him inside, and they would be at the doors ... He came around the corner, McCoy following blindly, uncomprehending, and again there were more windows and beneath them cars closely parked and near to the wall. Famy noted that and was satisfied. He glanced around him, for the first time a trace of anxiety showing through, then scrabbled onto the front of a dark car. It gave him the necessary elevation to see inside the lecture room, across the rows of pewlike benches and to the lectern where successive generations of dons and professors had attempted to impart information to their students and which on Tuesday night would hold the typed notes of David Sokarev. He jumped down from the car.

"Would you go inside," he said to McCoy, "and if there are curtains, draw them across this window, the middle one of the three." McCoy stood his ground, confused. "Just do it," the Arab said, his voice rising. "Just this window and draw them tightly. So I can see where they meet."

He waited a full two minutes after McCoy had gone, then the curtains swished their way across the broad window. He noted that when they closed, they were completely together, letting no light escape from the room. He bent hurriedly down, picked up a gravel stone and marked the wall at the place where they met. Almost immediately the drapes opened again. While he waited for McCoy he repeated the scratch in the wall over his original mark. This time he drew a six-pointed star a little more than four inches across from tip to tip. He was still smiling about it when McCoy joined him.

"We must get some gloves," Famy said. "Thick ones that will withstand broken glass, cover the hand and the wrist."

In the mind of Abdel-El-Famy the assassination plan was complete.

The drug scene in London, as in any major capital, is a brutal and violent one. Young detectives like Doris Lang, who attempted to infiltrate the market and supply the evidence required by the courts to convict the pushers, went through extensive and thorough training before they abandoned their conventional trim clothes for those of the teenagers and dropouts amongst whom they would now move.

She had taken a three-week course to learn the medical side of the menace and to be taught the arts of survival in an alien society, and had spent two concentrated days in a gymnasium with an instructor who taught self-defense. She was a capable young woman, used to looking after herself, and the detective inspector to whom she reported had few fears about her personal safety. What he was looking for from her was, first, patience, and, when that was rewarded, detail.

She had seen McCoy and Famy leave the house, and then spent another twenty-five minutes reading and gossiping casually and inconsequentially with her new friends before she excused herself. On the stair landing on the floor immediately below the room occupied by the two newcomers, she had stood stock-still for up to a minute listening to the sounds of the building, convincing herself that in the upper reaches of the house she would be alone.

She had been disappointed with her earlier search in the small hours. She had used the time on the clock that her training suggested, just after four, when the psychiatrists said the human physique was at its most vulnerable and yearning for deep sleep. But she had recognized that this would be only a cursory look, though she had weighed the chances of her discovery as being slight. In daylight she could be slower, more observant.

None of the locks were fitted with keys, and she was able to turn the handle and walk in. In her left hand was a small pad and a pencil stub. She worked through the men's possessions for a concentrated twelve minutes. Much of the time was spent rearranging the clothing in the Arab's grip bag and McCoy's old suitcase so that they would not detect her hand amongst the socks and the underclothes and the shirts. She found no papers belonging to either man—no passports, letters, driving licenses, no hint of their identity.

There was nothing remarkable about the clothing in the suitcase. It was the contents of the grip bag that fascinated her. The clothes in themselves were unexceptional, conventional for a young man, except that every maker's tag and washing and cleaning instructions had been removed. Not pulled away, but conscientiously unstitched.

She wrote that down on the pad; it followed the times of arrival and departure, and the descriptions she had taken of the two men. She felt the frustration that came from the failure to clarify their business in the commune. Perhaps, she thought, their trip out today would provide her with something; perhaps when they returned, there would be papers which she could find if she came again in the cold desolate hours before dawn.

At Scotland Yard, Jones saw the Assistant Commissioner (Crime) in his office close to the operations room on the fifth floor of the building. As a result of the meeting, two considerable and wide-scale programs would be set into operation. First, a dragnet to try and locate and then arrest the man McCoy and his unknown partner. Second, the gathering together of the security necessary to protect the Israeli professor when he visited London. It was the first plan that took the greatest time. Jones sketched through the information the Department had collected in the previous twenty-four hours, withholding in some instances, but allowing the policeman a detailed picture of the circumstances that surrounded the threat to Sokarev. He emphasized in particular the faint but possible connection be-tween the Irishman and the North London communes.

"You have a difficulty there straightaway," said the Assistant Commissioner. "We have several under surveillance. From the outside. I can call that sort of information in at any time. If your men are in one of those, we can identify them from the logs very quickly. But there are others where we have people living on the inside. I've been on the phone this morning and I'm advised that there are seventeen where that applies. They tend to come out on Monday mornings. There would be a fair deal of opposition if you were to ask me to break all those covers and get the officers out this afternoon or tomorrow. You appreciate a great number of detailed inquiries are going on through these channels. I think to justify such an action I'd need rather more positive information than you have been able to provide me with."

The Security Service is a force without powers. It can only request. Jones looked pained, acting up a bit. Face set with disappointment.

"I'm sorry, Mr. Jones. Tell me it's essential, tell me an address, give me something clear, and we can act. I think that's reason-able."

"Is there no other way of getting them out, other than de-stroying their position, your people's?"

"What's your suggestion?" The Assistant Commissioner threw it back at him. Like so many others who rarely came in touch with the Security Service, he distrusted them, remained unconvinced of their effectiveness.

"I don't have one," said Jones. "Not ready at hand." He felt tired, anger growing at the man across the desk. Unable to comprehend the scale of the problem, more concerned with heroin and cocaine than political assassination.

"I'll think about it, ask around," said the Assistant Commis-sioner.

That was the concession. Trifling, thought Jones. And half of another day gone, and nothing to show for it.

The security attaché of the Israeli embassy was late at the Home Office. Jones's ill humor, deteriorating fast and he recog-nized it, was not helped by the lack of any form of apology. But Jones had also recognized that there were times to bite on it,

not to make the hell of a scene he would have liked to. And the
Israeli brought information. Timetables of Sokarev's movements, hotel and room number, invitation list to the speech.

"And he will have two men with him from our own Protection Division of the Foreign Ministry. I can give you their
names. Joseph Mackowicz and Gad Elkin. You know it is our
policy, Mr. Jones. Since Munich we have become more aware
of the dangers. They are expressly charged with the safety of
the professor."

That was the best news of the day, thought Jones. If the
applecart goes, then those two bastards will be picking up the
load along with me. Nice to be in numbers.

He told him what was known of McCoy. The Israeli said,
"With respect I would suggest, from my observations of your
own problems and my knowledge of ours, that the one we have
to fear is not the Irishman. If the other man is a Palestinian, that
is the creature we have to be on guard against."

Too bloody right, Jones said to himself. And no name, no
description, no fingerprints, no file, no bloody history. "We
should meet again tomorrow. Same time, and here?"

The Israeli agreed, and Jones hurried to his car and drove fast
back to Curzon Street. It was his complete lack of knowledge
on what his next move should be that fanned his impatience.
His job only rarely required such a frenzied reaction as was now
demanded. It was a sensation he had not experienced before,
and he found himself looking at his watch as if the very minutes
that slipped away were precious and should not be lost. It was
a new form of warfare he had become involved in, where his
enemy was insignificant in stature and strength, had none of the
force and intellect that his own side possessed, and yet was an
enemy who dominated the initiative. For the first time in close
on three decades in the Department, he felt a sense of fear and
helplessness that was alien to the well-ordered and circum-
scribed career he pursued so diligently through his filing system.

Just before the light faded, the boy suggested it was time for
him to be on his way. David Sokarev was not surprised. It was
a long, exhausting drive between Beersheba and the IAF
fighter base on the road beyond Afula. He knew his son would
be on duty in his flying suit, waiting in the squadron ready room,

at five-thirty on the Sunday morning on three-minute warning. He would need the sleep, and the drive would take three hours, even in the tuned-up Mini.

As the boy stood up from the chair on the balcony that looked over the town, and then far into the Negev where the sun was reddening, Sokarev said quietly to him, "There is a matter I want to talk to you about. Can you come to my room? It will not take long."

And when they were together inside the room that the professor used for his work and his correspondence, Sokarev spoke to his son, shyly, without confidence. "Don't interrupt me. Not till I have finished. And I have not told your mother this. There is a threat against me when I go to London. There were two men from the Foreign Ministry who came to see me two days ago. They are to guard me, and they told me. It is not an important visit. I had been looking forward to it. Just one speech, and the chance to meet old friends and talk. Talk with different people. But it is something that could be canceled, and the world would not topple. I do not know how to react to the situation. If there was a risk, I would have presumed the Ministry, the government, would have canceled the visit themselves. But they have not done that. They have just sent men to me to tell me that I will be guarded. That is all there is, my boy. But what should I do?"

He looked at the boy, pleading, seeking for assurance. But his son answered him predictably enough in the language of a serviceman who executed orders, believed in the inviolate authority of his commander.

"If they did not think that it was safe, they would not allow you to go. You are too precious to us all, Father, for them to risk you if there was real danger. If they have not suggested that you cancel, then you should have no fear."

Sokarev kissed the boy on both cheeks, easier in his mind now, dismissing the thought of a telephone call to the director of Dimona, and together they came out of the office. But the gun, he would take that anyway.

Jimmy had shaved, put on a clean shirt and the old squadron tie, brushed his suit and cleaned his shoes before he came to Leconfield House. He'd sat in the outer office beyond Jones's door for more than half an hour, exchanging small talk with

Helen as she typed, while he waited for his appointment to be kept.

He was past fifty. Grey hair slicked down same as Jones's. Not much flesh on his face; the years of living and fending for himself alone had seen to that. There were dark blotched patches, fierce and red, on his cheeks, not as bad as before he went to the clinic, but still evident. A blood vessel had fractured in his left eye, leaving a small oasis of crimson in the extreme corner closest to the bridge of his nose. He was tall, not overweight, partly because he exercised in a private gymnasium, partly because his life style denied him regular food and meals. Helen could see that he was ill-at-ease, almost nervous, as he constantly shifted his position in the chair. Come on, you bloody man, he thought, don't keep me bloody hanging about all day. It was the time he loathed. The time that elapsed before he was briefed, before he was back inside the team again and a part of the new operation, when his mind raced with unsubstantiated ideas. Leaves you like a bloody vegetable, in limbo.

Jones came in. Nodded to Jimmy, but spoke first to Helen. "Any messages, anything new in?"

"Nothing," she said. "The DG would like to see you before six. He rang through. Nothing beyond that."

Jones masked his disappointment. He walked through to his office and opened the door and asked Jimmy to follow. Inside, he offered him a chair, and then went to his own behind his desk. Jimmy could see the pile of slim cardboard folders on the desk top.

Jones was expert at setting out the skeleton of a problem. Wasted few words. He took Jimmy through the information that was already available. There were no interruptions.

"That's the background, not everything we have. You can pick that out of the paper work when we've finished. In ideal times we'd concentrate the major effort on lifting the bastards before they hit, but as you'll see from situation reports that we've been doing, we're cold on that score." Just as Jimmy would have wanted it, thought Jones. When the rest of us are getting tired and looking to steer clear of the big ones, Jimmy'll be cheering from the top tower. Proper job for him, one to tax him, one to test him. We're different people, Jones knew that, the one played out and trying to avoid the fracas, the other

leaping about like a schoolboy. Not quite a smile from Jones.
"We have to be prepared for an actual attack, and I want you,
Jimmy, to be right beside our Israeli brother. Adhesive close,
not out of your sight except when he's safely locked in the
bloody loo. He'll have his own men with him, a cattle herd from
Special Branch, all falling over each other and arguing protocol,
but I want you a little bit tighter on him than any of the others.
Normally we wouldn't still be in a thing like this, it would be
straight police, but the ramifications on this one are too big if
it goes wrong. So you have no doubts about your position,
Jimmy, I'll spell it out. If you see anything that bothers you, you
act. If you see a gun close to him, you shoot. Don't concern
yourself with the bloody paper work and the rule book."

Jones looked thoughtful. Needed to be stronger than that,
needed to elaborate, leave him in no doubt, owed it to the man
at the sharp end. "And if you hit some poor devil out for a walk
in the park with his dog, we'll cover for you."

"You always say that," Jimmy said.

Would he cover—would he, hell. But it was a form of words.
Means not a bloody thing, Jimmy thought. What they feel they
have to say. But if the balloon filled up—what price immunity
then? In the courts like every other bugger, and double fast.

"What I need, Jimmy," Jones went on, ignoring him. Best way
with Jimmy. "What I need is the very clear knowledge that I
will be informed of every movement Sokarev makes. I don't
want it via the Israeli embassy, I don't want it via Scotland Yard,
I want it from you."

"If everyone is twisting their knickers at this rate, why isn't
the visit called off?"

"God alone knows. If anybody else does, they haven't thought
fit to tell me. The Israelis have known for some days of the risk;
they haven't opted for cancellation."

Jimmy left it there. He could see the other man was close to
the end of his patience, not ready for a gentle chat on the
theoretical.

Jones said, "I'll circulate your name to the Israelis and to the
Special Branch, and have it backed by the Home Office. You'll
need some time to work through the papers. Tomorrow I'll
want you with me when I see the Israelis. They'll want to run
the whole bloody thing. The DG is mildly anxious it doesn't

happen that way. You'll need some weapon practice. Fix that for the morning. You'd better get back to your place now and pick up some clothes. Fairclough and Duggan and I are sleeping in. You'd better join us. You can have Helen's office."

As Jimmy walked through the outer office he stopped beside Helen's table. "Unlucky again tonight, sweetheart. We're all kipping on the job."

"I told you they were in a flat bloody panic," she said.

Nine

When they left the university building, McCoy drove across the artery of Tottenham Court Road, and in the maze of side streets behind the Middlesex Hospital, found a small Indian restaurant. They spent a long time over the meal, while they talked. The abstract background of their lives. The Irishman mostly, with Famy listening, while they picked and pulled at the chappatis, toyed with the rice and the sauces and meats, fractured the popadums into tiny pieces. And then they took coffees, and after that more beer as the evening went by.

McCoy talked of Crossmaglen and Cullyhanna. He spoke of the sharp rising hills, with the farms that barely supported life, of the large families, of the economic hardship. He told of the fierce independence of the people who lived there, how they had transferred their old enmity of such everyday figures as the customs men and the tax collector to the soldiers of the British army. He related the story of Mick McVerry, killed in the attack on Keady police station, how they had placed nine gunmen around the building, and a rocket launcher, and how McVerry had died, shot down as he planted the bomb against the building—which when it went off had left a complete wing demolished. He'd been in the Kesh then, he said, otherwise he would have been there with his Armalite with its plastic stock, made in Japan, paid for in Boston, Massachusetts. Famy had raised his eyes inquiringly when McCoy mentioned the Kesh, and the Irishman launched into his stories of the prison where he had been held. How they, the prisoners, ran the premises. How they held their courts and punished those they deemed guilty. How they organized their escape committees, dug their tunnels, worked their switches with visitors. How they held their weapons and explosives classes. How they jeered the governor as he made his rounds. How they rioted. How they went on hunger strike. How they dominated Catholic public opinion in the province outside the wire.

Famy had looked uncomprehending, disbelieving. He tried to suggest that this was something the Israelis would never have tolerated behind the high yellow walls of the maximum-security prison at Ramla where they held the fedayeen. There were many things McCoy said that night that Famy was amazed by. No penalties against the families and property of those arrested on terrorist charges. Detailed fire-control orders for individual soldiers. A piece of paper that gave the military the circumstances under which they could shoot. A hundred paratroopers locked up in Crossmaglen police station whose food and ammunition came only by helicopter because it was too dangerous to drive lorries along the roads—too many culvert bombs on the roads, too many control wires in the ditches.

But what astonished him most of all was that McCoy was there sitting across the table. "Why when they had caught you, when you had done these things, why did they release you?"

And McCoy had just smiled, and laughed, and known that it was not possible to explain the gestures of the Secretary of State for Northern Ireland to a man whose knowledge of guerrilla warfare was based on that fought against an enemy as hard and intransigent as the Israelis.

McCoy wanted to talk, and Famy was relegated to listen. He moved on to the politics of the Irish Republican Army, Provisional wing. Left the other far behind when he spoke of six counties, and twenty-six counties, and thirty-two counties, and then of Ulster, which he said was theoretically nine counties. And regionalism and federalism and Fianna Fail. The Arab was lost. As his mind drifted from the slowly slurring speech of

McCoy, he could reflect that about his own cause there was nothing complicated, nothing that could not be taught to the child as it first walked, nothing that could not be understood by the simplest in the camps.

Because we know what we want, he thought, we are prepared to strive with sacrifice for our victory. Not in a pathetic cowboy world of minimal heroics, shooting down one soldier and claiming that as a victory, killing one middle-aged policeman and believing that changed political strategy; that is no course to fight. Perhaps because they do not know what it is they struggle for, they cannot steel themselves to acts that will shock and stagger on the grand scale. He will learn, this Irish boy. He will understand what it is to kill when the diplomats of every major capital in the world will react. He will find out what it is to earn the hatred of one half the world, the gratitude and adulation of the other.

But Famy enjoyed it, felt the security of the restaurant around him, realized that no eyes were transfixed on him, that he belonged to the scene, and was amused at the conspiratorial whisper with which McCoy kept up his personal patter of exploits. It was not till McCoy was peeling out the pound notes and paying the obsequious waiter that Famy thought again of the darkened figure that had searched his room last night, and of the girl who had stared at them as they left the building back in the midafternoon.

When they were in the car, Famy spoke of that. "We will sleep in different places tonight. You go to the far wall, and I will be close to the door. If someone comes again, they will have to move deep into the room, and I will be behind them then."

She had seen them through the open door of the living room, when they came from outside into the hallway. They had paused for a few moments as if undecided whether or not to join the group in the room, and she had heard their voices, indistinct against the record player. They had decided not to, and she had heard them walk away toward the stairs, and there had been the noise of their feet on the steps. Through the early part of the night, every half-hour or so, she had turned away from her book to look at her watch, waiting till the time was right. Gradually the room emptied, as the young people, singly and in pairs, drifted toward their mattresses and sleeping bags that lay higher in the house. When most had gone, and there was no longer the music and conversation to keep company with her, she felt the cold. If one went to bed early, the chill in the house was not felt, but by the small hours the warmth of the day had vanished, dissipated in the high rooms, the old walls. Few in the building spoke to her, but that was the life style they chose, the lack of commitment that brought them there. If she had wanted to talk, she would have found the ears she sought. As she did not, she was left to herself.

She wriggled inside the hard wool of her jersey, screwing her muscles closer to her body, fighting to maintain the personal warmth that seemed to be steadily eluding her. There was a child crying on one of the upper floors; it generally did, most of the night. The stupid bitch who was its mother had little to give it but a vague animal affection. In the days she had been in the commune, Doris Lang had grown to hate that woman for her incompetence and carelessness in the treatment of a two-year-old. She yearned to intervene, and every time dismissed the possibility as being out of context with her cover. Probably hungry, poor little bastard, trying to grow on toast and warmed tins of beans and spaghetti.

At a few minutes before four the last of those who had sat up in the room with her stretched and staggered, as if sleepwalking, toward the stairs. She was used to lack of sleep, and was able within moments to drag together the concentration she had allowed to fade and leave her as she had whiled away the time. It was papers she wanted, indications of identity, indications of purpose. The reason these two unlikely figures, out of shape with the other jigsaw pieces of the commune, had come to spend their time there. Her watch showed just past four o'clock when she slipped out of the room and went slowly, with great care, testing each footstep, toward the attic rooms of the house.

She wore heavy rubber-soled tennis shoes. Dirty exterior, long without any whitener, but totally efficient for moving without noise. With one hand she hitched up the long skirt to prevent it from brushing against the steps. Outside the door of the attic she paused again, listening to the night sounds, of traffic, the heavy breathing of deep sleep coming from many directions, the far-distant chorus of an ambulance on emergency call.

From behind the door there was silence. Complete quiet. She eased her hand onto the rounded handle of the door, pushed it open an inch, waited and listened again, and went in.

Famy had not heard her on the stairs or on the landing. But the movement of the door-handle mechanism alerted him, a minutiae of sounds, as the bar was withdrawn inside the old, unoiled lock. From his half-sleep his eyes focused instantaneously on the white handkerchief he had tied to the handle on the inside of the door. He could see that, however blurred and greyed its brightness was in the near-dark. He saw it move, fractionally at first, then swing out, opening into the room. Then his sight of it was obscured as the faintly silhouetted figure came past it. He felt a sweat rise high up in the trousers that he had worn when he had climbed down in the sleeping bag, felt the sticky cloying moisture search over his skin, finding havens in his armpits, in his groin, behind his knees. He fought to control the regularity of his breathing.

They are in no hurry, thought Famy. Waiting their time, waiting for the light to become natural, easier. Then there was movement again, and with it the soft scuffing of material on the floor. That told Famy that his intruder was a girl, and as he strained into the nothingness of the room, he pictured the one he had stared at downstairs, with the white sun-forbidden face and the hair that had not been brushed and the cumbersome dress that would reach down to the boards. His own part of the room was the darkest, but the street light made vague shapes of the end where McCoy slept. He could see clearly her outline when she approached his sleeping bag, saw her bend down and open the case, heard her hands among the clothes.

That she had found nothing which she sought he could understand by the way, unhurried, unexcited, she put down the top of the case. Then there was indecision, confusion. She looks for me, the little whore, thought Famy. Remembers where I was last night, is searching with her eyes, but she'll need the torch over here. He closed his eyelids tight, unwilling to risk the involuntary blink if the light should suddenly come on. The footsteps came closer to him, warily, seeking out the ground, testing the pliability of the boards. They were very near when they stopped and on his face he felt the thin beam of the torch.

He had put the grip bag close to his head, and he could feel her breath on his face as she bent low over him, painstakingly sliding back the zip fastener. She shifted her foot, leaving it just three or four inches from the sleeping bag, then her hands were inside it, following the line of the pencil torch. It was as she straightened to move away that Famy thrust his hands from under the cover of the bag and grabbed at the leg that was closest to him.

For a moment his fingers were lost in the folds of the skirt, until just before panic he clasped at the hardness of her ankle. His whole weight followed, dragging her off balance and pulling her down. The torch fell to the floorboards, clattering and then shining its beam away from them. Her surprise was complete. By the time she had realized what had happened, she was on the boards, face down, her right arm twisted high behind her back, gripped by Famy, whose knee was indented into the pit of her back. The shock had been too great for her to scream.

"McCoy, McCoy, come here." He hissed the command out, and the other man stirred on the far side of the room.

"What is it?" The voice came low across the floor.

"I have the little bitch, I have her here."

There was a flurry of movement and McCoy crawled through the darkness till he bumped into the mass that was the girl and Famy. His hand reached out for the torch, and he shone it into the pale, fear-stricken face. She tried to swing her head away from the light, but he grasped at her hair, and as she cried out he pulled her back into the beam.

"Get your fucking hands off me." She spat the words at him, and with his free hand he hit her hard across the mouth, and the metal of the battery container caught her lip, bulging and reddening it as the blood welled into the wound in the moment before the skin broke, and the trickle, highlighted by the softness of her skin, skidded a way downward to the side of her throat. She started to struggle then, without feeling the pain in her head as McCoy clung to her hair, oblivious of the numbing ache in her arm where Famy had twisted it behind her. With her other hand she reached into the void behind the light, found the flesh of McCoy's face and with extended fingernails gouged for his eyes. They were long nails, and she heard him cry out in a mixture of pain and astonishment as they bit down through the skin before she raked across his cheeks. The hand let go of the hair, and before she could affect the grip across her back, McCoy's foot had lashed into her head. She tried to turn away, but again the foot came back, guided now by the light. Accurate and vicious, striking against the long hair that offered no protection to her ear.

Then McCoy was on his knees beside her, hands in her hair again, and this time there was no resistance. She moved her head toward him, following his will, and saw the long jarring weals across his face, saw his eyes alive with rage.

Famy tightened the grip on her arm, so that she convulsed, then lay inert. The struggle over.

Famy said, "She searched your things, then mine."

"Roll the bitch over." McCoy was panting, and they pushed her so that she lay on her back. The Arab had his weight across her legs, high on her thighs, and now pinioned her arms to the floor above her head. She closed her eyes and felt McCoy's hands begin to search her. He started at her neck and worked quickly, expertly across her body, running over her breasts but not lingering, down her waist, rough and uncaring, till they fastened on the notebook in the wide pocket at her hips. Fingers forced their way inside the fold of the material and pulled the pad out. When she moved her eyelids fractionally open she could see him peering at her close, tight handwriting, flicking the pages over, torch close to the paper.

"What does it say?" said Famy, impatience growing as the other man concentrated.

"She's a bloody tout," said McCoy.

"What's that?" said Famy, voice rising.

"An informer. A spy. There are names here, people living in the house, times and dates of arrival. We're here too, when we came in, when we went out yesterday. She's a clever little cow. You've no tags, no maker's marks in your clothes, right?"

"We took them out before we came."

"Well, it's written down here."

McCoy waited, the big eyes delving into the young face beneath him. She could sense the chill in his voice, horrible and frozen, without pity. He said, "Who are you? Tell me why you came." The glazed fear-filled face peered vacantly back toward him and beyond.

"Who are you, you cow?" And he hit her again, with the edge of his hand, finding the tip of her chin bone, jerking her head back, banging it on the boards. Still she said nothing, and he struck her with his fist clenched hard into the softness below her rib cage. She gasped for air, fighting to force it down into her lungs, tried to draw her knees from under the Arab to protect the defenseless body.

"You'll get it again." Remorseless, awful, the dripping taplike voice.

She started to try to speak, but there were no sounds at first, just the effort and failure. Her chest heaved and writhed before the words came. There was a final act of defiance. "Get off me, you pigs. I'm a police officer. Get your pig-shit hands off me."

The thought through Famy's mind was immediate. Just two days earlier on the road to Boulogne the police had been waiting for them, now here, in the supposed safe house, the police were again close to him. "How did they know?" he shouted. "How did the bastards know we would be here?"

McCoy saw her reaction to what Famy had said. Saw her flick her head forward to stare at the shadowy face above her. It was that movement that sealed his resolution. His hands came down, settled on her throat, and tightened. She tried to speak of drugs and hippies, but the air was already denied her. Then there was nothing, only the sinking pain and pressure of the hands and the blackness when she tried to see.

When McCoy had finished, he realized that Famy was no longer beside him; he heard him coughing, heaving his stomach in the far corner. It had come easy to McCoy. In the world in which he moved and fought, the penalty for touts was clear-cut.

"Pull yourself together, you stupid bugger," he said. "Get your things in your bag. We're moving out."

The house was quiet, at rest, as they went down the stairs, through the door and onto the street.

While McCoy drove, fast and with studied concentration, through the deserted streets of the capital, heading south toward the river, Famy sat rock-still beside him. The Arab's mind was moving quickly. It was the first time that he had encountered violent death, and the speed with which the life had been crushed from the girl amazed him, its simplicity, its suddenness. And the doubts he had felt about McCoy had vanished in those few seconds. When the time came the Irishman, too, was prepared to kill. Famy knew, and it was a feeling he had not entertained before, that they were now a team. In the darkness of the attic bedroom the link between the two men had been irrevocably joined, and with that, his last lingering uncertainties about the success of his mission had gone.

"Where are we going now?" Famy asked.

McCoy did not take his eyes from the road ahead. "Down into the hills south of London. Into Surrey, where the guns are."

"And where do we sleep?"

"We sleep rough tonight and tomorrow. We have to ditch this car, get another. Come back to London on Tuesday, probably late. This car will do us for a few hours more, but when the balloon goes up we'll have to have another."

"How long do you think before they find her."

"Sometime, not immediately. And when they do they'll have the bloody commune on their hands. And they won't make much headway with them."

"It was necessary to kill her." Famy said it quietly, but as a statement.

" 'Course it bloody was."

"She knew who we were?" The question again.

"Shouldn't think so." McCoy sensed the other man's surprise at his answer. He went on, "Probably there on the drugs scene. Could have been bomb squad and out Provo hunting. You've got two alternatives—bluff it out or the other. And when you start knocking shit out of the girl, that narrows it down to the other."

"How far do we have to go?"

"About another hour and a half. Get some sleep." It was an instruction. McCoy wanted to drive without chatter in his ear.

Famy closed his eyes. The Irishman, he thought, he would have been able to sleep. But with himself there was no possibility of it. As the car jolted its way along the road the image that endlessly repeated itself was of the girl and her eyes that bulged and pleaded, and of the hard, calloused fingers on her neck.

*　　　*　　　*

But the killing of Doris Lang had not gone entirely unnoticed.

On the floor below, the woman who had nursed her child to sleep had lain with her eyes wide open, staring at the blankness of the ceiling. The sounds she had heard had baffled her at first. There had been bumps on the boards above, a half-stifled scream, recognizable as such, though short and cut off. There had been the footsteps that came hurriedly across the floor, then the noise of the struggle, then the shouts, too muffled to understand. There had been a scuffling, indeterminate, difficult to follow after that, and then more quiet before the footsteps came hurriedly past her door. The main door had slammed and there had been noise on the pavement, and the sound of a car starting and driving away.

She had clung to the sleeping child, not prepared to go and see for herself whatever had been left in the room. It was light before she summoned the courage, and the men had been gone nearly two hours. When she did go, her child left behind on the mattress, still curled fetuslike in sleep, her screams, hysterical and piercing, woke the building.

Henry Davies was drinking tea in the police station canteen. It was thick, strong-brewed, laced with sugar and hot. He could only sip at it, but always regarded his early-morning cup as the essential way to end night duty. He had signed off now, but usually spent fifteen minutes in the canteen, waiting for the day-shift handlers to come on, to exchange a few words, gossip, police talk with them.

On his radio net he had heard of the flap over on the far side of the area covered by the station, but a dog had not been required, and he had methodically continued his slow and lone patrol, checking factory, shop and warehouse doors.

He was sitting by himself when the sergeant came in.

"Lad, the DI's been on the radio. Wants you down Englefield Road. Number 112. Wants you down there as fast as you can." It was the standard joke in the station that he called everyone under the age of forty "lad."

"What for?" Davies asked.

"I don't know," the sergeant lied, but did it well and Davies couldn't read it. "He asked specifically for you. Slip on down there, lad."

They'd radioed ahead when he drove out of the station yard, and the detective inspector was waiting on the steps of the house for him. There were three police cars parked haphazardly at the side of the street, and a small knot of half-dressed onlookers. A constable who stood on the pavement and who knew Davies looked away.

When he got out of the car the inspector walked toward him, unshaven, roused from his Sunday-morning bed. "I've bad news, Henry. I'm very sorry . . . It's Doris. Some bastard's killed her." He stopped. Let the words sink in, saw the mask of overt self-control slide across the police constable's features.

"When did it happen?" Davies said, remote, far distant, something to say.

"Early this morning. We had a call about forty minutes ago. I've identified her. Do you want to go and see her, Henry?"

"There'll be all the cameras there, prints. All the bloody paraphernalia. I don't want to see her like that. Not with them all working round her."

"Is there somewhere you can go?"

"I'd like to go to her Mum's. Has she been told?"

"Not yet."

"I'd like to go there, then. Thank you, sir."

"I'll get someone to drive you round. Fred can come down and pick up your motor, and take your dog home and give it a meal. You can collect him tomorrow."

"Do you know who did it?"

"I think so. But they're long gone. Two of them. They're telling us a bit inside. More than they usually do."

The inhabitants of the commune were herded into the main living room on the ground floor while the coffin with Doris Lang's body was carried down the stairs and to the unmarked hearse. The detective inspector watched it go, then walked back into the room. He had spotted the spokesman for the group, older than most, a fragile and defiant figure. He called him out and went with him to the room behind, used as sleeping quarters and littered with blankets strewn where they had been left when the screaming had started.

"You've been helpful, quite helpful, before I was called out. I want it to go on that way."

The other man looked up at him without responding.

"The woman who found the body, she tells me two men left after she heard noises upstairs. Sometime after half past four. Who are those two men?"

The man said nothing, pushed his fingers, like a comb, through his shoulder-length hair.

"Now, don't mess me about, sunshine. It's a murder inquiry. We get impatient quickly."

"We knew one of them."

"Which one?"

"One was an Irishman."

"I said, and I said it clearly, don't mess me about. I haven't got all bloody day to be playing games."

Their two faces, the one bearded and with traces of acne, the other stubbled and tired, were less than a foot apart. The commune man looked away, then said, "There was a girl who used to live here. Eilish McCoy. One of the men was her brother. He's called Ciaran. I know because she once showed me a picture of him in a sort of uniform. Taken back in Ireland. He just turned up here about a week ago, asked for a room, said he had some people coming. Said they needed . . ."

The inspector said, "Somewhere quiet, somewhere to lie up?"

"Something like that."

"And the other one, the second one?"

"We never heard his name."

"Was he Irish?"

"No."

"Look, boy, last time, don't screw me about."

"I'd say he was an Arab."

"And no name—didn't McCoy call him anything?"

"They didn't mix with us. They were either out or in the room. The second one only came the night before last. There was no name."

"You say McCoy said he had 'some people coming.' "

"He told me there were three others; only the one showed up."

A detective came into the room. He held in his hand, gingerly and between thumb and first finger, a four-inch by two-inch pad.

"It was over in a corner. Left behind. It's Doris Lang's writing, no doubt on that. I've seen it in the station. Her week's log of the comings and goings. Seems she searched these buggers' room on Friday night, again yesterday afternoon. There's a bit about what she found, and a description of the two men. Proper detailed one."

The inspector went out of earshot into the corridor and said to the detective, "Get onto Division, tell them to call Special Branch, and shove over all the stuff on McCoy. And tell the people upstairs to get a move on, we'll have half bloody Scotland Yard here by lunchtime."

When he reached his office back at the police station an hour later, he was told by the desk sergeant, "There's been a man called Jones on the phone for you. One of the spoofs from the Security Service. Said something about a note pad. Wants to come up and see you as soon as you've ten minutes to spare him. The number's on your table."

"Coming up in the bloody world, aren't we?" said the detective inspector as he went into his office.

Ten

Like an incoming ocean tide that thrusts its way into rock gullies and crevices, so the name of Ciaran McCoy swept through the many departments of Scotland Yard. Photographic section, fingerprint section; Special Branch and its Irish section, Murder Squad; Criminal Records; Liaison Regional Crime. The name was telephoned to the Commander in charge of Special Branch, and to the Assistant Commissioner (Crime). Meetings were hurriedly convened, and at the center of them were the suitably doctored files passed on from Leconfield House the previous night. The photograph of McCoy was rapidly reproduced and dispatched to all police stations in the Metropolitan area. The photokit team began work on a compilation of the unknown Arab's features, using principally Doris Lang's description, written by a trained hand, and also including the sketchier accounts of his appearance as given by the occupants of the commune. Teleprinter messages from the Royal Ulster Constabulary headquarters at Knock Road on the east side of Belfast carried more information on the Irishman. The decision was made to release the picture of McCoy at lunchtime for the Independent Television current affairs program that would be on the air at that time, and for a BBC news flash.

That was where Norah saw the picture.

Her father always insisted that the television should be on during the formal eating of the Sunday roast, because he liked the farmers' programs. After the music had faded away and the end-title threshing machine disappeared behind a hill, the screen went to black before the appearance of the "news flash" symbol. The three around the table, Norah, her mother and her father, all stopped eating and turned their attention to the set, food left on the forks. The item lasted a minute or so, the first forty seconds taken up by pictures of the comings and goings in Englefield Road. A policewoman had died, strangled, found in a commune.

"Bastards," Norah's father muttered to himself. "Bloody bastards."

Police were anxious to trace a young Irishman. Name—Ciaran McCoy. The picture came up then, stayed on the screen for twenty seconds. Half of the time had elapsed before she recognized the boy she had lain beside at the swimming pool, the boy she had kissed, the boy who had left her so abruptly last Thursday night. She could see it was a police photograph, a man just taken into custody, aggressive and caged. But it was still the same man, the lines of a mouth whether set in anger or friendship change little, only superficially.

"Little swine," her father said. "We should string them up. Only bloody thing they understand."

Norah had said nothing. She put her head down and close to the food lest her parents should see the tears that welled in her eyes. She had bolted her food, made an excuse and run through the front door. She walked endlessly that afternoon, conscious of an overwhelming feeling of shame, of having been dirtied in some way.

When Jones came back from the police station he brought with him photostats and transcripts of the note pad. Duggan and Fairclough were waiting in his office.

Duggan said, "He's blown it, hasn't he, our little boyo? Lost his safe house, lost his base. His picture will be plastered everywhere by tonight, all over the television, front pages of the papers tomorrow. And now he's running, concerned with his own survival. Not what you'd call an auspicious start for what he's after."

"Meaning what?" said Jones.

"That it may well be over for him. His concentration now is how to stay free. Does a man in his position go walking through a police cordon—cordon forewarned, cordon with a description? Does he, hell. He stays out. Packs it in."

"That's one viewpoint," Jones acknowledged the argument, looked skeptical.

"The other view takes a different course," Fairclough joined in. "If we look at the Palestinian, or Arab, or whatever he is, we can come out with a different answer. He's been through crisis before in France on Thursday, and is still on the move. Look at it from his point of view. If he doesn't go on, what does he go back to? They won't welcome him with open arms back in his camp. He'd be a miserable failure. Fiasco. It's when the suicide mentality breaks through. The harder the going gets, the more he will be prepared to risk his own life in order to succeed."

"And the conclusion from that?" asked Jones.

"The conclusion from that is that the Arab is now extremely dangerous. Tiger in the long grass with half his guts shot out. He's a killer still, more so, but he's at a disadvantage."

"The picture of one of them, detailed description of the other. Available to every man round Sokarev. That stacks the odds a bit against our two friends." Jones was able to smile, rare over the last two days. "But if the Arab wants to go on, what about McCoy?"

Again it was Fairclough, hunched forward in his seat, using his hands to emphasize the points he made. "One of them has killed this morning, but they're both in it together. The critical factor is whether they fall apart, how much of a bond they have made. From what I've read of McCoy, I think he'll stay right in, right up to the end, providing he thinks there's a chance of living through it."

Jones wondered how he could be so sure, envied the younger man the certainty of his opinions. But it was not a time for sarcasm, not a time for academic discussion. So many of them had breezed their path through the Department over the years, knowing all the answers, having an explanation for every half-truth situation. The ones that stayed on were the ones who recognized that there were no simplicities in the business. Problem was, and Jones could see that much, that this wasn't the operation the section heads were familiar with, inexperienced at tangling with the short-term affairs. Pretty good when they had the space to spread themselves, to get through on the inside, to win time to build up the overall picture. But this was a sprint, and didn't really depend on men like himself. Hadn't much to contribute. When there wasn't any time, the whole bloody thing came down to Jimmy's level. Who shoots best? Us or them? That's why he'd brought Jimmy in on the effort. Liked the man in a distant way, was vaguely fond of him. But to be dependent on him, to recognize he had more to offer now than Jones himself, that left a taste in the mouth, a sour taste.

Jimmy took considerable care with his firearms.

For close protection work he favored the PPK (Polizei Pistolen Kriminal) Walther. And this was the gun he drew from the armory set behind reinforced walls in the basement of Leconfield House beyond the area used by the monitoring team. It was a small weapon, manufactured with great skill by the workers of the Karl Walther factory at Ulm near Donau in West Germany. Its length was little more than six inches, its weight just over a pound. It was not new, manufactured in 1938, and had come to the Department's collection after the war, but the armorer maintained it with studied attention, knowing that this, amongst all the others, was the weapon that Jimmy asked for on his occasional visits to the underground room. On most occasions the gun had been returned unused, but a few times the armorer had noticed that the magazine no longer contained its seven shells and that the barrel needed cleaning.

The two men had talked about Jimmy's choice the time the newspapers had been full of how the PPK being used by a Royal detective had jammed during a kidnap attempt, and how it had been withdrawn from use by the bodyguards. Neither the armorer nor the marksman had been impressed by the reasons made public for the switchover to the British-made Smith and Wesson, the traditional police weapon. Jimmy's loyalty was unmoved.

With the gun signed for, and two dozen rounds along with it, Jimmy drove north to the police firing range in an old building the far side of Euston Station.

There were policemen there, members of a pistol shooting

club, complete in their denim overalls and ear pads, firing at targets twenty-five meters across the floor from the painted white line that ran across one end of the range.

Jimmy showed his identification card to the instructor, and the policemen were called back to the shadows away from the shooting line. They watched as Jimmy loaded the magazine, then stood apparently relaxed, facing them and away from the human-shaped target, gun pointing to the floor, loosely held against his trousers. The instructor let fall a box of matches. By the time it had bounced twice and come to rest Jimmy had twisted, body crouched, knees bent, two hands together outstretched and both on the butt of the pistol, and his first shot hit the target. Three more followed.

"About a six-inch group," the instructor said, and Jimmy acknowledged, expressionless. Where else did they expect the bloody things to be? He went to the side wall, by the door, waited a moment for his legs to loosen, then flung himself forward on the floor, rolling all the time before there was an instant of steadiness and he fired twice.

"Eight inches or so apart, both in the chest area," said the instructor.

Jimmy fired all twenty-four rounds. Some in near-darkness, some with a bright light shining at his face, some on the move, some stationary. All hit the target; all the puckered holes had gathered in the torso area of the shape at the far end of the shooting area.

"Bit of a bloody show-off, isn't he?" said one of the watching policemen, but his whisper was overheard by the instructor, who walked across and said to him, his voice booming, result of the deafness accrued from eighteen years in the underground range, "Look, boy. There's a fractional possibility he might miss. And there's a fractional possibility you might hit. That's the difference between you and him."

Jimmy was well pleased with the morning session, and it was over quick enough for him to fit in a drink before he was due back at the Department.

The two of them were asleep in the car.

McCoy lay on his side across the front seat, head just beneath the steering wheel. Famy was curled up in the back, his coat off and covering his shoulders. The car was parked deep in a grassy clearing far from the road and visible through the high summer foliage only to someone who approached to within a few yards of it. There were many such places in the line of Surrey hills between Guildford and Dorking that block the route to London. Later they would become a haven for Sunday walkers and picnickers, but in the early morning the two men had the clearing to themselves.

"We must sleep now, anytime we bloody well can get it," McCoy had said.

They missed the breaking of the dawn, when the darkness gave way to the half-light, and then the sun began to cast its steadily shortening shadows across the grass. They didn't see the rabbits that came to eat and preen themselves, and the fox that hastened them back to their burrows. It was the noise of children that aroused them. Two boys little more than ten years old, faces pressed against the steamed-up windows of the car, peering in at them, and running, giggling, away as McCoy started up from his sleep and swore inaudibly. The children had sprinted away, leaving McCoy to collect his thoughts as he gazed around the empty panorama. There's always that moment immediately after waking before the bad news of the previous night is remembered. When it remains obliterated before the later recognition. McCoy couldn't place straightaway why he was in the car. It came to him soon enough, and with the realization came the memory of the events of five hours earlier.

He shook Famy. "Come on, lover boy. Time to be on our way."

"What's happening? Where are we?" Famy, too, had awakened confused.

"Out in the deep countryside, taking in the sunshine. Remember?"

Famy inclined his head slowly, deliberately, understanding.

Neither saw the two boys who lay in the thick green bracken watching the men as they rubbed their eyes and stretched and pawed at the grass, throwing out the stiffness that had accompanied their awkward limb-twisted sleep. McCoy beckoned with his hand, an abrupt gesture, and the two began to walk the length of the clearing to the path that meandered away amongst the pine trees and the birches and the undergrowth.

"It's a fair walk, we don't want to hang about," said McCoy over his shoulder as he led the way. Neither wore the shoes for the country paths, and both slipped and stumbled where the last week's rain had made the surface glistening mud.

They walked in silence for more than twenty minutes, then Famy noticed that McCoy was slowing down his stride, searching for a sign. When he found it he stood, pleased with himself, beside the old rusted-up pram chassis.

"That's the first marker," he said. "It's easy enough from here to find the place. We go fifty paces now down the path. Measure them out, and we'll be just about there."

Famy let the distance between them grow as McCoy, his step accentuated by the care he was taking, marked out the distance.

"At home," said McCoy when he had counted out loud to the number fifty, "we have to hide our guns. We keep them out in the countryside, but somewhere you can get them night or day, so you need markers so you can find them on a path in the dark. Has to be straightforward and obvious to the man on the pickup, but giving nothing away to the Brits. Now look, and what's the most prominent tree close to us? Has to be the one with the ivy up it, easy to see, would show up by torch. That's the main marker. Now we have to look for something else that's off the path but equally clear . . . stands out just as much. You walk round the tree, trying to line it up with something that stands out. Right? If you draw a line between this tree and the big one over there, the one the lightning hit, you go on and into the bank. There are rabbits' holes all the way down and along the bank. Well, what we're looking for is the hole in the straight line beyond the two trees."

He walked forward past the ivy-coated branches, past the dead tree. "The Brits are too bloody impatient to work it out like this. But once there was a chap on the television, and his men called him 'Sniffer.' He found more of our guns than any other soldier in the province. And what did the buggers do with him? Sent him first to the Tower of London on guard duty, then packed him off to Cyprus for nine months."

McCoy was still laughing as his hands sunk into the rabbit hole. Famy watched fascinated as they emerged again, clutching the whitened plastic of a farm bag.

"I had to dig the hole out a bit," McCoy said. "But who's going to notice fresh earth at a rabbit burrow."

He pulled the bag out onto the bank, scanned the path in both directions, listened for a moment and then, satisfied that they were alone, started to unwind the sticking tape that sealed the top. From the bag he took three rifles, small, narrow, seemingly ineffective by their very abbreviation. Each was only marginally more than two feet in length with the steel skeleton of the shoulder rest bent back alongside the barrel. He placed them on the plastic, handling them with delicacy and concern, and with them two bulky cloth bags.

"What are they?" asked Famy.

"It's a version of the M-1 carbine. World War Two American. These are the paratroopers' ones, with the folding stock. They wouldn't give me Armalites, the bastards, said three was too many. These are old, but that doesn't mean there's anything wrong with them. They were test-fired ten days ago, across the water, then stripped down and cleaned—"

Famy interrupted, anxiety in his voice. "There were no Kalashnikovs?"

"We never get a sight of the bloody things. They've tried to bring them in, but we haven't had any reach us. Our stuff is American. One of the reasons our big men got involved in this was to try and guarantee a supply of Kalashnikovs."

"To you it will sound ridiculous, but I've never trained with any other sort of rifle," said Famy.

"There's nothing wrong with these. They've packed enough coffins. Three-hundred range, more than we need. Fifteen-round magazine—if we need more than three, we're screwed anyway. Small, light—just about six pounds. The Yanks ran off more than three and a half million of them in the war. They're untraceable."

"Why only three? There were going to be three of us, and then you."

McCoy was taking loaded magazines from one of the cloth bags. He looked up and into Famy's face. "You were going to do the shooting. The deal was that I looked after the accommodation and the car. You looked after the rest."

"And now."

McCoy laid the magazines out side by side, twelve of them. "Well, it can't be done by one alone," he said, still gazing directly at Famy, "so we'll need two of them, and have one spare."

There was a huge smile across Famy's face as the strain of the last few hours fled from him. God, the bastard's been suffering, thought McCoy. He's had enough bloody hints, and not believed them. McCoy opened the second bag.

"We may not have done you well on the rifles, but on the grenades we've the best. We get a lot of our stuff via the dealers in Holland. These are Dutch, called the V-40 Mini, less than half the size of a normal grenade. Tiny, but the sales talk is sensational. Four hundred chunks flying out, hundred-percent casualties guaranteed at ten feet. It's what we want, something for close work, not a bloody great bomb that'll demolish half the audience, but one that can land nice and near your man and take him out."

There were twelve of them; he held one in his hand, nestled in the palm, where it fitted snugly, less than an inch and a half in diameter and deadly. McCoy packed the grenades and the magazines back into their separate bags and dropped them into the bigger plastic one. The rifles followed, and he again taped the top, and then they both walked up the path toward where the car had been left. McCoy's mind was now tuned to the next problem. Transport. Where to ditch his present car, where to get another. Where to sleep, where to lie up for the next two days. Famy could see he was thinking and did nothing that might break the other's train of thought. He felt complete confidence in the Irishman who carried under his arm the vital weapons that would be used against David Sokarev.

The Prime Minister cut short his Scottish weekend and flew to Northolt, the capital's military airfield. His surprise move aroused little press speculation amongst the journalists covering his foray into the North. It was generally believed, and not denied in official circles, that the country's economic plight had led to the abbreviated schedule. It was less well known outside his immediate entourage that the workings of the security and intelligence services that were ultimately answerable to him, fascinated and exhilarated the head of government. In his first-floor office, overlooking the immaculate flower-decked gardens of his Downing Street residence, he met the Director General of the Security Service.

The Prime Minister was prepared to listen to the exposition of the problem, and hear the results and actions that would follow from the series of meetings that had gone on through the morning between the police and officials from the Department. He had shown concern that at this stage of the operation no leakage of information to the press should happen, required maximum detail on the two potential assassins, and already knew of the remarks passed between the Israeli ambassador and the Foreign Office. When the Director General had finished, the Prime Minister turned away to the window, searching for the words he wanted, weighing them before speaking, face serious and intent, pencil twirling in his fingers.

"There is a chance, then, that a massive screen round the man will deter any attack. When I was in Germany for the football some years ago they adopted that policy. Total saturation. Nothing happened, and whether they were successful or nothing was planned, we have no way of knowing. But I think from what you say, you don't believe that to be a likely eventuality, the deterrent. We will now move, Director General, into the realm of what is called 'late-at-night thought,' not to be attributed to this building. I would like to think that should the Arab, if that is what he is, be taken prisoner, arrested, that he would violently resist such action and that in his escape attempt he should be shot dead. We've had one package of hostages on a VC-10 sitting it out in the Jordan desert, we've had another VC-10 wrecked at Schiphol, we've had another held at gunpoint in Tunis. I don't want a fourth. I don't want to have to hand this man over at the point of a rifle with a planeload of lives at stake, and that is what will happen if this man is taken and put through the courts. The Irishman in that context is unimportant."

The Prime Minister wished the Director General luck, smiled bleakly at him as they shook hands, and showed him to the door.

In their small bedroom the Sokarevs were both involved in the packing of his suitcase for the visit to Europe and the United States. While his wife took the clothes and folded them and laid them on the bed, Sokarev placed them with care into his old suitcase. He chided her against giving him too many shirts, and spoke of the services of hotel laundries, but she said she was not concerned with that, and had her way. The shoes, the shirts, the underclothes, socks, pajamas, dressing gown, a thick jersey—all went into the case before his two suits. The suits were the only two he possessed—one for best, for making his speech; one for wearing in the daytime. And for traveling she selected his jacket and a pair of slacks and hung them out on the edge of the wardrobe. When they had finished, the case was bulged and both of them had to press hard down on its top, compressing the linen and cotton inside, so that the locks would fasten. The case meant something special to him, and he had cared well for it since it had brought his many fewer belongings to Israel on the long journey from Frankfurt thirty-nine years ago. It was rarely used and treated with consideration, and had taken on special importance in the life of David Sokarev because his father had bought it for him, and carried it to the station, and handed it up into the train, before waving goodbye. His father had disappeared from view as the train pulled out from the platform, lost in the pall of engine smoke, and had returned to wind up the family affairs, full of promises and assurances that he would follow his wife and son to Israel when that was completed. David Sokarev never saw him again.

The key that locked the case had long since been lost, and Sokarev used a wide leather belt to hold down the top in case the clasps should fail during the journey.

She fussed around him that evening in the bedroom. It was a rare event for him to be away from home for anything more than a single night, but she could see that the anxieties and worries that had oppressed him two and three nights before were now something of the past. They laughed with each other, and smiled a lot, and sometimes he put his arm around her shoulders, and he talked of the friends that he would be going to see in London, men that he had met on previous visits or who had come to Israel, and with whom he corresponded. When the packing was finished he went to his study to work on the draft of his speech while his wife moved to the kitchen to cook his dinner; it would be something light, with cheese, as he liked it.

He wrote the speech in a spidery longhand, frequently crossing out and correcting what he had already set down. He would talk on the need of his country for atomic power to ensure self-sufficiency in the fields of agriculture and industry and to reduce the necessity of oil. It would not be a fine speech, he knew that. He shared the problem of many brilliant-minded men that he found it arduous and awkward to cannibalize his detailed work of the laboratory into the language of a lecture theater. He had sketched what he would say, unsatisfactory but the best he could manage. There would be paragraphs included on the survey of the terrain, using isotopic technique with a view to disclosing the quantities and distribution of natural resources, and he would finish by discussing the detailed new work going on in the field of enriching uranium by means of lasers.

There would be no mention of the energy of the atom when directed for military purposes, and in the well-mannered and professional group to which he would be speaking, there would be no questions on that count. It was understood. Accepted.

He had worked for more than an hour, and was still regretting that Anna would not be accompanying him, and that he would be dependent on a typist from the embassy in London, when the telephone rang.

"Mackowicz, here," said the distant voice after Sokarev had given the number. Thoughts of neutrons and atomic piles and reactors fled from him as his mind cleared. In their place was nothing. Clouded, vacant and hesitant.

"What do you want?" he said, his voice showing the resentment he felt at the other man's intrusion into the private oasis of his study.

"I was just ringing to make sure that all would be well for you tomorrow."

"There are no problems," said Sokarev.

"You need have no fears of the visit to London. The British authorities are taking many steps to ensure that no incident will take place."

"I have no fears." Sokarev spoke sharply.

There was a pause at the other end of the line. What more do you want to say? thought Sokarev. Why burden me at my home? For the next ten days you will be there to hold my hand, dictate my movements, govern my actions.

"I will be picking you up myself tomorrow . . ."

"But I have a taxi ordered. It is all arranged. There is no need." He was close to anger.

"It has been decided that I shall take you to Ben-Gurion. Elkin will be with me. You can cancel the taxi."

"Who has decided it?"

"It has been decided in the Ministry, by the superiors in our department."

Sokarev sank back in his chair, the telephone still to his ear. There was no fighting them. They had taken charge. The depression surged again through him. He was weak, pliable again in the hands of the young men who would accompany him. Like a toy passed from hand to hand.

The younger of the two boys who had played in the clearing in the early morning saw and recognized the picture of McCoy when it was shown again at teatime on the television. His father telephoned the village policeman. There was a series of calls that followed the sighting, and from county headquarters at Guildford some twelve miles away a tracker dog was sent. Special Branch officers drove down from London, and in the fading light the dog found the rabbit hole where McCoy had secreted the rifles and grenades. It had taken the Labrador a long time to discover the hiding place, but eventually he stood by the entrance whining and impatient. The policemen had moved with caution lest they should disturb the footprints in the fresh soil. They would return again on the Monday morning for a more detailed examination, but in the meantime the ten yards square in front of the hole was covered with plastic sheeting, and a constable was left to spend a lonely night to prevent interference with the evidence.

From Scotland Yard the report of the identification and subsequent discovery was passed on to Jones, along with the conclusions that had been drawn from the find in the woods. So Fairclough had been right, and Duggan wrong, in his assessment. The bastards weren't running; they were on course still, and visiting a cache. Collecting something. And only one thing they'd need such a hiding place for. They'd have their bloody guns now, thought Jones. He looked at the picture of McCoy on his desk, face puffed out where he'd tried to distort his face as the shutter had gone on the army camera—old trick, to try and make the official record useless. Hard, mean face, thought Jones. The photokit picture of the Arab was with him now, fresh from the printing press, and alongside it an artist's impression in semi-profile.

Jimmy came into the office, following his knock by a couple of seconds. Jones could see the well-scrubbed chin and cheeks, bright and shining, knew it was the sign of too many at lunch-time and a head under the tap. Cold water, to regain control.

Jones pushed the pictures across his desk toward Jimmy and said, "Those are our little boys. Get those bloody faces stuck in your mind."

Eleven

From behind the driving wheel Elkin watched Mackowicz emerge from the doorway of the flats, carrying the professor's case, and a few steps behind him came Sokarev and his wife. He saw the scientist kiss his wife hard on both cheeks and cling to her for several seconds before breaking away and almost running to the door Mackowicz had already opened. She stood and waved long after the car had gone away up the road, but through his mirror Elkin could see that the passenger in the back never turned his head. The face behind was taut, stretched with emotion, that much Elkin could see before he settled onto the long winding road to Ben-Gurion Airport.

There was little talk in the car on the journey; Mackowicz tried several times to get a conversation going, but was rebuffed by Sokarev. By the time they were through Kiryat Gat, nearly halfway there, he had given up and sat quietly beside Elkin, leaving the passenger to whatever thoughts he cared to occupy himself with. The two security men were not unused to this. It was frequent that men who required bodyguard protection should resent the presence of those sent to ensure their safety. If the little bugger didn't want to talk, then that was his concern, thought Mackowicz; he and Elkin had enough to concern themselves with.

They had been out of Israel on this duty before, but always in a bigger team, once with the then Prime Minister Golda Meir, when the detail had been nine men; once with Abba Eban in his days as Foreign Minister, when there had been four others. This was a different situation for them. Just the two of them, which made their success or failure more dependent on the effectiveness of forces completely outside their control. In particular, when they had traveled with the Prime Minister they had been in sufficient numbers to organize a complete security screen around their charge. They had not been obliged to rely on the departments of the countries they visited. But since they were simply a pair, they would be forced to accept the guidance and knowledge of the British police. It was not the way they liked to operate.

Their selection for the task of watching over the small, stout man who slumped across the back seat of the car had not been accidental. Both were expert shots with handguns, both were thorough and painstaking. When the threat had become known, they had been the two obvious choices. The head of the Protection Division of the Foreign Ministry had had no doubts that amongst the men under his control, Mackowicz and Elkin were the most efficient and professional. They traveled light. Two canvas bags in the back alongside the professor's larger bag. They contained just a few changes of clothes, and the suits they wore in the car would see them through the public functions. In one bag were the files, marked *Secret*, which contained all the available Israeli intelligence information on the threat, and a complete dossier on Sokarev, from his blood group to his family and financial arrangements. In the other bag, wrapped in shirts, were the personal two-way radios, which would be modified to the wave lengths of the Israeli embassy by the resident communications and wireless expert, and the issued firearms.

They had left at seven, and turned into the driveway of the airport seventy-five minutes later, which left them a little over an hour before takeoff. Sokarev could sense that the two men in the front of the car understood his nervous hostility to them. He was dominated by a feeling of isolation and loneliness, and an inability to communicate with them. They were so much younger, so assured. Nothing to talk to them about, no mutual point of sympathy. Killers, he decided—and how different from the men who awaited him if the fears were true? Cloaked in legality, given the seal of approval—but how much were they separated from the terrorist? Both killed from a sense of duty, both acted without hesitation, ferret-fast. He recognized that he was afraid of the men he had been given as travel companions. Only the gun could give him confidence, his own gun, the unused Mauser, and that was a step into their world, one that he could never sympathize with, barely understand. It rested in his coat pocket, beside his spectacle case, awkward, forcing out the material of the jacket, the single magazine in the inside breast pocket placed between the folds of his wallet.

The baggage check took half an hour. Thirty minutes of shuffling the cases forward inch by inch as he stood behind a crocodile of blue-rinsed lady tourists who even at that early stage of the morning were strident in their retelling of alimony suits, lost husbands and necessary hysterectomies. He was surprised they were not taken through a side door and spared the routine, but neither Mackowicz nor Elkin made any move to suggest that that was possible. When they came to the young man in the orange jerkin who was searching the cases, it was only Sokarev's that was opened. Once it had been checked, closed again, and scribbled on with chalk, his bodyguards produced their identity cards, exchanged a quiet word with the airport security man, and were allowed on their way to the ticket desk. Sokarev felt the indignity, near-humiliation of it. Elkin saw the chin jutting out and the thin-lipped anger of his mouth, and said, not with pomposity but with a degree of kindness, "It's routine, Professor Sokarev. It's nothing personal about you. All passengers are searched. All, that is, except us. We carry papers and equipment. Perhaps it would not be suitable for those to be seen by others standing in a line. So we go through. If it is of comfort to you, we are all searched when we leave Heathrow."

Sokarev fumbled for a reply, unnerved by the accuracy with which the other had interpreted his thoughts.

From the ticket desk the three of them walked toward the staircase that reached up to the departure lounge. Sokarev noticed now that Mackowicz was to his right, Elkin to the left. Not out of my own country, and already they have taken up their positions, he thought. Leaving me like a prisoner under escort.

They dwarfed him, eyes already watchful. Elkin's jacket was buttoned, and close to him Sokarev could see the bulging shape of the strap-fastened holster. They went through passport control, the official barely looking upward as he flicked through the passports, stamped them, and handed them back.

Elkin said, "You have to go through the body search now, Professor. We again are excused that. We will collect you on the far side."

In front was a long row of curtain-fronted cubicles, where from time to time a young man or woman, also in the orange jerkin, would appear. Like a whore waiting for trade, thought Sokarev. And the next customer would step inside and the curtain would be drawn back. Once a man, swarthy in complexion, was led back out of the cubicle, his face betraying self-consciousness as he walked in his stockinged feet, the security man behind him holding his shoes outstretched as they went to the counter that contained the X-ray equipment.

It was the embarrassment on the face of the victim that jolted Sokarev's mind to the weight in his pocket. It was a situation he had not considered. He had not thought out how he would carry the Mauser on board the aircraft; he had vaguely presumed that his escorts would be with him and would see it as a *fait accompli,* look pained for a moment, perhaps shrug, and allow him to carry on. The curtain was opened again; the man gestured him to come forward.

He stood with his legs apart and arms outstretched shoulder-high. There was fear now. Fear of discovery. The fear that comes to a small boy caught stealing, found playing truant away from school. The hands started at his collars, feeling under the material, tested the area under his armpits, loitered for a moment on the shape of his wallet in the breast pocket. Sokarev thought he was going to be sick. He watched as the wallet was withdrawn from the pocket and opened. The magazine lay there, pristine, unbelonging amongst his papers. The security man stiffened, set his face, muscles tensed on the top of his wrists.

"Do you have a pistol to go with this ammunition?" said the security man evenly.

Sokarev nodded. "In the pocket," he said, still keeping his hands out. The hands found the Mauser there, withdrew it

sharply. There was a moment when the security man's eyes
were off him as he checked the breach of the pistol, assuring
himself it was not loaded.

"I am Professor David Sokarev. I am a nuclear scientist. My
work is at Dimona. My flight is to Europe . . ." Waves of wretch-
edness overcame him, and his voice tailed away. His eyes were
now fixed on the floor, not caring to see the keen gaze of the
man who stood close to him in the cubicle. When he had collected himself sufficiently, he went on in low, barely audible
speech, "There are two men from the Foreign Ministry traveling with me. They are to guard me. They are waiting on the far
side. I had not told them that I was taking the weapon."

Ten minutes after they had taken Sokarev to the offices of the
security department of the airport, Mackowicz was shown in.
His face was controlled, betraying no emotion, and he spoke in
a huddle with the senior officer there. He never looked once at
the Mauser that lay on the desk, the single rectangular magazine beside it. Whatever business was conducted, Sokarev took
no part in it, then Mackowicz walked to the door, and opened
it and waited for the scientist to go through.

When they were alone in the concourse Mackowicz said, "It
was unwise of you to try to take the gun through. There is an
important thing that we must now establish. Neither my colleague nor myself would consider ourselves fit to make judgments on your work, at which you are an expert. We expect that
you would treat us with similar generosity. We do not expect
you to make judgments on security matters. If you have no
confidence in Elkin and myself, you are at liberty, as you have
been since we came first to Dimona, to telephone to Jerusalem
and explain your objections to our superiors."

The voice was icy, scything through Sokarev's defenses. He
shook his head, staggered now by his own stupidity. "I am
sorry," he said. "It has been a great strain since you came to see
me."

"We are responsible for your security. We have the right to
demand your full cooperation. There will be no repeats of this
situation. Not when you are in our care."

Sokarev's head was down on his chest as he shambled after
his captor toward the lounge seat where Elkin sat. The three
men sat in total silence till the flight was called, the guards

reading newspapers, the professor staring emptily through the windows and out onto the tarmac. He felt he wanted to discard the whole journey, go home to his wife and to his laboratory, and shut out forever the nightmare world of guns and searches and terrorists. When the flight was called, Mackowicz was up first, athletically rising onto the balls of his feet, then he bent down and took the professor's arm and helped him out of the low leather seat.

Elkin said, "I think we should remember, Professor, that we are going to be together for some time now. Whatever has happened is in the past. It should not linger on." And he smiled. Sokarev again attempted an apology, but Elkin shook his head. "It is in the past. Forgotten."

They walked together down the steps and past the young soldier who wore an automatic rifle slung across his shoulders, and out into the blazing heat of an August morning in Israel. The sun beat into Sokarev's eyes, causing him to flatten the lids together to keep out the very brightness that sprang up at him from the tarmac. Away to the front, acting as a giant reflector, was the 747 Boeing jet, its white underbelly and roof gleaming in the harsh light. There is no going back now, thought the scientist, there is no escape. Whatever happens now, he said to himself, it is out of my control.

Sokarev mounted the steps to the plane. Mackowicz and Elkin were a pace behind him.

Along the corridor from the control room, and high in the Scotland Yard tower block, they had taken over the main lecture theater for the Monday briefing of all those detectives and senior uniformed officers involved in the hunt for McCoy and his colleague, and in the protection of David Sokarev.

Jimmy sat at the back, far behind the rows of neatly clipped necks, looking down on the proceedings. If anyone had turned to watch him, they would have detected a faintly bored, disinterested face. That of a man who has been through it all before. Not that Jimmy ever felt totally at ease in the company of policemen. And they didn't react well to the presence alongside them of what was virtually a free-lance operator, not conditioned to their code of discipline and their rule books.

The details that were read out concerning the timings and

locations of the visit failed to hold his attention. The big man in uniform did the talking. Like it's evidence in a dangerous driving case, thought Jimmy. Solid monotone, dull. Never make it on the stage, you won't, brother. Drawing on the blackboard isn't much better. All those lovely colored chalks. How they adore it, like dressing up for the pantomime. Green lines and red circles and blue crosses.

What a way to go to war. Has McCoy got a big map, does he stick his finger on it like bloody Rommel? Can't fight these bastards with maps and diagrams, old soldier. Looks good, sounds good, doesn't work that way. There's only one place you'll get Master McCoy and his little friend, and that's beside Sokarev. That's the only place those bastards will show. Wasting your time in transit with all the motorcades and all the escort riders. Doesn't happen there. Happens when he's on the bloody pavement or at the speech. Stands to reason, if you're planning a show like this for a dozen weeks, forking out your piasters for the air fare, you're not going to risk your one-and-only on the off chance you might manage a pot shot at a cavalcade. And when the old drone had finished, time then to get up to the university and have a look, and come back via the hotel, and still have some minutes to spare before the plane arrived. Should have done the reconaissance yesterday, Jimmy lad, not been in that bloody boozer half the afternoon talking sweet sod all with a load of idiots. Should have given the place the look-over, not a thing that ought to be done in a hurry, should have been thought out, Jimmy.

He knew it. Didn't have to argue the toss about it, comforted himself only with the thought that he would be close to Sokarev. Human wall, and no pension rights. But perhaps it was a safe old number for all that. Whoever heard of the bodyguard catching it? JFK, RFK, right down to Faisal; all had the detail round them, who lived to file the reports on what went wrong and still had time to go to the funeral.

Forty men in the room, all of them brass, and how many taking orders . . . another three hundred, four hundred? And they're just two, so what goddamn chance have they got?

That was where the careering of Jimmy's thoughts came to a stop. Below him, pinned to the side of the blackboard, were the pictures, McCoy's and the man whose name they still searched for. Nasty rough bastards, Jimmy said to himself, very hard, very serious people. And what do we have against them? This bloody crowd, dragged in from murder inquiries, bank robberies, and demonstrations on Sunday afternoons in Trafalgar Square. Jummy's eye rolled around the room. Many of the officers were taking notes, all listened intently, following the speaker as he took them slowly through the maps and diagrams. If these two bastards decide to come on in close, thought Jimmy, then this lot'll find themselves in a different league, wish they'd never got out of bed.

The big jet had swung out over the sea, deep and distant beneath them. Sokarev saw the beach at Herzliya, could make out the people on the sand who looked up at the wallowing giant as it surged toward its necessary altitude. Four and a half hours would take them to London, thirty-one thousand feet and cruising speed of six hundred miles an hour, hurtling across the Mediterranean, then the Italian coast and the huge expanse of France before the descent and the shoreline of Britain.

Elkin sat beside the window, his charge beside him, and then Mackowicz in the aisle seat. Sokarev dozed till Mackowicz's voice overrode the hazy dreamy thoughts he was entertaining, and he opened his eyes. The man talking to his guard was like a replica, the scientist thought. Same assurance, strength, poise and ease of movement. And wearing the same heavy jacket, even in the sweat-making atmosphere of the cabin, to hide his weapon from the sensibilities of the passengers.

Mackowicz turned to Sokarev. "We used to work together, this layabout and Elkin and I. Then he took the easy life. He just flies with the airline. Logs more hours than the pilots."

Sokarev said, "I did not know that you people were on board . . ."

"Two, sometimes four. Always two. We have no option. The orders are very clear. Our planes are not to fly to Arab countries. If there is a hijack attempt, all you can do is shoot, and hope."

"And the pressurization, what if that is broken?"

"The pilot will dive. He will try and throw the terrorist off balance, he will also attempt to get below ten thousand feet."

"And the passengers, what of them?" asked Sokarev, impatience in his voice.

"If they are Israelis, they will understand. If they are not
. . . then they use another airline."

"But the guns you have. The moment you fire you will puncture the fuselage."

"The bullets are restricted velocity. You need have no fears,
Professor, it has all been worked out."

So they were at war. Even in the womblike casing of the
airliner, they were in a state of conflict. Not great armies, just
tiny fragments of platoons. But just as lethal, just as capable of
inflicting misery as the big battalions. Sokarev reflected that the
front line was now under two hours away. It might be in a car
on a three-lane motorway into the capital, it might be the pavement outside a hotel, it might be a lecture hall packed with
distinguished academics. It was a new war, as unfamiliar to him
as it was commonplace to the men who now rested, their eyes
closed, mouths sagging, in relaxation on either side of his seat.

Jones was a long time staring down at the twin pictures that
lay on his cluttered desk. They'd found their way to the top of
the pile of files and maps of Central London, and the plan of the
university complex and its immediate surrounding streets. He
supposed he was expected to loathe the pair, have a great and
consuming hatred of them, but it never worked that way. Before they'd pushed him into "Middle East" he'd labored for a
dozen years on the Soviet bloc/Czechoslovakia desk—where
the then DG said the real work was done. Not hard to remember the attaché, trade of some description, that they'd picked
up after months of trailing and surveillance. Was reckoned to
have been a big man, "incalculable damage to the national
interest" was what the judge had said when he'd been through
the courts. But he hadn't seemed that formidable in the interview room of the police station they'd taken him to after the lift.
Rather ordinary sort of man, more anxious that someone should
give him a cigarette than anything else. Hadn't said anything,
of course, just smiled at their questions in a rather apologetic
way, embarrassed that they had to play such games. The section
had used a major manpower quota to track him, classified it as
a "priority" operation, and Jones was one of those closely involved. Afterward it was just anticlimax, unimportant, devoid
of stimulus.

He wondered how much different he'd find McCoy and his friend, whether they'd be any more fearsome face to face than the quiet little man from Prague. McCoy was easier to evaluate—because his photograph had been taken in custody and his eyes and mouth showed all the aggressiveness of a trapped man. But the other picture, that was the one that held Jones's interest. Quite a pleasant mouth the photokit and the artist had given him, and eyes that were large and not set with fear. Hard to see him as something special, something to be exterminated and eliminated because the threat that he carried was so contagious. Didn't look like the rabid fox he was categorized as. Just a boy, really, and nothing in his features to betray his potential.

Helen came in, no knock, walked across the room, and peered past his shoulder at the pictures. "Those the clever pair causing all the fuss?"

Jones felt his age—ridiculous, wasn't it, unreal, so much attention on such insignificant faces? "Those are the ones."

"And you've set the big, bad Jimmy loose after them?"

"Slipped his collar, right."

"And how good are they compared with our Jimmy boy?"

"They'll do all right. They'll give him a good run, he won't have to worry about that. He'll get his full out of them."

"And then they'll send him home in one piece?"

"Probably," Jones said.

Before she went back to the outer office he saw the whiteness of her cheeks. Should have taken it more gently. But it was the one point that nagged him, worrying at his composure as to whether Jimmy would beat these two at the close quarters where he was certain they would meet. It was difficult to believe in the danger if he stared at the face with the close mesh of curled hair that the police artist and the eyewitnesses had given to it; he had to go to the file to find the real man, even that was still sparse, no flesh to hang onto the skeleton information they had so far accumulated.

He took a drawing pin from his desk drawer and used it to hang the Arab's picture on the wall beside his filing cabinet. Where he could see it at any time he wanted, where he could study it, learn from it, understand it.

$$* \qquad * \qquad *$$

The effect on McCoy was less violent than on Famy. The Arab looked with ill-concealed horror at the pictures blazoned across the front pages of the papers. They were standing outside a small newsagent's shop in South West London beside a bus stop where they hoped to board the transport they needed to return to the inner suburbs. The pictures had been reproduced hugely, and in the squat popular papers, covered half of the front page. There were banner headlines, screaming at them across the pavement: THE KILLERS. THE MOST WANTED MEN IN BRITAIN. HAVE YOU SEEN THESE MEN.

"Don't bloody gawp at them," McCoy hissed in Famy's ear.

"It was that notebook, the one that we left behind. That is where they have taken it from," said Famy.

"Bullshit. They'll have talked in the commune. Got my name there. That's a Northern Ireland picture of me, taken when I was nicked. They've got an artist to do yours from all the descriptions. It's not particularly good, yours."

"It is sufficient for them to discard many men. They have given a height, and a weight, the general detail. Not adequate for positive identification but enough to come close. And they have the clothes, the colors, the trousers and shirts that we still wear . . ."

"Get back from the bloody thing. There's no place better for anyone to spot you than if you're pressed tight up against the damn thing."

"They have no name on me," Famy said as he moved away from the shop front and the two men resumed their position at the back of the queue.

Famy felt the uncertainty again that had dogged him throughout his first hours in London. It should not have been happening in this way. They should have been safe and secure in the house, not needing to venture out, dependent on the Irishman for their supplies. There was to have been no question of their hanging about in crowded streets; orders had been specific on that point. Every time a man or woman or child turned to him he imagined the dawning of recognition, and he shuffled his feet, and attempted, badly, to maintain his casual relaxed front. How do people make the recognition? he wondered. How can they translate something so distant from their lives as a wanted picture splashed across a newspaper into the flesh and blood beside them on the street? It's a difficult and long step to take, Famy told himself. Would take great certainty, would take a person to peer again and again to convince himself he was right, and that there was more than similarity to a picture he had merely glanced at.

To McCoy it was a less awesome experience. He was accustomed to having his picture in the front pocket of the bottle-green RUC uniforms and the camouflage tunics of British soldiers. He was familiar with life on the run, avoiding capture under the very eyes of men who had studied his features. But he realized a fundamental danger in their present position. The newspapers put two men together, identified them as a partnership, and that was how they were traveling, in tandem, linked to each other. But isolated, moving as loners, how much safer they would be. It was turning over in his mind when the single-decker green bus pulled in at the shop and the queue began to move forward. They must separate—but where to, easy enough for him, but what to do with the bloody Arab? Couldn't have him wandering the streets solo, insecure and liable to panic. So what to do with him? There was no immediate answer, only a vague plan slowly ebbing into shape.

McCoy bought the tickets from the bus driver, and they made their way to the back seats where they would be behind the other passengers, where their faces would suffer least exposure. Famy had the grip bag, which contained a selection of both their clothes, and the rifles and the magazines and the grenades. It was heavy and the handle straps strained against the metal hoops that held them to the framework of the bag. McCoy's own case had been left in the back of the Escort, packed with some of his clothes, some of Famy's. The car itself was off the road in the woods that surround the Surrey town of Esher. It would be difficult to find, and he had prised away the number plates and thrown them far into the undergrowth. The ground had been hard and the tire marks had been slight, and then they had brushed the ground with hazel saplings, leaving a light scuff covering the trail of the wheels.

While the bus made its way toward Hampton Court, where it became attached to the growing spread of the London conurbation, the two men sat in silence, McCoy working on his next move, Famy suffering from the tension of having seen the pho-

tograph and the drawings. When they had become locked in
the traffic flow, McCoy said, low and direct, talking from the
side of his mouth and close to Famy's ear, "We have to separate
today. The danger lies in us being together."

There was startled surprise on the other's face, the flash in
the eyes that suggests the moment of betrayal. McCoy saw it.
"There's nothing for you to worry yourself with. But we have
to be apart for today at least. There are eight more hours till
darkness, when we should meet again."

Famy turned his head, the tightly clamped lips giving warning of his suspicion. "Where would I go? What do I do," he said.

"I don't know yet. We can talk about it. But we have to get
apart. The two of us together is too much of a risk."

"We could have stayed with the car in the woods . . ."

McCoy cut into him, anxious lest he should lose control, sacrifice the initiative to the Arab. "It would have been possible.
But we could not take another car there, and we had to change
motors. We have to get a car in the town. In the country they
can block you too easily, it would be reported faster."

Famy did not reply.

"Look, you silly bugger"—McCoy was talking quickly, urgently—"I've told you I'm in this with you. You don't have to
worry. I'm not bolting on you. It's a judgment I've made, and
a necessary one. Am I going to ditch on you now? Think about
it. After the girl, after taking you to the guns, am I going to bunk
out?"

Famy nodded. He was exhausted from four broken nights
without adequate sleep; there was no spirit for an argument.
"Where do we get off?" he asked.

"Further on there's a town. About another fifteen minutes.
There's tubes and trains there, cinemas. Whatever you want."

"And you, where will you go?"

"I'll just lose myself for a few hours," McCoy said, "till the
night has gone. Till we can meet up and get a car."

Famy saw the hesitation, had the ability to sense a lie. Again
he had no reply. The sense of loneliness and isolation welled
inside him. How far could he trust the Irishman? He was unsure
now, certain there was a further reason for the split, certain that
he was not being confided in. What could he do? On a bus,
where ears would flap and quicken if he raised his voice. He was

powerless, and the knowledge was followed by the dejection.

Five stops later McCoy rose up out of his seat and started down the length of the aisle. Famy took his cue and followed. Then they were out on the pavement, amidst people who hurried past them, intent on their business. They stood for a moment before McCoy saw the tea bar down the road and across the street, and began to walk toward it.

"Just round the corner and up the main drag, that's where the cinemas are. There's one there that shows three films, separate theaters, all divided up. That'll lose you for some time, and it's dark in there, you'll be okay. We'll meet back in the tea bar. Eight o'clock. Now don't just walk around, get somewhere like the cinema and bloody well stay there."

Famy looked at him as they went in through the door of the café, quizzing with his eyes, searching for the truth of the other man's decision. He found no answer.

When McCoy left, the grip bag and its contents stayed with Famy. "Safer with you," he'd said, "tucked under your legs in the cinema. Out of harm's way, better than me lugging them round."

He ducked out into the sunlight and vanished beyond the doorway, hurrying along the pavements, sidestepping to avoid the lunchtime crowds of shoppers. Free of the bugger, he thought to himself. Free at last, without the nursemaid millstone round the neck and pulling down. What a boring sod the bloody man was. The relief at being on his own again flowed through him, a river that has broken a dam and finds again the dry stone bed, and its expression rampant and without check. He was half running when he reached the supermarket.

McCoy went inside, through the electrically controlled glass sliding doors. The cash registers, a bank of them where the girls punched the keys and took the money, were at the far end. He took a basket and put a single bar of chocolate in it, something that would stave off the hurting pain of hunger, and walked down past the stacked counters and shelves to the queue that had formed for the privilege of paying. He watched the girl as she deftly handled the bags and packages and tins, eyes never on the customer she served, always on what she took from the wire baskets and put further down on the flat surface beside her while her hands played the numbers on the machine. Her face was set, expressionless, dedicated to her task of extracting the right money, giving the right change.

When he put the basket down, the slim hand was there in an instant, pulling clear the chocolate, mouthing the amount that showed on her machine as a tiny row of trading stamps reached out from the mechanism.

"Hello, Norah," he said. Very quiet, conscious of the people behind him bustling and impatient at being delayed. And she looked up at him. Startled recognition, rabbit fear because she was sitting down and he loomed above her. Taut, strained, wide eyes pierced at him. The will to say something but no voice. "I have to see you." He angled the words to give the stress of dependence, and waited for her to react.

"What are you doing here?" Bewilderment, but conspiracy also, hushed so that the words would carry no further than the two of them.

"I have to see you." He repeated the words, greater insistence. "Outside, make an excuse. I have to be with you this afternoon. I'll be outside and waiting." The two tenpence coins, whose value tallied with that shown on the cash machine, were beside her hand. He took the chocolate and walked back out onto the street.

On the far side of the street he waited—twenty minutes perhaps. Then she was there, looking for a gap in the traffic. Blouse and jeans instead of the overalls she wore for her work. Just before she saw the opportunity to cross she looked over to where he stood. His smile was not returned, and then her concentration was with the cars and the lorries.

He took her hand, soft, small, fitting inside his fist, and kissed her without pressure on the side of the cheek, and felt her drag herself back from him.

"You didn't tell me inside there. What are you doing here?"

"I've come to see you." Inadequate, need more than that. Fatuous.

"You've seen the pictures. You're in the papers, on the telly."

"I know."

"Well, what have you come here for?" There was a demand for an answer.

"I wanted to see you, girl. I wanted to be with you. I wanted . . ." He did not finish. What can you tell her? He clenched her hand tight, enveloped in his. How can you tell her that you have to get away from it? That you're not just a machine, a killing apparatus. That there's need for a break, away from the awfulness of the running. From the concealment and the chase and the ultimate confrontation. There was a girl on the farm near Cullyhanna, and a place in the gorse and bracken on Mullyash Mountain where she would go with him and let him talk to her and love her and relax with her, till the sleep came and the understanding. Then he could go back to his war. But how to tell the little shopgirl from South West London that a man who fights must one time fall asleep in arms that hold no danger. That the time comes when the company of men is repulsive and rejected. Another day beside that bloody man and he'd come to loathe him, not through any fault of his. McCoy knew there was no fault in him. But it did not lessen the need to escape, and to exist again in the world which he had denied himself.

"I needed to talk to you, somewhere where we could be alone," he said.

They walked together through the town and into the vast open expanse of the Royal Park. There were roads that divided and cut across the landscape, leaving great segments of virgin ground covered by sprouting grass, and the delicate-shaped fronds of the bracken, and where the sun shone down. And there were woods where the birches and oaks filtered the light and cast a haze of shadow. It was as he had wanted. He had found what he sought.

They went deep into the bracken, along a path used only by the big red deer that scampered and leaped as they approached, making good their escape. He put his coat down on the broken stems and they sat together. There was no horizon beyond the immediate wall of green that surrounded and encompassed, hiding them from all eyes. McCoy sank onto his back, reaching up with his arms and pulling the girl down onto his chest. Her head rested underneath his chin, and against his mouth he could feel the strands of her hair, and there was a scent to them, freshly washed and clean. They lay there a long time, and his thoughts were of the hill farms and the other girl, who was dark and more heavily built and who comprehended the need for release that overwhelmed him, and of the buzzards that would circle and swoop above them across the hills of Armagh County.

It was Norah who broke the spell he had woven for himself.

"Is it you they are hunting? It was your picture on the TV that we saw?" Frightened, small voice, and his dreaming reply failed to take her fear away.

"It was me. I'm the one they're looking for. They're a long way behind me, and they won't find me."

"But you killed a girl, strangled her, that's what it said."

"What do you want me to say? What do you want me to pretend?" He rolled over on his stomach and leaned on one bent elbow above her, his free hand in her hair, stroking, caressing it into shapes. "It has nothing to do with your life. It is something separate. I won't tell you I didn't, and you wouldn't believe me if I did. There's nothing I can say, nothing you should know."

His hand came down from her hair, and a fingernail flicked carelessly at the plastic buttons of her blouse, held by frail cotton to the material. He saw the tears coming, the tightening of the muscles close to her eyes and the reflection from the moisture that ran beside her nose, and found a track that skirted the fullness of her cheek and then was lost on the broken grass. He came down to her mouth and kissed her, and there was nowhere for her to back away to. She felt her body pressed hard against the unevenness of the ground as his weight eased onto her. And the hands began to go free, and search out the places they quested for. When they had unfastened the clasp behind her back and removed the soft protective covering from her breasts, she put her arms around his neck, and sobbing, dragged his head close down beside her. She could not account for her actions, could not justify the tenderness with which she ran her hands over the harsh bristles below the hair at the back of his neck, could not reason why she flexed her legs slowly apart in the hope that his hand would find its way there. When she opened her eyes his face was very close, and he kissed the lids, closing them, and there was just the darkness and the sensation and the knowledge that the hands were moving again, demanding ownership, seeking new territory. The button slipped loose at the waist of her jeans and she wriggled as his hands eased them below her knees, and still there was the darkness and the desperate requirement for him to move on. He lingered at the soft, scarce-formed line that led down to the gentleness of the soft hair, and she moaned his name without sound into the roughened cheek joined to her own. When he came into her there was pain, and a power she had not known before, and she writhed and tried to force an escape. But there was none. Only the thrashing, pinioning weight that held her, till at last, after eternity, he sagged, spent and exhausted.

Norah lay on the hard ground, unmoving, the sun playing its warmth on her skin, the wind blowing its patterns, while the man beside her slept, his face with the quietness of a child's, the smoothness of his skin broken only by the trim lines worked by the nails of Doris Lang.

From the bank where he had changed a ten-pound traveler's check, Famy looked for the bright-red cubicle that he now identified as a telephone box. It took him fifteen minutes and brought him back to the station that he had walked past when seeking the bank. The bag weighed heavily, and it was with relief that he dropped it down onto the floor of the box. He had no difficulty remembering the number, nor the extension to ask for when the switchboard operator answered. As he had expected, the figures of the extension were given remotely and above the crackle of the connection.

"It's Mushroom here," Famy said.

There was a scuffling on the line, the sound he recognized as a receiver being placed against the material of a shirt or jacket, and indistinct words spoken into a void. Clearing the room, thought Famy.

"What is it you wish to say?" The telephone was active again.

"I wanted to know whether there were further orders, whether there were new instructions." Was that all he had telephoned to discover, when there was no chance of further orders? His tone echoed the hollowness of his request.

"Nothing has come through."

Famy paused, waiting, wondering what to say. He could not speak of his desolation and isolation, of his fears, of the horror of seeing his picture plastered across the newspapers. "Nothing at all? There is no word from home?"

Perhaps the man at the embassy sensed something of his

feelings, recognized the helplessness of the other. "There is nothing, but that was not to be expected. It is the style of the leadership to allow a free hand in such matters. Your arrival has been communicated." There was a sharp click on the line, and the sound for a moment was blanked out. But in less than a second it was back, Famy able to hear the breathing regular and without emotion of the man he spoke to. "There are difficulties?"

"It is so confused now. We have lost our place, because of the girl . . ."

The voice cut in, interrupting. "There was a clicking noise on the line. We must not speak any more. Ring off, and move away. Do not stay near the telephone. Very briefly, is there anything else?"

Famy was confused. He had heard the noise but had not interpreted it.

"The Irishman. I do not know at what stage I can trust him, whether I am better on my own. We have the guns now, but . . ."

"Is there nothing of importance that you have to say? If not, ring off."

". . . it is the Irishman. He said we must separate for to-day . . ."

"Ring off. And get away from the telephone box. Right away from it."

The voice was at shouting pitch, and the line went dead, returning to its continual, miasmic purr. The urgency had at last communicated.

Famy picked up the bag and ran from the station hallway.

Twelve

With the talkative, restless Jimmy out of the office and on his way to the airport for the reception committee, Jones's office had reverted to its normal hushed calm. He was poring over the files, alternately concentrating on the growing information on McCoy and the maps and plans that covered the Professor Sokarev visit, when his internal phone rang.

"Monitoring section here, Mr. Jones. Your embassy number is on. Chatting away. We've routed through to intercept . . ."

He waited to hear no more. He ran through the open connecting door, past the desk where Helen was typing, and out into the corridor. Fifteen paces to the staircase, not bothering to wait for the lift, and down the six flights in a headlong race to get to the basement before the call terminated. He was panting when he reached the cubicle where the big man was hunched, checking the dials for sound level as the tapes beside him spun slowly around. The spare earphones were already plugged in, and he jammed them lopsided over his head and then pushed the righthand-side black plastic shape against his ear.

"They've just heard the intercept switch go, the embassy's trying to wind it up," he was told.

He was in time to hear the reference to "guns," then the shouts of the other voice. One more half-hearted sentence and the line was cut.

A white telephone on the table inside the cubicle rang, and Jones instinctively reached and picked it up. "Intercept here. The call was made from Richmond in Surrey, a public telephone. Checking the location now."

Jones dialed the special number that had been assigned to the Scotland Yard operations room that was concerned exclusively with the hunt for McCoy and the unknown Arab. He spoke briefly, passing on the relevant material. No more. And rang off. Time to get out of their hair, leave them a chance to get moving. Best bloody break we've had, thought Jones. Something real to bite on for a change. They played him back the tape and he asked to hear it four times.

When he walked into Fairclough's office, Jones said, "The nerves are fraying a bit in the team. The Arab onto the embassy, doubting McCoy. Says he's been left on his ownsome, and doesn't like it. Sounded depressed, miserable, not having a happy time, wanting instructions from home. But he says they've retrieved the guns, which confirms that stuff from the hills we had in last night. But he sounded unhappy, really bloody miserable."

"Did he say whether or not they were still going to have a go at it?"

"Nothing about that. Said McCoy had told him they must separate for today."

"Well, that's clear enough, then. And not bad thinking. They're more vulnerable like that, together. They'll resume harness tonight. I suggest they're still operational."

Jones made a slow way back to his own office. Knew what he had to do when he reached its quietness and sanctuary. Had to understand them, had to find a way into their thought processes, had to make the men who were just pictures and closely typed words into human beings. That was the way, the only way, you could anticipate their next decision and action. But they were so remote, and he so out of touch with their world, that he evaluated his chances as only minimal. That was why he was not hurrying.

                    *   *   *

In the town on the outskirts of London, police personal radios had begun to chatter instructions, locations, descriptions, facial features, clothes. Men were hauled from traffic duties, serving summonses, investigating larceny and vandalism.

The chief superintendent who controlled the local police station concentrated his men in three directions. First, he blocked all major roads leading out of the area; that was his major and initial priority. Second, a vanload of police took over the hallway of the station that served British Rail Southern Region and London Transport District Line Underground. Third, he concentrated those cars not involved in the roadblocks in the center of the town, put them to cruising and observing the hundreds who swarmed on the pavements and around the shops. Revolvers were issued to car crews leaving the station, the required and formal paper work left till the end of the day. When he was satisfied that the town was sealed as well as was possible at the time, he came on the radio net himself to issue a clear and uncompromising instruction.

"The man we are searching for is dangerous, is probably armed, and should not be approached by any police officer who is unarmed. If you see him, call in; we'll have the reinforcements you need."

That was the message which first excited the radio ham who sat in his terraced house whiling away the time till his night shift began at the Hawker Siddeley factory down the road in Kingston. He ignored the stringent code set down by the Wireless Telegraphy Act that forbade any member of the public to listen to police messages and make use of them, and left his set tuned in to the area police frequency. He had turned the set up when he had noticed the rapid upsurge in traffic, and was in time to hear in full the words of the chief superintendent. He had a list of the numbers of the news desks of the Fleet Street papers, and had taken a note of their edition times, being a conscientious man. The *Daily Express* was traditionally the best payers for news tips, and there was no necessity to explain where the information originated from.

As the net was closing around the town, Famy was paying his money underneath the glass grill at the cash desk of the cinema. James Bond was in town—double feature.

       *   *   *

"You've nothing to fear. Just do as we say, don't hesitate, whatever it is, and everything will be fine. The British have a big force out. Our own people from the embassy will be close by. But do as Elkin and I say, with no questions." Those were the last words Mackowicz said to Sokarev when the plane had finished its long taxi and the doors to the stifling-hot cabin had at last been opened.

Other passengers were already in the aisle, waiting to leave the plane, when the chief steward and the man that Sokarev knew as El Al security transposed themselves across the corridor, leaving the route to the steps clear for Mackowicz to lead, followed by Sokarev and Elkin. The scientist saw the resentment etched in the faces nearest to him of those delayed, wondered why people always looked so hurtful and embittered when they have just successfully negotiated an air flight. What have they to face, he thought, that justifies their puckered and peevish stares, pecking with their beaks, and all because they must wait another seventy-five seconds before following down the steps?

It was warm, a comfortable, gentle heat, not aggressive like that of Israel, that greeted them on the tarmac. And there were the Special Branch men. Six of them forming up, three on each side of Sokarev and walking with him, faces turned outward toward the black Mercedes of the embassy that waited close to the steps.

The security attaché spoke briefly to Mackowicz, shook his hand, and then came alongside the professor. "There are people to welcome you, sir. They are in the lounge at the terminal building."

Sokarev started to speak of his baggage.

"Just give me the tag, sir. On your ticket. It will all be taken care of while you are in the terminal."

When the car started up, Sokarev could see two heavily laden unmarked vehicles take up position in convoy behind. He sat in the back seat, squashed between the attaché and Mackowicz. Elkin was in the front with the driver, and between them another man who was middle-aged and had a faded autumn look in his features, a man to whom nothing had the freshness of surprise. From the windows Sokarev looked into the expressionless faces of uniformed policemen who waved and gestured the car across the traffic lanes. There were dog handlers in the background, and men who stood in civilian clothes but with their right hands resting on the top buttons of their coats. More policemen were at the entrance to the VIP suite, tall men in their blue-serge uniforms who discussed his progress from the car to the doorway via hand-held radios, and who failed to meet the smile, almost of apology, that he gave as he walked by them.

They sat him down in a comfortable low-slung settee in the suite, choosing one far from the door, and a lady in black with a white apron brought him tea in a china cup and saucer and offered him with her other hand a plate of biscuits. She at least returned his smile, muttered the word "love" to him, and was gone through a doorway, not to be seen again. The man who had sat in the front of the Mercedes was moving across the room toward him. Sokarev could see that his suit was old, not cared for; there was a nick of blood on his collar, his tie was sufficiently loosened to reveal the top button of his shirt, his shoes had been cleaned but in haste and without thoroughness.

"The name's Jimmy, sir. Security. I'm to be with you right through your stay here. I hope we'll get along. Which are your men?"

Sokarev gestured first toward Mackowicz, who hovered close to his shoulder, then pointed to Elkin, who stood across the room by the door.

"There is Mr. Mackowicz and Mr. Elkin. I am glad to meet you . . . Jimmy." He laughed quietly, waiting for the other to offer a surname. None was forthcoming. "I had been told that I would be offered help on the visit. I am grateful to you."

"There's more than just me, sir. About another two hundred. The ones you'll see, at any rate. But I'm the one you'll be aware of. I'll be beside you the whole way."

"You'll have competition," Sokarev quipped, warming at his first impression of the man. "Mr. Mackowicz and Mr. Elkin told me they had booked those places for themselves."

"Well, it should be crowded, then. Which is just about right for you."

Thank God, thought Sokarev, they are not all like those men that have come with me. This one at least one can talk to, has a sense of humor, not like those who pad round in my wake, with their orders and ultimatums, and their soured faces. He could see the man who called himself Jimmy was talking out of earshot with Mackowicz, folders passing between them. All the men in the room were in huddles, talking, chattering like sparrows, exchanging sheets of white paper, drawing them from folders of green and blue and red and brown.

And I am the supernumerary, thought Sokarev. Nobody talks to me, nobody has even the time to say a "Hello" or a "Welcome." Everybody talks about me, about my movements, my sleep, my meals, but I am not consulted. Even the one who joked with me has nothing substantial to say; all that is kept for Mackowicz. If I wanted to attract attention I would have to shout, throw an epileptic fit, take my trousers off. Otherwise they would all go on as if I did not exist. Perhaps for some I am an exercise in strategy, a game to be played with, and when the time has come for me to leave, packaged up, shipped home forgotten. For others I am a source of anxiety. Not that they would mourn David Sokarev if his body lay in the gutter with blood in the mouth; what they would mourn would be their careers, their futures, and above all, their reputations.

He was far away and enjoying the self-pity when the security attaché spoke to him. "We have your bag now, Professor. We are ready to leave."

His tea was half finished in the cup. It mattered to no one. The circus was ready to entrain. It was not intended that David Sokarev should delay it.

A reporter with the airport news agency, Brenards, with a clearance pass that gave her access to the area of the VIP lounge, saw the convoy leave. She was there to interview a prominent industrialist returning with major export orders from the United States. Courteously but firmly a uniformed policeman told her she was not permitted to go within twenty-five yards of the lounge doorway. She had already watched the cordon stiffen up, seen the drivers start their motors, taken in the scale of the police operation, when the little man was brought out of the VIP suite. He was barely visible between the larger bodies of the Special Branch men who hemmed him in. As the last of the guards clambered aboard, the cars were on the move. She would not have known what airline the passenger who warranted so much attention had flown with if she had not recognized the features of the El Al station manager. When the cars had gone she had moved up beside him and asked him the identity of his passenger. He had shaken his head, given no explanation, and turned on his heel to walk back to his own transport. There are few things that irritate reporters, even trainees, as much as the studied brush-off.

Her telephoned call to her news editor reported "massive security, an unknown and anonymous Israeli VIP, police tracker dogs on the tarmac, an escort of armed Special Branch men, the waiving of customs formalities, and a high-speed convoy into London." The news editor liked it too, gave it a further gloss of his own, and put it on the wires, along which it would be carried to the newsrooms of all Fleet Street papers.

Immured between the shoulders of the security attaché and Mackowicz, Professor Sokarev saw little of the countryside bordering the M4 motorway link between the airport and Central London. If he strained his head, there were occasional glimpses of fields and football pitches before the cars sped onto an overpass, and only the roofs and upper office windows of the taller buildings were visible. He could sense the tension that now gripped Mackowicz, the way he peered into the cars that they passed, the way he heaved himself across the glass of the window when they slowed, clogged in traffic as the motorway narrowed from three lanes of traffic to two, pressing his whole upper torso against the glass. Sokarev had looked hard in the other direction for the moment or so before the convoy had started off as the bodyguard had armed the heavy black pistol that rested again back in the shoulder holster. It was an unpleasant, angular weapon, outside his experience, and he was unable to give it a name.

At the far end of a second overpass they halted at traffic lights, and then the talk in the front had stopped, and the relief in the crowded Mercedes had been almost audible when the red had given way to amber and green and they were moving once more.

In thirty-five minutes they were at the door of the hotel that had been chosen for him. More detectives waiting there, easily recognizable, and his own car jerking to a halt, and Mackowicz saying in his ear, "Don't stop, don't hesitate, straight inside," and there had been an arm that had taken his and half bundled him into the traveling swing doors.

Across the hallway of the hotel a man stood half in the lift, holding the button to keep the door open. Sokarev was kept in motion across the lavish carpet, bustled inside the lift. As the doors closed he found himself pressured by the shapes of his own men—the attaché, the one who called himself Jimmy—and the elegant dark-suited fellow he presumed to be from the hotel. They went to the fourth and top floor. At the extreme right-hand end he saw two men rise out of chairs, one of them turning to unlock and open the door of a corner room. The pace was maintained till the door slammed shut behind him.

"Welcome to our hotel, Professor Sokarev," intoned the man in the dark suit. He spoke with the necessary formality that concealed the management's displeasure at playing host and having responsibility for such a guest. There had been no breath of this when the reservation had been made, no sign of policemen and detectives who wanted to sleep in corridors, watch the front desk, slump in the lounge chairs. That had all started early in the morning and too late for a cancellation to be insisted upon.

"There is a connecting door to the other room for your two colleagues."

One room only for the two of them, thought Sokarev.

The attaché read him. "At night one will be sleeping, the other awake. They will take it in shifts. In addition, there are the men outside."

The crowd made its exit—management through the main door; Mackowicz, Elkin, Jimmy and the attaché into the adjoining room. Sokarev was alone. Able to unstrap his case and begin to put into drawers the clothes that his wife had folded with such care, to hang his two suits in the wardrobe. He could reflect that whatever fears he himself entertained for his own safety, they were matched by the anxiety of the security services of Israel and of Britain. The realization chilled him as he put away the few personal belongings he had brought from Beersheba.

Next door, Jimmy was on the telephone, through to Jones, and the other men waited in silence for him to finish and then relay to them the latest information. Jimmy's face gave nothing away to those who looked for a sign. Poker-straight, he listened, said he'd be in later that evening, and rang off.

"There's been a flap since Friday morning, but it's really buzzing now. Bit over an hour ago one of them called the contact man. We've traced the call to the South West. They're saturating a town called Richmond. Nice, comfortable, posh place. And it's crawling with coppers now. They think there's a good chance they have the bastards bottled up. But then, they always say that. Make the excuses twenty-four hours later."

"How many of them are there?" Elkin spoke.

"Just two," said Jimmy. "One from Northern Ireland. Cut above the usual grade. Good record, good operator. The other we think is from your part of the world. No name, but we've a face, not a bad one we think, to fit to him. He's a bit homesick, made a telephone call he shouldn't have. That's how we're pressuring them right now. Special Branch will be round in about twenty minutes, an inspector, he'll have the files and the pictures for you."

Jimmy sensed he was the odd man out in the room, that they wanted to talk in their own tongue, discuss their problems amongst themselves. It was the time for him to assert himself, make the position clear. There must be no doubt, no misunderstandings.

"My orders, gentlemen," he said, "are very clear. I have to be beside your man every moment he's out of that room. Not five yards, or four yards, or three yards away from him, right beside him. My orders are very explicit on that. He's not to leave this building without me knowing it. This isn't a scene you'll run yourselves. We are in charge, and you will listen to us. And a final point. If I see something out on the street and open fire and hit the wrong bloody target, there'll be a hell of a row, but it'll blow over. If one of you does it, you'll be in court before you know what's hit you; it'll stink for months. So go a bit careful."

Jimmy went out into the corridor, to have a smoke, chat up the Branch men, and to allow the men he'd left behind in the room to vent their feelings. With amusement he heard the raised voice that he recognized as Mackowicz's, rich in aggrieved anger, and Elkin's, quieter but in a harmony of protest, and then the calmer tones of the attaché soothing the hurt pride, salving the wounds.

That poor little sod in the other room, Jimmy thought. Lonely, frightened, and going through this hoop just to make one bloody speech. He could just as well have put it in the post, all neatly typed out, and everyone would be just as wise. But that's not the way it works. He's going to stand out there like a tethered goat, bloody great bait, with us up in the trees and him praying we get the bastards before they get to him. Jimmy went back into the room. Mackowicz still hard-eyed, uptight; Elkin a bit better, not much. But they knew where they stood. The attaché had done a good job. Their clothes were already scattered around the room. The radios and the Uzis were on one of the bedspreads; they were settling in.

"No appointments tonight, right?" Jimmy said to the attaché.

"Correct. He was to have dined at the university. We've put that off, said he had a heavy cold. He'll eat in the room tonight. He'll be tired from the journey. Tomorrow he can stay in till we go out in the evening."

"And Wednesday to the States?"

"He goes to New York on Thursday. His arrangements there are from that day. We saw no reason to change them."

"I hope he likes his room, then," snapped Jimmy. "Because if he's going to be here for an extra day, that's where he's going to have to stay."

The wind had raised its pitch, gathering power and determination as it swept across the great open spaces of the park. It sought out the body of McCoy where he lay, shirt unbuttoned to the waist, forced its currents across his chest, so that in his sleep he shivered and wriggled to hunch his frame and protect himself. And then he awoke. He saw the girl beside him, with her clothes still in the casual disarray that he had left them, legs outflung, arms behind her head, staring vacant and uncaring into the deep distances of the sky.

He looked at his watch. Past seven. Less than an hour to the rendezvous, and the light beginning to drift away. The afternoon had been lost; soon would come the cover of darkness that he needed for movement.

"Come on, girl. I said it was time to move."

There was a cutting edge in his voice, sharp, unfamiliar to her. She reacted, fumbling with her jeans, pulling them over the slight hips, twisting her body away from him as she fastened the button, drew up the zip. She turned away from him to contort her arms around her back to refasten the clasp that he had unhooked. He brushed the grass and dried earth from their clothes, and together they started to walk toward the heavy wrought-iron gates through which the cars flowed in and out of the park. They walked in silence, Norah with her head down, avoiding him.

They were still a clear hundred yards from the gates when McCoy saw the policemen operating the roadblock. He counted six of them. One far in the distance on the road toward the town waving his arm languidly in the air, slowing and warning the oncoming traffic. Another with a clipboard taking down the registration numbers. Another talking to the drivers, peering inside, scrutinizing the passengers. A fourth and fifth searching under hoods and in the trunks of the cars. And a sixth sitting in a police car facing away from the block, his engine ticking over. McCoy understood the scene. Last man there for a breakout, revved and ready to give chase. It was professional, he accepted that.

Too many for anything routine. Too heavy a force for local crime. He thought of Famy then. Unwilling to be left on his own, nervous of what might happen to him if he were abandoned to his own devices for just a few hours, suspicious of where McCoy had gone. And now the roadblock; not a casual one, but thorough and painstaking. He had to be sure where the bloody Arab was. Had to know what had happened.

Stretching on either side of the gates were the eight-foot-high walls of matured brick that ringed the park.

"I can't go through the check," he said. "I have to get across the wall, somewhere away from the main roads but near to the town."

The girl hesitated, uncertain. The policemen would hear her if she shouted. One scream and they would be running, sprinting toward her. And what then? That was where the equation defeated her. What would she say? Tell them the man they sought had lain with her, that she had opened her legs to him, pulled him down to her?

She was not long in deciding. She took McCoy's hand and led him across the grass, cut short by the sheep, past the great oak

trees, and then where the wall dipped down following the contours of a gully, she stopped.

She had chosen well, he could see that.

McCoy reached up to the top of the wall and levered himself
a foot or so off the ground. It was perfect. The wrong end of a
cemetery, where the trees grew close together, where the leaf
mold and grass cuttings had been piled against the bricks. He
slipped over, landing easily on the piled vegetation. He put his
right arm back over the wall, grabbed Norah's wrist and heaved
her over the barrier. They crouched behind one of the big yews,
the necessary precaution till he was certain they had not been
observed.

"I want somewhere that I can lie up, somewhere safe," he
whispered to her.

"Just out of the cemetery there's a building site they've
cleared, there's nothing there now. Just scrub and that. What
are you going to do then?"

"Get me there, I'll tell you then."

They walked along the narrow tarmac path between the
disordered rows of stones, past the jam jars that held single
wilting tulip stems, skirted the fresh rectangular shapes of
earth, and came to the gate.

"Where to from here?" McCoy said.

"Across the road and about a hundred yards down, that's
where the site is."

"But there's a bloody great fence round it. I can't climb that
on the main road."

"Down at the side, the second turning, no one'll see you
there." She was involved now. Part of his team. The moment
of crisis had come, and gone. She would do as he told her, he
had no doubt of that. Usually did, the little bitches. He sensed
he now had in his possession something quite priceless. He had
a courier. Someone who could run for him, who could be his
eyes and his ears. God knows why they want to dip their fingers
in, he thought. But they do. Don't think it out, too stupid to do
the addition and multiplication.

There was traffic on the road, but no policemen. He had his
arm around her shoulder as they waited for an opening and
then crossed. They fitted a conventional image, boy and girl out
for a walk, fond of each other, and very distant from the picture

any motorist who saw them might have of a wanted, hunted Provisional IRA killer. They walked down the side road, not fast, taking their time. McCoy spoke to her closely, and anyone who saw them would have imagined it was endearment he was whispering against her hair.

"Listen carefully," he said. "Do exactly as I say. Near the station there's a tea bar, on the far side of the road, toward the river. You'll find a man in there, a darkie. Taller than me, no mustache or anything, short hair. He'll have a grip bag with him. Just say the word 'Mushroom' to him, and tell him to follow you. Take him through to here, not on the big roads, down the side streets—and get him here. And tell him to go carefully."

"Is he the other one they're looking for?" Norah said it with excitement pitched in her voice.

"I've told you. You don't need to know. Just go and do it, girl. The way I've told you. If he's not there, wait for him. At least an hour. But get him here."

He scanned each end of the road. Empty, deserted. Then he was on the bucking, bending wire, monkey-like, before he fell and tumbled on the far side and was gone. She heard his running feet crashing in the undergrowth, and after that, nothing.

Famy heard the sirens in the street outside. He remembered the urgency of the instructions over the telephone to set distance between himself and the station, and he huddled in his seat in the darkened theater as the raucous noise blotted out the sound track of the film whenever the police cars passed outside. He bit at his fingernails as he watched the technicolor heroics that filled the screen. The images meant nothing, failed even to divert his attention from the problem that now preyed on him. It was the immediate problem of survival. The bag was there against his legs, reassuring in its bulk, and he quietly slid open the zip and felt with his hand for the cotton surface under which were the awkward, angled shapes of the grenades. He lifted one out, small, the size of a shrunken apple, and put it in the pocket of his coat. The rifles were too large, too cumbersome, but one grenade would be sufficient to stave off immediate pursuit. It could be concealed, not like the guns, and it gave him the confidence that he would need to walk out in the unknown of the middle light of the evening.

Sometimes his thoughts wandered back to his friends, the
men he had hardly known but whose companionship he had
valued, to Dani and Bouchi. Their laughter on the plane out of
Beirut, the banter about Nablus and the olive groves as they had
driven across France, and the fear that had bound them on the
route to Boulogne. He remembered again—so that it overwhelmed him and blotted out the meaningless antics of the
celluloid pictures—the blood of his friends that had spattered
and soaked the seats of the car. He could still hear Dani's words.
Their exhortation before the color in the soft brown cheeks had
faded to the greyness that preceded death. The words knifed
through his subconscious, controlling him, providing the momentum he needed to go on.

He left the cinema before the completion of the second film.
He wanted away before the big rush to the doors, and the exit
he chose was at the side. It was simple reasoning that if a hunt
for him were in progress, the entrance hall of a cinema would
be an obvious place for them to look. With the bag in his hand
and the grenade in his pocket, he slid back the iron bar that
kept the fire door shut. He went unnoticed, without impedi-
ment.

It took him many minutes to make his way to the rendezvous.
He walked with a shuffling, almost sideways, gait along the front
of the shop windows, ready to spin his head toward the loaded
shelves of merchandise on the occasions that the squad cars
cruised past. There were men on foot too, and to avoid them he
twice entered shops, mingling in front of the counters till he
had seen through the plate-glass windows that the danger had
gone. With each step he took, there was greater confidence.
They're stumbling about, he told himself, uncertain what and
whom they seek, thrashing in the dark.

In the café he took a seat at the back, again sideways to the
door, where he could observe the comings and goings and at the
same time swing his head away should he wish to obscure his
face.

He saw the girl come in, noticed the nervous, switching eyes
that took in the customers sitting at the tables and on the stools
at the counter. The look of grateful recognition she gave him
stiffened Famy and his hand moved instinctively to the pocket
that held the grenade, his fingers seeking out the circular pin
that was the safety device of the V-40. He stared at her, hand

clasped around the metal as she came closer, eyes rivited to her pale, pretty face.

She bent down toward him as she reached the table. She was trembling, and when her lips moved, at first there was no sound. "Mushroom," she blurted out. "He said you were to follow me. I'll take you to him."

And Famy understood. Why had he been so anxious to split up that afternoon? Needed a girl. Not a woman who would reason things out, but a girl who would follow blindly where he led. Dangerous, he thought, but probably better than someone older. As she turned back toward the door he saw the hard-etched creases in her blouse. Not bad, McCoy, he thought. A roll in the grass and you have the loyalty of the whore.

She took him through the back streets of the old town, climbing the hill over which sprawled the fashionable residential homes of the previous century. Past almshouses and churches, past homes that had been neatly outlined in white gloss, past blocks of flats where those for sale were advertised as "luxury" on the estate agent's boards. Sometimes the streets were narrow, in other places they widened out, but none of them were busy with cars. There were children playing their games with balls, men walking in company to the pubs, women hurrying home with their baskets of late shopping, and no policemen. Famy held the girl's hand, and she let it rest there, inanimate and without feeling. But it was better that way, safer, more secure. They went mostly in silence, Famy occasionally speaking, but meeting only noncommittal response.

In front of them was a wall and daubed on it the words *Park Hill Was Home to Me*. A relic of the time there had been a great house set in its own grounds on the site, and there had been protests before the demolition men came. Now there was only a tangle of bushes, cut-down trees and neglected shrubs.

"That's where he is," she said. Her voice was detached, as if she realizes, thought Famy, that her usefulness is expended, and is resigned to it. "It's time I was getting home, my Mum'll be going out of her mind."

"Where do you live?" asked Famy.

"Chisholm Road. Just round the corner. At twenty-five."

"I hope we see you again. You have been very kind to me . . ."

She was running away into the night. He was different from

the other one. More gentle, wouldn't have hurt her like that bastard Irishman. But probably wouldn't have done anything, sat there all afternoon pulling grass up. It still ached where McCoy had been, and there was a bruised raw feeling at the top of her thighs. And he hadn't used anything, the bastard.

Thirteen

Even as security-conscious a building as Scotland Yard is susceptible to leakage of classified information. In the drably painted ground-floor pressroom the crime correspondent of the *Express* heard the first whispers of the mounting of a major security operation to protect an unnamed Israeli VIP.

The anonymity of the man being guarded was broken by the paper's science correspondent, who had received an invitation seventeen days earlier to attend a lecture by Professor David Sokarev of the Dimona Nuclear Research Establishment. His casual call to the embassy's press spokesman, and the flat refusal to his request for information on the professor's itinerary, served only to confirm that Sokarev was the man being subjected to intensive security. The Brenards report of armed Special Branch men at the airport to guard an El Al passenger added further color to the story. But it was the chief subeditor's intuition that turned the story into the front-page "splash." At his desk, where he collected the various typewritten sheets and the agency copy, he began to shuffle together what had up to then figured as quite separate material. He had in his hand the stories now catchlined "Sokarev" along with those on which he had scrawled "Manhunt." And it made good sense. Heavy pro-

tection of an Israeli nuclear scientist married with a vast police
dragnet for a known Provisional IRA killer traveling in the
company of an unidentified Arab.

By the time the third edition was on its way by van to various
railterminals, the headline ARAB DEATH THREAT TO ISRAELI
H-BOMB SCIENTIST blasted its way across the top of the front
page.

The Prime Minister's anger when he read the story before
retiring to his Downing Street flat for the night was stonily
rejected by the Director General.

"No leaks from this Department" was his riposte. It was his
policy to strike an independent posture for the Security Service,
and one thing he was traditionally quick to show intolerance for
was ill-informed criticism of its work. "From what you've told
me, sir"—and the courtesy was purely formal—"I think you'll
find it's straightforward reporting of a series of facts visible to
any trained eye."

That went some way to calming the head of government.
"But it doesn't help the position," the Prime Minister said.

"There's not very much that does help the situation in times
like this."

"What I mean," said the Prime Minister, "is that if anything
happens to this man Sokarev after this, we are all going to look
almighty stupid."

"That's a fair point, sir," the Director General replied.

Not a great deal to say after that. Only the obvious, that they
had problems, that they were coming from behind, that there
was huge ground to be made up. The silences grew longer, till
termination point in their conversation. He wished the Prime
Minister a good night's sleep.

So they'd the wind up in Whitehall. It always amused him.
Meant the telephone would be going every five minutes in the
morning. Politicians crawling in on the act, and nothing they
could do about it. For that matter, he thought, not much any
of us can do. He checked with Jones, still in his office too, but
with no new developments to report from Richmond. It would
be a long day tomorrow, long and trying.

Before they had set out into the open and silent spaces of the
darkened park there had been fierce words between Famy and
McCoy. Ostensibly it was over the question of whether or not

they should leave the seeming security of the undergrowth at Park Hill, but in effect it concerned the leadership of the two-man team. Famy had wanted to stay put, and was impressed by the semiconcealed basement of an old long-gone building that McCoy had been hiding in while waiting for the Arab's arrival. The Irishman was for getting on the move immediately.

"We have to sleep somewhere tonight. We have to have some rest, and this is as good a place as any," Famy had said.

"With the police about we have to quit, get out and fast" had come the answer from McCoy, who was accustomed to command, was used to men reacting to his orders without hesitation and arguments. He had assessed his colleague sufficiently, felt the time of deference had died its death.

"We are completely hidden here. We would not be found."

"All we are doing is staying inside whatever cordon they've round us. Giving them time to get organized, bring in reinforcements. It helps them, louses us. And in the morning, at first light, there'll be dogs, helicopters, the whole bloody works. They know we're here. Christ knows how, but they know it, and we have to shift our arses, and on foot, and in the dark." McCoy was suppressing his wish to shout, turning his voice to a subdued snarl.

"But they will concentrate their efforts while they believe in their information. When they have been unsuccessful they will relax—tomorrow it will be easier to move. We should stay till tomorrow." The top of his cheeks were flushed red as Famy stabbed with his finger at McCoy's chest to reinforce his point.

"They don't work that way, little boy. They're bloody policemen, not soldiers. They do it by the book, solid and thorough, they don't get bored and go home to put their feet up—"

"You have endangered us," Famy interrupted, unwilling to let McCoy dominate. He threw his ace card, unsure where it would take him, what dividend it would bring. "You have risked us. And what for? So you could lie with that girl for the afternoon—"

"Shut your fucking mouth." McCoy spat the words at him. Famy could not see him, just hear his breathing, feel the closeness of his body. "Shut your face and don't open it again. And just think back a bit, over what you've done today, try and remember where they picked you up."

The memory of the agitated diplomat on the far end of the

telephone seared through Famy's mind. The sense of shame was too great for him to tell the Irishman what had happened. He was defeated. "Where do we go?" he said.

McCoy made no capital from the submission, applied no salt, and spoke with the heat gone from his voice. Silently Famy thanked him for the concession. The pivot that controlled who dominated the team had shifted—it was inevitable, given the circumstances, also irreversible.

"We're going on foot into the park. There's a place near here where we can get over the wall. It's a couple of miles across. If we keep off the roads, we'll be all right and out the other side. Another couple of miles, and if we're lucky, we'll get ourselves a car."

Famy followed as McCoy led, blindly. The truth of his situation was clear to him: without the Irishman he was doomed; so too would be his attack on the Mushroom Man. He could yearn till it bled for the companionship of Dani and Bouchi, for the warmth of comradeship at the camp in Fatahland, but on his own in another continent, in a strange country, he needed the Irishman.

They blundered across the rough ground, tripping on fallen branches, stumbling in water ditches, always seeking the total black void away from the lights of cars. Once they saw the revolving blue light on the roof of a police car and flung themselves flat on the ground, and waited long after it had gone before resuming their progress. They climbed the chain-link fence that demarcated the park and a golf club, handing over the weighted bag one to the other, made their way across the greens and fairways till they came to another fence which shielded a neat, tended row of back gardens. They went with care over that fence, having sought out a garden into which no lights shone, and then were out in a short and rounded cul-de-sac, well illuminated by the tall sodium lights.

McCoy said, "I'll go ahead. Twenty yards or so and on the other side. You take the bag. That way we're not so bloody easy to notice. And go slow. Look as though you belong."

They walked another hour and a half till they were in the wide and deserted Wandsworth High Street.

"Somewhere off here," said McCoy. "Out of the mainstream we'll collect a car. The new ones'll have locking devices on the wheels. We want an old one, something with a 'D' or 'E' or 'F' after the numbers."

They were together now, mutually belonging; the immediate threat of the police cordon was far behind them.

"It was easy, as it turned out." Famy smiled, shy, wanting to end what tension still existed between them.

"There's no way they can stand shoulder to shoulder round a town that size. All they can do is block the main routes and hope for luck. If you keep your cool, you'll win."

McCoy didn't regret the hard words of their clash. Be something wrong if we weren't at each other's throats on a caper like this. Not enough sleep, not enough food, eyes running the pavements over your bloody shoulder half the day, hours spreading themselves and reluctant to pass on, clock hands desperate in the pace of their passage.

Less than a full day to go, and then, Holy Mother . . . the mad scramble to get clear of the sodding place. No clear escape route, not like it had been planned. Should have been sitting quietly in that attic, hearing the fuzzers and the politicos spouting on the radio, spieling their inanities to the goddamn reporters. Should have been all ready and waiting, safe in the nest at the top of the house, stacked up there while the temperature stayed cool. And now . . . Where to go now? Where to shift to, where to lie up . . . ? One at a bloody time, my Provie boy.

Let it work itself when you get there. Get the priorities sealed up first. But this bloody carry-on is not the way you do it. You don't stand up in Crossmaglen market square and blast a para and then wonder which way you'll run. Doesn't work that way. You plan it all out, think about it, have your watchers and your spotters and the woman who'll take the gun in her pram and the man who'll leave his back door open and the car that'll be waiting. Don't leave it to chance. Donal hadn't a route planned when he fired, seventeen and couldn't read. Died in the alleyway behind his house, and everyone in the section shot him, big bloody guardsmen, and they'd laughed. Sean hadn't thought it out when he drove the bomb to Newtown Hamilton and they stopped him at the checkpoint. Wasn't usually one there, not on that crossroads, and he's fifteen years in the Crumlin Gaol to think on it. The bloody eejit way of getting stuffed, he'd told his men, to be out on the business without the preparation. You don't survive if you're in a hurry.

They'd expect something better of you, Ciaran McCoy, he thought. Piss themselves laughing in the boozer. Off on the big one, off on the spectacular, and no plan out. The beer would swill round their guts but there'd be no tears if the bastards shoot you, no protests if they nick you alive and lock you up the rest of your natural. Drink themselves stupid and talk and talk and talk, and all to say that Ciaran McCoy had done a job across the water and hadn't thought the way out. They'd hiccup and belch their way home, down the streets off the square, and think: Stupid little bugger, and him the one that was always telling the rest.

But there'd be no more trouble from the Arab. He saw that, the way Famy followed him like a bloody dog, half a step behind, frightened of disapproval. There'll be no more shouting. He'll do as he's bloody told. McCoy knew the dispute of leadership was a thing of the past, would not rise again.

Off the main roads the streets were deserted. Televisions had played the national anthem and were now quieted, the bedtime cocoa had been taken upstairs, doors locked and bolted, cats shoved into the night. Behind the drawn curtains awareness was extinguished. No one curious of the sounds came to an upstair window as McCoy prized open the hood of an aging Ford Cortina. From his pocket he drew a packet of cigarettes and took one out. He slid his thumbnail down the join where the two ends of paper met and brushed out the shredded tobacco, then squeezed off the filter end, so that it fell into the gutter. With one hand he felt across the iron frame on the top of the engine till his fingers, guided by knowledge and experience, rested on the vital terminals. Into the gap between them he inserted the sliver of paper. Without asking, he moved to Famy, took the grip from him, unzipped it, and pulled from the inside a shirt, folded as he would have wished. He placed it against the triangular glass partition at the front of the driver's window, paused, and then smashed his hand against the cotton. The blow was sufficiently muffled. There was no alert from those who slept the night away. The glass tilted on its axis. There was room for him to insert his hand down alongside the interior handle and carefully release it. When he had opened the driver's door, he leaned across and freed the lock on the passenger side, then motioned for Famy to take his seat. When the Arab was there, door closed and the bag on his knees, McCoy returned his attention to the engine. Again his hands moved across the greased bulk, searching for the rubber nipple-like button that he needed. When he found it, he glanced again toward Famy, gave him the half-smile that meant success, and pressed. As the mechanism shook into life, he eased the hood down and slipped his way into the driving seat. There was a last look up at the undisturbed drapes across the windows and he had edged the car out into the width of the road and driven off. He left behind him a gap amongst the tightly parked cars, like that where a child waits for a last tooth to come, and which would not be discovered till the panic of dawn and the readiness for work.

He headed east, away from the policemen who shivered, bored and listless, at their roadblocks.

"Piece of bloody cake," he muttered to himself.

"What now?" Famy asked, cautious and uncertain of the Irishman's mood.

"Get some distance behind us, about half an hour's worth, and across the river. Find somewhere off the tracks, and get some sleep. We'll need a garage when it's light, where we'll get some keys to this bloody heap. Out on the other side of town, where there are woods, and we'll lose ourselves there for the day. We don't come back into town till the evening."

Famy nodded. He was conscious he was being told what he needed to know, nothing more. No frills on it, no embroidery and, above all, no discussion.

McCoy sensed the mood. "Don't fret yourself, lover boy. This is your day, not mine. I'll get you there. I'll prop you up just when the curtain rises. You think about that and leave the transportation to McCoy. Don't concern yourself with how we get there. You'll be on hand, just when you need to be, to see your man. There's a sod of a lot to get through before that, but it'll come soon enough. The time won't stand back for you, it goes on its way, till it's you and yer man. And don't go ballsing it on me."

McCoy laughed, selfish and introverted. Private thoughts, not to be shared, and as they drifted along the broad empty vistas

of a deserted night laden city, he sang, quietly ignoring his
audience. They were the songs of his movement that passed
over his lips, soft, delicate, finely woven words of death, martyrdom, adulation for the fallen hero. They're all like that, and
there was a bitterness there. Need to be stiff, cold, broken and
shrouded before the music men get round to you. Get their
fiddles and accordions out then, when the grass is sitting on you.
Not before. Don't find you the price of a pair of shoes till then.
But let some bastard soldier gouge your guts out, and they'll be
round the clubs, strumming and crooning your name. That's the
way of the music men. Never a song about the living, only the
dead. Only the little bastards stupid enough to get in the way.
He'd walked at Donal's funeral. Tramped his way far behind
the family, deep in a mass of bodies and beyond the range of
the army cameras and snatch squads, hidden and anonymous,
and made a lone exit from the graveside while orations and
epitaphs were in full flow. But they had an effect on him, those
great and endless trails of silent men and women who formed
the processions behind the cheap box, draped with the flag and
mounted by the black beret. He could recognize the emotional
dragnet that caught him up and welded him further into the
cause. When they buried one of his men, there was immediate
retaliation, a soldier died. It followed with an inevitability, night
after day. Clear, easy to understand. But the death of the Israeli
—was it worth the journey, bumping on the shoulders across
the long, ill-cut grass of the churchyard? Never heard of the sod,
hardly knew what he looked like, one piss-poor photograph.
Fat, insignificant little bugger, living on the other side of the
world. Just an order, McCoy. Leave it at that, and leave the
thinking to your superiors, soldier boy. Do as you're told,
obey your orders. Somebody else's war, this one, but can't be
fought unless McCoy stands the line. Famy would die, no hesitation, but Ciaran McCoy—what would he do? How hard
would he press home his attack? His mind was too tired to
react to the intricacies of the problem. Shelve it. Pray Jesus
that it doesn't come to that. And if it does . . . ? Think about
it then.

    Famy was asleep when he brought the car to a halt. They
were back north of the river, and the rough ground behind the
flats would suit him for the two to three hours before the grow-

ing dawn and the light of the day would drive him once again to seek obscurity and a more settled hiding place to while away the hours before David Sokarev was to make his speech.

It was hours now since the planes had come. Without warning, the sound of their vast thrusting engines left far behind as they swooped over the hills, flying the contours of the ground, hurtling toward the plotted coordinates of a map reference. Young men, expert and trained in the sunshine of faraway Arizona till they could handle the multimillion-dollar complexities of the Phantom cockpit, straining with their eyes for the crisscross of wheel tracks on the sand five hundred feet beneath them, then searching for the discreet, camouflage-muffled outlines of the tents before they let loose the awkward torpedo-shaped cannisters containing the petroleum jelly that had been given the title of "napalm" by a nameless scientist. The pilots, carried away toward the next target that had been designated for rockets, did not see where the canisters landed. The navigator would twist his body, difficult in the all-encompassing, padded-out "G" suit, but he, too, would recognize only the column of thick black smoke and have no knowledge whether the mission had been successful or not.

The leader of the General Command was in his tent. The hair stubbled, worn face resting on his clenched hands. There was a candle held upright in a Pepsi-Cola bottle on the table on which he leaned his elbows. The light faded and rose, at the whim of the cool night that eddied through the flap on the tent, finding the flame and bending and brushing it. It was a time that he loathed and detested. A time when he was helpless and unable to hit back. Four men dead, burned beyond recognition, life cut short as they screamed. And the technology of his enemy, his speed and his knowledge, took him far away from the puny retaliation possible to the men on the ground. Nothing, only the oaths and obscenities shouted into the dirt as they had lain in the fragile cover between the rocks and waited for the echoing noise to pass. And the men who had died, buried already, not deep down, the parched ground prevented that, but hurried into shallow pits at dusk.

His subordinates had left him when he had retired to the tent, recognizing the signs that he wished to be alone. Others would care for the morale of the young men who had filed past the bodies, would take care that the sight fanned their hatred of the enemy across the border. There was a solitary piece of paper on his table, brought by the journalist from Beirut, who had visited and left before the arrival of the jets. He had read it over and over again, keeping the information even from his closest colleagues, savoring amongst the disaster and horror of the day the news that it carried. The one they called Saleh Mohammed was there, on target and meeting his rendezvous contact. The best boy that he had, the one he had willed to survive.

It would devastate them, he knew that. A plan of such detail and skill that he had hugged and kissed the shy, bespectacled recruit who had worked on its conception—not a youth who could himself go across the border, the right claw foot controlled that, but one with brains and with foresight and who had talked not just of the operation but of its consequences, its wounding potential to the State of Israel. It would hurt them, twist behind the nation's rib cage . . .

The old man who acted as his bodyguard came noiselessly into the tent, "Some food for you, Ahmed. It is time to eat. One cannot sit and starve and grieve."

He was the only one in the camp who would call the leader by his given name. It went back a long time, eight years. They had held the house together at Karameh when the Israelis had swarmed in brigade strength into the refugee village beside the River Jordan ten months after the Six-Day War. It should have been so easy for them, but for the first time the Palestinians had stood and fought. The cynics said it was because they had been left no escape route. There was truth in that, but for once the fedayeen had not thrown down their guns and surrendered. There had been mourning in Israel when the casualty figures were announced, more than twenty dead, more than seventy wounded. There had been dancing in Amman as the captured Centurion armor was driven in triumph through the ancient, winding hill streets, and amongst the Palestinians there had been much to remember and heady praise and the start of resistance. The hours in the wrecked building, hammered by the tanks and hitting back with the rocket launchers and the Kalashnikovs, had forged the association between the two men, one a leader and the other a follower. The relationship had not changed. It was acceptable, and the old man knew when he was required.

The old man put the plate in front of the leader. A mess of beans and rice and sauce with lamb's meat cut in small squares. "They have had their day, the Israeli. We will have ours. There is no sudden way to victory," he said.

"What they have accomplished against us is a mere nothing to the blow that awaits them." The old man was rarely taken into the leader's inner confidence. He said nothing, and arranged a spoon and fork alongside the plate in front of the sitting man. "Within the next hours, perhaps as long as two days," the leader went on, "we shall hit them so that they will yelp like the dogs."

"Across the border?" With a burden of sadness. He knew the risks, had cleared too many bundles of the possessions left behind by the suicide squads.

"Across many borders. Far from here. Bouchi, Dani and the third one—you remember? They went to Europe. Bouchi and Dani are dead; the other alone has gone through. He is on course, on target. Today or tomorrow he will move, and then the world will know of him." He spoke the words hurriedly, interspersing them with pauses as he scooped up the food from the plate, cramming it without finesse into his mouth. He did not look at the man who stood behind him. When the plate was cleared, he sat back in his chair and addressed himself to the empty screen of canvas to his front.

"His target is David Sokarev. Of the utmost importance to them, but a man of whom you will not have heard. He is from the world of science, of the very fundamentals of science. He concerns himself with the structure of the atom, and with the breaking of the atom, and with the release of its energies. They are jealous of their anonymity, these men, they do not seek to be answerable to their fellow species. They hide themselves away like slugs underneath wet rocks. It is rare for them to emerge into the open light, but Sokarev has come out. To London. That is where we will meet him, and will kill him."

The old man watched as the leader turned toward him. He saw the excitement in the eyes, deep and brown and shadowed in their sockets. Not since they had waited for news of the raid into Kiryat Shmona, when the orders had been to eliminate as many of the enemy as were within range of the guns, men or women or children, had the old man seen a similar look—the fanatic awaiting his fulfillment.

"Eight bombs they have, perhaps nine by now," the leader went on, staring into the other's face, the voice quavering on the verge of self-control, "not big. The size of Hiroshima and Nagasaki. In a city they would kill ninety thousand, up to one hundred thousand. Suck the air from their lungs, burn the bodies of our people, blind them, maim them, infect them so that those that live from their breeding would produce grotesque mutations. They would not make what their American allies call the 'clean bomb.' They will not waste effort and expense on such refinements. It will be a weapon of filth and of poison, and it is their ultimate defense. They hide behind it, in the knowledge that the very mystery of its existence gives them strength. The man that we will shoot is the man who has created this bomb, loved it, sucored it, spent his working life refining the effectiveness of its yield."

"And when he is dead, what will have changed?" said the old man.

"It will take the elimination of Sokarev to awake the world to the Israeli power. When he is dead and the news has been carried from continent to continent, the world will wonder why the Palestinian people have chosen to exact retribution on one who seems so mild, so quiet, such a harmless-looking little man. And we will tell them why he was chosen—we will tell them of Dimona, of the plutonium schemes, of the reactors there. And with their knowledge, so too will come their fears. Fears of a mushroom cloud settling the 'Middle East problem,' as they call it, fears of an annihilation more ghastly than the world has experienced since its cleverer men developed this horror. All the world will be talking about the bomb of the Israelis, not just the peasant peoples, but in the embassies and the chancelleries and the senates and the palaces. There will be demands for inspections and controls—the Americans will want that if only to silence their critics. If their bomb is muzzled, their ultimate defense is taken from them, then they are weak, then they can be beaten. All their men are replaceable. Dayan was replaceable, and Sharon of the Canal, and Rabin, and Eban, and Peres —all have others who wait to take their places. Sokarev too.

Other scientists can move behind his desk, but nothing can replace the bomb. It is final, the complete answer to their defensive strategy when future war goes against them. If it happens as we believe it will, if the governments of the world demand to know of this weapon, exercise control over it, then ultimately Israel will lose and go down stripped of her last and most powerful weapon of defense. That is why we will kill Sokarev."

The leader smiled like a man who has outlined to his friends his plans for the conquest of a woman they all consider unattainable, and beyond reach.

The old man ran his fingernails across the days' old bristle of his chin, pondered, his brows lined with deep confusion. He had not heard the other talk in that way before. "It is strange, is it not," he said quietly, "how the death of a man can move the world more than the life he has so long striven to perfect." He let himself out of the tent, taking the plate with him, and was gone, moving his way with familiarity across the sand, by-passing the ropes that held the tents. The night was very clear, a slight moon and the endless abyss of stars.

The leader snuffed out the candle with his thumb and forefinger, and stripped off his denim camouflage coat and trousers. He felt his way across to the narrow canvas bed and edged his body under the single blanket that he allowed himself. He had no difficulty in finding sleep. The images of the four burned carcasses had long since passed, and he dreamed of the small, sad-faced man whose picture he had seen. And the face dissolved into terror, and there was a gun blotting out the picture, and he could hear the man's scream and then the staccato roar of the automatic rifle. Beyond his canvas walls the camp was quiet. Only the shuffling movement of the sentries and at the village a mile away a dog calling for its bitch broke the unmeasured silence of the night.

It was past three on the Tuesday morning that Jimmy returned to his flat. He'd been conscientious enough, nothing to drink, and he'd made his calls. He'd been to Leconfield House and reported back to Jones; he'd returned to the hotel and seen that Sokarev was in his bed. For half an hour he'd padded around the hotel, checking the fire doors to convince himself they were closed to outside entry, satisfying himself that the Branch men were in position. He'd spoken briefly to the Israeli who was sitting up; it was the one called Elkin. The other slept noisily in the bed close to where they had talked in whispers. The connecting door to the scientist's room was open and the Uzi lay on the bed beside them. They talked inanities—Jimmy cheerfully and Elkin with caution, as if unsure of himself with the strange man. Jimmy had said he'd be back by early morning, and repeated that under no circumstances were there to be visitors allowed to see Sokarev or that the man under threat should be permitted to leave his room.

There was a Branch man in the corridor outside the room, another beside the lift shaft, two more in the ground-floor lobby of the hotel. Too many for them, thought Jimmy; hopeless for the opposition. It relaxed him enough for him to wander out of the front door easy in his mind that no harm could come to his charge during the night.

From the hotel he drove south and west for twenty minutes till he reached Richmond. The roadblocks were in position still, searching the cars traveling in the other direction. He found the police station easily enough, in a side street close to the bridge, where the scent of the low-water river drifted up to him. It was a chill, damp night, and he hurried from the car across the parking area at the back of the station to the rear door. There was a bustle of activity there, an ants' nest which a spade has pitched into. In more normal times there would have been three, perhaps four, officers on duty, whiling away the darkness and waiting for their reliefs to come in.

Instead, the lights were on, blazing throughout the building, corridors noisy with hurrying men, some in uniform, some in plain clothes; teleprinters chattered messages to and from Scotland Yard; telephones rang. At the front-hall desk Jimmy showed his identification card and watched as the bored features of the sergeant who looked at it awoke with interest. He was ushered up two flights of stairs and shown the open door of an office where a group of men sat around a table. The air was heavy with tobacco, the flat surfaces littered with maps and plastic coffee beakers.

The senior officers didn't waste Jimmy's time. He was grateful for that. They explained what they had done, what they were currently involved in, what they planned for the morning. It was thorough and painstaking, left nothing out. They showed him where they had already searched, where their roadblocks were in force, where their patrols, foot and mobile, were operating, the locations of the houses they planned to raid at first light. But he could read the answer he was looking for in their drawn, humorless faces. There was none of the anticipation that catches hold of a huntsman's eyes when he thinks he is closing on his goal. It was routine, good routine, and that he conceded, but there was insufficient material for them to go on, and they knew it, and understood that for them to catch the men whose descriptions were plastered across the district, they would need extraordinary luck. Policemen don't expect luck, don't count on it, Jimmy knew that. He sensed that for all the effort being put into the search, there were few in the room in which he sat who expected that the night would be crowned by success.

As he drove back to the flat he could reflect that it had not been a totally wasted journey. Jimmy liked to know where he stood, and the monotone description of the police action in the town had provided him with the information he sought. They were loose again, the two little bastards. Free and with their guns and with a plan and inching their way closer to the target. They had two full days in which to launch their attack. When they're that close, Jimmy boy, then they have to be in with a chance. No doubt about that. You're enjoying it, you little bugger, he said to himself, it's the way you would have wanted it. You'd have crapped yourself if they'd been picked up and you had to hand the PPK in, unsoiled and unused. Nobody likes a fox that won't run, that goes to earth too fast, and you, you daft little sod, you're looking for a good long ride and a good kill at the end.

He let himself into the flat, took off his shoes by the door, and tiptoed into the bedroom. Helen was there, scarcely covered by the sheets, arms and legs heaved apart in the abandon of sleep. Not a stitch on her, poor bloody girl. Destined for disappointment again. He undressed, letting his clothes mingle on the carpet with hers, and eased his way onto the bed, careful not to wake her. Something in his presence must have aroused the girl. She hooked an arm across his waist, feeling out the crevice underneath his armpit, but she did not wake, and Jimmy lay still till sleep came to him too.

He never found it difficult, not even on the nights he might shoot or be shot at, or when another man's life might rest on his wits and alertness. There was no tension. There had been none the night before he met the Foreign Office defector in the hotel outside Utrecht; whose last living sight had been of a man who had enjoyed a good rest previously.

Killing was not important to Jimmy, which was why the sleep came to him fast, which was why Jones championed him, which was why the Director General tolerated his presence on the payroll.

Fourteen

It was the cold that woke Famy. He had been in a half-sleep, tossing under his coat in the back seat of the car, searching for warmth, wriggling to escape the chill that had settled on his body and gnawed its way beneath the light cotton of his clothes. For a few moments he could not place where he was as he stared up at the roof of the car, then swung his head up to peer through the window. There was a noise, but far away, the sound of children shrieking to each other, of the revving of starting cars; a city starting out on another day. Beyond the glass he saw the tired, untidy shapes of the tower flats, soaring up in composite and identical rows to high beyond his view. Grey and streaked from years of exposure to the weather. There was a woman there, shouting instructions into the void to a man going to his work. Between the flats and his position were the lines of prefabricated garages, and then nearer still, seven feet of chain-wire fence, buckled and bent where children had scaled it. To the far side of the rough, broken ground where the car was parked was another fence, and beyond that, a railway line. There were other cars alongside, but different from the Cortina —without hoods, without tires, wheels askew, doors gaping open, deserted as useless and too complicated to dispose of.

Famy stretched to see over the back of the seat, anticipating
the huddled shape of McCoy prone across the width of the car.
It hit him a cruel, winding, sledge-hammer blow. The emptiness that he saw. He rose on the back seat, jerking his sleep-stiff
limbs forward, searching for confirmation as the messages raced
through his brain. Two seats, gear handle, steering wheel, dashboard—nothing else. The sweat started to run, there was a
tremble in the fingers, weakness in the legs. He peered again
through the windows, revolving around in all directions, before
sagging down upright on the seat. With a quick movement he
felt down to the floor for the grip bag and ran his fingers over
the outside till they rested on the hard shape of the rifles. The
guns were there, but where the bastard Irishman?

The argument and the hard words of the previous evening
came back to him, verbatim and exact, and the long silences as
they had walked and then driven through London. You cannot
trust any but your own, he should have known that. Putting
trust in a stranger, one whose involvement was no more than
partial, it had been madness. Famy felt a great exhaustion
sweeping over him. On his own, how could he go forward? Was
it possible to continue by himself? Tears drove their passage
across his autumn-brown cheeks. He had no strength to fight
them, interrupt their path to the stiffness of his collar. He had
not wept for many years, not since his youngest sister had died
at the age of a few days in the front room of the bungalow in
Nablus. But he had been only a boy then, and since adulthood
he'd prided himself on his ability to keep his emotions tight and
controlled. But that the Irishman had left him asleep and defenseless, betrayed him, made an escape without having the
courage to face him directly . . . that was a total wound, painful
and throbbing.

He opened the door of the car and eased himself out. His
watch showed past eight, and the sun was coming high from
behind the flats, casting great shadows and playing patterns on
the weeds that grew unchecked on the open ground. He
walked warily away from the vehicle, taking in his surroundings, till he came to the opened gateway which led to the made-
up road and further away to the lines of sand-brick terraced
houses that lay behind the long tin fence. There were more
people there, none concerning themselves with the tall young

figure who watched them. As his eyes played on the short horizon of chimney tops and television aerials, it took him little effort to realize that he had no knowledge of his whereabouts. They had driven a long way since crossing the bridge; he had known that as he jolted in the seat with the motion of the car. Then he remembered the A-Z guide he had bought, and he looked for a street name that would help him to identify his exact location. It would be at the far end of the line of houses, where the junction was. But there were too many people out on the pavements, readying themselves for work and school and shopping. Later they would be gone and the houses would settle into a midmorning listlessness, too preoccupied to notice the hunted man. That would be the time to walk the whole length of the street to find its name.

By the time he turned on his heel and drifted slowly back toward the car, his mind was made up. There was no possibility that he could follow the path of abject defeat taken by the Irishman. When the men of the General Command went across the enemy's border, there was no retreat if they were cut off and surrounded short of their target. They stood and fought and died where they were trapped. Few returned to receive the adulation of their comrades after a successful mission; none returned to admit failure. Failure and surrender, those were the cancer growths in a movement such as his; despair would be close behind, and hopelessness, and then the victory for the enemy. If we lose our courage, he thought, we can lay down our rifles, fold away the denim fatigues, and go back to plowing the fields of Lebanon and Jordan; we will never see the hills of Nablus and the groves of Haifa.

There was a poem he had read in Beirut, written after the degradation of the Six-Day War. One verse alone remained in his mind, clear and without complication:

> People may be divided into two classes, those who grin
> Vacant and lopsidedly,
> Who've given in,
> And the rest of us who grin
> To prove he isn't there,
> The worm within.

It would be a sentence of death to go on. A conscious and measured decision. But it had been so for his brothers at Beit Shean, or on the sea front of Tel Aviv, or at Nahariya. They had stayed to die, accepted its inevitability. He felt a great calmness now. The tears ceased to roll on his face; deep in his belly the tightness had gone.

Mackowicz did not inform David Sokarev that a visitor had arrived at the hotel expecting to take breakfast with the scientist. He was left in his room, playing with the toast and the little packages of butter and the plastic marmalade jars, unaware of the heated dispute being fought out in the lobby. When the tall, white-haired, upright figure of Sir Humphrey Talbot, Fellow of the Royal Society, glasses half-moon and far down the bridge of his nose, had come to the reception desk and asked for the Israeli's room number, a Special Branch man had folded the newspaper he had been reading and walked to Sir Humphrey's shoulder, indicating to the girl behind the desk, with a regular shake of his head, that the information should not be given.

"Can I help you, sir?" His voice was pitched low, inaudible to the other guests who milled about the counter, handing in keys, seeking directions, writing traveler's checks.

"I don't think so." He turned back toward the girl. "Young lady, I was asking you the room number where Professor Sokarev is staying."

"He's not taking visitors, sir," said the detective.

"And who might you be?" snapped the other man, already in poor humor at the frustration of the delay coupled with the early hour he had risen in order to travel from his university home in Cambridge to keep the appointment.

"Detective Sergeant Harvey, Special Branch, Scotland Yard. I'm afraid the professor is not able to see anyone this morning. It's a very clear instruction we've had, sir. I hope you haven't been inconvenienced."

"Of course I've been damn well inconvenienced. I've come up from the country to see the man. I have a letter from him inviting me." Sir Humphrey reached into his faded leather briefcase, rifled through the papers, and with a look of triumph on his face, produced a single-page letter. "There, read that. Very simple, I would have thought. Clearly typed and with his signature at the bottom, on headed paper from Dimona."

The detective read it through, motioned for the visitor to wait, and picked up a house phone. He spoke quickly and out of Sir Humphrey's earshot, put the receiver down, and came back to Sir Humphrey's side. "One of the professor's colleagues will be down to see you directly, sir. To explain the position."

"But he's traveling on his own. It says so in the letter . . ."

"I think you will find that things have changed somewhat, sir, in the last few hours. Have you seen a newspaper this morning?"

"Of course I haven't. Not read one, anyway—just glanced. Been traveling, haven't I?"

"If you had, perhaps it would be clearer to you, sir."

The lift door opened and Mackowicz emerged. His coat had been hurriedly put on, tangling with his shirt collar. At least he's hiding his bloody shoulder holster, bloody cowboy, thought the detective. Might have shaved by this time in the morning.

Mackowicz read the letter, and handed it back. "I regret that your journey had been unnecessary. Professor Sokarev is receiving no visitors before his speech this evening. I am sorry."

Sir Humphrey's voice rose in anger. "But this is absolutely ridiculous, damned ridiculous. I've traveled halfway across southern England to get here at the professor's invitation, and you, without even the courtesy of introducing yourself, tell me I shouldn't have come. What sort of nonsense is this?"

"My name is Mackowicz, I am with the professor's party. I can only repeat my apologies that you were not forewarned by our embassy that it would be impossible for Professor Sokarev to keep his appointment with you."

"I demand to speak to him on the telephone. He's an old friend."

"That, too, I am afraid will not be possible. He is taking no calls. I am sorry, sir."

Sir Humphrey was not used to being spoken to in such a way. He was accustomed to deference, a smoothing of his way. He was uncertain how to react toward the young man, with his open shirt and the casual leatherjacket and a day's growth on his chin, who met his gaze so unswervingly.

"Well, when in heaven's name will I be able to see him?"

"Are you going to the professor's speech this evening?"

"Of course I'm going. I'm chairing the damned thing."

"There will be an opportunity then," said Mackowicz. "I see from the professor's letter that he was expecting you to drive him to his speech this evening. That, too, I am afraid has been changed. But at the university you will have an opportunity to meet with him and talk."

"And perhaps you would be so kind as to inform me the reason for this lunatic carry-on."

The detective sergeant handed him a morning paper. "You seem not to have taken in the headlines, sir. Perhaps that will help you to understand our problems . . ."

"Of course I've seen the papers, but you're not for a moment considering that I pose a threat to—"

Mackowicz cut him off. "Because of the situation, it has been decided that the professor will receive no visitors. There are no exceptions." He went back to the lift and disappeared.

Flushed with embarassment, Sir Humphrey walked to the door, and the Special Branch officer settled again in his chair, molding into the background, inconspicuous and unnoticed.

Four floors above, Sokarev had finished with his breakfast and was pacing dejectedly about the room. Elkin was now asleep and Mackowicz made poor company. More than an hour to go before the typist came from the embassy to take the dictation for his speech, but that at least would be a diversion, would distract him from the company of the young men and their submachine guns and radios who shuffled about with their fixed humorless stares. The speech would take the morning to prepare, and after that perhaps he could sleep. There would be many distinguished men of learning to hear him in the evening; he wished to be at his best and most incisive. An afternoon rest would help.

Jimmy slept late, deep in a meaningless dream that involved images of the countryside, hedgerows, overgrown fields and the animals who made their homes there. He fought to retain it against the ever-increasing competition of the daylight that surged an uninterrupted assault through the window, curtains not drawn. Silly bitch, he thought when he woke up, always leaves them open; probably undresses there as well, right in front of the glass, handing out orgasms to half Holborn.

He hadn't noticed it when he'd come back to the flat. Stayed up too long. Too much talking with Jones before going to the hotel and to Richmond. Bloody man didn't seem to want him to go. Wants to be loved, Jimmy could see that, lonely boss man with all the chaos piling up on his desk and having to rely on someone else to steer him through it. Jones under strain, talking more than he usually did, fidgeting with his pipe and pulling at the skin at the graft points below his mouth, reddening and irritating the lines. And he'd wished him luck when Jimmy went on his way. Never done that before. It had been a bit ridiculous, a sort of paternal send-off, and Jimmy not three years younger and as much in his twilight as the other man.

The girl was still sleeping. One of them always was; seemed the most consistent fact about their life together. They laughed about it to each other, and cursed privately. She looked good, always did when she was asleep, and too vulnerable to be wakened. She'd be late already for the dingy room where she spent her days sandwiched between Jones's office and the corridor. He wouldn't wake her yet. Jones could wait and it wouldn't do any harm, slave labor he had from the girl. Jimmy told her that often enough, and she ignored him. Jones could get impatient for one morning, wouldn't take her so much for granted.

He reached across her prone form, careful not to disturb her and deny to the girl the deep relaxation of sleep that showed in the way her mouth had drifted open, awkward but at peace, too many teeth showing. Not at your best, sweetheart. There were lines, beside her lips, alongside her eyes, under her chin, that in a few hours would be camouflaged by the cosmetics. Jimmy wasn't concerned with that; the rivulets of age that were forming on her features caused him no dismay.

From the bedside table he lifted the telephone receiver and dialed the number of the hotel where Sokarev was staying. When it was connected to the top-floor rooms where the Israelis were encamped, Jimmy recognized Elkin's voice, softer and more conciliatory than the other bastard's. He sounded cheerful, said they'd had an uneventful night, that their charge had awakened, taken his breakfast, and was now working on his speech for the evening.

"And no visitors, under any circumstances, right?" Jimmy said.

"That is the instruction. A guy came and wanted to see him, a scientist. Mack dealt with it. He was a bit bothered, but left."

Jimmy shuddered at the prospect. He could imagine the tact that the gorilla would have employed to make his point. He said, "I'll be down quite soon. A few things to sort out, but it'll be before lunch, and for God's sake, no room service or anything sent up from the kitchens direct to the room. If he wants something, he'll either have to do without or you get it yourselves."

"There's enough of your police outside the door to serve a banquet, cook it, and wash the dishes afterwards."

"Don't worry about them. They're there to make up the numbers, make the circus look good. Do it yourself. I'll be there in an hour."

Jimmy crawled out of his bed and made for the bathroom, out through the door and across the corridor. There wasn't much else of the flat, just a kitchen. Bachelor Towers, and he wanted it that way. Needed someone like Helen to visit once or twice a week, and clean the place up while she was waiting for him. But not to live there, they'd be on top of each other, argumentative, pulling hair out, claustrophobic. It was not a bad arrangement. Gave each sufficient companionship and the mimimum of commitment.

Those in the Department who knew them both and who knew of the limitations of the arrangement put the bond down to a mutual passed-over loneliness. Jimmy would have denied that, probably violently. Helen would have smiled and changed the conversation. It was generally agreed amongst their friends that neither allowed the relationship to impair their individual effectiveness at the Department.

After he'd shaved, and scrubbed with his toothbrush to eradicate the taste of last night's whiskey and the cigarettes, he dressed. He did it slowly and with thought, as if getting himself prepared for an important engagement, an interview for a new job, an evening out with a girl friend. But it was the clothes themselves that let him down. His trousers were heavily creased, not just at the seams down his legs, but all over, a legacy of the nighttime hours that they had lain crumpled on the carpet after he had kicked them off. The shirt that he chose was clean, not worn yesterday, but it had been on his back for many other days before that and the collar showed the frayed outline where the cotton had rubbed against the unshaven bristles on his neck. A button was missing, but would be hidden by his tie. The socks were clean, unholed, perfect, and he could smile quietly and secretly to himself as he pulled them on— three pairs he'd bought, one of his few concessions to the semi-domestication Helen had tried to enforce on him. Beside the bed were his shoes, brown and lace-ups. The toes were scuffed and needed the attention of polish and a duster. He pulled the handkerchief from his trouser pocket, checked to see that Helen was still asleep, and then rubbed the white cloth square hard across the leather. She'd seen him do that once and screamed a protest. His habits hadn't changed, only the discretion that he employed.

From the drawer of the table on which the telephone stood, he took the pistol he had drawn from Leconfield House and the shoulder-holster apparatus that was his own. The holster, of strengthened black plastic, fitted across his upper back and chest like a carthorse harness. It had been made to fit, and until he placed the gun itself in the pouch provided, he was hardly aware of the straps that looped around his arms and across his back. But the gun gave the holster a weight and presence. His jacket hung across the chair he had draped it over, and when that was worn, the PPK and its props were decisively hidden. Same time as yesterday—RAF Escapers Club. Nothing dramatic for the motif, just a pelican bird, and not many who would pass Jimmy on the street and know its meaning.

He shook her shoulder, gently and with kindness that few who knew him casually would have believed he possessed.

"Wake up, girl, time to be on our way."

"What time is it?" She said it sleepily, resisting the intrusion, eyes squinting into the sudden light.

"Bit after nine."

"You pig," she shouted, scrambling from the warm security of the bedclothes.

"It's a beautiful sight to start the day with." Jimmy was laughing as she struggled to cover her thighs and breasts with the scraps of lace and nylon that she scooped from the chair near her side of the bed.

"You're a pig, Jimmy. A mean, miserable, bloody pig. All

bloody dressed yourself, and not calling me. Jones'll be off his bloody rocker when I drift in at this time." She wriggled her long legs into the trousers she had worn the day before. Jimmy didn't like her keeping spare clothes at the flat, so what she arrived in the previous night she went out with the next morning.

"Won't do him any harm, let him sweat a bit," Jimmy said.

She said nothing else, fiercely concentrating on her dressing and then the attack on her face in front of the mirror. Hunched over it, eyes intent on the reflection as she worked the pencils and brushes around her eyes. The lipstick she put on with a bravado that ensured disaster. There was a low oath, in a pitch she seldom used, as she tidied the indulgence with a flick of the Kleenex tissue that had remained overnight on the dressing table.

"Are you coming down to the speech tonight?" Jimmy asked as they stood on the pavement beside her Maxi car.

"Only if I'm needed. I don't want to be there just to rubberneck. I don't know whether Jones is going."

"I'd like you to come, might want the car there. If I've one from the Department, I'm saddled with the damned thing. If you come, slot in behind the convoy, and when we've dumped the little bugger back in his bed we can shove off somewhere. I can call you later on."

"There cannot be much chance of Jones going. He may want to be at the Yard, or by his phone, but it's not like him just to be there if there's no purpose to it. There's enough of the thickies, you included, lined up for the evening without him shoving in and getting in the way."

"Whether he comes or not, I'd like you to be there with the car."

She unlocked the driver's door and sat far back into the seat, and as she fastened the safety belt across her chest she said quietly and with a suspicion of mockery, "Want me to see the hero boy in action? Roy of the Rovers defies Amazing Odds. Triumph of Virtue. Good wins Through. That it, Jimmy boy?" When it came to needling Jimmy she was the great expert, few could compete with her.

"Bugger off to your boring office," he shouted. "I'll call you, and I want you there. If you want a bloody meal on the house, that is."

The car was away and lost in the traffic, leaving Jimmy searching the street for a black cab.

They were not easy to find in the final throes of the capital's rush hour, and he paced impatiently for a full fifteen minutes before he could hail one and then sprint a weaving path between the oncoming cars to the other side of the road where the driver waited for him.

When they were on the move Jimmy sagged deep into the seat, peering, half aware of the scurrying masses going about their business beyond the window. This was the ideal guerrilla country, the perfect territory on which to wage the sharp and cruel form of warfare that the enemy had perfected. Thousands of faces were swept past his vision from the window, their preoccupation with their own affairs total, their knowledge of the threat minuscule. The perfect unnoticing hiding ground, where anonymity remains a virtue. In this huge, diverse antlike society, what hope could there ever be of selecting out just two who were different from the rest by virtue of the fact that they had declared hostilities? Where to find them, where to start to look? Impossible, thought Jimmy.

There can be only one killing ground. The one right beside David Sokarev. Not ten yards from him, or even five, but right up against his shoulder, poor little bastard, that'll be the killing ground. Jimmy felt no sense of fear at the prospect of physical injury. What screwed up his guts into that tight cold mindless state of apprehension was the possibility of failure. It always dogged him, that horror. That he could end up as the ultimate loser. He could picture the little man with the blood and the surprise in his face, and the look of betrayal that would dominate his eyes. That would be the awfulness for Jimmy. The unmentionable and unspeakable disaster, if he lost Sokarev.

By the time he reached the hotel, where he would spend the rest of the day before leaving for the Senate House, the very image of failure and the chance of it that had crossed his mind had rendered him irritable and tense.

From where he crouched inside the small car Famy saw McCoy appear around the corner from the street and walk warily toward their hiding place. Twice he looked behind, to satisfy himself he was not under surveillance. He jogged the last ten yards to the car.

Under his arm was a brown paper bag, and he reached inside his pocket on the left of his trousers when he reached the window through which Famy stared at him. McCoy took in the numbed astonishment in the other's face, and the sad, emotion-drained look in his mouth.

"I've got the keys. No problem, an old fool in a garage up the road, spilled him a yarn and had them straightaway. Got the whole bunch and said I'd return them later. Piece of cake. I've got the gloves we need for the window too, motor-cycle sort, with protection halfway up the arm. Made of leather and bloody expensive. Hope your mob are good on expenses."

McCoy laughed, then let the humor dissolve as Famy's face failed to react. "What's the matter?" he said. "You look like someone's just parachuted you into bloody Jerusalem."

"I thought you'd gone," Famy whispered, frightened of the words but with no option but to speak them.

" 'Course I'd bloody gone," said McCoy. "I told you last night we'd need the keys. You said we'd need gloves. What's special about that?"

"I thought you'd gone for all time. That you were not coming back."

McCoy spat back at him, "How many times do I have to fucking well tell you? We're in this fuck-up together. I've told you that. For once in your suspicious, miserable life, try believing what you're told." He stomped around the car, angry, kicking at a tin and clattering it away across the stones and debris of the site.

Famy climbed out of the car. "I'm sorry," he said. "It was shameful to doubt you. I am abject to you." He paused, let the seconds of confrontation flitter away. "How do we spend the rest of the day?"

McCoy nodded. He had the imagination to feel the Arab's sentiments on waking in the empty car. "I should have woken you. Forget it now. We stay for the rest of the day. It's as good as anywhere. We'll go direct from here to the Senate. No sense in just moving about unnecessarily. What we need now is some bloody sleep. I don't want to be yawning and looking for my bed tonight."

*   *   *

The few tourists who had gathered on the pavement across the road were all unaware of the identity of the man who stepped from the black Humber car and hurried into the extended and tranquil-lit hallway of 10 Downing Street. No better informed was the police constable at the door, nor the morning-suited usher who glanced from the proffered card to the book listing the day's appointments with the Prime Minister, and matched the printed name on the card he had been given with the typed list that rested on the lobby table.

The Director General was taken by lift to the flat on the top floor that the country's senior politician had turned into a miniature home when pressure of work prevented him from using his more substantial town house. It was well known that the Prime Minister's wife disliked having her living rooms tramped by civil servants and members of Parliament and visiting delegations, and so when her husband had early business to conduct he slept "over the shop," as he delighted to tell those who called on him at the start of his day.

He was at breakfast, but immaculate and ready to present a public face, with the only concession to informality being the absence of a jacket to cover his waistcoat. As he pushed the marmalade onto his edged squares of toast he motioned to the head of the counterespionage force to take a chair opposite and pushed the china coffee jug in his direction.

"I've seen the Home Secretary this morning," the Prime Minister said. "He's told me what the police are doing concerning the professor and his problems. I wanted to know your feelings about the affair as we go into these crucial hours. No minutes to be kept or anything like that, just your opinions, and what your own Department's state of readiness is. That sort of thing."

The memoir business that retiring political leaders entered into with such enthusiasm on retirement was sufficient to keep the Director General on his guard. He regarded the Prime Minister's request for information as legitimate, but saw no need to expand at too great length.

He chose a cautious path, describing what the other man already knew. He started with the police operation at the hotel, listed the precautions that would be taken to transport Sokarev across the city. Official-style decoy car driving from the hotel at

high speed, while the target left via the kitchens in a closed
police van, switching to a more formal type of transport in the
concealed yard of Tottenham Court Road police station before
arriving at a normally locked side entrance at the university's
main building. He spoke of the scale of the escort that would be
used during the transit period, and also of the numbers of men
on guard at the building, and of the search procedures that had
been adopted inside and outside the hall where Sokarev was to
speak. He mentioned the gelignite-sniffer Labradors, and the
metal detectors that plainclothes troops had employed before
the room was sealed the previous night. He talked of the police
liaison that had been set up with his own Department. He went
into the degree to which invitation holders to the lecture had
been vetted, and lingered for a moment on the problems of
body searches without giving offense to the members of some
of the most learned institutions of the country. He touched on
the convoy and the protection screen that would be used to
return the professor to his hotel. And then he stopped and
waited for the Prime Minister's questions, which were not slow
in following.

"Well, that covers the police side of things. Everything in fact
that the Secretary of State told me. What are you doing?"

The Director General was in no hurry. His long pauses could
be infuriating and he knew it, but he did nothing to alter the
pace at which he delivered his answers. "I have the men who
head the various departments involved in constant meeting,
and they have a liaison line to Scotland Yard. We have endeav-
ored to provide the Metropolitan force with all information,
relevant information, that is at our disposal."

"Do you have a man on the ground with Sokarev?"

"I have a man right beside him. He is my direct liaison with
the police protection force and with the Israeli Foreign Ministry protection team that is accompanying Sokarev."

"What sort of man?"

"Experienced," said the Director General.

"Experienced in what? Running an office, liaison, Arab
affairs?"

"He's a marksman."

The Prime Minister stared directly at the DG. A piece of toast
remained uneaten and hand-held half an inch from his mouth.

"There are enough police there for that, surely? I would have thought that you would have put a senior man with liaison capabilities rather than a gunman."

The Director General was patient, leading a small boy through an algebraic problem that he might one day answer, but not in this school year. "I have placed a gunman, as you describe it, alongside Sokarev because the greatest risk to the life of our guest is close-range shooting. The man I have there is far advanced to anything the Metropolitan police can provide. He will not be taking a subordinate role in this day's movements . . ."

"It would seem," said the Prime Minister, "from the way you have dispensed your priorities that you regard an act of violence as a major possibility."

For the first time since he had sat down the DG poured himself a cupful of now lukewarm coffee. Before he began to drink it, he said. "Considering the known opposition, I regard it as an inevitability."

Fifteen

As David Sokarev walked through the door of the lecture room in the Senate House building of London University, he came unnoticed. He was late, and the attention of the three hundred men who made their living from the study of nuclear physics had long since been diverted from the huddle of plain-clothes policemen with their bulging suits who blocked the only entrance.

He was close to halfway down the side of the room and heading toward the table adorned only with a stand microphone and a glass water jug that sat on a tray between four glasses, when those that he had passed reacted to the short figure in the grey suit who shuffled past them, hemmed in like a convict by the taller and more heavily set bodyguards who jockeyed for space at his side. There were few who had come to listen who had not read their morning papers, listened to radio news broadcasts, or watched a television news bulletin. All day the headlines had blared the information that a major terrorist plot existed with the sole purpose of assassinating the scientist who was now making his way the length of the room. Those who first recognized him, from the pictures they had seen in the last few hours or who had met him in the past, rose from their seats and began to clap. Within seconds the entire room had taken their cue from those who had initiated the applause. The noise spilled into a cheer, self-conscious at first, from men used to working in silence and unaccustomed to venting their thoughts in such public manner. Those that were close enough saw the sad eyes of Sokarev, saw his tongue run with anxiety over his lips, seeking to moisten their desert dryness. Perhaps the acclamation confused him, but as he turned to look behind to gauge the size of the room, his feet entangled the one with the other and he pitched forward a few inches before one of the many hands of the men who surrounded him arrested his stumble.

By the time he reached the table, everyone in the room, excepting the security men, was standing, pulping palms together in a concerted gesture of solidarity. The smile that dawned on his face was one of helpless gratitude. He tried not to look as they beamed and shouted their support for him; instead, contenting himself with cleaning his spectacles, and when that was exhausted, sorting his notes for the address.

It all meant little to Jimmy.

He had permitted Mackowicz and Elkin to flank the scientist and had positioned himself a pace or so behind. That had been the inner yoke of the shell around the Israeli. Beyond had been the Special Branch men, six of them, two carloads who could get no closer than five to six feet from the man they had been ordered to protect. Now the shell fragmented as the guards moved to their appointed places, where they would stay for the time Sokarev was in the room. The only door had been locked behind him, a plainclothes and unmistakable police guard on either side and equipped with walkie-talkie personal sets to coordinate any turning of the key. There could be no sudden and surprise entry from that quarter.

The two Israelis were at the raised table: Elkin standing to the side where the door was located; Mackowicz opposite and close to the windows now draped in long brown-velveteen curtains. Jimmy saw that Mackowicz had brought his mackintosh; warm summer evening, clear sky, indisputable weather forecast of sunshine for at least the next three days. The coat, held across his thighs, meant the Uzi was concealed there. Wonder if the bugger's put the catch off, thought Jimmy, cocked the bloody thing. Down the long walls that stretched the length of the room were four of the Branch men, two on each side. Remaining two at the far end, facing Sokarev and the committee that had assembled to host the meeting. Nine armed and trained men in the room. Has to be enough, Jimmy said to himself, has to guarantee it. But the knowledge that Mackowicz had the submachine gun grasped in his right hand aggravated him. Without permitting anyone in the packed ranks of seats to observe his action, he drew the PPK from his holster and held it low behind him against the wall, separating buttock from plaster, and positioned himself so that he faced the windows and could see Sokarev to his left and the men by the door to his right.

When the silence at last settled on the hall, the chairman rose to speak. He had already glanced at Mackowicz with as great a force of anger and contempt as he could command. He found no reaction, but his experience of the morning in the hotel lobby still stung at the vanity that he so rarely displayed.

"Ladies and gentlemen." He threw his voice to the back of the hall, correctly gauging that some of the elderly might have difficulty hearing in spite of the amplification system. "It gives me the very greatest of pleasure to welcome to our gathering this evening that most distinguished of colleagues from the State of Israel, Professor David Sokarev." He paused, and the clapping began immediately and with great fervor, till, Christ-like, he raised his hands to quell it. "I think we are all aware that the professor has done us a great honor in coming to visit us. If we believe only a half of what we read in our daily journals, then there is no doubt in my mind that Professor Sokarev has displayed great courage in coming to our shores to honor this engagement. I think we can accept that in the highest offices of our land the dangers that Professor Sokarev is running are believed to be genuine. Witness the number of gentlemen with us this evening who, I regret wholeheartedly, are going to find this evening's lecture extremely tedious."

There was a ripple of laughter as the greyed and balding heads of the audience strayed around the walls, searching out the men, with their close-cuts and the two-button suits and suede shoes, who stared back at them. But the laughter did not last, and it was at best brittle and nervous. The presence of the interlopers was a factor beyond the experience of the men who had come to listen to the professor.

"Because of the difficulties that have surrounded Professor Sokarev since his arrival here, I myself have not yet had the opportunity of speaking to him, but when I extended the invitation that he should come and talk to us, I suggested he might care to discuss in our company the distinguished work connected with lasers that has been associated with his name. Now, whether that is what he has eventually decided on, I do not know . . ."

It was clear the chairman had more to say, and Jimmy was prepared to shut out the rest. The gun, he had now decided, was unnecessary. It could rest as easily in the holster, enough of the bloody melodrama. He turned to the wall, as a child does when it wishes to urinate out of sight of the adults. With the PPK again weighted against his chest, he faced back into the room, wondering how many had seen his movement. The speech of introduction droned its course, Jimmy's attention lost. He felt himself beginning to relax. Two moments of priority danger, he told himself, and one already successfully negotiated. Arrival and Departure. Those were the hitting times for the opposition. Not in here, not with the screened and searched and checked-out audience. The Departure would be the time for maximum vigilance—not Jimmy's phrase but Jones's. And Helen was out there waiting. Soft and comfortable. She'd follow them back to the hotel, and when they'd dropped Sokarev off, all tucked up in his pit, they'd go back to the flat together, and stay awake together.

The policemen who were beyond the locked door, outside in the corridor, shared Jimmy's feelings. They had formed a close knot together, sufficiently at ease to light up their cigarettes and talk about the ordinariness that dominated their lives. Mortgage rates were swapped, the cost of holidays, gossip about superiors and deskmen. And in the creeping darkness beside the towering shape of Britain's largest university complex, the officers posted there also felt an easing of the tension that had gripped and alerted them at the time the professor had driven to the building. There would be ample warning of his exit. Then the pocket radios would chatter and there would be the noise of the car engines revving. Time enough to supervise their closely chosen watching points. One group had gathered at the main entrance, dwarfing and formidable. Another had drawn together by the side door through which Sokarev had entered the building. From neither position was it possible to view the windows of the lecture hall, as that part of the building butted out too far for them to see beyond its corners.

The constable who had been assigned the duty of watching those windows lay now at McCoy's feet. He had not been armed, and even if he had carried a gun, it is doubtful whether he would have had the opportunity to use it. Nor had he spoken into his radio, attached to his tunic lapel, before the crashing blow came down on the soft rear area of his head, below the line of his reinforced helmet and where skull base and vertebrae joined. It had been mercilessly simple . . . Famy advancing with his tourist map, stuttering in ineffective English, distracting the constable's attention as they peered together at the street divisions while McCoy moved cougar-quick with the metal tube of plumber's piping. The thieves' charter of keys McCoy had gained at the garage in the morning were next employed. A parked car opened, hand brake suppressed, and the vehicle pushed in silence to the place of the scratched star underneath the window.

Famy saw that the Irishman never looked at the sprawled figure beneath him. Again the glossy coldness that meant there would be no hesitation at the moment of contact, and all who trespassed in the way, obliterated without concern. It was as he would be when the time of firing came. Famy was aware of the flooding excitement bursting through him. Now at last they would savor victory, triumph over endless obstacles. It was the ultimate moment of his mission.

McCoy said, quietly and slowly, so that he would not have to repeat it, "There's been one round of clapping. That's the entry. The next one means he's on his feet. We go, straight then."

Famy extended the shoulder rest of the M-1, locked it in its extended position, checked that the magazine was in place, cocked the gun quickly and fearfully lest the noise of the mechanism arouse curiosity, eased the safety catch.

Beside him McCoy had pulled the heavy black glove onto his right hand, the metal tube grasped in the grotesque finger-shapes. But no gun. Famy saw he had picked up no weapon.

"You should have the other M1 with you," he hissed, amplifying his worry.

"No need. Your pigeon now, remember? I'm going to give

you the clear shot; then it's all yours, baby boy."

"It will be a famous success for our people . . ."

"Keep that fucking nonsense till you've hit the bastard."

They heard the swell of applause build behind the blackness of the curtain, prolonged fierce clapping and shouts. Famy went up the back of the car and onto the roof, which bent and heaved under his weight. Needed to steady himself with the free hand, nerves gripping at his legs. McCoy came the other way, climbing over the hood and stretching up past the windshield till both stood together, uncertain of balance on the shifting platform. They were exactly above the mark Famy had drawn against the wall, and level with the join of the curtains.

The Irishman pushed his face close to Famy's. "Remember it, then. When I've done the window and got the curtain back, he'll be forty-five degrees to you. And don't bugger about. If they all start blasting, chuck the sods the grenades. Right?"

He waited for Famy to bring the rifle up to his shoulder in the aim position, waited till it was snug against the shoulder and the right cheek, then smashed the tubing into the expanse of glass. Famy winched away from the noise, as McCoy's fist, protected by the glove, beat at the obstinate and remaining slivers still fastened in the mortarwork of the frame. The hand grabbed for the curtain and pulled it back, and instinctively Famy lunged forward, still in the fire posture, raking the brightness of the room for his target.

Where was he? Where was the whore? Which was the one he sought? Which of the uncomprehending, blank faces that had turned and now stayed motionless and transfixed, peering at the source of the commotion? The clarity was not long coming. The man who stood at the table while all around him sat, the man who had begun to cower, who knew the blow was near and sought to avoid it, who could not urge his muscles to follow the racing orders of his brain. That one—that one was Sokarev.

Famy steadied to fire. Aiming for the chest where the white shirt and the dark tie disappeared into the greyness of the suit. So big, so easy, through the shape of the gunsight.

"Speed it up, for Christ's sake," screamed McCoy, and as the finger closed round the trigger, squeezing as he'd been told, Famy twisted his gaze to the agony of impatience on the Irishman's face.

When he looked back he saw the man at the far end of the

table thrusting a way toward Sokarev, and the man closer to
him was wrestling with a coat, swinging the billowed shape of
it up toward his shoulder.

Famy fired.

As the curtain exploded with the noise of the breaking glass,
Jimmy's hand moved to the holster under the breast pocket of
his jacket. His fingers found the harshness of the handle, fasten-
ing on the ridging to aid his grip. Then there was the protruding
gun barrel, barely thirty feet from him. The pistol was coming
fast, out in front, arm extended, level with the eyes as he heard
the shout from far in the night, and then the first shot. Fractionally later Jimmy pulled the hair trigger, without finesse and
conscious of the need not for accuracy but for a volume of shots.
Some were to hit the curtain, some to disappear he knew not
where.

Jimmy fired six times, shouting all the time in the direction
of Sokarev, "Get him down. Get the bloody man on the floor.
Get him under the table."

Elkin reached the scientist first, taking off in a leap when still
five feet from him, pinioning Sokarev to the floor amongst the
tangle of chair and table supports and feet. Jimmy saw the
chairman sag in his chair and his upper torso fall forward, casually and without effort, onto the open surface of the table.

Again and again the rifle at the window fired, and with each
succeeding shot Jimmy was surer in his knowledge. "He's
missed, the little motherfucker, and he knows it." Almost a
shout, exhilaration at the contact, half-smile playing on the
mouth, but the eyes, cold, focused, taking in the scene around
him.

The two Branch men along the same wall as Jimmy had
begun to fire, not standing, but crouched, in the taught posture,
classic but slower. He's not going to take it, too much for him,
it'll finish him, the little rat, thought Jimmy. He saw Sokarev far
under the table, Elkin covering him, saw Mackowicz bring the
Uzi to his shoulder, rid himself of that bloody useless coat, and
he began to make for the door. He had reached it, elbowing
aside the policemen, shouting for the door to be opened above
the nerve-shattering noise of the long burst fired by Mackowicz,
when from the corner of his eye he saw the puny dark-grey and

rounded shape loop its way from the window toward the table. Mackowicz, far back in the room, shouted the one terrifying, choked word: "Grenade!"

Seemingly consumed with inertia, it bounced on the floor between the table and the front row of the audience's seats, made a gentle parabola before bouncing again and then rolling unevenly, because it was not a perfect sphere, toward the shelter of the table where Elkin protected Sokarev. Mackowicz jumped for it. There was a moment when he was airborne and Jimmy could see the grenade wobbling, nearly stationary, then it was gone underneath the big body. Stillness, fractional but complete. Then Mackowicz was lifted high toward the ceiling. Jimmy did not see him fall; he was through the door, now unlocked, and running toward the main entrance.

The detonation of the grenade was still battering in Jimmy's ears as he went down the corridor through the confusion of the milling policemen. Because the shots and the explosion had come from inside the lecture room, every man, in or out of uniform, saw it as his duty to crowd as close as was physically possible to the source of the gunfire. Behind Jimmy, as he shouldered his way through the advancing charge, was the cry for "Stretchers!" He knew where to go. Dug his heels into the soft gravel immediately outside the doorway, ran out into the night and to his left, and then swerved again to get himself along the side of the building and to the marksman's position. In the shadows far in front he saw two men jump from the roof of a parked car and start to run for the low boundary wall that separated the university precincts from Malet Street and the free-flow traffic. Still sprinting, Jimmy fired—stupid, really, carried away with the cowboy game, only one shot, and the magazine was expended. There was a shot in return, wide and high and to the right, barely close enough for him to distinguish the "crack" that signaled incoming. As his finger moved uselessly on the trigger, bringing home the message of his wastefulness, he slowed, couldn't get close now, not with an empty bloody shooter. Across the road he heard the frantic, piercing sound of dispute, and the noise, belatedly, of a car being revved. Jimmy was panting now, out of condition, not enough time in the gym, striving to fill his lungs with air.

"Helen. Helen. Where in God's name are you?"

It seemed deep eternity before the car pulled up sharp alongside him.

"Get out. Get out of the bloody thing." His voice came in short, staccato bursts. She hesitated, disorientated by the distant noise of gunfire and now the heaving wild-eyed form of Jimmy.

"Get out, you stupid bitch. Get out of the bloody car."

She began to unfasten the clasp of the safety belt worn across her body. Always in position however far she went, a reflex. Jimmy wrenched open the door and took hold of the collar of her coat and pulled her from the wheel. One action, out of the seat and clear of the door. The background cacophony: of police whistles blowing, of a radio screeching with static, of orders being bellowed. Jimmy had taken her place and the car was already spinning in a full one-hundred-and-eighty-degree half-circle as he headed for the one gap in the wall and toward where he had seen the running men and the starting car.

Seventy yards in front, the Cortina struck out into the mainstream. It was a labored movement, that of a winged animal, one certain in the knowledge that it must escape but with its limbs damaged and impaired. Jimmy heaved with relief. He was in contact; the vacuum space between the cars would lessen. He cut right from the center of the road to avoid a racing police car, light revolving, siren at volume, traveling in the other direction. Flashed his headlights, but it was past him, his gesture unseen by driver or navigator. No system of communication from Helen's car, no radio telephone. He pulled out again, avoided the bus that lumbered in front and cursed that the girl had purchased a slow-acceleration family car. But the gap would close.

The Cortina went through the traffic lights on red and was in Goodge Street, long, Georgian and geometric, heading south. Jimmy followed, was faintly aware of the car that skidded to an emergency stop to avoid collision, and settled himself easily into the seat. Not good yet, Jimmy, had you with your pants on your knees, not often it goes that way, but it'll get better, and the little bastards up front'll wonder what hit them. The PPK rested on his lap. Another magazine was in his jacket, right pocket. He would wait for an opportunity to reload.

*   *   *

They had run from the window close together. Famy with his head bent around, covering the area behind them, the small rifle ready to fire, ready to head off pursuit. McCoy leading, with his right arm pressed hard against the upper shoulder.

When Famy had turned once to fire away into the distance, McCoy had savagely pulled him forward, destroying his aim. "It's bloody distance we have to have. Hang on here and we're screwed." The words sobbed out, but with little tone as they emerged from the clamped and pain-creased mouth.

When they reached the Cortina, McCoy had thrust his left hand across his body into the opposite trouser pocket and pulled clear the laden key ring. It took him several seconds to select the one he wanted, small and bright and fresh-cut. He tossed it to Famy. "You drive," he said, and flung open the passenger door, left unlocked when they had parked there barely forty minutes earlier; should have left the keys in the ignition and all.

Famy had the rifle to his shoulder. It was small, a child's toy, too insignificant to be a killing weapon. The people who had paused on the far pavement did not believe in it and now stood and watched. Not with great fear, not petrified beyond movement, curious. He was jolted from the image by McCoy's words.

"Come on, you stupid bloody eejit. You'll have to drive."

Still Famy held the rifle up, peering over its sights, watchful of pursuit.

"Shift yourself, you bastard."

And Famy lowered the rifle and held it at his side, as a man who walks with a stick and is resting. "I cannot," he said.

McCoy seemed not to have heard him. "Don't piss about. Get behind the bloody wheel."

"I cannot drive." Famy said it slowly. Humiliation abject and total.

" 'Course you can bloody drive." McCoy's voice rose in exasperation and temper.

"I don't know how to. I have never driven."

McCoy waved his right arm in Famy's face. "Can't you see, there's a bloody great bullet in there. Stop farting about and move the car off."

"It is impossible. I have never driven. I cannot."

The monotonous recitation slid home to McCoy. The obscenity he yelled at the Arab was vicious and wounding. McCoy ran around the car and draped himself into the driving seat. He lay his right arm along the wheel for support, and by the street light Famy could see his face whitened and there was the sweat bead of deep hurt on his forehead. With his left hand McCoy inserted the key into the ignition, and then put the car in gear. By pushing his whole body forward he was able to turn the wheel toward the direction of the road before he could bring his left hand into play again with the gear stick.

Famy wondered whether the Irishman would faint. He wound down the passenger window and looked back across the road, rifle aimed again. In his jacket pocket three grenades, he could run his fingers over them. Grip bag in the rear, where it had been left, more ammunition, more grenades, needed the reassurance, and then the car was moving. He cringed as they went through the lights, bracing himself for an impact that did not happen. And another car came through the lights, clearly visible to him, unmistakable.

"Another car followed us." Near-panic, near-hysteria.

"What am I supposed to fucking well do about it?"

"I cannot see it now, not as an individual car, there are just lights."

"Forget it," said McCoy. "If it gets close, blast it. If not, forget it."

McCoy could tell that his concentration was sapping. Felt the weakness drifting uncontrollably over him. The wound itself fascinated him. Little to see, but he glanced obsessively at it. Just the neatly driven hole that lay in the center of the blood patch where the cloth had darkened and stained on the upper forearm. The pain ebbed, rising only when he tried to use the hand, and then sliding into numbness when he rested his fingers on the wheel.

"Did you get the bastard?" McCoy said.

They were successfully on the move now. If he did not have to go fast, and drive under pressure, then he could manage. If there was pursuit . . . There was a vagueness, absence of care, caused by the loss of blood, but that was the option that he did not care to consider.

"I don't know." Little more than a whisper, Famy's reply.

" 'Course you bloody know. Either saw him go down or you

didn't. You know when you've hit a man, the way he goes."
McCoy said it with patronizing knowledge. Seen it at first hand.
The way a man was raised in the air, thrown-up rag doll, and
the way he then slumped out of control, unable to protect his
head. There was a lapse of the coordination that maintained the
living.

"It was difficult to know." Famy paused. Studied the road in
front, the thinning traffic of late evening in Central London,
glanced behind. Only a myriad of jumbled lights, some stationary, some on the move, none so close as to threaten danger.
Famy wanted to explain, wanted the other man to understand.
"I was about to fire at Sokarev when you shouted. There was
distraction. As I fired, there was a man across the room who
began to shoot. One of the men pulled Sokarev under the table.
I was firing all the time he did that, but he was on the ground
and then was gone from my sight. The man who sat beside
Sokarev, he was hit . . ."

"Big deal, they'll be singing and dancing in Beirut if you've
drilled a Brit geriatric."

Almost amused, McCoy, bloody man's discomfiture. And it
was a failure, that much had penetrated to him, through the
cloud and the haze, bloody failure. Without his wound he would
have felt savage hatred at the association with the fiasco, but the
injury dissipated his anger, rendered it obsolete.

". . . There was shooting from the wall facing us. Three or four
men. And the bodyguard near the table, another one, not the
one that went to Sokarev, he had the small machine gun. He
had started to fire when I threw the grenade. The grenade
would have taken Sokarev, but the man fell on it. Then I could
see nothing. He just exploded and then there was smoke. The
men who were shooting had an aim by then, one could not stay
at the window."

"One of those bastards took me." There was finality in
McCoy's words. To Famy it seemed the pain of the inquest was
over, and the car was still moving, McCoy could cope with the
disability. Famy watched the cars behind and those alongside,
but could find nothing to sustain his earlier anxiety. He put the
M-1 on the floor, under his legs, easy to reach but invisible to
any driver who might glance at them casually from an adjacent
car.

McCoy said, and there was the trace of a smile playing at the side of his mouth, "I thought this was the one where you stood up and had yourself counted, where you took Sokarev, or they took you. Bugged out early, didn't we?"

"It was impossible to continue shooting with all the firing from the wall."

"Handgun stuff, not accurate at that range. Lucky shot hit me."

"You started to run, and you were pulling at me."

"But it's not my war, remember? You could have stayed. You were the bloody marksman. Me, just the chauffeur. So why did you do the scamper?"

"I couldn't see any more . . . only the smoke . . . I couldn't aim." But Famy knew they were just words, explanations and excuses. There was no recollection of making a decision to run. Already moving, long before the awareness of it. Never been the moment when he had the choice, choice of life and death.

They had swung to the west now, and the traffic was lighter as they navigated a by-pass route, avoiding the heart of the city. McCoy was able to keep the speedometer flickering a path between twenty and thirty miles an hour.

"They won't react well, your masters. Won't have wanted you hanging about able to fight another day and Mr. bloody Sokarev coming out clean." McCoy was turning the screw. Knew it, and enjoyed the process of demolition. Retribution for his pain.

Famy stayed silent.

"My crowd wouldn't take kindly to it. Not with all the investment. If it's cocked, then it would have been better it had never started. Victory for them, bad news in your parish."

McCoy was talking as if to himself, softly, and winning no response.

"The Provos have their own way if it doesn't work out. If it's yellow, if the bugger sprinted to save his neck, then it's court-martial. Not as formal as all that, nothing pompous. Half a dozen guys—in a barn, in a garage. Sentence comes a bit formal, though. Hood and a pistol shot behind the ear. Leave a note on them too, so the next lot know why."

Famy had his eyes closed, lids tightly drawn together, but unable to shut out the message as McCoy expanded.

"If it's just because they didn't think, mucked the scene, then it's easier. Call it kneecapping. Bullet through each, from the back. They walk again, but they never run, stand out from the crowd because they're on sticks for weeks. The Proddies, the other mob, they're worse . . . use a Black and Decker. It's a drill, used for putting holes in the wall. Takes longer than a bullet, obvious, isn't it?—but they're real bastards those Proddies."

Famy said, "There was one who went into Israel, and came back alone. All the rest were taken or killed, only this one survived, and they found his Kalashnikov had not been fired. And they took him with ten of his friends to the open ground. He had a start of fifty meters, and then his friends began to fire. They all had to shoot, and the guns were checked afterwards, and they were watched to see they did not shoot wide. He did not go many meters, and it only happened once. There was no need for a repetition."

"You'd better think of something good to say," said McCoy. The game had gone far enough. Blood sports when the chase is over are seldom savored.

There were other preoccupations for McCoy. Where to go, what to do about the wound. All men who go to the lonely war, the guerrillas' war, have a common fear, multiplied in their fantasies till its control grips and dominates them. It is the horror of sepsis, of gangrene, of the putrefaction of their flesh. Needed a den, where he could go and curl his legs and watch the entrance, and be safe, and needed it for many days, with hot water and clean towels . . . What to do with the bastard bloody Arab? No place for him in the den, the lair for one only. Perhaps kill him, easiest solution, attractive. Something to think on, half an hour more for the driving, and a decision by then.

The problem engrossed him as he drove, and Famy, too, was quiet, but with what thoughts, McCoy neither knew nor cared.

For a full three minutes after the firing of the last shot Elkin covered Sokarev's body. When the scientist tried to move and shift his suppressed left arm from under his body, the security man firmly pressed him down again flat on the polished boards of the floor. There was a great calmness about Elkin's face, and the eyes were very clear, traversing for any further threat, and outstretched in front of him like an antenna his arm and the service revolver he preferred to the Uzi.

The Branch man who had taken a position nearest the table had bent down and asked the one inevitable question. Was Sokarev hurt? Elkin had shaken his head.

"Keep him there, then," the detective said. "First we'll clear the casualties. Then empty the room. After that we'll work out how to shift him."

Sokarev was aware that his legs were trembling, uncontrollably, the flesh of his upper thighs lapping together, and he was powerless to stop it. He could remember little of what had happened. Just the noise of the window, and then the sight of the shortened barrel of the rifle poking and weaving in the curtain gap, locking onto him. He could recall the moment that Elkin had hit his legs and pulled him down, and then the horrific, unending exchange of gunfire. He had seen Mackowicz dive and lie still and then lift off into the air, and his ears felt pierced by the shock wave of the grenade.

The stretchers came fast. That on which the chairman lay was covered, end to end, by a grey hospital blanket and left at the far end of the room. What remained of Mackowicz was beside. The policeman who had helped the ambulance team to lift the Israeli's disemboweled corpse onto the stretcher had vomited as soon as the pink and softened organs were covered over. The ambulances had come from the University College Hospital less than half a mile away. It was to there that seven casualties were hurried: four suffering from gunshot wounds, one from grenade shrapnel injuries and two from heart attacks.

The detectives had already started to examine the fire position outside the window when one of their number, walking beside the car used as the platform, stumbled on the body of the constable. When they lifted the young man onto the stretcher it was with care, a degree of gentleness, conscious that they were handling their own.

In strange, shuffling silence the guests were ushered from the room and across the wide corridor to a similar lecture hall. Their patience was requested and it was explained to them that though they would not be detained for long, it was impossible that they could be allowed to wander from the building and head for their cars and public transport while the large-scale search of the immediate area of the university was still under way. After the door had been closed on them, few had anything to say. The conflict between Israel and her neighbors was not a thing that many understood; briefly they had been exposed to the unfamiliar. For only a few moments, but the experience would do little to aid their comprehension.

When all had gone Sokarev was helped to his feet. They stood him back to the wall and hemmed in by policemen, Elkin right beside, shoulders rubbing, the gun still in his hand but resting against his trouser pocket.

Later they brought him a glass of water. He found he could scarcely hold it, and Elkin took the glass and put it against the professor's lips and tilted it to such an angle that some spilled from his mouth and dribbled on the front of his suit.

Jones had stayed in his office alone that night. Helen, vague about her movements, had been gone three hours. From a long way down the empty corridors he heard the labored footsteps of the messenger from Communications. Too old to hurry, and why should he in his ignorance of the folded teletype message he carried to Room 3/146. He was a little out of breath when he knocked hesitantly on the outer door, and surprised that the section head had bounced across two offices to be there to snatch the paper from his hand. There were no thanks from the man who now concentrated on what the messenger could see were three bare lines of type.

They didn't tell him much. An attack on Sokarev—unsuccessful, rifle fire and an explosion. Casualties. Large local-scale hunt started for two men—no immediate result. In his office, he sagged back into his chair, reread the message three, four times, looking unsuccessfully for any word of interpretation that he might earlier have missed. And nothing from Jimmy. Where was he when all this was going on? Why hadn't he intervened? Why hadn't he called? Half the reason for the bloody man being there was that he'd be on the bloody phone, so the Department wasn't relying on the police for information. Should have called in. He swiveled half around in his chair and looked at the picture, in deep shadow now because of the angle at which the lights were hung. Pretty little boy, nice smile, big eyes, neat head, looked as harmless as a bloody butterfly, and he'd concealed the wasp sting. Bloody near pulled it off, him and that Irishman. Jones felt a great sadness, which pulled him down, slumped in the shoulders, his head deep in his arms on the table.

What was the bloody point of it all, when all the king's horses and all the king's men could be pushed off center stage by that little rat? Shouldn't have been an equal contest, shouldn't have been allowed to throw the sucker punch, and he had, and bloody near won.

The Soviets sniffing round the defense establishments, or the Czechs, or East Germans . . . they were so straightforward. Bit of a game when you became involved with them. Reckoned on the odds, didn't they, and if they didn't think they could win, they didn't come in. But this little sod, he hadn't worked out his chances of survival, couldn't have, or he'd have stayed at home, and yet he was in there thumping. Jones didn't know what his feelings were toward the young Arab. Probably there was a tinge of admiration, that of the older man for youth. But it was balanced quickly by the anger of frustration that the little bastard had put them through the hoops, and laughed at them and lived.

Had to be brave too, Jones acknowledged that. The old labels weren't any good. Courage if he was from your lot, fanaticism if he was on the other side. He'd learned the futility of the tags when he was still young, when he saw an ME-110 night fighter with its two-man crew peel away in its tail of flame, known they wouldn't survive, and known, too, that they'd pressed their attack long after the chance of success had vanished. They were brave men, and they were the enemy, and they'd earned respect, and been prepared to die. The Arab had been prepared to die, too, as a sacrifice for his army, whatever bunch of twisted idiots they turned out to be. And all such a bloody waste, and everyone scared out of their bloody wits by the implications of it all, everyone except his Jimmy.

The telephone broke in, shrill and insistent, bursting over the quiet room. Helen on the line, chill and matter-of-fact, without emotion or involvement. Jimmy in her car . . . hot pursuit . . . a getaway vehicle disappearing from the scene . . . God only knows where he's gone . . . shots in the street . . . she was coming back to the office. Just the staccato statements, and she'd rung off. Jones put the receiver down. Funny the way she'd used Jimmy's name; usually the laugh when she mentioned him, not this time. Jones had long been sensitive to intonation, emphasis, noted it, and then wondered what the bloody hell she was doing there anyway, and then put it from his mind. Unimportant, silly girl, should have stayed at home, and his thoughts were surging with Jimmy. Just what he would have wanted, Jones thought, the big challenge and the chance to prove himself where all else had failed. And he'd have to kill him, wouldn't he? Have to kill the Arab. Only way now.

Under pressure Jones would normally have resorted to the palliative of work, buried himself in the paper work of the operation, twisted his mind away from the generalities with the specifics of detail. But he had no function now; all out of his hands; nothing he could usefully do. That's how far down those bastards have brought us, he thought, right down to the base area, where the Jimmys are waiting.

He screwed up the teletype message, harshly crumpling the paper in his fist, and tossed it unsuccessfully in the direction of his tin wastebasket.

None of the photographers and television crews who had been covering the arrivals and who were scheduled to film the departures had any worthwhile pictures of the event. Now they crowded against the side door from which they believed the Israeli scientist would emerge. A fierce argument broke out when a police inspector called them to silence and informed the gathering that under no circumstances would flash bulbs or arc lights be permitted. Thirty voices were raised in protest, but when they died, the inspector's message was even more explicit.

"Gentlemen," he said. "I am not prepared to have the person of Mr. Sokarev either impeded or in any way illuminated on this step. If you think about it, there's no way I can say anything else. If you don't play ball, you're down the station, charged, and in court tomorrow, and I wouldn't vouch your cameras will survive."

The Prime Minister, called from the dinner table, suffered three agonizing minutes of uncertainty. The first message relayed to him by the Commissioner, telephoning from Scotland Yard, merely stated that there was heavy shooting and an explosion inside the room where Professor Sokarev was speaking. More details would follow.

He had waited for them alone in his personal office, unwilling to face his guests again before he knew the worst. When the telephone rang again he expected catastrophe, but was told that whereas there were casualties, the professor was not amongst them. There was no more reliable and confirmed information.

He had barely resumed his meal when his parliamentary private secretary brought in a folded slip of paper. The Israeli ambassador was demanding a meeting, and that night.

"Put the bloody man off till the morning," he said, and motioned for the butler to replenish his glass. "Right to the top," he urged.

Sixteen

It satisfied Jimmy that the car he tailed should be unaware of
his presence. Like a marriage, tied together, but neither showing indication of the bond that linked them. They were in
concert, in harmony, elastically held. It was as it should be,
professional but not easy, not one for the kids in the Department, they'd have been up close, blowing the contact. But
Jimmy kept back from the other car, leaving it room to maneu-
ver, far from the bumper and the rear red lights that shone at
him, that gripped his attention. No question of an attempt to
ram or force it off the road. Idiocy if he tried it, would leave him
with two men to handle, both armed and with all the dangers
of losing them both in a foot chase. It was better this way.
Eventually the bastards would stop, and that would be time
enough for him to make his presence known. Because of their
speed they were not hard to follow, yet there was surprise in his
mind, the analytical mind that worked out such problems, that
there was not more speed and more effort to put greater distance between themselves and the university. Jimmy sought to
interpret his opponents, fancied he could understand them, all
part of his training, but this lack of urgency confused him.

There was a roadblock outside Richmond. Uniformed police,

torches, arms waving, but all in the lane that ran toward the city and showing no interest in the cars that traveled the other way, from the direction of London. Typical, thought Jimmy, no bloody liaison. The wireless nets must be jammed with traffic on what's been happening, and nobody's told these poor sods that the birds have upped and flown, and that the only purpose of the law being there was because they might come back to the nest to roost. It was a wide and open road, well laid down by a fully endowed local authority, with a grass space with bushes and small trees separating the two routes. Slow as it was, the car he followed went through, carried by the flow, too fast for him to shout and attract the attention of the policemen on the other road. No chance of stopping, couldn't risk severing the thread that bound him to the Cortina.

The PPK was loaded now, empty magazine discarded on the floor by the foot brake. It was not difficult to rearm the pistol, on his lap when the men in front observed the red traffic light and waited for the change to green. He weighed in his mind when would be the predictable moment to open fire. Perhaps when they stopped the car, when they were out on the pavement and unaware, when he was in the darkness of the car and they were in the open, free for him and naked, illuminated by the street lights. A possibility, a good one. Attractive, because then there was the chance that they would be together, close, the one to the other, and the burst of shots might cover the two of them. When the traffic closed and he was but two or three car lengths away from the Cortina, he could see the two heads. That of the driver bent low, in supplication, over the wheel, the other more upright and turning every two minutes or so to look behind him. How did they rate themselves? Jimmy wondered. He knew where he'd have put it. Fifty-fifty, at best. Escaped, but hadn't taken the professor. Perhaps not as good as fifty-fifty. Chap needed a score to measure his performance against; important that, competitive world. Not as good as evens, Jimmy's reckoning. Perhaps only the professor counted. Buggered it up, hadn't they? And for all the security, they'd won their surprise; must have wanted the surprise factor above all else, and they'd achieved that. Good groundwork, but the rest screwed. Not like McCoy that, Jimmy thought, not if you read his file. Couldn't have been him on the gun, must have been the other bastard.

Taken too long, hadn't he, not the way you'd have done it, Jimmy, you wouldn't have left the rifle hanging through the window half the night. Silly bastards. Should have been on champagne now, and instead they're running, and don't even know what's right up their backsides and waiting to belt them.

Jimmy could see they had slowed in front of him. Nearly there, he told himself, but unsure of the right turning. Lost their way, but they wouldn't be in the side streets unless that's where they're headed for.

The pistol was in his right hand, flat against the wheel. His window was down. Not long now, my little darling; he muttered it casually and without emotion, but would not have denied the excitement.

To kill the Arab or not. It had bounced around McCoy those last miles into the town. He was expendable, and from the way he turned and fidgeted in his seat, was aware of it. Knew what his own people would do to him if he crawled home, the surviving straggler, in the first true flush of failure. Better off face-down on the refuge of the building site, with the weeds and undergrowth and rats for company. He'd had his chance of immortality, if that mattered to him, and had messed it. The alternative, to rot in a cell as a lifer in the Scrubs, and no one coming in a hijack jet, the freedom bird, to lift him out and take him home. Good for nothing, wasted material. A bloody great beacon of fiasco to his colleagues and commander; McCoy liked that, rolled off his tongue well. He'd be paraded, sunken and sheepish, through the British courts, after the spooks had finished with him, after the chatter, after the debrief. Be a killing for the Ministry of Information back in Jerusalem, worth a public holiday to them—"Day of Arab Balls-up." And the bugger knew it all, could see that from the way he sat, misery from ear to ear, the little chokes, the set firmness of the mouth. And his chances of making out on his own, getting clear, McCoy assessed them as minimal to nil. If he needed his hand held for the attack, how much more would he depend on the nanny protection for escape.

McCoy was close to resolve when Famy broke the long silence that had permitted the flow and insinuation of the Irishman's thoughts.

"You are going to the girl's home, right? To the place where you hid when she came for me? That is the place that I will leave you." Perhaps he looked for reaction, expected startlement, but there was none from McCoy, just eyes on the road, hands on the wheel, and the bead of lit sweat high on the forehead. "There was an idea when we were planning the mission at home, that the attack should be mounted at Heathrow, at the airport as he flew to the United States. It will be harder without my friends, but it is the only possibility. I will go on foot, across country, to the airport. They told us that it was not difficult to gain entry to the perimeter, and I will see the El Al land. He will not board till the end, and I will have time, with the rifle, to get as close as I need."

"Impossible." McCoy never moved his head, just the word of dismissal.

"It is not impossible, only difficult. I have the resolution now, not earlier, but it has come to me. It was different earlier. I have now the will that I should have possessed when Sokarev was on the gun. But it was the first time that I had ever fired on a man. It is not easy, not the first time. It is not simple to stand and expose oneself to gunfire. I have learned much in the last hour, more than they taught me in the camp. More in the hour than in three months."

"They'll gun you down before you set foot within two hundred yards of the plane, and you don't even know which one it will be." Perhaps McCoy was less certain of himself, the quietness of the Arab disconcerting him. The strange confidence that he hadn't witnessed before, something novel, delicate, and which he did not wish to fracture.

"The plane will be the one that is most heavily guarded. I have ideas, and there are many grenades. The Israelis say, and they are right, that if one intends to kill, there is no favor to be found in starting far back, relying on aim and the steadiness of the hand. The Israelis say you have to be close, body to body, that you have to be prepared to die yourself. They are correct. They are experts in the art of killing, and we are not. We can only learn from them."

"We part company then. It's not part of my game."

"Your side is more than complete. You carried me to the target, you placed the rifle in my hand. You have fulfilled your order. As long as I live I shall remember you with friendship."

No risk of that being long, thought McCoy. Right bloody hornet's bed we've put our stick into. But if the boy wants to go gloriously, his problem, his concern. Not the style of Crossmaglen. Happened once in Ballymurphy, up in Belfast, when they all went twisted after Internment, and half a dozen guys went for a trot down the road and firing Thompsons from the hip at the biggest pile of sandbags and bunkers you ever saw. Had their bloody heads blown off, one after the other. Did anyone thank them for it the next week, or the next month, or the next anniversary? Did they, shit. Just called them eejit bastards.

"I'm going to the house," McCoy said. "She'll put me up somewhere. I have to wash the arm. Doesn't hurt so much now, but it needs the cleaning. Last time they had me over the border and into Dundalk General, and on the table with the knife in less than half an hour. You can't bugger with gunshot, have to clean it."

"Where will you put the car?" asked Famy.

"At the end of the street by the house. It's a dead end, no one'll see it there, come looking for us. We'll do the goodbye bit then."

He'd hesitated at several of the road junctions in the last half-mile, searching for the landmarks of the streets known from the single occasion that he had walked the girl to her front door. And then there was the spread of ivy on the end brick wall, and the tree with the whitewashed number on it, that was cancered by disease and that would have to be cut. She had said it was a shame, for the tree. He turned into the girl's road.

After McCoy had stopped the car he reached, feeling the awkwardness of his injury, toward the back floor space of the car, feeling for one of the M-1s in the grip bag and for another magazine. From the cloth sack he took two of the grenades, slipping them into his pocket, where they banged together, a dull, hidden noise, without the ring of softer, less lethal metal. He crooked the gun in his armpit as with his left hand he opened the door of the car. Famy waited for him, then pulled the bag over his seat. His rifle was loose, trailing one-handed as he walked around the front of the car. Simultaneous with McCoy, he was aware of the lights of another vehicle that turned into the street, and reacted as fast as the Irishman in shielding his firearm alongside the silhouette of the leg.

"Stay still till he's parked and switched off," McCoy snapped at Famy, concerned at the intrusion, wanting to be on his way, unwilling to face interruption. They were both illuminated by the powerful undipped beams that blazed at them from twenty yards down the road. There was a sense of foolishness, of conspiracy that was unnerving.

"As soon as he's gone, disappear." McCoy trying to take control, knowing it was for the last time, but a pride dictated that at this moment, even as he relieved himself of his commitment and responsibilities, he should still lead. "It's been strange. Not much to say now . . . but, I'm sorry, for your sake . . . and I mean it . . . I'm sorry it loused up . . . What's the matter with the bastard, why doesn't he kill those bloody lights . . . ?"

McCoy felt the searing surprise of pain as the first bullet struck his shoulder. It spun him half around in the fraction of time that it tore a path deep into the softness of the flesh, smashing into the boned strips of his upper ribs, before disintegrating in an aerosol of smoothed and roughened particles. Famy reacted well. Crouched beside the car door he fired six individual and aimed shots at the car, hunting for the lights, seeking to destroy them, and when that was complete, blasting into the darkness above his memory of the bulbs. He paused, studied the silence that had spread at desolate speed across the street, and grasped for a grenade. Pin out, lever free, left arm extended, and then he hurtled it, as the instructor had taught them, overarm and toward the car. The moment before the blast he saw a shadow, down low near the pavement, scurry for the protection of the nearest front garden.

Drunkenly McCoy regained his feet and lurched through the wicket gate to the front door of the girl's home. With his rifle, held one-handed and high, he hammered at the wooden paneling. There was one more shot, but wide and far into the night, insufficient to deter him.

"It's a pistol. Out of range. Give him a few more. Have the bastard keep his head down. And listen. When we get inside, just do as I say, don't bloody argue."

Famy saw he was ashen, his face screwed tight around the mouth and chin, the reaction sharper and more acute than the previous bullet had achieved.

In front of McCoy the door opened. Silhouetted by a light from the back of the hallway that stretched the length of the house was the girl. There was an older woman behind her. Further back, a man, top collar button undone, staring without understanding.

McCoy pushed the girl savagely to one side, sending her spinning onto the floral-patterned carpet. Satisfied that Famy had followed him in, he kicked back with his heel and heard the door slam behind him, the Yale lock engage, the portcullis down on the outside world of the street.

"Whoever the bugger is that's out there"—and McCoy was speaking only to the Arab, ignoring the others in his earshot as if they did not exist, had not yet been reached in his agenda of priorities—"he's seen us both go in. Double yourself out the back, through the kitchen door, over whatever fence there is, and run, run till your legs won't carry you. I'll hold here with this crowd. It'll take the fuzz light-years to work out what to do, and all the time they'll be thinking it's the two of us that are sitting inside. It'll give you hours of start on the bastards. But don't hang about now. Move yourself . . ." The pain came in a great spasm, seeming to catch hold of the wound and pluck ruthlessly at it before letting the sinews fall back into their torn but ordered place. "For Christ's sake, don't mess me, be on your bloody way."

Famy said nothing, just ran on past them. Past McCoy and the girl, past the parents. The light from the kitchen ceiling threw the small garden into shape and he saw the fence, five feet high and sixty feet away. He trampled through some plants that clung tackily to his ankles, then swung himself onto the wattle-embroidered barrier and was over. There was a path, and beyond his eyes nothing but the close darkness.

When McCoy spoke again, it was with great deliberation, his defense bunker against the flowing agony. "I have a rifle, fully loaded, twenty-six rounds in the magazine. I have hand grenades. There will be no hesitation in killing you if you do not do exactly as I say. And any bloody heroics and the women get it first. The old one right at the start. If the police come, God help you." The girl, upright now and joined in fear to her mother, began to weep, quick, sudden little choking sounds, delicate convulsions at her throat, head hanging. "You, father" —and McCoy gestured with the rifle barrel to the man—

"you're to go round the house. I want all the outside doors and windows locked, and I want every curtain in the house drawn, and I want the keys brought to me."

He looked at them for the first time, turning his head from face to face, lingering on each till they averted their heads, unable and unwilling to meet and sustain the gaze of the deep, hate-consumed eyes. "I've explained it, then? And it's understood? Don't mess me about. Don't play games with me. I've said what it means if you fool with me."

As he took the mother and daughter upstairs he could hear the noise of the locks being turned, the bolts driven home, and the curtains sliding on their plastic runners. He was so very tired, so near to sleep, yearning for it, and for an escape from the pain and the awful hallucination of fighting in another man's army, another man's war.

On all fours Jimmy edged his way along the pavement toward the end house of the terrace. Helen's car was alight, flames careering through the interior. In a few moments it would explode when the heat reached the petrol tank. Shouldn't have happened to her, not her pride and joy, only bloody girl he knew who washed her car, poor cow. He went without haste, without panic, feeling the growing heat playing at a distance on the raised seat of his trousers, watching all the time at the house, expecting the gun, the black barrel. Next round due, bell should be clanging, and he was short of seconds, no one to hold the stool, but no one that he would have wanted there. What you joined for, Jimmy boy, the license to play the grown-up games. He saw the curtains in an upstairs room abruptly jolt across the window frame, noted it as an essential step in the protection and precaution process against siege and eventual attack. Nothing else he could register on, and then he smiled to himself, nothing but the tacky and small pool of blood, reflecting, by the front gate. One of the bastards with problems. The Irishman, it would be his cupful. That was the one he'd aimed for and who had spun against the bodywork of the old Cortina too fast for him to be on the evading kick. The move of a man who's been hit, and the blood, the amount of it, that meant an effective and hurting wound. Incapacitating, what old Jonesey would have called it. Cuts the odds, getting onto an even chance now,

Jimmy. One by one the lights were doused in the house. Good thinking again, obvious, really, but meant the homework had been done, necessary if they want to see out. Only have to move the curtains a fraction of an inch and they can see the whole street, and they stay hidden, invisible. Four houses down and on the same side of the street, a front door opened and Jimmy saw the man who peered at the burning car. Others would follow when curiosity overwhelmed the baser instincts of self-preservation and the barricading of doors in response to the gunfire.

The man backed away when he saw Jimmy's gun, seemed to see it before he fastened onto the crouched figure beside his hedge-enclosed front garden, and hurried toward his door, seeking to shut out the threat. But Jimmy was faster, had his foot there, his worn leather taking the force of the swinging wood-work.

"I want the telephone," Jimmy said. "And while I'm talking, write me the names of the people in the end house, this side, everyone who might be in the house at the moment. And don't go back on the street, not unless you want to make the front page of the papers, picture and all."

For the man it was instant nightmare, too consuming for him to question Jimmy's identity, and there was the gun. With a meekness that his friends would not have recognized he led him to the back room and pointed to the telephone; with an automatic response he subdued the volume of the television program he had been watching. Fingers spun the dial. Jones's direct outside-line number.

"Jimmy here, Mr. Jones. They're holed up in Richmond. Chisholm Road, just by the park. One's in difficulty, not fatal, but he'll have a hard time. They've rifles and grenades, same stuff as earlier. Police aren't here yet, but they'll be coming when the local worthies report gunfire up and down their discreet little track. First impression is that they know what they're at, taking all the basic precautions . . ."

Through the house Jimmy heard the penetrating wail of a police siren. He put the telephone down without explanation and ran back through the house and front door, out into the center of the road to wave down the patrol car. He saw the officers inside flinch away, remembered then he still held the

PPK. Showed them his plastic-coated identity card, answer to all problems, with the black-and-white mug-shot photograph from the days before his face filled out with age.

"Don't go any further," he snapped. "First thing, one of you get round the back, the other clear the street. Boyos from the London effort tonight are in the end house, one on the right side. They're littered with hardware, so go careful." And as an afterthought he asked the obvious. "Have they issued you with firearms?"

The policemen were both young, not out of their twenties. They shook their heads, fast reaction to his question, apprehension running deep.

"Well, don't just sit there. If you haven't got them, it's tough. Show biz. One of you'll have to shift round the back, the other call up the bloody cavalcade."

Within a quarter of an hour the house was sealed to the outside world. Police marksmen with FN rifles had taken up positions across the street facing the house. Others lay in the garden at right angles to its front door. Four were against the back fence and with them were the local force's two attack-trained Alsatian dogs. A portable searchlight, short and tubular, erected on a tripod and powered by a noisy, insistent generator, projected its narrow high-intensity beam against the face of the house. The home was eerily still, as if plague-contaminated, quarantined, no movement and no noise around it, great shadows thrown on the brickwork by the roses that the family had so carefully nurtured. At the bottom of the street were the fire engines, motors ticking over, blue hazard lights circling perpetually, and further back the ambulances with their rear doors opened and the red-blanketed stretchers laid ready at the roadside. This was where the other residents of the street had gathered. Adults still dressed, children in their nightclothes and wrapped in anoraks and overcoats against the chill of the evening. There was little talk amongst them, just the overweening sensation of shock that such a thing should happen in their street, in their private preserve.

The order had already been issued that no instruction concerning reaction operations should be broadcast over police short-wave radio, and no information issued to the press unless from authorized police public relations at Scotland Yard.

"We have to cocoon them," the station superintendent said. "Cut them right off till the VIPs arrive and announce the great plan. In the meantime, no sense letting them just twiddle a few knobs on a radio set and have an earful of what we're up to."

"Who's coming down?" asked Jimmy.

"Half bloody London. They're leaving the PM and the Queen in charge, far as I can make out. The rest are hotfooting it over here. Assistant Commissioner, Home Secretary, Defence people, a man called Jones from your crowd, scores of them."

"Let's hope they bring some changes of socks," said Jimmy. "They can take a long time, these things."

"It can take a long time, or it can take five minutes. That's the political decision." The superintendent walked away.

In the back of the black official car that was speeding southwest out of London toward Richmond, Jones felt an overwhelming sense of relief. Had the pair of them boxed up, that had been the gist of the message from the Scotland Yard operations room. Would be just a matter of sitting it out, waiting for them to get tired of their predicament once they'd been convinced of the hopelessness of their situation. Might lose a hostage or two, unlikely, though, and anyway, they were expendable, weren't they? Probably get everyone out alive; reasonable to assume on past performance. That would tie it up nice and neatly, avoid the martyrdom that Jimmy would want to award the Arab. No more killing, no more slaughter, and a finish to this lunatic hysteria that had been gripping everyone in the Department these last five days. And the Department had done well, that would have been noticed.

The Prime Minister sat at the end of the table, the cigar nestled in the fingers of his right hand. It was unlit and little more than a theatrical prop, but he liked to have it there, particularly when decisions had to be made. There were four other men at the table. On the Prime Minister's right, the Commissioner of Police for the capital and the Permanent Under Secretary for the Ministry of Defence; on his left, the Director General of the Security Service; and further away, a middle-ranking civil servant from the Home Office.

The Prime Minister had opened the meeting, which had

started as his dinner guests were still finding their way onto the pavement outside Number 10, by asking the Commissioner to report on the latest situation at the house.

A detailed, clipped account. Without waste, no adjectives for effect, rhetoric far removed. The policeman concluded, "It's basically a classic siege situation, of which we have some experience of our own, but on which there is much international information to fall back on. They have three hostages, they are proven killers, one of them is confirmed injured. As yet we have no demands, but it's early for that, they'll follow, and when they do they'll be wanting a plane out. These men are liable to be in a highly unstable condition after their failure earlier in the evening. In my submission, time, as much as anything else, will calm them down. Otherwise you have a bloodbath potential."

The Prime Minister shifted his weight, faced the Director General.

"I've not much to add to that. Except that we believe that our man has wounded—"

"Your marksman," the Prime Minister interrupted, "the one that you put such faith in."

". . . our man has wounded the Irishman, McCoy. Our assessment is that McCoy would probably be the more skillful of the pair, in the tactical sense, that is, but that his resolve may not equal the Arab's. We would believe that if it came to a shootout in the house, then the greater threat to the lives of the hostages and of the storm party would come from the Arab."

So bloody ridiculous, thought the Prime Minister. Intelligent men all of us, people to see, work to be done, beds and families to be getting to, and all sitting round a table in the seat of government discussing the form, the betting card on who kills best—the Celt or the Oriental. Bloody nonsensical.

"Mr. Dawson, we move into your realm. What are the considerations we have to weigh in contemplating the storming of the house." The Prime Minister was looking past the Director General to the youngish, lean and shadow-pallored man who had to that moment taken no part in the discussion, only scribbled comprehensive shorthand notes on a small lined pad.

"With respect, sir"—Dawson spoke at speed that matched his writing, not looking up from his papers, but with a low voice, so that the others had to strain forward to hear him—" the business we face is not that different from the proceedings of the Lord Chief Justice's court. We can only deal with previous case histories, with other judgments. It is unlikely that there will be special circumstances here that will give us an option that has not faced other authorities here or on the continent or in the United States when challenged with the same problem. I submit that we have to look at the solutions that have been attempted or discarded in the past. First, the best-documented —the Olympics attack. In Munich the Germans were confronted with an end-of-terrace building, but they were dealing with a larger group of hostages, and many more men in the attack squad. The police president of the city considered the use of incapacitating gases, and eliminated them as too slow. They also considered gaining access to the house next door and placing explosive charges against the common wall and blasting an entry that way. This was rejected too; potentially dangerous to the hostages and also unsatisfactory if their exact location in the building could not be pinpointed. So they relied in the end on luring the Black September team into the open and assaulting them with selected marksmen. Result, a fiasco. In the United States, in the Washington courthouse siege, the authorities took their time. Stalled. After many hours they managed to provide a key to the hostages, secreted in the supplies they were permitted to send in, but they had some high-quality people imprisoned who were able to make decisive use of the help given to them. I think that is unlikely to apply in this case. The Israelis themselves, and they believe they have a certain unmatched expertise in these matters, stake all on heavy frontal assault backed by diversionary fire, heavy fire. They risk everything on speed and finely worked-out timing. You will be aware, sir, that the terrorists die, but they take a high proportion of the hostages with them. Probably unacceptable in our circumstances."

There was no shuffling of papers, scraping of feet, stifled coughs. Dawson was the expert, with a mastery of a vague and untested subject. It was easy to see that on his ability and conclusions rested the lives of many.

"The Dutch faced a different type of situation in the prison siege at Scheveningen in the autumn of 1974. They determined to enter one heavily locked door, the only point of access to the prison chapel. But they had certain knowledge through eyewitnesses and electronic aids of the precise positions of hostages and captors. They waited till they were satisfied the terrorist faction had been lulled into false confidence, then used a laser beam to burn out the lock, accompanied by massive diversionary noise. That operation was completely successful. I should stress that British experience is in the field of the waiting game. It is the tactic most generally advocated. As a strategy it is probably applicable more to the domestic problems of criminals or IRA-type terrorists, less useful in dealing with international groups—Palestinians or Red Army of Japan. If you freeze the latter type out, you are then faced with the legal processes and the probability of reprisals, aimed at freeing your prisoners."

"How soon could we mount an effective attack on the house?" The Prime Minister wanted it over, completed. The other men could see that. Easy to recognize, the fear of a long-drawn-out bartering for life. Endless negotiations, as they had witnessed in Germany and France and Greece and Italy, and then government capitulation to the power of the automatic rifle, the primed explosives.

Dawson said, "It's well documented that the most favorable time for assault is just before dawn. Give or take a few minutes, but it's around four o'clock. Doctors will tell you that medically this is the time of least resistance, it's when the elderly die. The blood gets colder. And we start with the advantage that these men will be tired already. They have been under pressure for many hours now, since the weekend. They need to rest. If one is hurt, then that puts greater stress on the other, but he too must relax at some stage. So tomorrow morning, it could be done then, as soon as that. But the earlier you attack, the greater the risk. Whatever their capabilities, these two men will still be attempting maximum performance. You would be leaving no time to wear them down, blind-alley them."

The idea of the laser appealed to the Prime Minister. He talked frequently in his public speeches of the need for technological advance in the country; his opponents said he was obsessed with gadgetry, more interested in the machines of industry than in the men and women who manipulated them. He was close now to the decision for which the four men waited.

"Two questions, Mr. Dawson. Could we produce the laser by the time tomorrow morning that you have specified, and what sort of diversions would you think necessary?"

It was William Dawson's value to those that he advised that he seldom answered unless certain of himself. The availability of the cutting beam caused him to hesitate before committing himself.

"Probably we could get a laser from industry, certainly from Imperial College. It does not have to be a particularly refined or sophisticated model. Whether the necessary authorization and personnel could be obtained in the next five hours . . . As for the diversions, I would suggest considerable noise for five-minute periods, every twenty minutes or so. Engines revving, fire-brigade sirens, shouting, radio chatter. Build it up, then let it fade, but keep it up in the pattern through the night till the small hours. They'll be accustomed to it, familiar, by the time we want to use the laser, its noise will be covered; it would take about fifteen seconds to open the front door, not more."

"You have the authorization, Mr. Dawson. Get the damned thing." The Prime Minister was bubbling now, effervescent, decision-making, the broth of politics. Facing the civil servant who sat beyond the Commissioner of Police. "Mr. Harrison, I want the Special Air Service to assault the house in the small hours of tomorrow morning. I would be unconcerned if the Arab should not survive the entry."

The Commissioner reacted quickly. "With respect, this is a Metropolitan police district. Several serious crimes have been committed in that overall responsibility area, and we are quite capable through Special Patrol Group of mounting a necessary assault to make our own arrests. It's a slur . . ."

"Commissioner," said the Prime Minister coldly, folding his spectacles, readying them for their case, the discussion completed. "I am interested in results, not sensibilities. If you ask Mr. Dawson, I am sure that he will explain in great detail that one of the few successful legacies handed down by the Munich police after Fürstenfeldbruck was the certain knowledge that in future all similar operations should be placed squarely in the hands of the military."

The messages went out, coded and fast. Thirty-five minutes after the Prime Minister's advisors had taken their leave, and still short of midnight, the SAS anti-hijack force had been lifted by Wessex helicopter from their base camp in Herefordshire.

They represented some of the most highly trained and re-
sourceful troops in the British armed forces. There was little
equipment stowed on the floor of the helicopter, just an awesome variety of firearms.

The spasms in his shoulder came and went with increasing
frequency as McCoy moved about the house, so that he needed
to steel himself for the onset of pain that caused him to stop and
lean for support against the nearest wall. There was much
movement, much that he had to do, aggravating the wound, but
his persistence was uppermost. Structure had to be built, the
rest would come after that. He took the parents upstairs, one at
a time, and lay them face down on the beds in the main sleeping
room and in the spare bedroom. It required great effort for him
to rip up the top sheet of the front-room double bed into the
narrow strips that he sought. Using his undamaged hand and his
teeth, he tore at the lengths that he needed to tie them. Neither
of the elderly people, separated the one from the other, was in
a state of mind to resist him, too horrified by the suddenness of
the incursion. But if they had, then one well-placed blow would
have won them their freedom. As it was, they obeyed meekly
and followed exactly the orders that he gave. When they were
prone on the beds he bound their hands behind their backs,
threatening to each that he would be watching the lifetime
partner, and that if he heard the sound of attempted escape,
then he would kill.

When he had finished he felt his strength drained; totally
weak and mingling with the pain was a rising nausea. He
flopped back against the wall behind the headboard, on the
sparse single bed in the girl's room, his feet on the yellow cover-
let, smearing it with street dirt. He angled his body so that his
weight was borne on the left side, and in that hand he held the
rifle, pistol-like, the shoulder support still folded. Like a grotesque interloper he dominated the tiny room, blond hair disheveled and lost in a myriad of Medusa patterns, face with its
color from the fields of South Armagh now vanished, only the
anger of the eyes and the ferrule lines of exertion. Overall, the
jacket, with the stains, not rich and red, but stark, damp and
soiled. He lay the rifle across his lap and pulled the grenades
from his pocket and placed them beside his hip and the good

hand, the one he now relied on, then resumed hold on the trigger guard of the M-1.

Till she followed him into the room she had not seen the wounds, but when he shifted on the bed, awkwardly and seeking the comfort that the pain denied him, then the blood was visible and, set in its heart, the twin places of the holed cloth. She sat on the edge of the bed.

"Why have you come back here? What do you want of us?"

"Time, my little girl. Time, my little shopgirl. Time for a friend."

"For the Arab?"

"Time for the Arab. Time for him to stretch his legs, get on his wings."

"He has gone?"

"You saw him, he's moved on. Further to go than I have. This is where I finish, his post is a long way yet. It's as if he hadn't left the starting line. He's the whole course to run. I'm his handicapper. Big Ciaran ensures he starts in front, out ahead of the bastards. That's the way it is, my little cash-machine girl."

No need to talk to her, nothing that could be said that mattered, just an empty face and fingers that punched a till. Meaningless. Time to think of yourself, Ciaran boy. Famy off on course, but the fences are higher and the ditches are deeper and they've extended the track, the bastards. We held all the cards, he thought, now none of them, and the silly bugger's gone on, and to his death, and he's taking you with him, Ciaran. His eyes were open, but he did not see her, just stared at the darkness of the ceiling. He had wondered how he'd go. How death would close in on him. Had thought it might be in a ditch, or in the mess of a farmyard as the cordon tightened, or on the high wire of the Kesh, or being pulled by the legs from a sniper pit by a para. But never thought of it like this, not in a room eight by ten with rabbits and daffodils on the wall, and the smell of scent and a folded nightdress under his arse.

But even as the barometer of pain circles to hideous levels, the preciousness of life remains hard to pass up. His eyes closed, clamped shut, his upper teeth hard on the bottom lip, and he waved with the rifle barrel for her to come closer. He put the gun down beside the grenades and began to drag with his left hand at the jacket. She slid along the bed to him, and as he levered himself away from the wall, she looped the jacket over his shoulders and down his arms. Once he cried out. When it was off and he was free of it and she had dropped the garment on the fluffed sky-blue rug on which she first set her feet in the mornings, then he rolled on his side, doubled up and panting for relief.

"Get some water, and something to clean it"—she barely heard the words.

He opened his eyes when she switched on the light and came back into the room with a saucepan and the steam rising from it and a wad of bright cotton wool. With his help she took off his shirt, and with care lifted his undershirt over his head. The blood had caked far down his chest, dark, dried rivulets leading to his navel. With the swabs she worked her path closer to the neat, circular, organized wounds in the flesh. Not much time on the arm, priority to the shoulder. She felt the skin tighten, striving for escape as she neared the place of that bullet's entry. Instinctively she leaned him forward to clean the expected exit wound in his back and saw only the skin unbroken and stretched across the tightened back muscles.

"It's still in there"—half a statement, half a question.

He nodded, and for the first time she saw him smile.

"It has to come out. It'll kill you."

"All in good time," said McCoy. "The lad has a long way to travel. I want him far on his journey before the heavies find it's just wee Ciaran McCoy that's holding the baby."

"What will they do, the police?"

"They'll huff and puff a few more hours, then they'll call for surrender, and we'll do nothing, then they'll have a bash at us . . . Switch the light off." His voice was suddenly urgent, incisive.

When the room was in darkness she could listen. Close-by down the road the roar of a heavy engine as if the driver was pumping his foot up and down on the accelerator. Across from the window muffled shouts. She eased the curtain back, giving herself visibility of the road immediately in front of the house. "There's nothing moving there," she said.

There was some brightness from a street light, augmented by the searchlight beam, and though his face was half in shadow she could make out the line of his features. "Why is it necessary to do what you have done to my parents?"

He anticipated her. "They stay tied, and they stay separate."

"They couldn't do anything, they couldn't hurt you."

"I said they stay like that . . ."

"You said the police would break in. How soon?"

"Not for a day or so. They'll want time to work out a plan. Take them half a week." He reached forward with his left hand and took hold of her arm, vise-grip, and pulled her so that she stretched across the width of the bed, and his head sank into her lap where her thighs came together. He remembered the afternoon in the park. Not thirty hours before, half a bloody lifetime. In the darkness his breathing slowed and he lay still. Had to rest, had to go back to Cullyhanna, had to climb the hills again.

"Why didn't you use anything yesterday?" she said.

"I don't know," said McCoy. "I don't know."

Seventeen

Once the doctor had gone they left David Sokarev alone in his room.

The tablet he had taken, washed down with tap water drunk from the tooth mug, was not slow to operate, bringing on the drowsiness that chemically conquered the terror of the earlier evening. After the noise-filled, siren-blasting convoy had carried him to the hotel, they had hurried him to his room, aided his undressing, and readied him in his bed for the arrival of the Jewish doctor. Elkin had hovered close and maternal as the doctor bent over his patient, but Sokarev could see that his calm acceptance of the situation was waning, replaced by a morose silence, the lion that had lost its mate. The two men had hunted together, worked, planned, eaten and rested together, bound in their opposites by a comradeship. All destroyed now, by the pathetic and harmless-seeming grenade.

The assurance and confidence around him when they had left for the university was another casualty of the attack, replaced with a diffidence that alternated with the fraying tempers. The Englishman should have been there, the one Sokarev remembered above all others, the one with only a given name and with the old suit. He was the one who had promised he would be beside Sokarev, who had made a joke of it all, who had laid his professionalism out for all to see in the very relaxation he had demonstrated since they had met. But he was absent, the one who was needed now. The man amongst all others that Sokarev had believed in, had placed his trust with. There had been a promise.

Sokarev felt a great helplessness, felt isolated and remote when he spoke from his bed, the neat folded hotel blankets high up against his striped pajamas and across his chest. "Where is the Englishman, the one who called himself Jimmy?" It was an interruption and cut across the low-pitched conversations that were being pursued out of his earshot across the width of the room.

"He left in chase," said Elkin. "After Mackowicz was killed he ran for the door. He had been shooting. There is no word of him since then."

"He said he would be with us. Continuously."

"Well, he's not here. No sign of him. Running the bloody streets, no doubt, trying to pull back something from the chaos. But something dramatic it has to be, after what has happened. The security was like a sieve. Disorganized, unprepared. A shambles they made for us." He came close to the bed, words under bare control, spitting his anger. "You can understand, Professor, that from now it will be we who supervise all movements. There will be no more outsiders making decisions. No more delegation. The Englishman that you want beside you made a grand speech about responsibility to Mackowicz. Where is Mackowicz now? Where is the man who gave those orders?"

The Special Branch inspector, already feeling the frigid ice wall that divided him from the Israelis, made no comment. Irretrievable situation. No verbal points worth scoring, and short of currency anyway.

With the arrival of the ambassador the men had withdrawn through the communicating door. The ambassador, not attempting to disguise his fury, the security attaché, Elkin, two more men from the embassy that Sokarev had not seen before but who carried hand radio sets. They closed the doors after them, and the English policeman, unwanted and ignored, made his way into the corridor outside. Last to go had been the doctor. Just a specimen to them, thought Sokarev. Like a box of bullion, to be displayed when necessary, shifted when convenient. Not to be consulted, not to be taken into confidence. In the last minutes before the pill took its action he heard the raised voices seeping through from the next room. Shouting, and Elkin's voice loud and demanding to be listened to, the security attaché attempting to act as intermediary and being sliced into irrelevance by the clear-cut words of the ambassador.

The point at issue was simple enough. The movements of Sokarev. Elkin insisted on an immediate return to Tel Aviv. The ambassador, with his superior diplomatic rank but without the specific responsibility for Sokarev's safety, required clearance from Jerusalem before the visit to New York could be canceled.

"It is impossible to justify the continuance of his journey," shouted Elkin.

It is a way of life in the Israeli community that title and position count for little when the question of security is at stake. He could browbeat a senior diplomat in a way unthought of throughout Europe.

"If they can attack here, they can attack in the United States. One of our men has died already that this one speech could be made—not completed, only started. How many more do we lose protecting him if we go to America. And for what . . .?"

"He goes for precisely the reason that he came here in the first instance. The threat was known, but we do not bow to threats . . ."

"He is a scientist, not a damned target dummy."

". . . The decision was made at Cabinet level that he should come. We will not be cowed by these people."

"Before, that was a reasonable risk. Not now. They did well tonight, those bastards. That they missed was our luck. Not credit to us. Luck, and Mackowicz."

"The decision must come from Jerusalem." The ambassador spoke with finality.

"The decision is easy, Excellency. Very simple, no doubt you can answer it for me. Which way is the professor more important? A household name, famous, and dead. A martyr to the cause of the survival of our country. That is one option. Or more important in his office, in his anonymity, with his papers and his tables and his work. It is sad you cannot consult with Mackowicz; he would pick between the options."

There was a purple-veined flush high on the ambassador's

cheeks. He turned to the door. "As I have said, the decision must come from the Foreign Ministry, I will relay your comments, and they will have consideration."

"And what of Sokarev? What of his ability to go on? Will that have consideration?"

But the ambassador and the security attaché were gone. Elkin looked at the two new men who were to share the room with him, then twisted away lest they should see the tears that now lapped at his eyelids. Like a brother to him, Mackowicz. An elder brother, protective, dominating. And now without his stomach, intestines splayed to the winds. He crumpled himself full-length on his bed. That Sokarev was alive and breathing heavily a few feet away was an inadequate consolation for the loss.

The ambassador, an experienced diplomat, was well versed in the art of professional self-preservation. His request to Jerusalem for guidance contained no suggestions of his own, and contained, with prominence, the concern of Sokarev's remaining bodyguard. The coded reply he awaited, a jumble of numbers, arrived in the embassy communications room within two hours. After it had been deciphered it was brought to him.

XXCLL478219

FOREIGNMINISTRYJERUSALEM

0018298 PERSONAL FOREIGN MINISTER TO AMBASSADOR UK ITEM HIS EYES ONLY ITEM AFTER URGENT CONSIDERATIONS SOKAREV'S MOVEMENTS AYE INFORMING SIMULTANEOUSLY AMBASSADORUSA TO ANNOUNCE CANCELLATION OF ABOVE'S TRAVEL AND SPEAKING ARRANGEMENTS IN NY AND OTHERS ITEM SOKAREV SHOULD RETURN ISRAEL FIRST AVAILABLE NONSTOP ELAL FLIGHT ITEM WE DEMAND FULLEST SECURITY DURING REMAINING HOURS SOKAREV'S PRESENCE UK PARTICULAR LONDON HEATHROW DEPARTURE ITEM YOU WILL ISSUE STRONGEST PROTEST TO UK GOVERNMENT AT LEVEL NOT BELOW FOREIGN MINISTER PREFERABLY PRIME MINISTER AT LAX UK SECURITY STRESSING FULL INFORMATION AND WARNING PROVIDED BY OUR SECURITY SERVICE PRIOR SOKAREV ARRIVAL ITEM WE REQUIRE PUBLIC EXPRESSION REGRET ITEM COMMUNICATION COMPLETE

XXDYY478219

*   *   *

Alone in the flat in Beersheba, the scientist's wife heard over the Israeli Broadcasting Corporation's final radio news bulletin of the attack on her husband. The information came without warning, as the news media transmitted the story faster than those government authorities responsible for her husband's welfare could react.

In desperation she tried to telephone first her son: on operational stand-by and not available to take messages. Next her daughters: both out of their student hostels and not expected back till later. The director at Dimona, an old friend: away at a conference in Tiberias. The seemingly endless lingering of the disappointments as she had waited four times for a familiar voice to come on the line, and on each occasion had her hopes dashed, took a heavy toll from her. She sat in David Sokarev's chair, beside the fire that would not be lit till the winter came and the cold over the desert, and waited for the early-morning light still five hours away. That she knew her man was safe was of some small help. What caused her to sob soundlessly into the half-cast darkness of the center of the room was the knowledge of the deep fear and terror he would have suffered. So inoffensive, so mild, without enemies, with a voice that never raised in anger. Buried away in a cramped office, insulated against the hatred and hostility that lay rampant beyond the wire fences of Dimona. But would his work, and the implications of his study, provide him with an insight into this obscenity? She wondered about that. The preparation of the bomb itself, awful, grotesque, multidestructive—would that have prepared him to confront the viciousness of the last hours? But it was not his way to see the bomb as a finished and completed and cased article of war. Just figures and notes on paper. Drawings that were meaningless to others. Long hours and days and months of work. Calculations and equations.

He would not have understood. He had been too long absented from the world of the men who now fought around him to take and to protect his life. He would be alone, defenseless. That was why she wept for him.

The Special Air Service squad was brought to Chisholm Road in two Black Maria police vans from an improvised helicopter landing pad on the football pitches beside the main road that ran out of Richmond to the south. The men wore full-length black dungarees, were not encumbered with webbing and equipment, and none boasted badges of rank on their upper arms or shoulders. They jumped easily from the open doors at the back of the vans, casual, at ease, and then the heavy canvas bags were handed down.

Jimmy stood in the shadows and watched them. Not youngsters, but most of them still half his age, hair cut close, clean-shaven, disinterested faces visible only when the lights rotating on the roofs of the fire engines illuminated the path across which they walked. The killing squad. Different from Jimmy, not self-taught as he had been. Trained and practiced, funded by the government so that their expertise should be developed. Selected with care and toughened and primed. Taught not to act independently, but in the pack, deadly and irreversible when the leash was slipped. If they felt excitement, they did not show it, just trooped after the one who was their leader across the road to where the Home Office man waited. Some squatted low over sheets of paper half flat on the pavement; others stood in a circle peering into the area lit by torches.

William Dawson was a thorough man. He took them through the diagram of the outside of the house, all windows and doors marked in red, first the ground floor, then the upper story. The squad said nothing, two taking notes, the others watching and silent. Then came the plans of the interior of the end of terrace home. Drawn to scale. Red marking the doorways again, and blue crosses on those that the neighbors had reported to be fitted with locks and bolts. Fingers ran along the routes of the hallway, the stairs and the landing. Occasionally those at the back would crane their necks up the street to relate the floodlit frontage with the paper work. Jimmy stood half a dozen paces back from the huddle; Jones was far behind him at the steps of the police control vehicle.

Dawson was talking, fast and coherent, sketching the plan he had described to the Prime Minister. Diversions and time factors, and entry points and opposition capability, and the laser. There were precedents, and case histories and suggestions. The attention that the squad gave the civil servant was the accolade that he had done his work, was as expert in the planning as they would be in the execution.

When the group broke up, it was to appointed tasks. Four to unload the firepower they had brought with them, to lay the weapons out and to load them. Four more to begin a scrounging expedition amongst the fire brigade, for ropes and axes and the fifteen-foot ladders that would carry them to the first-floor windows. The officer and his sergeant detached themselves, and in the company of a ranking police officer, made their way past the front doors of the houses, traversing the front gardens, working closer to the house that they would storm. When they had seen the front they moved, silent and catlike, through another house and across its back garden till they came without warning on the police who watched the rear of Number 25. From the outside there was little to tell them of the situation beyond the brick walls. All curtains drawn, all windows darkened.

"They had the light on a bit ago. In the front upstairs. The small room where the girl sleeps. It was off within a minute. The men across the road from the front think the curtain there moved once, but it's bloody difficult to be sure. It was when we first started the noise business that the Home Office chap wanted. The second time we did it, nothing happened, not that we saw. There's been three more times we've used the noise since then, and nothing. No movement that we've seen." The chief inspector was depressed. That this was not police work, he acknowledged; he was grateful he was not asking among his men for volunteers for an attack party, but the very competence and hardness of the new arrivals had shaken and concerned him.

"What chance have you got of getting those people out alive." That was the nub of the problem as he saw it, and he raised the question as they slipped back toward the concentration of vehicles and men.

"Can't say," replied the officer quietly, as if their voices would carry. "Depends where the family are, whether they're together. What state the wounded fellow is in. How much speed we can muster. If we're fast enough, there's a good chance. The theory is that it's difficult for a man to turn his gun on his hostages as we're coming through the door. He has no protection. He goes with them. There's not many relish that; that's what the handbook says, at any rate. But it's all theory, there's nothing cut and dried."

Before they reached the fire engine closest to the house, and where men in uniform had gathered, and where there would be ears to listen to their conversation, the officer said, "Don't misunderstand me, but isn't there some question about priorities? The hostages aren't at the top of the list, as I see it. If they were, we'd be talking, negotiating. Spinning it out. I have the priority as the two blokes. If we get the family out, that's a bonus. Hitting those two buggers in there is what we're here for."

Jimmy's eyes had seldom left the house. Its very ordinariness fascinated him. Uninteresting, unremarkable, undistinguished. Forty-nine others like it in the road. A personal habited box. Lived in by people who were as stereotype-produced as the bricks and mortar they surrounded themselves with. And their visitors, they also were from the depths of mediocrity, without identity—totally irrelevant without the guns and the grenades. The only things of significance about them were their rifles and the explosives. But that to Jimmy was muscle, that was the center core of terrorism, the power of the corkscrewed barrel that violated the norms of behavior, lifted the nonentity onto the pedestal he sought. Jimmy had heard that in a lecture in the Department, had listened, which was rare, and agreed. Behind him was the Home Secretary, arms either akimbo or flattened against his backside as he looked solemnly at the tarmac and heard out the Assistant Commissioner. Only one reason he's here, thought Jimmy, the hardware. Doesn't matter how screwed up the little bastards with their hands on it are, the hardware brings the big men out. To all of them standing round the house with their guns and their dogs and their truncheons, McCoy and the Arab were just pictures, two-dimensional, black and white. Not to Jimmy. Jimmy had seen them, seen the character of their faces, the shape of their mouths and the slouch of their movements. And Jimmy had tried to kill them that evening, counted himself unlucky that he hadn't. It tied them together, Jimmy and McCoy and the Arab. Perverse but a brutal liaison. And they had seen him, twenty yards away, and there had been the rifle fire and the thrown grenade. So they knew each other, understood the stake money. When he looked away from the house, Jimmy could see the SAS men making their preparations. But these were strangers and outsiders, not a part of it till little more than an hour earlier when their helicopter had lifted off from the far west.

Jimmy walked across the road to where the army officer stood, concentrating on his notebook. When he was beside him, he tapped the shoulder and pushed forward his identity card. The officer glanced at it, acknowledged by diverting his gaze to Jimmy's eyes. He's impatient, the bastard.

"Jimmy's the name. From the Security Service."

"George Martin, captain."

"I've been on this one. Full time. Since the flap started. I'd like to go along with you."

There was a faint smile at the extremes of Martin's mouth. Not quite as tall as Jimmy, looking up at him. Unsettling, unhelpful, difficult to communicate.

Jimmy went on, "I'd like to go into the house with you. I know what they both look like, could be of use to you."

The smile broadened. "Sorry, father, no passengers this time round. If you want to come and identify them after, there'll be no problem."

"Don't give me the father crap . . ."

"And don't get in my way. We've work, and no time . . ."

"Listen," said Jimmy, face close to the soldier's. "I'm in the protection team. Right beside Sokarev, the Israeli, this evening, appointed to guard him."

"You're a touch off course, then. Nobody told us he'd joined the party in there. I'd have thought your best place was at the hotel holding your baby's hand. Must be looking for a bit of a lullaby after the hoop you put him through tonight."

Cool's going, Jimmy. Double fast, like it always does with these uptight swine. "If it hadn't been for me, he'd be in the morgue now. And when you get in there you'll find one of the bastards half dead with my bullet in him . . ."

"Come to the wrong chap, then. It's the Birthday Honours you're looking for. I don't hand bloody medals out. Right now I'm busy, got my hands full, and no one goes in alongside my team. Understood?"

"You stupid bastard," said Jimmy.

The captain smiled again, almost a laugh, and walked away.

It took Jimmy some minutes to find Jones. He was in a group amongst men of equal status, discussing the problems that confronted them. How to introduce, before the scheduled dawn attack, the fisheye visual surveillance lens that would arrive in a few hours from London, the merits of the various audio electronic devices that were available, the question of news releases. Jones was rarely in such company, unfamiliar with the bright excitement his companions felt at whiling their evening away waiting for the disaster or success that the morning would bring. He felt his years shackled to the desk had cheated him of something he vaguely saw as precious. Too much time on paper work, while the knowledge of the techniques that dominated the world of his new companions was denied him. That he was accepted amongst them pleased him, but he recognized it was not because of his contribution but because of his rank and title. And then Jimmy was at his side, pulling at his coat, right as he was in midsentence, and drawing him away. Jones saw the warning signs, noticed the blink in Jimmy's left upper eyelid, knew it from years back. And Jimmy launched off, "Bloody army, bloody pigs. I've been with this one right the way through, did you well tonight, bloody well, and now I want to go in there and finish the bloody thing, and that little prig, the bloody army man, treats me like I'm out for some bloody Cook's tour. All patronizing and 'Come in when we've finished' and that crap."

"What do you want to go in for, Jimmy?" said Jones.

"To finish the bloody thing, finish what started this evening."

"Be in at the killing, right? That's what you want?"

"Right first time. I bloody started and . . ."

"It's not a quota job, Jimmy boy. You don't need notches on your pension book. What's the matter, short this year on your numbers? You're not a bloody policeman. Haven't got to get twenty traffic bookings a month to hold down a reputation."

"You're not going to tell them to count me in?" There was doubt now for Jimmy. Jones always backed him, always had in the past—why different now?

"Of course I'm not. What do you expect me to say: I've got a man on my books who's a bit short of stiffs this month; comes out in a rash if he doesn't nab a couple each thirty days? Snap out of it, Jimmy. You've had your scene tonight, done well, bloody well. You should be off home, and in your pit by now, and sleeping so you're not a bloody zombie tomorrow when God knows what happens."

"Straight bloody heave, then?"

"If you see it that way, Jimmy, that's your problem. But do us all a favor and shove off back to town so you're not nackered in the morning."

"I thought there'd be some bloody clout from you," Jimmy was shouting, his words carrying across the still of the night, loud enough for those who could not avoid hearing to shuffle their feet and cough.

Jimmy swung on his heel and walked through the cordon, side-stepped the newspaper and television photographers, past the sightseers who would wait till there was any action of any sort at whatever advanced hour. He walked down the hill toward the town. There would be a taxi rank there, and then there would be the hotel close to the flat where the night porter would fix him up with a half-bottle. As he went he wondered about the life and times inside Number 25. Thought of McCoy with the hole in him, thought of the Arab. Pictured the faces as he'd seen them in the glare of his headlights the moment before he'd fired. Wondered how they'd cope when the military came in. Wanted to be there, missing his bloody treat, and God, he'd deserved the party. The tin that he kicked in his frustration careered clumsily and raucously down the road in front of him.

She knew that if she moved, McCoy would waken. It was awkward, half propped on one arm and lying across the narrow width of the bed, with the weight of his shoulders and his head flattened against her stomach. His sleep was light, punctuated by convulsions when he twisted his body over from right to left, felt the pain, and swung back onto the undamaged arm. The wound through the upper chest was near to her head and it oozed strange and unknown fluids that showed in the half-light as opaque dribblings. Sometimes she turned her eyes away from the hole and its debris, but then her imagination took over and besieged her more fearfully than the reality. Nightmarishly she could see the stunted column of lead striking the softness of the skin, could feel the splitting and carving of the tissues, and wonder at the sensation of the fragments making their uninterrupted passage in the void beneath the flesh. And he had said it would all happen again. Told her, hadn't he, that they would come. Policemen with rifles, more bullets, bursting through the door from which her dressing gown hung, kicking their way across the tiny floor space, brushing aside the white-wood and wicker chair on which she had laid his stained jacket and shirt and undervest. And what would he do when they came? His rifle was half under his legs, still held close to the trigger guard by the left hand. So small . . . And beside its shallow length, the grenades, miniaturized. They didn't have the scale and size for her to believe in them as killing weapons. Too sparse, too insignificant. But when they came, when the police came, he would try to fire, try to pull the absurd circular pin on the grenade. And they would shoot. They would be quicker, organized, without pity. Then there would be the profusion of holes, beating formations in his chest, slicing through the rib cage that showed clear as he lay in his sleep. When they came, it would be to kill, not to capture. Norah knew that.

Even had she not been so tired she could not have analyzed her feelings for Ciaran McCoy. Love was the magazine word, written in stories with wind-swept hills, and boys who were dark and tidy, and girls with wasp waists and unbuttoned blouses and long hair. Infatuation she understood, read of it in the agony columns, real enough, able to match it with her own emotions; the boy last year who worked under Father at the factory. Temporary and heartrending, nice to cry over. But McCoy, this was something unique for her and surpassing her vocabulary. She could not envisage herself in love with a man capable of such horror as the strangulation of the policewoman whose picture the television had shown, not in love with the man of the hateful, animal-wild eyes imprinted in her mind from the newspaper picture. Yet she had lain with him in the grass of the park, and taken him in her arms, and pressed his head against her breasts, and said his name, and felt the warmth and the pain of him deep between her legs. And he was to die. Snuffed out. Shot dead by the guns of men in uniform.

Norah reached down to the floor, to the square of carpet that covered the center of the room, and felt under her bed for her shoes, careful not to disturb his sleep. All her shoes were under the bed; the room was too small to provide the adequate cupboard space she required. Two pairs were there—her evening going-out ones and the flats for work in the supermarket. Further under were the back numbers of the magazines that came on Thursday mornings and that caused her to linger in bed and be late for breakfast and run for the bus. She straightened, gently and slowly, taking time till she could ease out the pillow that had nestled in the small of her back. Together they were sufficient. First the magazines, then the shoes, then the pillow. With one hand she steadied his sleeping head while she wormed as far back toward the wall as her body had room to move, and then there was the space for her to build the counterfeit lap. The height was the same, and when she eased his head onto the softness of the pillow his eyes stayed tight shut, and there was only the forced and erratic breathing.

It was not that she was betraying him, she told herself, only offering him salvation. This way he would survive. Go out of her life, that was inevitable, but survive. On her window sill were the keys to the outside doors that he had brought upstairs with him. It was easy for her to select the one that opened the front door.

Past three she saw on her watch when she stepped out onto the landing of the house and went barefoot, and on her toes, without sound toward the staircase. At the head of the stairs she stopped and waited to listen to the night noises of the house. McCoy's breathing, audible, painful. Fainter movements from the rooms where her parents lay.

Pray God he doesn't wake, she said to herself, and eased onto the first step.

Famy had gone over the wall and into the park. Inside, he ran till his legs would carry him no further. Fast, hard and direct toward the southwest, sprinting so that many times he had plunged without warning into bushes, stumbled in the grassed-over drains. His hands were cut, and the knees of his trousers torn. The rifle made it difficult, clutched as a talisman, only one hand free to protect him when he pitched forward. But McCoy had made the sacrifice. McCoy had stayed behind to win him the distance he now sought to put between himself and the pursuit. No idea how many hours' start he would have, whether the hunt had in fact already begun, whether it would come at dawn or not for a full day. But the Irishman had sacrificed himself, probably given his life to gain him the ground he now swept over. It clinched his motivation, and when his legs sagged under him, he rested only for the muscles to tighten, the control to be regained, before starting once more.

When the brickwork of the park wall swung away from the direction he sought, exhausting its usefulness, he looked for escape in the streets and roads outside. It took great effort for him to force his way up onto the summit of its height, and he toppled rather than jumped onto the ground on the far side. Soon he was out of the cover of the trees and under street lights, passed by late traffic, and running by houses where lights still shone and from which came the flicker, blue-grey on the wall-papers, of television sets. When he came to the river, he walked along the bank, anxious lest he should miss the bridge marked on his pocketbook map. But when he had found it he quickened his step. There would be no more such barriers for him now, the map showed that, just a network of streets and roads and gardens stretching across his path, separating him from the great open space of flattened concrete that was the airport and from which David Sokarev would fly.

He knew his way, was unerring in tracking his route. Every ninety-five seconds a jet-powered passenger air liner roared above him on its descent to the tarmac, red and green belly lights flashing the message to the Arab far beneath that he was on his course.

Eighteen

It was the policeman crouched in the shadows of the doorway directly opposite Number 25 who first heard the faint whisper sound of the bolt being withdrawn behind the door across the road. He stiffened into an aim position, the FN self-loading rifle at his shoulder, barrel pointed across at the floodlit porch, and talking all the time into the radio that clipped to his tunic. Within seconds of his first message he could hear the scraping of activity around him, others alerted, more marksmen preparing themselves. The superintendent's voice was relayed to him over the miniature loudspeaker set into the same instrument. Distant, disembodied, unreal, came the instructions: "If the men come out, shoot. Only if their hands are up and they are obviously not armed do you hold your fire. If they have hostages with them, shoot. Under no circumstances are they to reach the darkness, either of them."

All right for him to bloody say that, the policeman thought, all right if you're down in the control vehicle. The door edged open, two inches at first, time for the constable to ease off the safety clip on the right side of the rifle, an inch or so above the magazine. He was sweating, could feel the moisture on his hands. He'd only fired in practice, and the last time eight months before. Then the door swung fully back on its hinges, but the light from the beam down the road came at such an acute angle that it threw no clarity into the hallway, left only a black rectangle of darkness that he strained without success to break into. They'll all come in a rush, he told himself, all together, the parents and the girl in front, the men behind. And his orders were to shoot. God help us all, he thought, lips bitten tightly, hands shaking fractionally, causing the needle sight on the end of the barrel to waver in gentle, helpless meanders. In normal times he drove a squad car, the marksman's role was something he had never taken on before; only his eyesight, which was superb, qualified him for the shooting position he occupied twenty short paces from the doorway.

His finger tightened on the trigger, and then he saw the girl come from the shadow and hesitate on the step. There was a surge of relief through him; at least the bastards were not right behind her. It would give him a chance to miss her, perhaps hit them. Very quietly, little more than an aside, he broadcast her progress along the four yards of paved path to the front wicket gate. Here again she stopped, and the fifteen rifles that had covered her as she walked forward traversed their aim back to the dark recess of the doorway.

A hundred yards away and watching now through binoculars, the superintendent called into his microphone, "Tell her to get into the middle of the road, and keep the bloody door covered."

The constable stretched up, straightening his legs against the stiffness that had long crippled his knee joints. The girl wouldn't have seen him yet, wouldn't have seen any of them, would be bewildered by the silence and the emptiness of the street.

"Keep walking," he said, more staccato than he would have wanted. Nerves he put it down to. "Come out into the street, hands high. Out in the middle."

Still the girl seemed unaware of his presence, simply obeyed the commands. She came to the center of the road, and the constable could see the glazed eyes, could see the bloodstains, too, on the white of her blouse, the scattered hair strands, the uncertain steps. Like a bloody sleepwalker, he thought, like someone learning to walk again in a hospital. "Walk down the road, and slowly. There's a rope across it about a hundred yards down. They'll meet you there. And don't run." The girl veered to her right, reacting to the instructions, and began to walk, and the policeman's concentration returned to the open doorway, rifle grip marginally relaxed, waiting.

When she reached the rope a host of hands greeted her. Under her shoulders lest she should faint, hands of comfort around her back. She felt weakness till two detectives frisked her, and she was alive again, backing away from the fingers that ran down her body, circling her waist, on the inside and outside of her legs. "Just formality," said the voice behind her, but close and reassuring, and then there was one arm around her, strong, protective. She made no effort to stem the flow of tears that shook and racked her as they led her without more comment to the control van. They helped her up the steps, and the superintendent muttered to his men, "Keep it very gentle. When she starts to talk I want it coming easily. Rush it now and we'll screw it for all time." He was old enough in the knowledge of interrogation to know that hasty, capsulated and impatient questioning could cause the girl to freeze, make the progress endlessly slow and confusing.

They gave her a chair, and the superintendent said, "It's Norah, isn't it?"

She nodded, blank agreement.

"Tell us what's happening, Norah, in your own words."

She smeared her arm across the upper face, diverting the tears, snuffled, and started to talk. Her voice was very low and the policemen and the SAS captain who had crowded into the van had to stretch forward to hear.

"He said you'd attack, and when you came in you'd be shooting. You'll kill, I know you'll kill him. You'll murder him in there." The faces of her listeners were impassive, showing no reaction to what she said. "I couldn't see him die, not like that. He's hurt, there's a terrible wound, blood . . . and he got me to clean it. He's sleeping now, he was when I left him . . . I made a pile for his head so that he wouldn't know I'd gone. He needs help, he needs a hospital. I thought if I let you in, you'd take him alive, you wouldn't shoot him."

Behind her a detective whispered, half to himself but not subdued, "Little cow. Little bitch." She seemed not to hear.

"The door's open. He's up the stairs, in the small room at the front. It's my room. He's on the bed there. Asleep. He doesn't

know I've come. He'd kill me . . ." The tears came again and
her head sank forward on the smallness of her chest.

The army captain leaned close, one question to ask. "What
sort of guns does he have . . . where are they?"

"There's a rifle, a little one; it's in his hand. And there are
some grenade things; they're beside the rifle. That's all he has."

"Norah, listen, because this is very important if we are to help
this man." The superintendent spoke softly, paternal, a voice to
be trusted. "You have to tell us where in the house is the other
man. The one on your bed is the Irishman, where is the other
one, the Arab?"

She looked into the face that was very near to her—tired and
bagged eyes, stubble beginning to show, white collar fringed
with grime. So he knew what he was up to, the man McCoy. She
wanted to scream her laughter. It was as he'd said it would be.
Buying time for his friend, and how much purchased? How
many hours? Four, five perhaps. And they didn't know. Tricked
by a man with one good arm and half his chest shot out. All these
bloody coppers, and McCoy had done them. But there was no
hysteria, too exhausted for that. Only a slow smile that rimmed
the bottom of the young fresh cheeks, almost of sympathy.

"He's been gone a long time," she said. "He went right at the
start. Just ran through the house. There's only Ciaran . . ."

"Bloody hell," said the superintendent, kindness evaporating
from his mouth.

"We'll go and get the bastard." The captain said it over his
shoulder, already half out of the van.

The superintendent sat back in his chair. "And you haven't
come to tell us this to save your father and mother, haven't
mentioned them. Nor to help the troops who were going to
break in, less than an hour from now, and risk their bloody lives.
Not on your list, right? Only thing that matters is that Ciaran
gets his bloody treatment. Straight in on the National Health,
makes you want to puke."

She was satisfied with herself now. They saw the defiance
come to her, chin butting out.

"So where's the Arab?" Different tone, harsher, games completed.

"He didn't say. Just ran through the house. Went through the
back. Hours ago." The last spat out with relish.

"Where to, for Christ's sake?"

"I said he didn't say. Ciaran said the whole thing was to win him time."

"And how long have you known him, this McCoy?"

"Two weeks."

"And you knew what he'd done?"

"I knew." And she smiled again.

Pretty smile, the superintendent thought, pretty face. Just as bloody stupid as they all are when they meet their McCoys. Screwed her, and screwed her life. Par for the bloody course. He climbed out of the van to begin formulating his plans for the manhunt that would not get operational till first light, still more than ninety minutes away.

The split board that Norah's father had so long meant to repair betrayed to Ciaran McCoy the approach up the stairs of the SAS sergeant. The creaking whine when the soldier eased his weight onto the divided wood broke through the thin sleep, causing him to sit up sharply, a reflex before the agony jolted him down. He was aware of the rifle immediately, nestled in his hand and pressed to his thigh, but when he moved his shoulders, seeking the shape and familiarity of the girl, he realized she had gone. He took his hand from the butt of the rifle and felt the pillow and the shoes and the magazines. Confirmation, if he had needed it. There was a whisper from the stairs, a hiss for quiet, then the drumming of feet, the moment of assault. For a fraction of a minute he had the capability of making the decision that would determine whether he raised his gun and armed the grenades, or whether he submitted—but his mind was incapable of thought processes, and his instinctive reactions too dulled. When the sergeant came through the door, finger poised on the hair trigger of the Stirling submachine gun, McCoy lay where he had slept, gun barrel prone on the bedspread and offering no threat. That he lived through those three seconds as the SAS man acclimatized himself to the light of the room was due to the soldier's training and expertise, and his knowledge of when it was necessary to shoot, when not. At electric-shock speed he assimilated the atmosphere of the room, saw the crumpled figure, the barrel that pointed nowhere, the hand removed from the immediate proximity of the grenades. And then there were others crowding into the bedroom, three and four and five more, standing high over McCoy. The light was switched on. One pulled the gun from his hand, snatching at his fragile grasp, removed the bullet from the breach, scooped up the grenades. They ran their hands over McCoy's trousers, checking him for more weapons, and lifted him without violence from the bedclothes before ripping back the pale-blue sheets. When they laid him down again, it was on the hard coiled springs of the bed.

Ciaran watched them as they worked quickly and with thoroughness around the room, no words spoken, acknowledgment that each knew what was expected of him. End of the road, Ciaran boy, but not the end his imagination had ever entertained when he played his war games. He'd thought they'd shoot. Flattering himself. Couldn't take the great Ciaran alive, without a whimper, without the mighty bang-out. Too big just to finish up this way. Deceived himself. Unimportant, though, and he didn't care. Get so tired, such far exhaustion, that you don't give a damn what happens. Glad in a way that it's over. Whichever way, with the living or the dead, unimportant, just the relief that it's completed. And the Arab had had his start, had his opportunity. And he must go through it all again, the poor little bastard. And on his own. And you're out of it, Ciaran boy, clear and finished and safe.

The captain bent over him. "Get the doctor up here." He said it without emotion, matter-of-fact. "Pity the bloody thing wasn't six inches across. Would have saved us all a load of bloody trouble."

Through the door McCoy could hear the voices of Norah's parents, frightened, gabbled and seeking the reassurance of the soldiers. There were feet on the staircase, a diffusion of voices, orders being given, and then the arrival of the doctor.

"Make a habit of this caper?" The doctor had his hand on McCoy's pulse, but his eyes, puckered with the distress of an old man, wandered from the wounds to the already healed scar in McCoy's side.

"I don't mind shifting him," said the superintendent. "But I don't want him under anesthetic yet. He's some talking to do before we get that far. We'll chat him in the ambulance and when they're cleaning him up."

The father and mother were still on the landing when they carried McCoy, bound to the stretcher, past them. They looked at him as if staring at a rodent, vermin. Hate-consumed, but schooled by fear. The progress down the narrow stairs was difficult and slow, and before they were halfway and maneuvering on the bend, McCoy heard Norah's mother, plaintive and appealing: "Where's our girl? What's happened to our Norah? What did he do to her?"

You'll find out soon enough. It amused him, without the pain he would have laughed. You'll find out and wish you'd never asked, and if they tell you, you'll wish they hadn't. But always the bloody same. Always the girls in tow, attracted like dogs to a bitch's fanny, flies in a jam pot. And always they cock it up. You're not the first, Ciaran. Just like the big boyo in Belfast. Took his bird along when they holed up in the big posh house, in the posh road, and she still went in her slippers and curlers to fetch the morning milk from the corner shop. Rest of the road had it delivered. Gave it away a mile off once the copper on car patrol spotted her. Got him nicked.

He was still wondering why the girl had betrayed him, when the stretcher party carried him out onto the street.

There were television arc lights there. They'd allowed the cameramen up from the corral at the bottom of the hill. Give 'em a show, McCoy. Give 'em a picture. Don't let the bastards see you down. The spotlights were aimed at his face and blanched the skin on his bared chest, accentuating the whiteness that surrounded the bullet hole with its sparse patch of covering lint.

He shouted, "Up the Provos," and the policeman holding the stretcher handles behind his head jolted them hard, sending the rivers of pain flowing fast and deep. Pigs, bastards. And all up to the bloody Arab to wipe the victory smile off their faces. The bloody Arab and his Mushroom Man.

Before they lifted him into the ambulance, McCoy had lost consciousness.

The cures he'd been on, the expensive, the unpleasant and the not so cosseted varieties, had never lasted for Jimmy. The craving for excess of alcohol, a dose sufficient to immunize him against pressure and anxiety, remained, lingering and nagging in his life. They'd tried most of the accepted methods to wean him away. The health farm in Hampshire had cost the most, and lasted the least time when he was back in the outside world. The withdrawal program practiced at the clinic behind Brixton Station had been the most ferocious, the most scarring and the longest-running. But all broke down at the stages when Jimmy went back to his breadwinning and the sepia world of his activities demanded some softening of its intensity. He was now a low-capability drinker, a short-capacity man. When rational he could recognize the problem; when angry and disappointed he turned away from the consequences.

The flat had been empty when he returned to it. Helen not there, gone to her own place. Could hardly blame her, didn't know what time he might have shown up or in what state of tiredness. Bed wasn't made from the previous sleeping. Washing-up not done, never was, tea leaves settled in an eddy around the plug hole of the sink. Clothes not picked up. If she'd come back, she would have done the tidying ritual. At least, wouldn't have to tell her about the car. Insurance . . . ? Didn't know, be some difficult talking. She'd hate him for it. Couldn't blame her. Pride and joy . . . and up in smoke.

He unscrewed the top of the bottle, cheap brand. Filthy expensive by the time he'd paid the porter his chip, lose it all on expenses. They looked at them hard in the Department, but he could lose that, hadn't eaten all day, funnel it through there. Straight, no water. Tap water would be warm, and he hadn't filled the ice-cube box in the fridge. About an inch to start with, four gulps, needed forcing down, coiled up his guts, blazed a trail through them. Sagged in the chair, the easy one, springs still kept in check by the upholstery, the only one, feet just reaching the table, laces at eye-level, loosened his collar. Coughed a couple of times, then corkscrewed his body forward to reach the bottle and the first refill. So tired, seemed to have been moving forever. No thoughts, just wanting to shut it all out. Jones pulling his bloody rank, the SAS captain and those bastards in the house. Should have been your day, Jimmy, and sent home early, and told to work a bloody shift pattern.

At first the telephone was simply an accompaniment to his thoughts. It took time for it to communicate urgency, and even more for it to instill the submission required for him to give up the comfort he had established for himself and hobble across the room to the table beside the bed. He deliberated whether to answer its insistence, but the discipline won through. He picked up the receiver and gave out the number, had it right too, and that surprised him.

"It's Jones here, Jimmy. It's all over down at this end."

"Congratulations." Jimmy had difficulties, the word was slow coming.

"It's not like that, Jimmy. We have McCoy, but the Arab's gone. He's loose."

"Not so bright, then. Which clever bastard let him slip?"

"He went when you were there, Jimmy, so cut the quips, before the cordon . . ."

"I was on my bloody own, wasn't I? Can't be round the whole house. He didn't come through the front." All the bloody same, bloody buck-passers brigade.

"Don't come the maudlin, Jimmy. No one's criticizing you. It's a statement of fact. He's loose, with a minimum of five hours' start. I want you at the West Middlesex, and now. Not hanging about, but down there now. They're patching McCoy up, and we're keeping the surgeons off him till we've had a preliminary. After that he goes under, has his surgery, and they dig your bullet out of him."

"Leave the bloody thing there."

"Don't screw me about, Jimmy. We have to know what the Arab is at. McCoy has to tell us."

"You've got others who can go and do it." Why wouldn't the bloody man get off the line and leave him to the bottle and the chair? Why Jimmy, why not any of the young ones who fancied their hand at interrogation? Budding Skardons all of them, looking for another Klaus Fuchs to break, looking for a reputation.

"Jimmy, stop waffling, stop boozing, and get off your arse. The Yard's down there. I'm on my way. I've sent a car for you, be at your door in about ten minutes. Put your head under the tap and be there. I want you to talk to McCoy, that's all."

Even with the drink, Jimmy knew why he had been called. Just like Jones, the way his mind worked. Who'd be on the same wave length as this Irish bastard, who'd be able to frighten him, or win him, or batter it out of him? Not a copper, not one of the bright lads transferred from Intelligence Corps, not old Jonesey himself. Another thug, that's what he wanted, and put them together. Two rats, both hungry, in the same hole. Two roaches disputing the one patch.

Jimmy sat up, breaking his catnap as the car drove through the wide gateway and into the hospital forecourt. Sleep when you can, basic rule, fit it in with the opportunity, always the same when the other lot dictates the timetable, hold the initiative. Time now to regret the whiskey, hadn't been much lift in the bottle, motion of the car didn't help. Head spinning, uncontrollable circles. The half-light was beginning to simper through and the nineteenth-century blocks were heavily outlined against the coming dawn. Blue-and-white signs pointed in every direction. CASUALTY. MATERNITY. X-RAY, OUT PATIENTS. Ward names, remembering local dignitaries. He saw the police van and the group of uniformed men outside Casualty, and the car pulled up there.

Jones was waiting for him. He saw Jimmy's appearance and winced, distaste on his face. "We don't have long. The surgeons are coming, impatient. Want to get their hands on him. Police haven't had anything out of him. Laughs at them. He's weak, but should survive. Reckons he's the cat's whiskers, probably the morphine."

He led the way through the corridors beyond Casualty, past the red-eyed junior doctors and nurses who slipped the night away waiting for the road accidents and the self-damaged drunks. By the staircase there were plainclothes men, cigarettes cupped in their hands, the whole place deathly quiet and accentuating their echoing steps. They went up the stairs onto the first floor and toward the ward entrance to their right. Jones said, "Fifteen minutes maximum. You and me, I'll take the notes. Just get the bastard talking."

He showed his ID card to the two policemen outside the door short of the main communal ward area, and went into the private room. Small, barely big enough for a bed, a table and an upright chair. They'd worked a small chest in there as well and the two men had to ease their way around the obstacles to get to the bedside. There was a nurse sitting at McCoy's feet, short and West Indian, her feet dangling above the floor, waiting the requisite time before removing the thermometer that stuck out like a battleship's gun from the Irishman's mouth. The two men said nothing, allowed her to wait till she was ready, examine the thin glass tube, and write down the results of her study on her clipboard. She moved past them, avoiding their eyes, and went out into the corridor. The detective who had been sitting in the room watching McCoy followed her. Jimmy took the nurse's place on the bed; Jones, the vacated chair.

Picking at his nose, Jimmy said, "My name's Jimmy. I'm here till we've finished with you. After that you'll get the surgeon. But not until we've chatted. Doesn't matter to us whether it's ten minutes, ten hours, ten days . . ."

"That's not what the doctor . . ." McCoy spoke with a faintness, whispering.

"Fuck the doctor, McCoy. The medics come back through that door when we say so."

"They said . . ."

"Well, they got it wrong. Don't you follow in their tracks. We've all the time in the world. You haven't. You're short of an exit wound, right?"

McCoy turned his head toward Jimmy, managed to lift himself fractionally so that he could see into the eyes, grey-blue and pitiless, rimmed with redness. There was a man like that in Armagh City, came to do the executions, seemed to matter less to him than culling a pig on market Thursdays.

"I know about that bullet. I fired it. Not a good shot, should have bloody killed you. Was ahead of you all yesterday. Fired first at the meeting when your gun was still waving about, followed you out, trailed you all the way. Then you gave me a good clear shot while you stood on the pavement, couple of bloody gooks. Pathetic stuff, McCoy, and you supposed to be a bloody expert. Short of men on your side of the water, are they?"

Good stuff, Jimmy boy, thought Jones. Nothing to write down yet on his pad, but setting him up well. Kicking the boy's vanity, needling him and hard.

McCoy could remember, though his concentration surged and ebbed, the time the army had lifted him years before. There had been a roughness, but a certain set of rules about it all. Pinioned him, not gently, but they'd never given him the fear that they'd kill him. This man . . . different. Not a soldier, not a policeman . . . different. An enemy.

"Wasn't me on the gun."

" 'Course it bloody wasn't you on the gun. That was the sharp end, wasn't it? Didn't expect you'd be there, didn't expect you'd be standing by the window when we all started blasting. Left the man's bit to the kiddie, did you?"

"Famy wanted to shoot, that's what he came for."

Jones's pencil started to move, first words on the clean paper. A name at last to put to the face. Not really important, but tidier. Made it all neater when you had a caption for the picture. And all those bloody hours they'd put in just to get the name, and now they had it, irrelevant, not worth a damn alongside the usefulness of having the face. Jimmy would have registered it too, would have given him the kick he needed to get on top. Be no stopping him now.

"He's worse than you, and that's fucking useless." Jimmy's voice was quiet, casual. As if the conversation were about the visiting center forward, between strangers on the terraces. McCoy could follow the technique, was aware of it, but too tired, too hurt, too drugged to combat his adversary.

"He's not finished, the boy."

"Only because he's running. Running with the mess in his pants and the paper in his hand."

"He'll bloody show you, you Britisher pig."

Out in the corridor where nurses and doctors waited, gathered beside the police guard, they heard the Irishman struggling to shout. Looked at their watches, noted how much longer the questioning could continue.

"He'll show us how fast he can run."

"He's not finished. What do you think I stayed behind for? Why hole up, if not to give him time? I wasn't there just so's he could scarper. He's set to blast you, you and the Yiddisher."

Jimmy laughed, exaggerated, loud, ridiculing. "He'll never see him."

"He'll see him and he'll get him."

"What do you think we're going to do, you pig-thick ape? Parade him up Whitehall? Stick him in a coconut shy? Had your bloody chance, and you buggered it."

"You can't keep him close all the time. He'll have to put his bloody feet on the ground . . ."

"There's only one place."

"Right," hissed McCoy.

Jimmy could see him quivering, chest shaking, breath panted in the emotion of the dispute. "The airport. Up the steps the little man goes and your hero makes his last stand." Jimmy gabbled the words out, maintaining the momentum.

McCoy was with him. "Right, right first bloody time."

Jimmy said nothing. Sudden, total silence. Quiet in the tiny room. The noise stillborn, the voices aborted.

McCoy's eyes closed tight shut. The enormity of what he'd said, slow in dawning, then overwhelming. Betrayed him. Ciaran McCoy, volunteer and officer of the Irish Republican Army, had betrayed him. "Holy Mother of Jesus, forgive me." His lips barely moved with the formation of the words that Jimmy did not hear.

Jimmy stretched off the bed and walked toward the door, Jones a pace behind. He said, distant, matter-of-fact, "The surgeon only gave us fifteen minutes. We reckoned that would be enough. And we were right, Ciaran, we've four and a half to spare. So it's over to his tender hands now. Hope the bloody knife's blunt."

McCoy did not see him go. In his life he had never known such abject misery.

The diversion along the park wall and then the search for the bridge crossing of the Thames had cost Famy a considerable detour, switching his journey from six miles to nearly nine. But the pale sliver of light was spreading as he came to the cohorts of warehouses and offices that marked the outer perimeter of Heathrow. New confidence, now that he was alone, held him, and on his back the new clothes—blue jeans and a pale-green shirt. It had been a clear night and the housewife, who worked a long day's shift, had seen the opportunity to leave her husband's washing out on the garden line. A bonus for Famy as he had gone on his way. New clothes that would render obsolete the description given to the police in Richmond.

Famy recognized the danger of moving too far a distance inside the airport before he had solidified the cover that he regarded as essential to protect himself later in the day. The detail he had studied and accepted as he had run. Now all he needed, he told himself, was time. Time to move to the position that he must have. Time to be ready when the El Al landed. Must be there for the first one. They'd take him out, send him home, rid themselves of Sokarev. And so easy to know, once he was there. Can always tell when a big man is flying, or one they think highly of. The security, that's what gives it away, what makes it so obvious. But had to get there, and then stay and wait and watch, watch for the signs that meant Sokarev was coming. Had to get there, to where the first El Al flight would take on its passengers, and then be patient and observe, and look for the security men, the hard-faced men who would tell him the quarry was close.

In Fatahland they would be waking now. In the tents set amongst the scrub and the rocks his colleagues in arms had passed a night spent dreaming of an opportunity such as he had been given, awaiting it as their own one-time destiny. The new day would be coming over the camp. The same sun rising across the mountain to the east of Nablus, where the road ran on down to the Jordan Valley, where his father would be out of his bed, and his mother already in the kitchen outhouse behind the bungalow, and his brothers dressing for school. And in Haifa and Netanya and Ashkelon and Beersheba the Jews would be waking too. All would say his name when the next evening came. Some with adulation, some with resignation, some with detestation. The blow he prepared to strike would be mighty, it would shatter the fetid complacence of many millions, and to those who lived on the far side of the wire and the mine fields and who longed to cross over, he would bring hope and aspiration. There was a pounding of excitement, close to purest happiness.

Inside the perimeter he skirted the road that ran adjacent to the runways and across the acres of dividing clipped grass, keeping back from the vague traffic flow, seeking the shadows. He appeared to any who might notice him as one more from the ranks of the thousands of immigrant workers, the lifeblood of the airport, on his way to another day at work, washing dishes, sweeping concourses, cleaning lavatories. His bag seemed not to weigh so heavily, the roar of the big engines lightening the load. He was very near to the end of his mission.

Back in Lebanon they had told him about the tunnel that was

the sole route from the outside conurbation to the heart of the
airport complex. They had showed him a photograph of its
entry, pointing out the footpath lane that ran its length, seper-
ate from the vehicle road. If there was security, that path could
be guarded—too simple, too easy, and risks should not be taken,
not when the scent was so strong. He saw the bus queue, a short
hundred yards up the hill from the entry tunnel, a straggled line
of brown faces, of turbans and saris, many carrying the bags that
contained their working overalls, bags that were so similar to
the one that rested by his feet when he joined them. Infiltrate
where you will not be noticed, that is what they had told him;
there is a time for combat uniform and a time for camouflage.
And the bus when it came would take him to the central terminals. He must look there for the canteens and rest rooms where
the workers gathered for their breaks. He must look for a man
whose job, whose appearance and whose identity papers would
give him the passport to the tarmac where the jumbo would
refuel and reload its seats.

One man, one man from so many who would be there, one
man alone was necessary.

Nineteen

The bus was hideously slow through the tunnel. Worrying its way down the underground passage, sandwiched between the cars and lorries and coaches. No speed, no hurry, no urgency. Flashes of illumination thrown into the interior from the big yellow lights fastened to the angle where the sides met the roof, causing Famy to turn outward toward the windows, obscuring his features from his fellow passengers. There was little talk on the bus. Eyes of the inmates remote and insular, men and women compartmentalizing themselves from their seated neighbors, minds dulled by the time of day and the anticipation of the boredom and frustration of their service tasks through the next nine hours. They were gelatinous, soft, thought Famy. Unthinking fodder, and with neither the power nor desire to question the humiliation of the role that had been awarded to them. Poverty of initiative, absence of hope. Facing another day of averted eyes, stumbling submission, far from their own country. Plucked from a great distance and brought here to serve. Pathetic people, without the arm of Famy and his strength, incapable of insurrection against the system, shackled. And they would have little comprehension of the Arab, fail to understand his mission and what he tried to achieve for them.

They would be unable to accept that the M-1 and its hitting capability represented a blow as much for them as for the men and women and children in the Chatila and Sabra camps.

Did not all the colonialists support the Israeli state? They paid lip service to the enemies of Israel, but only superficially, only for their gasoline. There was no sincerity. The white man identified with the Jew. When the day was over, and they sat again on the bus that would reverse its route and they went back to their homes, how would these people have reacted to the operation that Abdel-El-Famy planned for the last hours of their work shift? Too stupid, most of them. Few would acknowledge that his act was for them, for all the majorities that lacked wealth and opportunity. They were trapped, these people, as trapped and imprisoned as the Palestinians. Without homelands, without fields, without flocks, without expression. It is a daydream, Famy; tomorrow will be the time of dreams, tomorrow . . . but today there is not time. The bus increased its speed, surged into the selected lane that would direct it to the central airport buildings.

They swung across the traffic lanes, paused at the traffic lights, and then turned right toward the bus shelter where the night-shift workers waited. As the brakes were applied many were standing up, lifting their bags with them, and the prematureness of their movement jolted them when the bus finally came to a standstill. They were hurrying down the aisle, nervous of tardiness, and in their rush they swept Famy forward with them. His bag would have weighed heavier than the others, and it was the bag that made him different from them, separated him from their ordinariness and subservience. By the time they took to their beds that night, all would know his name. Emblazoned across their minds, unforgettable, a martyr for them, overriding their need for food, their anxiety about money, their desire for the naked comfort of their partners. But dreams again, and they must be curbed, emasculated, if the work was to be done.

Famy watched the way the men went as they left the bus stop. The procession had divided, men taking one course, women another, a splitting of the human confluence. There were other buses behind him, more in front that had already disgorged and were pulling away, and the stream took him toward the opened double doors of the red-brick building surmounted by the blue-tinged windows of the octagonal all-seeing control tower. There were signs beside the entrance. CANTEEN and ADMITTANCE TO STAFF ONLY. No security checks, none that were visible anyway, but early, that would come later. Nothing sensitive here, no threat presented. But it suited him well to be out of the rising sunlight, mingled and anonymous amongst the mass of people who belonged to the system. This was not where they would be looking for him. A place where he could rest, where his legs that ached and protested could relax, where he could doze and regain the sharpness of thought and clarity that he must have by the midafternoon.

The woman who served him at the long counter was surprised at the way his coffee cup and saucer rattled as he carried them away from the cash machine. She put it down to nerves. Like half these bloody Asians, she thought, scared half out of their wits, and what do they have to do, only clean out the loos and push a broom round. It amused her, gave a cherished feeling of superiority. She was wrong in her assessment. There was no fear in Famy now. That his hand shook was from the strain of carrying the bag for so many hours, fingers entwined around the plastic strap. But no fear, not now that he was without the Irishman. And confidence is of critical value to the assassin. The killer has to believe in his prowess as much as his cause, must believe in his ability as much as the God-given right to exact retribution. Those who saw the unfamiliar face sitting at the clothless table by the window would have latched onto the great contentment on his features. The gentleness that comes from peace of mind and the patience to consume time. He was now a more dangerous and potentially lethal figure than at any time since he had landed in England. He had come to terms with his mission, and with its implications. He was ready to kill.

He put three spoonfuls of sugar into the coffee, stirred it slowly, and looked about him.

Along the Great West Road leading toward London from Windsor, huge queues of traffic formed up behind the military convoy.

Land-Rovers front and rear, fifteen three-ton trucks, each carrying twenty soldiers. Alpha, Bravo and Headquarters Com-

pany. Grenadier Guards, long lines of battle honors stretching
back into three hundred years of history. Thin Red Line tunics
of the ceremonial discarded for mottled camouflage denims,
the uniform of urban guerrilla warfare on the streets of Northern Ireland. Four hundred men in all. FN rifles. General-pur-
pose machine guns. Hand-held Carl Gustav rocket launchers.
There to protect one man from the hands of an equally solitary
threat. The resident battalion at Windsor Barracks had practiced their recent responsibilities of Heathrow Security many
times on exercise, but there was a tightness and silence about
the men who sat on the slatted seats in the backs of the lorries.
Never before had they been told the risk was real, confirmed.

Interspersed amongst the trucks were the armored cars of
two Hussar squadrons, Saladins with khaki cloth tied across the
muzzle of the big gun, and the Saracen personnel carriers.

Police reinforcements were being mobilized from divisional
forces in the Metropolitan area. More would come from the
rural Thames Valley strength. By nine in the morning the perimeter of the airport would be sealed, the concourses would be
under guard, the tarmac patrolled. Later the plans for the security of the El Al flight to Tel Aviv would be thrashed out in the
squat police station on the far side of the tunnel, where the
various security forces would set up their control and communication posts.

The Prime Minister had rubber-stamped the guidance from
Home Office and Defence. Saturation. Forces of such strength
that the Arab would turn his back on his target, dismayed. Box
the bastard out, deny him any chink of light, any opportunity
to attack.

Through the window he saw the deploying. Little strung-out
columns of troops. Rifles carried warily and diagonally across
their bodies, letting the bustling civilians fan out and find a path
to the side. Some draped in the belts of machine-gun ammunition, worn in cross-over sashes. One man in each patrol
hunched forward to compensate his balance for the weight of
the radio set with its quivering antenna that perched high on
the back. Amongst the conventional throb of the traffic, he
heard the piercing and complaining squeal of the big Rolls-
Royce engines of the armored cars, always seeming to protest

at the gear they were driven in. He saw the pedestrians out on
the pavement pause, and turn and stare at them. All had read
their morning papers, heard the radio news bulletins. They
would wait about for the show to begin. It amused Famy. One
against so many. No one to share the glory moment with him.
So much rallied against him. So many of them. After a while he
became tired of watching the crisscross motions of his enemy,
and finished his coffee. He walked back to the counter, ordered
a fresh cup, and with it a sandwich filled with dried and crum-
bling cheese and slices of overripe tomato segments.

There were many hours to be consumed before it would be
time for him to move. But the sights beyond the window fanned
his confidence, spread it like a brushfire. His best hopes were
confirmed. The troops and the guns had not come just to hunt
down Abdel-El-Famy. There was another more cogent and po-
tent reason. The Mushroom Man would be traveling, on course
for their rendezvous. The fly into the web, the lion toward the
pit. And all the soldiers and police would be like extras, like
onlookers.

From the next table he took a discarded newspaper and read
a version of the previous night's events. His English was adequate, sufficient for him to understand what had been written.
He was "fleeing," he was "probably on drugs," he was a "fanatic." The public was warned to keep away from him, not to
"have a go," told to phone the police if he was sighted. Guns had
been widely distributed to the police. He would be shot on
sight, the journalist had written. On the front page there was
a smudged and meaningless picture of the house where he had
left McCoy, a policeman there and a rifle in his hand, and the
story was topped with the news of the capture of his friend.
Described as "late news." He read that McCoy, though injured,
would live, and he was thankful. But they do not understand,
he thought. There is no word of Palestine, no word of the bomb,
no word of the camps and the suffering. It raged through him
so that he wanted to scream and shout at those who shared the
canteen with him. Do they care so little for Palestine that they
take no trouble to understand why? Why do they think we are
prepared to die? Stupid, goat-shit bastards, do we enjoy death?
Can there be no sanity in what we do? Can we never be right,
justified, driven beyond the boundaries? And then his temper

calmed. On the center pages of the tabloid was a photograph, blown large, of David Sokarev. More recent than the old snapshot they had shown him in Lebanon. He could dwell on the face in a way that had not been possible in the split seconds that he had peered into the artificial light of the hall. Remember it closely, study its detail. There will be little time when he is between the car and the steps, and he will be hurrying, and there will be men around him. Recognition must be instinctive. Not as it was in the hall when the eyes had to search and traverse. Faster this time.

He would know him. Whether he was crouched low, whether he wore a hat, whether he had his coat collar turned up, however fast he went. He would know him.

The alcohol that he had drunk in the small hours needed greater time to disperse through the bloodstream than Jimmy had permitted. Short of sleep and still wound at wire tension he came to the hotel. The adrenalin that for a short period had fought and overcome the whiskey for control of his veins, as he confronted McCoy, was now bested, back to second place. Johnny Walker supreme. Head aching with the pressure trying to break out and expand from the confines of his skull. Splitting pain, and self-administered. Wanted to rest, wanted just to fold up, curl in a corner and sleep it off. But no rest permitted. Told where he had to be, and that was with Sokarev. Back on course again, Jimmy, taking orders, doing as the gaffer said.

The Branch man in the foyer recognized him from the previous days, nodded a greeting, and described his passage into the lift over a small radio transmitter. New that, souping things up a bit, and so they bloody ought to. On the fourth floor he was met again, quizzically and with suspicion, by a man he had not seen before and who blocked his way down the corridor to the Israelis' rooms. Jimmy fumbled for his wallet and searched among the folds for his card. Should have been able to spot it straightaway. Knew where he put the bloody thing, but couldn't find it. Always put in the same place, but where? And then it was there, clearly to be seen, where he should have looked in the first place. Jimmy mouthed an apology, embarrassed. The detective was clean-shirted, shaved, dressed for work. And you, you look a bloody wreck, Jimmy. Bloody shambles. The policeman examined the card, searched back again into Jimmy's face, handed the card back, and stepped sideways to allow him through. There were more men outside the doors of the two rooms. They would have seen the initial checking, but went through the routine again. Bloody coppers. Jimmy knocked on the first door, opened in response by Elkin.

The greeting was mutually cool. Had to be after last night. No source of congratulations. Jimmy noted that the curtains of the room were drawn, bedside light on, no possibility of anyone outside the building being able to see inside the room, basic precaution, as it should be. Everyone learning what it's all about. There was a new man slouched on the far bed, the Uzi not more than six inches from his right hand.

Elkin went straight into the attack, had been accumulating it. "It will be different from yesterday. We have taken charge of the arrangements. Any plan will go through us, be approved by us."

"You'll do as you're bloody well told." Hadn't expected the assault that fast.

"After last night we make the decisions."

"You'll make the decisions when you're on that fucking aircraft . . ."

"We left it to you, and it was a fiasco."

"You'll be told what's going to happen, and if you don't bloody like it, you can get out on the bloody pavement and walk to the airport." When Jimmy shouted, the sledge hammer reverberated behind his ears. He closed his eyes. All so bloody daft, childish. When he forced the lids hard together he could squeeze out the pain. "Calm yourself down, for God's sake." He spoke like a man who wants to end the full drama of a domestic row, wants to pack it in and forget it by the morning. "Did you sleep last night?"

Elkin shook his head. Bags big and bulged, spreading to his cheeks, high red flush beneath them, eyes above soft and watery.

Bugger's been in tears, Jimmy saw. "We have the Irishman. Only leaves the other one. Fancies himself at the airport when your man goes out this afternoon. Be out of his depth. Less chance than a chicken in Biafra. He's no hope. They'll be working out a route later in the morning, nothing for you till that gets in the pipeline. You should put your head down till then."

Elkin walked back to his bed, sat on it heavily. Jimmy recognized he would struggle to stay awake, and lose. Poor sod, doesn't rate us, and why should he? Fearful that we'll cock-up while he's kipping. And everyone so bloody tired; never known an operation when they weren't all walking round like zombies . . . What Jones had said, wasn't it? Stupid old bugger. Jimmy took off his coat and slung it on the floor, lifted the pistol from the shoulder holster and pressed it into the waist of his trousers before dumping himself into a brocaded armchair. He had thought that sleep would come easy to him, pleaded for it, aware of how much faster the incapacity of exhaustion came to him as he veered between middle and old age. But the liberation was not at hand, made harder by the still figure of Elkin on his bed. Jimmy willed himself to follow, but without success. And his head throbbed, with the blood-scarlet flashes tracing across his vision.

Beyond the partition door David Sokarev, too, was asleep. Jimmy had heard no movement, no creaking of restless bedsprings, and turned the door handle, giving himself a few inches of vision. Like a little bloody angel. No nightmares, the pills had seen to that. Dead to the world, blanked out, insensitive to it all. Pray the drug keeps him there. Met a man once in a pub, where you meet them all, Jimmy. In his cups, deep. Said he'd been a prison screw. Once done the death-cell stint. Hadn't volunteered, the sick list had seen him on the rota, usual guys not available. Not the actual night, but the one before. And the man had slept, and they'd all marveled, and known the news the governor had brought the previous evening. Even slept through the shift change, and the new screws had tiptoed in. They'd let his breakfast get cold, fearful for him when the protection of sleep was gone. He'd been a crude bugger, the one who'd told him the story, but different when he spoke of this. And the more that Sokarev slept, the better. Cushion him from the carry-on. Only bloody defense he had. A weak face he had, unprotected, with its old man's stubble.

And by the late afternoon Sokarev would be gone, and his hands would be washed—and he'd be back with his girl, and no phone calls, and he'd retrieve the bottle. God, he wished his head would call a cease-fire. He'd be in lousy shape in the afternoon. Bloody lousy.

*   *   *

Famy had studied many of the men who came into the canteen through the early and middle morning. Some he dismissed immediately as being of no use to him, others he toyed with for longer, examining their features and their build, before rejecting them, too, as unsuitable for his purpose.

It was gone eleven when he saw the man he wanted. Indian, correct height, at a little below six feet. Youngish, early twenties, and not yet filled out with the obesity of his race. A turban, good because it distracted from the facial images, took attention away from them, white and cleanly furled. No mustache, no hair on the chin bone, but there was time for Famy to use his battery razor and match that. White overalls, emblazoned across the left chest with the British Airways sign and, more important, specked with oil spots and smeared with grease. Maintenance. A man who worked on the engines, tended the beasts when they were tethered, had access to them when they lay crippled. And where did the work go on? At the piers, on the tarmac, on the big concrete open spaces where the aircraft sojourned. Access dominated his thinking. The need to find an identity that ensured access. A job that provided access to the hidden and secret areas denied to ordinary civilians, the ticket behind the wire fences and the control points.

Famy left his table, and holding his bag, moved across the grimed floor of the canteen toward the table where the Sikh sat, solitary, unaware of the man who approached him.

As his car drove away from the cul-de-sac of Downing Street, the Israeli ambassador's acute concern was defused. He had taken his security attaché with him to the meeting with the British Prime Minister, but had left him outside the heavy oakwood doors to the personal office. Alone for an hour with the British head of government, he had discussed the previous night's attack. They had moved on from the past to the plans that had been drawn up for the departure of David Sokarev in the late afternoon.

"The Prime Minister put it to me," said the ambassador to his companion, "that his government could in no way be accused of dragging their heels on this matter. He said it was his personal order that preparations were made for an assault on the house where it was thought the terrorists had taken refuge. He said that the safety of the hostages was put at secondary priority compared with the need to avoid negotiating with these people. I cannot counter that. It was to be done as we would have hoped. And they have been fast with the interrogation of the one man they hold. They tell me that the Arab will attempt a final attack at the airport. It is admitted that there was laxity at the university, but I have assurances that it will not be repeated. It would have been difficult for me to relay the instructions of the Foreign Ministry."

The security attaché was unconcerned with the private diplomatic innuendo that had passed between the two men out of his hearing. "What are their plans for the airport?" More important, what had his civilian master, short of a military background, agreed to?

"They have moved troops to Heathrow. Guardsmen and light cavalry. They are bringing in more police. There will be around a thousand men from their security forces, many armed, they tell me. The Prime Minister informs me that the Arab is in possession of an M-1 carbine with a maximum effective range of three hundred meters. Therefore, they will put an army and police cordon in position of a circle with a radius of four hundred meters around the jet liner. There will be no admittance inside that area other than for vetted personnel, our own people and the security men. The plane will already be loaded when Sokarev boards . . ."

"How is he transferred to the airport?"

"It is the assessment of the British that a motor convoy is the best method. There are many points of entry into Heathrow, and they maintain that it would be impossible for the Arab to be correctly positioned, and knowing which one they will use. I see no reason for disputing that. It is their hope that the demonstration of force will be so great as to deter the man until Professor Sokarev is safely in the air. After that they will concentrate on his capture."

"So, again they have not consulted us." The attaché spoke evenly, not looking at the ambassador, watching the oncoming traffic.

"They have consulted me."

"You are not an expert in these matters."

"That is offensive."

"You would not know whether there were flaws in the plan or not."

"Where are the flaws that your experience warns you of?" Knife-edge sarcasm from the ambassador.

"How can I tell? How can I estimate? I had hoped to see the plans. Discuss them. Negotiate them. Be given alternates, told of the contingency fall-backs. There is no chance of that now."

The ambassador was silent, thoughtful of the way he had committed himself so few minutes earlier. Career, future, promotion to permanent position in the Ministry in Jerusalem—all might rest on the agreement he had made with the Prime Minister. The attaché said nothing else. The point had been made, there was no value in returning to it. They would do their best, the British. Probably haphazard, but their best. Only they were not experts. The Israelis alone were experts with these bastards. Europeans did not understand them, were naïve in the new science of counterterrorism. But so proud of their integrity, so determined to make their own decisions. And their own mistakes. So there had been no talk of decoys, or of helicopters, or of military aircraft. Do they comprehend the resourcefulness of the assassin who is prepared to die that he should reach his target? He doubted it, and the belief tightened the muscles of his belly, caused the perspiration to flow in his groin. He chain-smoked the remainder of the drive back to their fortress embassy.

Mohan Singh was happy at the other man's company. It was rare for him to have conversation during the early lunch break when his shift pattern decreed that he go sooner for his food than many of his work colleagues. The stranger listened to his problems, to the description of his life and his education, the circumstances that had brought him to England, and his difficulties in finding a job as rewarding financially as the one that he now held. He spoke of his family—his wife and the three small children—how they lived in two rooms at the back of an uncle's house in Hounslow, how he was obliged to send money back to Amritsar to maintain his elderly parents. He was not aware as he chattered on in his high-strung accent that the man with him spoke little, just nodded and smiled and encouraged.

There was not long, Famy knew that. Sitting at the table

already for fifteen minutes, there for another fifteen before the approach. How many more before he returned to his work? High wall clock turning, not much time. And all the while the plans racing, wasp fast, through his mind. They had more coffee, Famy going up to the counter and collecting the two cups. His hands no longer shook, relaxed and supple now, fingers eased, pliant, sensitive to touch. They would be able to seek out their target, cling to it, squeeze on it. And the strength had returned to his wrists . . . He set the coffee cups down and inclined his head to hear again what the Indian wanted to pour out to him. He had no feeling about the clear ice-water knowledge that he would kill this man. He was nothing. An arcade machine, currently activated by a coin. Not an enemy, not a friend, just a carriage to take him to his destination, to his destiny. McCoy would have done it better, would have had more expertise, but McCoy had made the sacrifice for him, and he must fulfill his trust.

The man was tedious to Famy. Grumbling, but frightened to be considered in that light, without the courage to fight for what he wanted. Like a carpet that complains but cannot shift itself from the trampling boots. He would die quickly, compliant with his fate.

The Indian had finished his coffee, coughed and cleared the sinuses of his nose, loud and guttural. "I must return, or I will be late for the afternoon's work. It has been nice—"

Famy interrupted. "I have to wash my hands. You will show me the lavatory?" A stranger, helpless, needing a friend.

The Indian responded. "I will show you. It is difficult to find if one is new here."

They walked together down the corridor, further into the building and away from the canteen. Twenty yards, perhaps thirty, and around two corners till they came to the door with the male puppet-trousered symbol set high on it.

The Indian smiled. "It is here. Not easy to find."

His inclination then would have been to leave and walk away, but Famy spoke quickly and at the same time pushed open the door, moving inside. "I would like to see you again. Where could we meet?" And the mayfly settled over the trout tunnel.

Mohan Singh followed him. Famy was no longer listening, was taking in the layout, the cubicles at the far end of the long side walls past the stand-up urinals. There was a man there, nearly completed, heaving his hips in flabby motion to shake off the last drops. He would be gone in a moment. Not a place that men delayed beyond their business.

At the washbasin, the water running, loud, interfering, Famy pretended not to hear. "Wait a minute. Till I have finished," he said over his shoulder. In the mirror he saw the man move toward the door, heard it slam in his wake.

Famy swept the water from his hands onto the front of his jeans and spun to face the Indian. No words now—and how many seconds before another man blurted in? The Indian had started to talk again when Famy's forearm, swung from far back, hit him on the protuberance of his throat, at the Adam's apple apex. A gurgling, choking moment of protest. Surprise in the eyes before the misting of insensibility. Famy caught him as he collapsed downward, and pulled him, limp now and unprotesting, to the furthest of the lavatory cubicles. Like a sack of the dried ass mess they took to the fields carved in the valley past Nablus town. A weight, unresponsive till properly maneuvered. Famy pulled the Indian through the door into the constricted space in front of the bowl. Not dead yet, not a body. But had to be killed, had to be silenced. He worked the shape in front of him so that the head faced inward and he had room to close the door behind him and fasten the catch. *Engaged* it would say to any one who came. And he would hear the door into the main corridor if it was opened and an intruder entered. That would hold him up. Time would be fugitive again. He had waited all morning for his man, was now impatient.

He closed his eyes, settled himself as if in a moment of prayer, seeking the strength that now was essential, knuckles whitened, nails in his palms. He raised up the Indian's head, took the turban from it, placed it carefully on the door hook, particular not to disarrange it, aware that he would not know how to rebind it. Then pulled the zipper of the overalls down to the level of the upper waist and clawed the arms of the garment from around the shoulders till it rested in a concentrated mass on his hips. The overall, as much as the turban, was too vital to be defiled if they were to serve his purpose. And now he was ready. A fearful clarity, in slow, stopped motion. Lifted the head again and with all the force in his shoulders slammed it down on the hard and cold and polished white china of the rim of the bowl. Once, twice, three times, till the bone of the skull no longer resisted the impact. Crude, irreversible, damage was what he sought. He could not hold the man in the upright position any more, slumped on his knees, blood finding independent paths into the water held at the bottom of the bowl, suffusing pinks and reds together.

There was no movement. The man had become matter. Insignificant, finished, completed. Famy heaved him once again upward so that he could observe the hurt he had inflicted, and more practically to see that the red ribbons had not passed onto the overalls that he so coveted. He stripped them off, twisting the body, lifting it, pushing it so that he could slip the garment down its length and over the shoes. It had been a hot day and the Indian wore only a singlet, deep-stained now, and pants underneath, not clean and with their own faint smell that competed with the urine stains on the floor.

He left the body, still kneeling but with the head deep in the bowl. An obscenity, but necessary to remove totally the horror of the face and the damage that he had brought to it. In the breast pocket of Mohan Singh's overalls on which the British Airways insignia had been sewn, he found the small plastic-coated Polaroid card, read the name of the man he had executed in the cause of Palestine, and looked at the photograph unrecognizable from the smashed features he no longer had the strength to gaze upon. Three minutes later, now wearing the overalls, he climbed up over the dividing wooden wall and into the next cubicle. He hurried across to the washbasins, scrubbed his hands in liquid soap to rid himself of the few blood spots that rested there. He checked in the mirror that the turban was straight and still fastened. His bag was where he had left it, under the basins.

Out in the corridor, Famy glanced at his watch. If the jumbo was on time, it would be landing in three hours and forty minutes. There would be another sixty minutes of refueling. He had far to go, each step more hazardous, more critical than the last. And he had killed for the first time, the first time in his short life. Yes, there had been men who had slumped in his gunsight in the lecture hall, but they were different, abstract, unconnected. This was with his own hands, using his own strength and his own will. It had been the irrevocable step and he had taken it.

Twenty

It was four years since the British had first awakened, and tardily at that, to the threat confronting their premier airport. The familiar Continental backdrop of patrolling troops and armed paramilitary police on the runways and in the terminals had been thought just another European eccentricity, until the Guards and their armor had deserted Windsor and rolled into Heathrow for the first time. Many had seen that as an erosion of something peculiarly British, a departure from a way of life long established, a further weakening of the nation's aloofness from the violent habits of the neighbors. But the times changed, and the troops came more frequently, their alerts reducing the bizarre appearance of their initial arrival. And the British Airports Authority, the managing body for the 2700 acres of billiard-flat grass and concrete that played host on a summer's day to close on a thousand aircraft movements, had called its charge a "national defense priority," and written in an annual review of the "formidable tasks posed by the new warfare" of terrorist attack. Familiarity, though, dulled the fascination of the armed men; the excitement died its death. Twenty million passengers came and went each year, and few could boast to their friends of having seen a rifle, a semi-hidden pistol handle at the hip of a policeman, let alone a light tank.

So on this Wednesday there was again a refreshing novelty about it all, and enough sunshine to bring out the crowds. Those who were flying arrived earlier than they otherwise would have. Those landing lingered in the anticipation of an event. Around the army, work, on the surface of things, continued uninterrupted; but ears were cocked to the wind, listening for sirens and gunfire, and above all was the perpetual drone of equally uninformed and ceaseless rumor.

The turban felt strange and unfamiliar on Famy's head. Not that it had weight, nor that it was ill-fitting. It was a constriction, the mark and uniqueness of an identity that he had not fully taken over. The overalls were right, loose and baggy, presenting no pressures on the shape of his body and masking the rifle, its barrel now pinioned downward in the belt at the front of his trousers. One of the minimal pieces of advice that they had given to him. Secrete a barreled weapon in the very front of your body. The hands always search at the sides, examine the flanks. The grenades would have been harder to dispose of on his person had the Indian not carried the small yellow plastic lunchbox in the deep pocket of his trousers. The V-40s wrapped well in the greaseproof paper that the nameless and faceless wife had packaged around her man's food in a back kitchen somewhere far away at the end of the dawn.

Famy walked with a boldness toward the security checkpoint between the two giant structures that formed Terminal Three. Departures to Right, Arrivals to Left, and straight ahead the pendulum bar, unmistakable in its red-and-white message, with the notice slung beneath, large and decisive: *Stop.* Beyond was the inner world that he had to join, the realm of the loaders and mechanics and airline personnel, passengers excluded unless they moved in their corralled herds on specific walkways. The BAA security man, blue uniform, white-rimmed cap, operated the movement of the bar from a glass-cased booth at the side. A soldier had crammed in beside him, and there was a Land-Rover behind daubed with the standard NATO camouflage parabolas. More soldiers beside the barrier itself. They were relaxed, confident, safe in the knowledge of their numbers and their firepower. Briefings had passed that down to them. Battalion commander to company commander, company commander to platoon commander, platoon commander to section leader. The word had been spread, circulated. One man was the risk. They had his picture in their minds, the description of his clothes.

An Indian in British Airways livery went no way toward fitting the requirement for vigilance and care that had been stressed to the Guardsmen. They looked in the bag, but cursorily, and laughed when he asked in a voice high-pitched by nerves, but which they took to be the flavor of his homeland, whether he should remove his turban. As they waved him through, he shouted to the men in the booth, "Good luck."

And their smiles turned to the sneers of the young. A thousand against one. So who needed luck, with those odds? Half a day more, and the rifles would be back in the armory and they'd be in the pub under the castle wall. They watched him go, and their attention was taken by the next vehicle. An airport catering van, and there was the requirement for the tedium of climbing inside and searching.

Pier 7, they had said back at the camp, was the one where the El Al would come to rest. Right at the extremity of the glass-and-prefabricated buttress down which the passengers would walk to the aircraft. Some days they would board through the tunnel that billowed out from the main construction; sometimes they would walk a few yards across the tarmac. One thing was constant, they had said, always the El Al was removed and remote from the other aircraft. Nearer to him was Pier 6, clogged with its quota of jumbo 747s—British Airways, Pan American, Trans World Airlines, Japan Air Lines, Middle East Airlines. He skirted them, measuring a distance that would cause no offense, draw no attention to him. Neither too close to the machinery nor so far out on the tarmac that his basic unfamiliarity with the surroundings would be exposed.

There were more soldiers to his front and an armored car, dwarfing them. Awaiting an arrival. Sitting and crouched amongst their packs, close to the one who had unslung the burden of the radio. Watchful, but not yet on alert. They had been right at the camp, and he praised their thoroughness, wondered where they accrued such information. This was where Sokarev would come. There were police standing in separate groups, distant and unwanted by the soldiers, a lesser force. And dogs that sat with patience beside the shins of their handlers. As he crossed beyond Pier 6, more of the reception group came into his view. Two more armored cars sheltered under the raised flooring of the further and final pier. Big, ugly, powerful. Huge engines. Mounted machine guns silhouetted against the sky. Firing power, hitting power, killing power. All there for Abdel-El-Famy. Twice he had seen the wounds on McCoy, seen his man's blood flowing from his body, seen the pain take his face. But they were pistol shots, not fatal, not lethal. Different from the force and velocity of the weapons that were now arrayed in front of him. These were stopping guns. Men did not climb up again, did not drive cars, did not see another day break, not when they were struck by this power. The M-1, difficult to forget, pressed against his groin, was unequal. Only the Kalashnikov could match. The rifle he had been trained on. A soldier's rifle, a rifle of war. Trained? Trained for what? So easy in the dry heat of the camp to talk of war, and to wave the farewells to the men who went without hope of return and whose places at the trestle tables would be filled by others with the bright eyes and the solutions and the unquestioning confidence. But what war is this? In a foreign, alien, hateful world. Reviled. Hunted. A war with only one victory, consummated only with the death of Sokarev. And if toward that victory, Famy died, of no consequence. Erased without trace if the big rifles take him. That Famy is prepared to die for Palestine . . . not important. An aggregate of irrelevance. Forgotten with the last tremors of his heartbeat. As if he had never been. But in the camp, would they not care there? Only from success can the martyrdom come. Success and only success, no other criteria. As in a dream he walked, argument and counterargument punching and confusing him, seeking answers his intellect could not provide. Why, knowing the forfeit, did we strive so willingly to be remembered? Why, when we know we will be dust, worm fodder, do we seek so hard to be recalled in friends' minds and in their voices? Famy did not know. Did not have the comprehension. Yearned only to be mourned. But understood the currency. To be remembered with tears, then Sokarev must die. Only then would they weep for him, the boys with the abyss-brown eyes who shared his tent in the camp.

"Where the bloody hell do you think you're going?" Strident, breaking in through his fantasies. The voice was rough, aged and foreign to him. "Get out of the bloody way."

Famy was rigid. Horror at discovery, disaster. His eyes flick-
ered, body still. The fork-lift cargo transport was five feet away
from him, directly in his path, painted strident yellow and blue.
El Al colors.

"You want to look where you're bloody going, mate."

"I'm sorry." Famy stuttered the words.

"Not half you won't be sorry, not if this lot runs over you.
What do you think those bloody lines are for, the white ones?
'Cos it's for trucks, right? Trucks corridor."

"I was watching the soldiers."

"Stupid buggers, goofing about because of this Arab and the
Yiddisher. If you worked for El Al, you'd seen enough of them.
Troops, police and their own crowd, and they're right bas-
tards . . ."

Famy had recovered, was steadier. He was not one of them,
this man. An employee, but not of their blood. "It will be a big
show this afternoon, all the troops and things, when the Israeli
comes."

"Not here it won't."

"But when he boards, there will be great security, surely?"

"Not putting him on here. Stands to reason. They're not
bloody fools, these people. Load up here, taxi onto 28L, across
to the VIP suite, lift him on, and up, up and away, and all the
squaddies and coppers can go home."

"I didn't know there was a VIP area there." Fishing, Famy.
Deep, black water, unable to detect what is at the bait, uncertain of the reward.

"The new one. The one the old girl uses when she's off to
Balmoral, where they put Kissinger down, right beside Cargo."

"I'm sorry that I was in your way." Famy smiled, and turned
and began to walk toward the nearest British Airways plane.

A fleet of company trucks hovered underneath the fuselage
belly. There would be a lift there. He would say he was urgently
required at Cargo. It would only take a man a few minutes to
drive him, and he would be close then. As close as he needed.
Within range, within the range even of the puny M-1.

The fleeting relief that Jimmy had succumbed to was broken
by the arrival of Jones in the hotel room. He was aware of the
voices, dim and thudding through his consciousness, before

his eyes reluctantly took in the scene, lids prized apart in protest at the sounds. Elkin looked to have benefited from the rest. He stood now on the far side of the room and close to Jones, and they were examining a sheaf of typewritten sheets. The security attaché was with them, and before he let his presence back with the living be known, Jimmy accepted that the conversation was between Elkin and Jones, the attaché on the outside, present but not partaking of the feast. No sign of Sokarev. Poor bugger, thought Jimmy, still holed up in his patch and waiting to be consigned. Wonder they don't give him a waybill, stick a number on his arse and freight him home. His head still hurt, not as acutely as before, but intermittently. Take the bloody pledge, man. Your age, and still don't know better.

Jones acknowledged him. Not with friendship, not with warmth, just recognition. Doesn't really like me, after all these years, tolerates me round. Accepts he needs me today, knows he won't have to go through the charade tomorrow. That'll be the ditching time, usefulness used up. Quick handshake it'll be, then piss off and don't show your face till it's been under the long-term tap and washed the bloody booze out. No obligation, not till the next time, till there's a bit of filth that needs scooping off the carpet, a drain that needs cleaning that stinks too much for him to put his pure white hands down.

"Glad to have you back with us, Jimmy," Jones said. "I was summoning the courage to kick you, you've been snoring like a sow in labor."

"Why didn't you wake me up when the confab started?"

"Nothing too complicated there, and you were much too pretty to disturb. Mr. Elkin and I have gone over it."

Pompous bugger. Wasn't like that when he wanted McCoy talked to. Means he thinks it's a piece of cake from now, all sewn up and can't go wrong. And it had to be. He'd be a gutsy bastard, the Arab, if they saw him again. If he puts his nose into this crab hole, then you'd have to hand it to him. Takes some balls to go where you're not wanted, not expected, only announced.

"What's my part in this show from now?" Jimmy asked, still slumped in the chair.

"You travel with him to the airport. Hold his hand all the way. Take him carefully up the steps, fasten his seat belt, and last thing before they shut up shop you vamoose down the ramp again. Very simple, very straightforward."

"Where's he going from?"

"South side, the VIP area. The plane will taxi across from Terminal Three and lift him up right under our supervision. For once it's all planned, nothing for your right index to get twitchy about."

"What news of Famy . . . ?"

Jones was growing irritable. Not pleased at being spoken to with such lack of deference in public, in front of foreigners, strangers. "No word of him. But the airport's sealed. Troops, police, armor—no need for you to be worried."

"It's not me that's worried. Not my bloody job that hangs on knowing where the little runt is."

Six thousand men work at the Heathrow Cargo Terminal, there to dispatch and unload more than a thousand tons of freight a day. That an outsider, an alien, should be in their midst would not be noticed.

Famy squatted low on his bag in the sunshine in the front of the big British Airways transit shed. There were others around him, watching the soldiers in the distance, statuesque and guarding a circle of empty tarmac. He spoke to no one, nor received any words of greeting or inquiry. It was of no concern to him, he did not seek communication and conversation. More troops on the corner of the building before the open ground that stretched to the white wooden fence that shielded the bungalow VIP lounge from his sight. The presence of the turbaned stranger would not arouse comment; freighters were traditionally the veterans of the fleet, converted as their passenger days were exhausted, and it was accepted that maintenance was in frequent demand.

There was a warmth in the air, and in the distance the shapes jumped and bounced and faded, hazed by the heat. He had to blink to hold his concentration on the big plane in full view across the tarmac. The sheen gleamed on the outline of the El Al jet less than six hundred yards from him. He could make out the armored cars, black in shadow against the light, and occasionally the figures of the soldiers around them would press into focus. Beneath the upright zip of his overalls the rifle worried against his body. It hurt, and would continue to hurt. There were many minutes before the plane would be ready to take Sokarev on board. He felt a curious calm now. No anguish and no stress. The desire to dream and fantasize was conquered. All so very clear. In limbo, sucked into a void, and awaiting the inevitability of the rendezvous. It was beyond interference.

Sokarev was past complaining, or feeling any degree of independence, as they led him through the kitchens of the hotel and then into the delivery area where food and provisions were unloaded in built-up bays. The escorts seemed to be too preoccupied with their problems and anxieties to explain to the scientist the departure plan that had been decided on. The van that waited was painted blue, unmarked and with the windows smoked to obscure outside vision of the interior. There were five men with him to share the two rows of seating behind the driver. The security attaché, still defensive and introverted. Jones, who ignored all around him. Elkin, fidgeting, willing the journey over, the Uzi across his knees and constantly referring to his wristwatch. Special Branch convoy coordinator, talking all the while into his handset, and then fiddling with the dials as his answers came back in differing volume. And there was Jimmy, picking with a matchstick at the dirt under his nails, with his coat open and his gun exposed, and his head down, thoughtful and concerned and not sharing his mind.

It is as if they are punishing me, thought Sokarev. As if I am in some way culpable, to blame for what has happened. He was still tired, not rested by the capsule that the doctor had given him. They put me out of their way while they worked out their plans, needed me absent, and the easiest way was with the pill, he told himself. But it does not bring real sleep. And he recognized that the men with him were tired, had seen it in their faces, and in their clothes, the way they snapped at each other, their impatience. The equation had often been proved for him in the work at Dimona; tired men operate at reduced efficiency, and that frightened him. He felt a shortness of breath and searched for air, loosening his collar and slipping off the suit jacket he had put on for the journey. All the ventilation slats in the van were closed. He would have liked one open, to release the engine fumes and the body smells, but did not feel the authority to ask for it. Incapable of soaking up more humiliations, he sat in his seat and suffered till he felt a shiver in his limbs and deep under his clothes, and a feeling of cold and sickness. There was nobody to tell.

In the yard of Hammersmith police station, a third of the way to Heathrow and behind closed doors, he was transferred to a car. There were escorts front and back, but nothing for the casual observer of the convoy to recognize.

The security attaché drove now, Jones and the Special Branch man crowded into the front beside him. Sokarev was sandwiched between Elkin and Jimmy.

As they climbed onto the overhead road, Sokarev felt the tug at his sleeve and looked at Jimmy.

"Don't take too much notice of these buggers," Jimmy said, for all the car to hear, "they're all as shit-scared as you are. And will be till we've waved you on your way."

Famy's whole being was riveted to the movement of the big jet. Three hundred and fifty tons of it, making the solemn progress from the end of Pier 7 toward the axis of the runways. Two Saracens came in front, where he could see them, dwarfed by the huge concentric lines of the nose. Small cockpit windows, high above the ground, where the pilot and his crew were sitting. All of them able to see him, but not capable of recognizing the face of their enemy. Remember Dani, remember Bouchi, remember McCoy. Endless, indistinct faces played through his vision, sometimes blotting out and obscuring the reality of the plane. The faces of his friends, of those who had believed in him.

The plane was waved inside the cordon of soldiers. More armored cars were awaiting it, policemen beginning to scurry, and the wind brought the talk of their radios, faint but recognizable. The soldiers faced out of their arc, stern-eyed now, keyed, expectant. The nearest was barely twenty feet from Famy. Corporal. Two blackened V stripes on his tunic arm; self-loading rifle, water bottle, emergency field dressing strapped to his webbing belt. Famy saw his hands as they cradled the rifle. Finger on the lip of the trigger guard, thumb for the safety catch, a second's movement and the gun was armed, deadly.

The soldier did not return his stare, gazed through him, used to being looked at. The Guards always were. And his position, the square of concrete on which he stood, had chosen to stand, made him Famy's opponent. As inconsequential as that, where a man placed his feet. That decided whether he would kill or be killed.

"Juno turning into Hatton perimeter entrance, sir." A corporal on the Land-Rover radio set to his company commander.

The major raised his hand in acknowledgment. Bloody stupid names they always gave these affairs. "Sunray getting it on the net?" the major asked.

"All getting it, sir, not just the CO, the convoy's hooked into all stations."

"Put out the Instant Readiness."

"Roger, sir."

Beyond his cordon the major saw a line of civilian trucks and cars and lorries held back a quarter of a mile from the plane. Have to wait till the show was over. No noninvolved persons inside his line, perfect field of fire around three-sixty degrees. Just about perfect, anyway. Only the corner hangar of the British Airways cargo complex jutting in and breaking the geometry of his protective circle. Saw the loaders there, standing and sitting and watching, anything for a chance not to work. Shouldn't have been there, but no harm done. The corporal dominating them. No need to throw weight about, make a scene, have them shifted. Saw the turban, creased and clean. It stood out in the light, the sun playing on it.

He turned toward the VIP suite past which the convoy would come.

The cars came fast down the straight line of the inner perimeter road, motorcycles in front and all oncoming traffic blocked far ahead. Sokarev saw the arrowed sign to the right marking the route to the VIP suite.

Jimmy said, "Just about there now, sir. No farewells out on the tarmac. The car goes right up to the steps and you're to be straight onto them. Don't stop. Don't hesitate. Just go straight on up. Inside, don't look out of the windows, just get into the seat. They're not going to hang about, you'll be straight off."

Sokarev did not reply. Jimmy could see the nerves on his aging face, wrinkles accentuated; eyes wide open, staring, but at nothing; and the lips clamped fractionally apart, breathing coming in irregular sucked heaves. Poor sod, not taking it well. Ten to bloody nothing his legs'll freeze, have to half carry him on.

The convoy swept past the low-built lounge with its decoration of hothouse flower plants. Marigolds and snapdragons and embryo rhododendrons. In front was the upper torso of the jumbo that loomed over the far fence.

"Goodbye, Elkin." Jimmy leaned across Sokarev, hand outstretched. It was not taken. The Israeli's attention was outside his window, fingers clamped on his submachine gun.

The cars S-patterned through the gap in the fencing and raced toward the jet. Amidst the protest of the tires, Jones found himself reflecting at the very vulgarity of it all. Big men, hunched and crammed together on the seats. All so difficult to take seriously, just a game for grownups. Only Sokarev playing, though. We're all in with the spectators, thought Jones, only the old man who goes out on the field. No dignity in the moment, nothing of the third floor at the Department, and Jimmy lording it over everybody. Intolerable, really; he'd have to be spoken to. The plane was huge now in its silver closeness, dwarfing them like a fortress in its own right. And the steps were there, in position, waiting for them.

The stiffening of the soldiers, the way their hands quickly changed the grip on the rifles, fingers to the trigger guard, telegraphed to Famy the imminence of the arrival.

His right hand ferreted down inside the overalls for the safety mechanism of the M-1. Already cocked, already a bullet nestled in the breech of the firing chamber. A hundred yards to the steps of the plane. Take him twelve to thirteen seconds. The problems were fading, over everything a devastating simplicity. When the cars came into sight that was when to start running. Fast, but weaving, ducked low, and the shot when the man was at the base of the steps. Bank on chaos. However much they have prepared for you, they will never quite have expected the presence, that was what the men had told him in the camp. There will always be confusion; it is the greatest weapon in your hand, they had said.

Three cars in the convoy, snouting around the corner, break-ing because of the angle they were negotiating.

Famy was on his feet. Without hesitation, a continuous rip-pling movement, he pulled the zip fastener down the length of his chest. The Guardsman was barely aware of the action that produced the rifle, before the bullet hit him low in the muscle wall of his stomach, throwing him back and clear from the path of Famy's sprint.

In front of him, as if in slow motion, the doors of the car were opening, the men in their suits jumping out. Unaware, they don't realize. The insane exhilaration of the achievement of surprise. Run, weave and duck, maintain the rhythm, give no one the clear sight. When do the bullets come? How long? The bundle in grey, half out of the car, helped by the darker suits, reluctant to come, slowing them, impeding. The first bullet spat into the ground close to his feet. Fools, idiots, crazy men, firing low. Halfway there. Sokarev in sight, his head clear, the body half shielded by the men rooted around him. The orange groves, upright, regimented, before the spring brings the sun of Palestine to make fertile their leaves and their fruit; merging together the fantasy of the trees and the sharpness of the men as he pounded his way forward.

More bullets now edging closer, the little puffs of nothing in the concrete, and the hostile, honed whine of the ricochets. And the ranging blast, wide but creeping, of the big machine gun. Sokarev near the steps, wrestling with the men around him. They taking him toward the plane. Doesn't want to go, the little bastard, wants to crawl and hide and bury himself. The moment to shoot.

In full stride Famy flung himself arching forward, swallow dive, with a strange grace, onto the tarmac. His knees and elbows took the impact, ripping at the cloth that covered his body. The gun was at his eye, down the barrel, down the V sight, down the needle sight. Eyes smarting, the pain from the fall, blinking the moisture out. The man in the grey still strug-gling. He fired, finger releasing the trigger. Knew with that deadening instinct that he was wide, high as well, knew it even as he felt the jolt in his shoulder, heard the empty clatter of the discarded shell case. A moment of silence, breath-taking, then again the machine gun.

No more to see of Sokarev, everything so still in front of him, no man standing. Gone, all of them, at a stroke. Disappeared, vanished. At the steps no target.

Four in a burst they teach the soldiers to fire when they feed the belt into the machine gun. More than that and the barrel waves too greatly for the accuracy to be maintained. One in the right foot, two in the calf, fourth in his hip. As if a man with a pickax were striking him. Not aiming at a rock-face but a muscle, vulnerable tissue, and the delicacy of his flesh. There was nothing in his hands, only the flat oil-smeared concrete for his fingers to grasp at. The rifle was far to the front, pitched clear, beyond reach, beyond his chances of hope and salvation. In the distance came the ordered shout, the voice of command, and to his ears the words echoed and had a strange quality.

"Stop firing."

Between them Jones and Elkin carried Sokarev up the flight of steps to the plane. The strength he'd summoned earlier to resist them was absent. Elkin at his shoulders, Jones at his thighs. Both men panting, and the narrowness of the steps preventing further aid.

Jimmy rose from his knees, where he had taken cover in front of the scientist between the steps and the still-opened door of the car, and began to walk toward Famy. Slow paces, all the time in the world now, the end of the stampede. Around him, soldiers were lifting themselves from their firing positions, uncertain what to do. Uneasy in the sudden silence. So many of them and so many rifles and revolvers, and only this one silly bugger in contention.

He saw the eyes of the prone man still locked on his rifle, tantalizing, out of range, far from the capability of heroics. Jimmy swung his foot, lazily, without care, and kicked it noisily into the middle distance.

"Good try, boy," Jimmy said, quietly spoken, a private remark. Famy watched him, awkward from the ground, neck stretched back, face unmarked.

"Good try, just not good enough."

Like they're talking at a bloody garden party, thought the sergeant who picked up the rifle but was out of earshot, could only see the back of the man in the creased suit who stood looking down at the fallen figure.

"McCoy told us you'd be here. Told us this morning. We didn't think you'd get this far. But it wasn't far enough, boy. One shot you got off, just one. Way off target. Looked good, looked dramatic, but set yourself too much. Should have been an aimed shot. Never works, all the running around, not with a popgun like that, anyway."

He saw Famy smile, overcoming the pain, mouth moving but no sound.

"That was what they gave you, the M-1? Not very generous, not very suitable. Would have liked something with a bit more guts, right, boy?"

Famy nodded, slight movement, agreement. As far around as his eyes could see the men were now advancing on him, soldiers and police, their guns no longer aimed. Pointed at the ground and the sky.

Jimmy put his hand in his pocket, under the cover of the cloth, and when it emerged, the PPK was there. He saw Famy begin to squirm away, trying to move but pinioned by the damage to his legs and his hip. Whimpering, like a dog that expects a beating but is too trained by discipline to run from the threat.

"Don't make it difficult, boy. You knew what it was all about when you came on the joyride. And you did well, considering."

Jimmy fired into the center of the pale-brown forehead, below the clear white rim of the turban. Even with a moving target he was usually accurate.

The noise of the shot was drowned by the four fanjet engines of the taxiing 747.

From beside the car, still stationary, still with the engine ticking quietly over, still with the front and rear doors open, Jones had watched it all. There had been words that he'd tried to say, some sort of call, helpless and faint, for Jimmy to come back, but the roar of the engines prevented his being heard by any other than those immediately beside him.

He'd seen the pistol in Jimmy's hand, small and blurred in the distance but silhouetted as a recognizeable shape against the great emptiness of the tarmac. He hadn't looked after that, unable to face the inevitable. The plane was turning toward the runway, its power rising into deafening, ear-blasting crescendo

as it eased its way clear from the group of men with their dark
suits and hardened eyes.

"Bloody good job and all," muttered the Branch man, whose
eyes had never wavered from Jimmy and who now stared over
Jones's shoulder.

Jones swung back. Jimmy walking toward him now; the one
he knew just by the name of Famy abandoned and unmoving
behind the erect and brisk figure. He was soon close enough for
Jones to see the almost boyish grin of satisfaction that wreathed
the mouth. Cat with the cream, thought Jones, like he's scored
a bloody try at Twickenham.

"Bloody good job, the way it should be every time," the
Branch man said again, and Jones bit on his lip, unable to speak
his mind, out of step with the mood.

Well, they'd had their money's worth out of Jimmy boy this
time. Earned his retainer, hadn't he? There'd be some paper
work to be getting on with, the predictable escape mechanism,
and Jones went in search of a car heading for Central London.
Knifing through his mind the continuous thought—it was what
they'd wanted, it was what they'd asked for, those bloody politicians with their directives from on high, and they'd been gra-
tified.

In the first-class cabin, occupying two seats at the rear, were
Sokarev and Elkin. The pilot had swung the plane hard around
and lined himself onto the 3600-meter-long Runway 5, given
precedence over all other flights. Clearance from the control
tower was immediate, and the aircraft hammered its way into
the slight wind down 28L.

Just before the moment of lift-off, Sokarev whispered, straining to Elkin's ear, that he felt sick.

"Don't worry," Elkin said. "It's all over. It's finished now. We
are going home. There is nothing more to fear."

They were all going home. Mackowicz in the tin box on the
freight deck beneath them. Elkin, who had been his friend.
Sokarev, who had been his charge. The security man noted the
pallor of the scientist, and the perspiration on his balding head
and the way that he struggled to reach upward to direct the
cold air nozzles toward his face. When they were airborne it
would be easier. He told himself that, and settled back, deep,
into the comfort of his seat.

Twenty-one

At first the pains were slight and concentrated in the center of his chest, but the nausea and desire to vomit were uppermost. As Elkin slept beside him, Sokarev was able to worm a path over the legs of his bodyguard and into the aisle toward the lavatories. He'd had little food and his retching was painful and hard. By the time they were overflying the Mediterranean the pain was spreading in area and intensity, and still Elkin's eyes were closed, insensible to the outer world. When at last a stewardess noticed Sokarev's distress, he was doubled in his seat, clutching his hands across his body. Over the loudspeaker system of the aircraft the chief steward called for a doctor.

Elkin stood out in the aisle now, for once helpless, for once unable to offer aid to the man he had been ordered to protect. The doctor reached low over the heaving form of Sokarev, whom they had stretched across the two seats, center armrest pulled out.

When he stood up, the doctor, young and in a T-shirt displaying the name of Hamburg, where he had spent his European holiday before joining the flight, asked if anyone was accompanying the passenger. "He is subject to severe coronary attack."

Elkin nodded, unable to speak, stunned at the revelation. Now of all moments, after all that . . .

"Has he been under strain?" The doctor's voice carried the
hush of concern.

"He is David Sokarev."

"I don't know the name, I have not been in Israel for some
weeks."

"He is the one the Arabs tried to kill. At the airport and
before that, last night."

"The reason for the troops? The passenger on the far side of
the airfield?"

"Yes."

"He has been under severe strain?"

"Total strain. They were trying to assassinate him." Enough
of the talk, bloody talk. There must be action that could be
taken.

"He needs morphine," said the doctor.

"And . . ."

"And I do not have morphine. I do not carry it with me."

Elkin looked away from the doctor, down to the pain on the
professor's cheeks. "Call the captain," he said. "Get him off the
deck and here."

The pilot, mid-forties, shirt sleeves, grey hair, a decision
maker, offered no options. "We go for Ben-Gurion. Lebanon
and Cyprus are nearer, but are out. Beirut, obviously, Larnaca
is too short for the plane. Athens might save a few minutes, but
it's marginal and the facilities at home are superior. We have a
little less than an hour till we are down. The necessary people
will be waiting."

The doctor said aloud as he bent once again over Sokarev,
"He is an old man to have gone through all this. Not fit. Overweight, not equipped to take such turmoil. The bastards always
hit when they are not expected."

Elkin could not reason why he spoke. There was no need, no
requirement, but he replied. "We have known for some days
that an attack was planned. The professor has known too."

"And you took him, and you exposed him. Knowingly you
brought him to Europe. At his age, in his condition."

"A decision had been taken."

"There is no wound on him. Remember that. You and your
people will have to make their own decision if he dies. You will
have to know who killed him."

There was darkness around the jet as it whispered its way, ten miles every minute, toward the coastline of Israel and the landfall.

On the intercom the personal assistant announced that the Prime Minister was calling from Downing Street. With resignation the Director General cleared the papers that obscured his note pad, took a sharpened pencil in his hand, and raised the receiver of the telephone. He heard the Prime Minister being informed that the link was now through, that the other party was waiting. There was quiet in the room, fitting for the moment before the commencement of the verbal assault that he had anticipated and predicted to himself. Understatement that the Prime Minister was furious. Voice raised. And the head of the Security Service held the telephone a clear inch from his ear.

"It was turned into a clear fiasco by your man."

"In what way, sir?" Don't give the blighters an inch, don't get into the apology situation, don't make it easy for the inquiry.

"In what bloody way? Because of what your fellow did on the tarmac. Right out there in the middle, with half the bloody world looking on."

"You'll have to explain, sir." Stall the inevitable. Let the heat cool, then counterattack.

"Don't play the fool with me. Your man has executed—only word for it—this Palestinian, or whatever he was, right out there, in public . . ."

"Your instruction was quite clear, sir. You did not expect the Arab to survive our contact with him." They'd be taping at Downing Street, nice to get that on the magic magnetic ribbon.

"Not like that. I didn't expect him killed like that, not . . ."

"He had grenades on him. Live and primed. He was still capable of using them. His hands were moving. He could have used the grenades."

"You're justifying your man?"

"His target was still armed and dangerous. My operative made a quick and correct decision. More lives could have been lost if he had hesitated. He acted quite correctly."

"It makes our position fearfully difficult." Always the same with these damned politicians. Can't take it on the chin, can't ride a right hand. Weakening already. The Director General had the telephone close against the lobe of his ear. "The shooting of this fellow could have very grave repercussions."

"I think our man would have felt that faced with the circumstances that confronted him, the actual danger to life was of paramount importance when compared with possible diplomatic repercussions."

Abruptly and without further comment the Prime Minister rang off. The Director General waited for his line to clear, then dialed the extension to Jones's office.

Long into the evening Jones sat in his office, alone at his desk. The coffee in the beaker remained undrunk and sealed with a skin surface. Helen had gone now, eyes reddened and aware of the conversation he had had with Jimmy.

Sod it, damn it, fuck it. Cock Robin kicked the effing bucket. Bloody waste, a man like that going, getting the chop. Still full of sap, years more of it. Awkward bastard, couldn't deny that, but then, Jones had always fancied he alone could handle him. Bloody-minded when he'd wanted to be, but not just now. Had gone with his own dignity, hadn't made a fuss, just let the blade run through the timber, and keeled over gracefully and without protest. Hadn't argued, just accepted it, made his excuses and disappeared out of the door toward the basement to check his gun in. From the upper window Jones had seen him walk out into the street and stride away toward the Underground station. Could have had a car home, but not his style to ask for one, not when he'd just had the push. Typical of the way the bloody Department exists. DG couldn't do it himself, had to get a minion to scrub the dirty pants, rinse the unmentionable stains. Told him what to do, told him what the PM wanted, and he'd carried it out. To the letter, careful and in copperplate, he'd done it . . . and that was why Jimmy was walking home. On the scrap-yard pinnacle and the best man they had.

Didn't any of the stupid bastards understand the new warfare? Gone past the Queensberry days. No rules that governed this combat. Have to fight the McCoys and Famys with their own kind . . . Would they have left Sokarev half dead for an ambulance to cart away? Would they, shit? He thought he'd never see Jimmy again. Wouldn't be the way of the Department for him to have further contact with a man he'd fired. Went back a long way, lot of years, lot of late nights and talk and togetherness. Now all screwed up because of a little swine from God knows where in a place called Palestine that doesn't exist.

When he telephoned home his elder son answered. Wife out at the Women's Institute Committee. They'd had their food before she went. Didn't think anything had been left for him. No reason why it should. It was a clear week since he'd last phoned and said he might not be home that night. It had been the best bloody week in his time at the Department and it had ended all loused up. Taste in his mouth like a monkey's crotch. And he scratched and worried at the irritation of his scars.

The detective had to screw his legs under the wooden chair to leave room for the nurses who worked around McCoy's bed. They fussed and pecked at their patient and then went in croco-dile line out through the door. There was light from the car park outside and shadows thrown against the wall. For what seemed an age, frighteningly long to the policeman, the Irishman lay still, unmoving, unblinking on the crisp white of the bedclothes.

When eventually he spoke it was too dark in the room for the detective to see his face.

"What happened to him?" The words were slow in coming, spoken so faintly that the other man had to lean forward, curs-ing in his mind even the murmur of the distant traffic. "Did he make it?"

The detective was uncertain what he was allowed to say, kept silent.

"Did he get the bastard?"

Conscientiously the words were written down.

"Did he get him, for Christ's sake, tell me?"

"He tried and he didn't make it. Shot a soldier, fired on the Israeli. Missed. He's dead now, they shot him on the tarmac."

From the bed there was a deep, heaved sigh, then only the regular, drug-controlled breathing. McCoy said nothing more.

Through the haze of images there was a certain hard-won precision. Of how the news would spread from Cullyhanna to Crossmaglen, what the talk would be in Forkhill and Mulagh-bane, what the men would say in the hills around Slieve Gullion and Lislea as they nestled in the bracken and grass and watched and waited with their binoculars and their Armalites. And he felt against the clamminess of his arms the white tiles of the cell walls that would be his. There would be bars and heavy doors, and iron-shod feet, and uniforms, and he would rot and desiccate and decay, and pray and hope each night for the mercy of sleep.

Behind the barman and hidden by the inverted liquor bottles the radio played music from the BBC Northern Dance orchestra. Jolly and conventional and designed to lighten and cheer the customers of the pub. There was much noise in the "Public" and the swill of beer before closing would soon be under way. There was talk of the day's affairs, not of the economy, not of inflation, not of sport, not of the boobs on the inside pages of the tabloids. Attention was gripped by the events of the airport. To be expected . . . the picture by the Agency man with his telephoto lens had made the final editions of the London evenings. Not much detail, but the figure on the ground and the man above him with the gun were recognizable enough. Art department had helped with the gun. Justified the headlines. EXECUTION and HIGH NOON AT HEATHROW.

Jimmy sat in the far corner, near the door, solitary at a table, uncommunicative and now on his fifth double of whiskey. He was slumped low, with his head close to the glass and his eyes deep in the amber, watching the stillness of the liquid, following its reflections, amused by the shapeless patterns of the bubbles that rose from the diminishing ice cubes. No bitterness. Just a sense of regret. Passing of time. Ending of an institution.

The barman rang the big ship's bell hanging above the polished counter. "Last orders, gentlemen. Last orders. One more gulp for the road."

Compulsive for Jimmy. Never could resist the last one. Had to have it, rain or shine. Success or cock-up. He was on his feet, pushing with the throng, thrusting forward his glass with the rest of them. The signature tune of the news headlines rose and faded above the shouting and demanding. First words indistinct, drowned by the big man wanting the big round. Fatuous face, filled out with beer and distended sub-skin veins. Heard the word "Sokarev." Heard the words "Heart attack."

"Shut up," Jimmy yelled. "Shut your bloody faces."

A score of faces were turned on him, saw the power of his eyes, of his chin, of his shoulders.

". . . an hour after Professor Sokarev had been admitted to the intensive-care wing of a Tel Aviv hospital it was announced by the Foreign Ministry in Jerusalem that the efforts of doctors to save his life had failed. The professor, who was aged fifty-three, was one of his country's principal scientists working at the nuclear center at Dimona in the Negev desert.

"In London, Scotland Yard has still not given any details on the unnamed security man who shot dead an already wounded Arab terrorist on the tarmac at Heathrow after the unsuccessful attempt on Professor Sokarev's life this afternoon. But our political editor reports that government ministers are demanding disciplinary action against . . ."

His deep, raucous, baying laughter shook the bar. Head well back, face taking on the crimson of exertion, body shaking from the distant belly sound. And all around, the faces of hostility and reaction.

"What's so bloody funny about that?"

"Nothing to bloody well laugh about."

"Warped little bastard."

"What's the matter with him, half pissed."

He ignored them with grand contempt. So bloody funny. Bloody hilarious. Laughed till it hurt in his guts, till the pain came to his chest, and was laughing as he stumped out into the coldness of the street. Cheated them all, you little bugger. Denied the bloody satisfaction to Famy and McCoy. Fucked the triumph of our side. What price now, Mr. bloody Elkin, or even old Jonesey? How much champagne already downed, and what now . . . a fair old belch there'd be back at the Department. And you, Jimmy boy. He screwed you too, and after all that. All the bloody heartache, all the bloody pain. You screwed everyone Dr. Sokarev, sir. The whole lot of us. Both sides. Didn't know you had it in you, you crafty little sod.

The flat would be empty. There was no hurry to approach its loneliness, its vacuum. Slowly Jimmy made his way down the pavement, and the hiccups were intermingled with the laughing that soon faded to little more than a giggle.

                    *   *   *

Failure had been a familiar bedfellow. So many missions
launched with high expectation, and rarely the wounding blow
that they sought. Barely a fortnight without the young men
departing for their objectives, erect in their confidence, and
then hard on their heels the devastation of disappointment.
Undisturbed beds, unused mess tins, shortened ranks in the
morning parade. And when does frequency become inevitability? When does the dimness phase into darkness? When is there
no longer hope of success? The leader of the General Command
had been brought the transcript of the World Service news
from London and had read without comment of the death of
Famy, the survival of Sokarev, the flight of the El Al jet from
Heathrow. He had walked into the sands, seeking solitude and
absence from the new recruits. It had been a good plan, he
reflected, and he had sent good men, and it had been insufficient.

He stood for more than an hour as the dusk came down over
the desert, so still that the earth-coated mouse ran close to his
feet as it meandered a path to the ambush of the adder. And the
killing was quick: startled eyes, frozen movement, and the job
completed. The land where the soft and the gentle and the
harmless did not survive. He yearned for the snake's speed and
resolution, remembered the cold, unfeeling and mechanical
strike of the reptile and craved the ability to impart the simplicity of that minute brain into the minds of the men who would
leave the camp before midnight and drive in the jeep to the
frontier and walk forward toward the minefields and the wire
and the enemy.

When the night had advanced and the stars risen, he
made his way back to the camp and went and sat with the
four who were eating together with their friends, perhaps
for the last time. He hid depression behind humor and quiet
exhortation and made no mention of the news from Europe.
When the time came for them to leave he walked with
them to the jeep and hugged them deep in his bear arms
and kissed each on both cheeks, and watched the taillights
till they were too distant and had gone amongst the shallow
hills. Afterward, in his tent, he lay on the canvas bed and
read again the operational plan on which they had been
briefed. He was close to sleep when the old man pulled

aside the tent flap, and illuminated by a storm lamp, came across the floor to him.

"They have been monitoring the Israeli broadcasts. Sokarev is dead. He died tonight in Tel Aviv—"

"From what?" The confusion of the Leader showed, half sitting up in the disarray of his blankets. "The reports made no mention of his being injured."

"The Israelis say he was unhurt in the attack, but that he suffered a heart seizure on the plane."

"So it was not us, not by our hand?" He sank back onto his roughened pillow, the momentary excitement extinguished.

"But he is dead."

"But not at our hand." Leaden disappointment.

"We sought to kill him, and he is dead, and—"

"Listen, old man." Weariness creeping through him, tantalizing and irrevocable, not the time for discussion. "Listen. His death is unimportant if it was not at our hand. We had to show we had the power to strike successfully at him. Instead we showed we were not capable. That is no victory."

"We could say . . ." And the old man, mindful that he had been interrupted before and aware of the leader's failing attention, let his words tail away.

"We could say nothing. To make people of whatever country, wherever in the world, aware of the mushroom clouds that can rise over our men and women and children, then we had to be triumphant in our attack. We were not. The mission is over and completed. Sleep well, old man."

When the light had gone and the tent flap had been folded back into place, the leader turned toward the canvas side that was close to his face. And before he slept he thought of the lights of the jeep and the bright furnace eyes of the men he would not see again.